U0004164

柳林中的風聲

The Wind in the Willows

中英雙語典藏版

肯尼斯·格雷厄姆———著

謝世堅———譯 亞瑟·拉克姆、曾銘祥———繪

晨星出版

導讀

漂流物

「一陣變幻莫測的微風從水面吹來，輕輕撼動山楊樹，吹動了帶著露珠的玫瑰，拂上他們的臉像是輕輕地撫摸他們的臉……」第一次讀到讚賞自然如此美好的詞句，感覺它就像首田園詩，卻不知這竟是英國作家肯尼斯・格雷厄姆的經典之作。肯尼斯・格雷厄姆出生於英國蘇格蘭的愛丁堡，一生喜歡自然和文學，業餘時研究動物和寫作，很早就是一位很有名氣的作家。主要作品有《黃金時代》（1895）、《夢幻的日子》（1898）及《柳林中的風聲》（1908）。他喜歡為兒子編講故事，兒子非常入迷，甚至暑假也不肯到外地去，他只好答應用寫信的方式，把故事繼續寫給兒子看。這就是《柳林中的風聲》一書創作的源起。

由於肯尼斯・格雷厄姆常酷愛大自然，在他的筆下，對自然描寫極為流暢有趣；而且他也喜歡研究動物，因而熟悉動物的生態，文中的鼴鼠、河鼠、蛤蟆是擬人化的動物，描繪得維妙維肖。然而《柳林中的風聲》與前兩部作品《黃金時代》、《夢幻的日子》有顯著的不同，故事裏的角色，從以往的小孩子變成了各種動物。對於格雷厄姆的這種改變，以往讚揚過他的評論家感到十分不習慣；因此，《柳林中的風聲》剛發表時，並沒有得到巨大的迴響。但它最後還是得到廣大讀者的喜愛，所以此書慢慢地得到評論家的承認，被稱英語文學作品中，最偉大的兒童佳作。由於此書的文字描述非常優美，還被譽為英國散文體作品的典範。甚至，《小熊維尼》作者米爾恩（1882—1956）還將此書改寫成劇本，取名《蟾蜍莊園裏的托德》，並且歷演不衰。不只在英國境內，這部作品的名聲遠渡重洋，還擄獲美國羅斯福總統的喜愛，甚至寫信告訴作者，說他一口氣讀了三遍。

整本書由十二個章節組成，每個章節是一個完整的故事，十二個故事組合起來又構成一個整體。書中的主要角色有河鼠、鼴鼠、獾和蟾蜍，每個角色的性格明顯。河鼠熱情帶有幾分浪漫；鼴鼠天真又富機靈；獾老成沉穩具有很高的威望；蟾蜍自以為是，最愛冒險。住在河邊洞穴裏的河鼠和鼴鼠是要好的朋友，他們互相關照。某天，鼴鼠在野林中迷路時，河鼠隻身進入野林尋找鼴鼠，並保護他安全脫險；當河鼠有心事時，鼴鼠給予他安慰。他們倆樂於幫助有困難的動物。水獺的兒子小胖子失蹤了，他們倆不顧勞累、困乏，連夜去找小胖子；更可貴的是，當他們找回小胖子，水獺父子倆歡歡喜喜地團聚時，他們卻悄悄地離開了。

　　文中的麻煩製造者蟾蜍先生，雖然坐擁豪華的莊園，但他厭倦富足平淡的莊園生活，一心一意想要尋求新奇刺激。自從喜歡上汽車後，他便為此吃上許多苦頭；再加上他一副自以為是、狂妄自大的模樣，不僅鬧出許多笑話，甚至闖出不少的亂子。獾是夥伴中最年長的一位，老成持重卻樂於助人；他率領河鼠、鼴鼠和蟾蜍打敗了黃鼠狼一夥，想盡辦法要為蟾蜍重新奪回莊園。而過錯不斷的蟾蜍，也在友情的支撐下認清自己的錯，痛下決心改過自新。

　　這是一本什麼樣主題的書呢？米爾恩曾說過，此書可測試性格，我們不能批評它，因為它批判著我們。但我必須給個告誡：當你坐下來看此書，千萬不要身陷我的品味，或是格雷厄姆的評斷之中，建議閱讀此書，可以用不同的角度來欣賞。你可以視此書是歌頌大自然的美好和浪漫，亦可以說書中彌漫宗教的奧秘之處。尤其河鼠和鼴鼠相偕尋覓失蹤的小水瀨，撞見拯救小水瀨那位半人半神的文字敘述：「我撫慰在林中流浪的小孩童……我幫助林中迷路的小羔羊……我撫平他們身上的一切創傷……囑咐他們把一切都遺忘！」不管那神靈有無恍若希臘神話中的潘神，莊嚴的文字都令人不禁神迷嚮往。你也可說此部作品描寫不同階層的各種生活風情，諸如野林子的白鼬和黃鼠狼，典型農民階級的河鼠，而蟾蜍則是隻可愛的反抗者，所以無法好好適應團體生活。甚至你可以認為，此書讚揚友誼和人性的美好之處，像是河鼠的善良助人；鼴鼠的溫順憨厚；獾的慈祥和藹；蛤蟆的魯莽愚蠢，但頗具坦率和慷慨。不管你用何種角度來切入此書，都可以發現其迷人風情。

目録

CONTENTS

柳林中的風聲

第一章　河岸

　　鼴鼠這天早上忙得不可開交。春天來了，他在給自己的小家進行一次大掃除。他先用掃帚掃，用抹布抹，接著一會兒爬上梯子，一會登上臺階，一會兒踏上椅子，用石灰水粉刷牆壁。最後，他的喉嚨和眼睛都進了灰塵，黑色皮毛濺滿了斑白的石灰漬，半天的勞累使得他腰痠腿疼。在外面的空氣中，在泥土裏，在他周圍，到處都彌漫著春天的氣息。春天挾著對現狀的不滿和對未來的期待，來到他那間陰暗、低矮的小屋。突然，他把手中的刷子往地上狠狠一扔，說：「該死的大掃除！討厭！眞討厭！」他邊說邊走，連大衣也沒穿上，把門一閂，就出去了。外面有種東西在召喚著他。他爬上一條陡峭狹窄的地道，這地道通向一條砂礫鋪成的行車道，屬於那些住得離陽光和空氣更近的動物所有。他用自己的小爪子扒呀扒，一邊忙著自言自語：「到地上去！到地上去！」接著「噗的」一聲，他的頭部伸出了地面。這裏陽光明媚，鼴鼠高興得在暖洋洋的草地上打滾。

　　「太好了！」他思忖著，「比粉刷牆壁好多了！」溫暖的陽光照在他的皮毛上，直晒得他暖洋洋的，和煦的春風也正撫摸著

他的額頭。在寂靜的地底隱居了很長一段時間後，鳥兒歡快的歌聲，在他那雙變得遲鈍的耳朵聽來，簡直就像在高聲喊叫似。他蹦跳著，生活多美好啊！此時的他，再也不用去想那該死的春天大掃除了。他在草地上奔跑著，一會兒就來到了一道樹籬前。

「站住！」一隻上了年紀的野兔，在樹籬的豁口前對他叫道，「這是私人通道，過路費得交六便士！」這時鼴鼠臉上立即露出不耐及不屑的神情，令野兔大為氣惱；別的野兔也急忙從洞中探出頭來，想看熱鬧。鼴鼠一邊繞著樹籬走，一邊揶揄他們，「笨蛋！笨蛋！」他嘲弄地叫道。野兔還沒能來得及想該如何回應時，他早已溜走，消失得無影無蹤了。於是像往常一樣，他們開始互相埋怨起來，「你真蠢！為什麼不告訴他……」、「嘿，你為什麼不說……」、「你該提醒他……」等等諸如此類的話。當然，這些話都太遲了，他們老是這樣。

這裏的一切是那麼地美妙，簡直令人難以置信。鼴鼠在草地上四處閒逛。在樹籬上，在矮叢中，他看到鳥兒在築巢、花兒在萌發、樹葉在成長——一切是如此地歡樂幸福，生機蓬勃而又緊張忙碌。擺脫了粉刷牆壁這件苦差事，他並不覺得良心不安，相反地，在忙碌人群中作為一個無所事事的人，他只感到無比地愜意。畢竟，假期最美妙之處，也許並不只是讓自己短暫地休憩，而在於悠閒地看著別人忙碌地幹活。

他覺得現在的自己幸福、自在。他毫無目的地閒逛著，突然來到一條漲了水的河岸邊。他這輩子從未見過河流——在他看來，這是一隻油光可鑒、蜿蜒曲折的龐然大物。他追逐、歡笑，

咯咯地抓住手中的東西,又大笑著把他們放開;他匆匆地撲向新的玩伴,而他們竭力地掙脫他的糾纏,但又被他抓住。這所有的一切都驚動河水,發出嘩嘩的響聲,鼴鼠觀賞聆聽著,並全然地陶醉於眼前的景象。他沿著河邊輕快地跑著,有如一個走在大人身邊的小孩,一邊牽著大人的手,一邊聽著大人迷人的故事。後來,他終於感到倦了,便坐在河岸邊。河水還在嘩嘩地和他說著話,似乎在為他講述世上最美麗的故事,而這些故事從地球的中心噴湧而出,奔向永不知足的大海。

鼴鼠坐在草地上眺望著河的對岸,這時,對岸的一個黑洞映入他的眼簾。他恍惚地想著:對於一心就只想在河邊有個小巧舒適的家,其餘別無所求的人來說,這該是一個多麼舒適的安身之處啊!在這裏,不僅洪水淹不著,而且遠離喧囂。突然他看到洞口裏,似乎有個明亮的小東西在閃爍,像一顆小星星似,飛快地消失,緊接著又閃了一下。顯然,那不可能是顆星星,而且那東西很亮、很小,因此也不會是一隻螢火蟲。就在他對著它看時,它向他眨了一下,彷彿告訴他,那是一隻眼睛。慢慢地,一張小臉在眼睛的周圍顯現出來,活像一幅畫的畫框。

那是一張褐色的臉,上面還長著鬍鬚。

那是一張嚴肅的臉,眼裏還閃爍著一種光芒,就是這種光芒先引起了他的注意。那一雙小而整潔的耳朵;那一身濃密而柔順的毛髮。

原來是一隻河鼠!

於是這兩隻動物站著,一動也不動,小心翼翼地互相打量。

「你好，鼴鼠！」河鼠說道。

「你好，河鼠！」鼴鼠說道。

「你想不想到這邊來呀？」河鼠接著問道。

「噢，說說話就好了。」鼴鼠任性地說。他第一次來到河邊，還不知道河邊的生活習慣。

河鼠沒多說什麼，蹲下身解開一根繩索，然後用力一拉，接著他輕輕鬆鬆地登上一艘小船。在此之前，鼴鼠根本沒注意到那艘小船；船的外表塗著藍色的油漆，裏面塗著白漆，這艘船正好能坐兩隻動物。此時鼴鼠對它已是心馳神往了，儘管他並不全然懂得船的用處。

河鼠熟練地搖著船槳，船很快便到達岸邊。當鼴鼠小心翼翼地向船走來時，河鼠伸出一隻前爪：「扶住我的手！」又接著說，「來，邁開步伐！」這是鼴鼠平生第一次坐船，他心裏又驚又喜。

在河鼠划離岸邊後，鼴鼠說道：「多麼奇妙的一天啊！你知道嗎，我這輩子還沒有坐過船呢！」

「什麼？」河鼠叫道，嘴巴張得大大的，「從沒有……你從沒有……呃，呃……那你都做些什麼事啊？」

「坐船真的很美妙嗎？」鼴鼠怯生生地問道。但他早已將身子往後靠，仔細打量著船上的坐墊、船槳、槳架，及一切使他著迷的東西；體驗船在腳底晃晃悠悠的感覺。

「美妙？這種感覺可是獨一無二的。」河鼠一邊搖槳，一邊莊重地說，「相信我吧，我的朋友，沒有什麼事情——絕對沒

第一章

有——比在船上消磨時間更好玩的了。」他夢囈般地說，「飄飄蕩蕩，悠哉……」

「河鼠小心！」鼴鼠突然叫道。

但是已經來不及了，船猛力地撞在岸上，船上那個做夢者——快樂的划槳能手被摔得四腳朝天。

「悠哉遊哉。」河鼠鎮靜地說完他的話。接著若無其事地邊笑邊站起身說，「坐在船上或者被拋到水裏都不要緊，一切都變得無所謂似的，這就是坐船的魅力。不管你要往哪裏去，還是坐在船裏哪都不去；不管你到達了自己的目的地，還是要到別的什麼地方；也不管你什麼地方都沒到，你總是忙著，而且你忙的又不是什麼特別的事。更何況，你做完一件事，你總是會有別的事要做，所以你想做就做，不想做就算了吧。哎！要是你今早真的沒什麼事，我們乘船順流而下，去玩上一整天怎麼樣？」

鼴鼠高興得直搖動腳趾，樂不可支地靠在鬆軟的坐墊上，心滿意足地讚嘆道：「這一天該有多美呀！」他說，「我們趕緊出發吧！」

「先不要急！」河鼠說完，立即把纜繩繫到碼頭的一個圓環上，然後爬到他在岸上的洞穴裏；過了一會兒，他扛著一個柳條編織的寬大午餐籃，蹣跚地走了出來。

「把這拿到你的腳下。」他一面把籃子遞上船，一面對鼴鼠說；接著他解開纜繩，划起槳來。

「籃子裏裝的是什麼？」鼴鼠扭動著身軀，滿心好奇地問道。

「裏面有冷雞肉，」河鼠簡單地答道，「冷牛舌、冷火腿、冷牛肉、醃黃瓜、沙拉、法式小麵包、三明治、罐裝肉、薑汁汽水、檸檬茶和蘇打水。」

「夠了，夠了，」鼴鼠欣喜若狂喊著，「這太多了！」

「你真的這樣認爲？」河鼠一本正經地問道，「這只是我往日遠遊時要帶的東西，其他動物都說我是一個吝嗇的傢伙，對什麼都斤斤計較！」

鼴鼠根本聽不進河鼠說的話，此刻他正專注地想著自己的新生活，沉醉於身邊河水的波光、泛起的漣漪、芬芳的空氣、動聽的聲音和燦爛的陽光。他把一隻爪子浸入水中，然後做著白日夢。河鼠這位善良的小夥子平穩地划著船，不忍心再去打擾他。

「我真的很喜歡你這套衣服，老兄。」大約再過了半個鐘頭，河鼠說道，「哪天要是有了錢，我打算去買一套黑色天鵝絨服。」

「對不起，你說什麼？」鼴鼠說著，他竭力從恍惚中清醒過來，「你一定覺得我非常沒有禮貌，這一切對我來說真的是太新奇了。這麼說來——這——就是河啦！」

「我們的河。」河鼠糾正道。

「你真的就住在河邊？多愜意呀！」

「住在河邊、身在河裏，河就是一切，」河鼠說，「它是我的兄弟姐妹、我的嬸嬸、我的夥伴、我的飲食，當然也是我洗澡的地方。這是我的世界，我別無所求。河裏沒有的東西我不想要，河不懂的東西我不想懂。嘿！想想我和它一起度過的美好時

光！不管是春夏秋冬，它都帶給我快樂和興奮。當二月的洪水來臨時，我的地窖積滿了水，混濁的河水還漫到我漂亮臥室裏的窗戶；當河水退去時，地面露出一塊塊散發著葡萄乾蛋糕氣味的泥巴，燈蕊草和其他雜草則堵塞了溝渠。這時我可以在河床上閒逛，還不會弄濕我的鞋子呢。在河床上我能撿到可口的食物，還有船上那些人不小心掉下的東西！」

「難道你沒有感到生活枯燥乏味的時候嗎？」鼴鼠冒昧地問道，「只有你和這條河，沒有人和你說話？」

「沒別的人了——唉，這不怪你，」河鼠寬容地說，「你第一次到河邊來，當然不瞭解這裏的情況。如今的河岸太擁擠了，整天人來人往。以前可不是這個樣子，如今全變啦。水獺、翠鳥、小鷺鷀、黑水雞，他們整天來找你，叫你做這做那——好像別人沒有自己的事情要忙似的！」

「那邊是什麼地方？」鼴鼠問，一邊用爪子指著岸邊草地後，遠處一片黑壓壓的林地。

「那邊啊？噢，就是野林子。」河鼠簡單地說，「我們這些住在河岸上的人，通常都不到那邊去。」

「住在那裏的人不是……不是好人嗎？」鼴鼠有些緊張地問道。

「呃——」河鼠答道，「要我說嘛，松鼠們還不錯，野兔——有些還不錯，但他們有好有壞。當然還有獾，他住在林子的深處，就算你拿錢跟他換，他也不願意住到別處去。親愛的獾老兄！沒有誰會去打擾他，最好誰也別去惹他。」河鼠意味深長

地補述。

「誰會去打擾他呢？」鼴鼠問。

「嗯，當然……有些……別的人，」河鼠有點遲疑地解釋道，「黃鼠狼……貂……狐狸等等。說起來他們還不錯——我跟他們還算好朋友——我們見面時還能一起消磨時光，但不可否認的是，他們有時會大發脾氣。總之，你不能真正信任他們，這是事實。」

鼴鼠很清楚，過多地談論可能會因此惹上麻煩——即使是暗示——亦違反動物間的規矩。因此，他換了另外一個話題。

「野林子那邊又是什麼地方？」他問，「遠遠看去是一片淡藍色，好像是群山又好像不是，似乎是城裏冒出的炊煙，或許只是浮雲吧？」

「野林子那邊是廣闊的天地，」河鼠說，「但那對你、對我都無關緊要。我從沒去過那兒，我也不打算去，如果你還算聰明的話，最好也不要去。不要再提它了，好嗎？好啦，終於到了小河灣，我們就在這兒吃午飯吧。」

船駛離河流，他們進入了看起來像是一個小湖的水域。水邊是綠油油的草皮，清澈的水現出褐色的樹根。樹根前有一道攔河堰，這裏有一隻轉個不停的水車，水車上方有一間灰色山牆的磨坊；水車輪發出一種令人心曠神怡的聲響，凸顯磨坊令人窒息的沉寂，雖然偶爾裏面也傳出歡快的聲音。一切都是那麼美妙。鼴鼠興奮地直舉起前爪，感歎道：「哎呀！太美好啦！太美好啦！」

　　河鼠把船靠在岸邊，繫好纜繩，扶著笨手笨腳的鼴鼠安全上岸，然後搖搖晃晃地搬出那只大籃子。鼴鼠懇請河鼠讓他獨自把籃子裏的東西取出來，河鼠樂得答應，便伸開四肢躺在草地上休息。此時，他那位興奮的朋友把桌布攤開鋪在地上，然後一包接著一包地，拿出籃子裏神秘的東西；打開包裝後整整齊齊地放在桌布上，每發現一樣新的東西，他都發出「哇！哇！」的讚歎聲。一切都準備好後，河鼠說：「好啦，吃吧，夥伴！」鼴鼠高興地從命了，因為他如許多人一樣，那天一大清早就開始他的春天大掃除了，忙得連吃飯的時間都沒有。從那時到現在，他經歷了很多事，覺得好像已經過了好幾天了。

　　「你在看什麼？」過了一會兒河鼠問道。這時他們已快填飽肚子，而鼴鼠也終於可以把目光從桌布上移開了。

　　「我在看水面上冒出的一連串氣泡，」鼴鼠說，「真有意思。」。

　　「氣泡？噢！」河鼠一邊說，一邊高興地咂著嘴，似乎在邀請什麼人。

　　岸邊的水面上露出一顆寬大發亮的頭，接著水獺從水中爬了出來，並抖落衣服上的水。

　　「饞鬼！」他叫道，同時撲向擺在桌布上的食物，「為什麼沒有邀請我，河鼠老弟？」

　　「是臨時決定的。」河鼠解釋道，「介紹一下我的朋友，這是鼴鼠先生。」

　　「幸會，幸會。」水獺說。於是兩隻動物便成了好朋友。

「到處都這麼熱鬧！」水獺接著說，「今天好像全世界的人都跑到河上來了。我本想到這個河灣來，找一個安靜的地方，沒想到會在這兒碰上你們！請原諒……我真的不是要故意打擾你們的雅興。」

這時，他們身後的樹籬中，傳來沙沙的響聲；樹籬下，鋪著一層厚厚的落葉；樹籬裏，冒出一顆有條紋的頭顱，頭後面是高高的肩膀，那雙眼睛正瞅著他們。

「快過來，獾老兄！」河鼠喊道。

獾往前走了幾步，接著嘟噥道：「哼！原來是你們。」然後轉過身去，便消失得無影無蹤。

「他就是這個樣子！」河鼠失望地說道，「一點也不喜歡和別人交往！我們今天不會再見到他了。喂，說說看，有誰到河上來了？」

「蟾蜍算一個，」水獺答道，「駕著他那艘嶄新的賭博船，披著新披風，什麼都是新的！」

兩隻動物對視片刻，並會意地大笑起來。

「他曾經非常喜歡帆船，」河鼠說，「可是沒多久就厭倦了，後來又喜歡上撐篙的平底船；他整天什麼都不做，只在那撐船，搞得一塌糊塗。去年，他喜歡上了遊艇，我們大家都不得不一起待在他的遊艇上，還得假意地對他的遊艇讚不絕口。當時他打算在他的遊艇裏度過一生呢！他就是那樣，不管喜歡什麼，慢慢就厭倦了，接著又搞新的玩意兒。」

「他其實是一個不錯的傢伙，」水獺沉思須臾又接著說，

「就是有點喜新厭舊——尤其是他對船的態度！」

　　從他們所坐的地方，可以看到不遠處的河流。這時，一艘賭博船進入他們的視線，划船者——一個粗短的身影——把水划得四處飛濺，但他仍賣力地划著。河鼠站起來跟他打招呼，但是蟾蜍——就是他——搖了搖頭，又認真地幹起活來。

　　「如果他這樣划槳的話，等一下肯定會從船上掉到水裏。」河鼠一邊坐下一邊說道。

　　「絕對會。」水獺咯咯笑道，「我跟你說過蟾蜍和河道看閘人的有趣故事嗎？事情是這樣的，一天，蟾蜍⋯⋯」

　　一隻蜉蝣在水面上逆著水流漂來漂去，那種自我陶醉的樣子，只有沒見過世面的蜉蝣才做得出來。此時，水面出現一個漩渦，接著撲哧一聲，蜉蝣便消失了。

　　水獺也失去了蹤影。

　　鼴鼠往水獺坐的地方一看，他的耳朵裏還迴盪著水獺的話音，但他剛坐的地方，顯然已空空如也。放眼看去，已看不到水獺的蹤影。

　　只見河面上又冒出一連串的氣泡。

　　河鼠嘴裏哼著小曲，鼴鼠想起：根據動物的規矩，不管什麼時候，不管任何理由或有沒有理由，朋友突然不辭而別後，是不允許隨便議論的。

　　「好啦，好啦，」河鼠說，「我想我們也該回去了。應該誰來收拾東西呢？」聽他的口氣，他似乎並不想收拾。

　　「噢，讓我來收拾吧！」鼴鼠說。於是河鼠便讓他收拾。

　　把東西裝進籃子並不比從籃子裏取出東西好玩，那可不是有趣的活兒。但是鼴鼠並不在乎，他覺得任何事都很有趣。當他把東西裝進了籃子，並緊緊地捆好後，他看見一只碟子躺在草地上盯著他。他放入這東西後，河鼠指著地上的一把叉子——這本來誰都會看見的，還有那只芥末瓶！鼴鼠一直坐在它的上面，卻毫無發覺。最後，東西總算收好了，鼴鼠一點也沒有發脾氣。

　　太陽漸漸下山了。河鼠一邊輕輕地把船划向回家的方向，一邊吟唱著詩句，沉浸在忘我的境界，似乎忘了鼴鼠的存在。鼴鼠中午飽餐了一頓後，感到心滿意足、自豪無比，他認為自己已經熟悉了船，於是興奮了起來。突然，他說：「河鼠兄！我要划船！給我船槳！」

　　河鼠笑著搖了搖頭說：「你划不動的，小夥子，等你學會了再說吧，這並不如想像中那般簡單。」

　　鼴鼠沉默了一會兒，但看到河鼠划得如此輕鬆有力，他越看心裏越不是滋味，一直嘟囔著，認為自己也可以划得很好。正當河鼠凝望著河面，口裏吟誦著詩句時，突然，鼴鼠跳起來，猛地搶過船槳；河鼠大吃一驚，又一次四腳朝天地摔在船底。勝利的鼴鼠霸佔了河鼠的座位，滿懷自信地緊緊抓著船槳。

　　「別鬧了，你這蠢驢！」船艙裏的河鼠嚷叫，「你不會划的！你會把船弄翻的！」

　　鼴鼠奮力搖起雙槳，然後使勁往水裏划；但船槳根本沒搆著水面，反而把他高高吊起，接著鼴鼠摔倒在船艙裏的河鼠身上。這下子他可被嚇壞了，使勁地抓住船舷，緊接著「撲通」一

聲……

船翻了，鼴鼠在水中掙扎著。

哎呀！這水真冷啊！天哪！衣服全濕透啦！他不斷地往下沉，耳朵嗡嗡作響！他掙扎著浮出水面，不停地咳著。此時的陽光多麼燦爛，多麼宜人！當他覺得又往下沉時，內心充滿了絕望！突然一隻有力的爪子，抓住他頸部的後背。原來是河鼠，他一定在笑——鼴鼠可以從揪住他脖子的爪子感覺到，他在笑。

河鼠抓住一根船槳，把它推到鼴鼠的手臂下，自己用一隻手扶著船槳，另一隻手划水，把可憐的鼴鼠推往岸邊，然後把他拖起，讓他在岸上坐著。可憐的鼴鼠，這時跟一團濕棉花沒什麼兩樣。

河鼠為他擦了一下身子，抹掉了他身上的水，說：「好啦，老友！沿著河岸的小道使勁地來回跑吧，一直跑到身子發熱，身體變乾為止。我還得潛入水裏撈籃子呢。」

渾身濕透的鼴鼠心裏既沮喪又羞愧，他照河鼠說的，在岸上跑了起來，跑到身體變得十分乾爽為止。與此同時，河鼠又跳進水裏，把傾覆的船翻轉了過來，拖往岸邊繫好；接著把浮在水面上的家當，一件一件撿上岸；最後潛入水裏，成功地撈起了那只籃子，又吃力地把它拖上岸。

他們把所有的東西重新裝上船後，鼴鼠垂頭喪氣地坐到船尾。當他們啟航時，鼴鼠激動得語無倫次，他低聲地說：「河鼠兄，我寬宏大量的朋友！我真心為自己愚蠢又討厭的行為，感到十分愧疚。當我想到，自己差點弄丟了那只漂亮的籃子時，我的

心都快碎了。我承認，我是十足的蠢驢。請你忘了這件事，原諒我這一次，我們還是像以前那樣，好嗎？」

「這沒什麼，上帝保佑你！」河鼠親切地說，「挨點濕對河鼠來說算得了什麼？一般來說，我在水裏的時間比在岸上還長呢！你不要為這事胡思亂想了。對了，我想你最好到我家住一段時間——我的家很簡陋，比起蟾蜍的家，差遠了——你見了就知道。儘管如此，我會讓你過得舒舒服服的。我還要教你划船、游泳呢！不久以後，你就可以在水上得心應手了。」

聽見他如此貼心的一番話，鼴鼠無比感動，不知道說什麼才好，他激動得用爪背拭去眼中的淚水，河鼠善解人意地望著別處。很快地，鼴鼠的情緒又恢復了，他甚至和幾隻黑水雞頂起嘴來，因為他們正嘲笑他那副落湯雞的模樣。

回到家後，河鼠在客廳裏生起了火堆，給鼴鼠拿來睡袍和拖鞋，並把他安頓在火爐邊的扶手椅上，給他講了許多發生在河上的故事，一直講到晚飯時間。對於像鼴鼠這樣住在陸地上的動物來說，這些故事是那麼地引人入勝。這些故事有的是關於攔河壩、突發的洪水、躍出水面的梭魚，還有那些往河裏亂扔瓶子的輪船啦——反正瓶子是被人們扔掉的，很可能是從輪船上扔下的；有的故事則是關於鷺鳥，他們跟別人講話時，總是一副居高臨下的姿態。河鼠還說了他在排水溝的歷險經過，與水獺夜釣的情景，以及跟獺到遠處去玩耍的經歷。

這頓晚餐他們吃得十分開心。但沒過多久，鼴鼠打起了瞌睡，周到的主人便扶著他到樓上最好的臥室去，不一會兒，他便

枕著枕頭安然入睡。他心裏明白，他剛剛認識的朋友——那條河水——在輕輕地拍打著他的窗戶。

　　鼴鼠終於從長年的地底生活中解脫了，但今天只是新生活的第一天，此後他度過了許多個快活的日子。夏日一天天過去，他在這裏的日子也一天比一天長，一天比一天愜意。他學會了游泳和划船，開始享受起流水的樂趣來。偶爾，他抓住蘆葦，把耳朵貼在上面，聽聽風兒悄悄地說些什麼。

第二章　大路

　　一個陽光燦爛的夏天早晨，鼴鼠突然對河鼠說：「河鼠兄，我想請你幫個忙。」

　　河鼠坐在河岸上，嘴裏正哼著歌；這是他剛剛編的曲子，因此唱得特別起勁，也就沒怎麼注意到鼴鼠和別的事情。一大清早，他便和鴨子朋友們一起在河裏游泳。當鴨子們像往常一樣，把頭潛入水裏時，河鼠也潛到水中搔他們的脖頸取樂，就在他們下巴的下方（如果那是他們下巴的話）；河鼠直搔得他們匆忙把頭伸出水面，他們氣得「哇哇」地叫喚，拍打著翅膀撲向河鼠。畢竟當他們的頭還在水中時，是沒辦法給河鼠一點顏色瞧瞧的。後來，鴨子們懇求河鼠走開，去做他自己的事，不要再打擾他們；因此，河鼠離開他們回到河岸，一邊晒太陽一邊想出了一首關於鴨子的歌，歌名就叫《鴨子之歌》：

　　　　河灣上，
　　　　席草高，

鴨子鬧，
尾高高。

母鴨尾，公鴨尾，
黃腳搖，
黃嘴巴，不見了，
埋水裏！

河草青，
魚兒游，
此間有飯食，
包你吃個夠。

各有所好！
我們喜歡
頭朝下，尾朝上，
樂逍遙！

藍天下，
和風吹，
我人樂逍遙，
尾高高！

「我覺得這首歌並不怎麼樣，河鼠。」鼴鼠小心翼翼地說。他自己不懂得寫詩，也不會把寫詩的人放在眼裏，他的性格就是這樣，喜歡直來直往。

「鴨子也不懂我的歌，」河鼠爽朗地答道，「他們說，『為什麼不讓人們做自己喜歡的事情呢？他們喜歡什麼時候做便做，喜歡怎麼做就怎麼做。別的人幹嘛非要坐在岸上，不停地看著他們，對他們說三道四呢？簡直就是多管閒事！』鴨子們就是這麼說的。」

「說得好，說得好。」鼴鼠滿心高興地說。

「胡說！」河鼠氣憤地叫道。

「好啦，是胡說、是胡說。」鼴鼠安慰他說，「但我還是想請你幫個忙，能不能帶我去拜訪蟾蜍先生呢？我經常聽別人提起他，所以非常想認識他。」

「當然可以！」好心的河鼠說完後決定先放下詩歌創作這回事，他站起身，「把船拉出來，我們現在就划船去他家。要拜訪蟾蜍什麼時候都合適。不管早晚，他總是那個樣子，脾氣很好，對客人老是笑呵呵的，客人要走時經常依依不捨！」

「他一定是隻很不錯的動物。」鼴鼠一邊說一邊上船，划起了船槳，而河鼠則舒舒服服地坐在船尾。

「他確實是動物中最好的，」河鼠答道，「單純，善良，又重感情。也許他並不很聰明——我們也並非個個都是天才；他雖然喜歡吹牛又自以為是，但他也確實有很多優點。」

繞過了河流的彎道後，他們見到了一幢漂亮、古樸而又莊嚴

的紅磚房，修剪得整整齊齊的草坪一直延伸到水邊。

「那就是蟾蜍的莊園，」河鼠說，「左邊的小河灣上有塊告示牌，上面寫著『私人碼頭，未經允許，不得停船』。從那往上便是他的船塢，我們就把船停在那兒。右邊那一排是馬廄，你現在看的那間是宴會廳——那可是古香古色的呢。蟾蜍非常有錢，這幢房子是這一帶最漂亮的，儘管我們在蟾蜍面前從沒這麼說過。」

他們讓船在小河灣上滑行，船駛入泊船處時，鼴鼠收起了船槳。他們看到很多漂亮的船，但沒有一艘是浮在水上的。它們有的吊在房樑上，有的擱在碼頭邊上。整個地方給人一種空蕩、荒涼的感覺。

河鼠看了看四周。「我明白了，」他說，「看來他玩船玩膩了。不知道他現在又喜歡什麼新玩意兒？走，找他去，我們很快就會清楚是怎麼回事。」

他們上了岸，穿過點綴著鮮花的草坪，四處尋找著蟾蜍。他們很快就發現他坐在一張柳條椅上，正神情專注地看著膝蓋上攤開的那張大地圖。

「嘿！」見到他們，蟾蜍高興得跳起來喊道，「你們來得正是時候！」他熱情地握著他們倆的爪子，也不等河鼠向他介紹鼴鼠。「真是太好了，」他說道，一邊手舞足蹈，「河鼠兄，我正打算派船去接你呢，而且還下令要求他們，不管你正在忙什麼都一定要把你請來。我太需要你們倆了。想吃點什麼？進屋去，吃點東西！你們這個時候來我真是太高興了！」

「還是讓我們安靜地坐一會兒吧，蟾蜍兄！」河鼠一邊說，一邊坐到一張安樂椅上。鼴鼠則坐在他身邊的另一張安樂椅上，嘴裏稱讚著蟾蜍的「漂亮府邸」。

「這可是整條河上最漂亮的房子，」蟾蜍補述道，「在別的地方也不會有更美的房子了。」

這時河鼠用肘子輕輕推了一下鼴鼠，剛好被蟾蜍看到，蟾蜍的臉立即紅了起來，接著是一陣令人難受的沉默。然後蟾蜍突然大笑起來。「好啦，河鼠兄，」他說，「你知道我就喜歡這樣。說起來，這房子可真不壞，對吧？其實你也很喜歡這房子吧？好啦，還是說正經事吧！我真的太需要你們了，你們可得幫我的忙，這件事意義重大！」

「一定是關於划船的事吧？」河鼠故意裝出一副天真的模樣說道，「你不是划得很好嗎？儘管有時還是會濺起水來。只要你有耐心，再加上適當的指導，你一定……」

「呸！划船？」蟾蜍不耐煩地打斷河鼠的話，「那是小孩的玩意兒，我早就不幹了，那根本是在浪費時間。看到你們這些傢伙，把美好生命浪費在那種沒有意義的事情上，真叫我難過。不，我發現了唯一一種可以做一輩子的職業，我打算把自己的餘生都致力於這個事業。我真為從前把歲月浪費在一些瑣碎事情上感到後悔。走，親愛的河鼠兄，還有你這位和善的朋友，和我一起到馬廄前的院子去，到那兒你們就會明白的。」

說完，蟾蜍便走在前面帶路，河鼠滿臉狐疑地跟在後面。馬廄前面的空地上停著一輛吉普賽大篷車，是一輛閃閃發光的新

車，車身是淡黃色夾雜著綠色紋飾，車輪則漆成紅色。

「看呀！」蟾蜍又開雙腿大聲說，「這輛小型車將帶給我們真正的生活：寬闊的大路、塵土飛揚的馬路、灌木叢生的荒野、牧場、樹籬，還有起伏的丘陵！到那時，我們可以在野外露營，或到村子裏投宿，我們可以到許許多多大城小鎮去！今天到這裏，明天換另一個地方！我們可以到處旅遊，樂趣無窮，多刺激呀！整個世界都鋪展在我們面前，地平線上的風光，每一刻都截然不同！還有，這輛車子是最棒的，在同型車子中獨一無二。進去看看裏面的設備，那可全都是我設計的！」

鼴鼠聽後激動不已，興致勃勃，迫不及待地跟在蟾蜍後面，進入車子裏。河鼠不屑地哼著鼻子，雙手插進口袋，站在原地不動。

車子確實十分靈巧、舒適，裏面有一張小睡床，一張折疊的小桌子，做飯用的爐子，以及櫃子、書架、裝有一隻鳥的鳥籠，還有各種各樣的鍋、盤、壺、罐。

「一應俱全！」蟾蜍得意洋洋地說著，一面拉開其中一格抽屜，「你看——餅乾、罐頭龍蝦肉、沙丁魚——要什麼有什麼。這是蘇打水，那是香煙，還有信紙、臘肉、果醬、紙牌、骨牌。」他一面說一面走下車子，「今天下午我們出發後，你就會發現，車上什麼都不缺。」

「對不起，」河鼠慢條斯理地說著，嘴裏嚼著一根稻草，「你剛才說什麼『我們』、『今天下午』、『出發』，怎麼回事？」

「哎呀，我親愛的河鼠老兄，」蟾蜍用哀求的口吻說道，「別這樣咬文嚼字、冷嘲熱諷。你知道，你一定得來，沒有你我怎麼能應付得了，就這麼說定吧！別爭了——我可不想跟你爭論。你總不能一輩子都在河上過那種乏味古板的生活吧，整天待在岸上的洞裏或困在船上，有什麼意思？我要帶你勇闖全世界！我要把你變成一隻名副其實的『動物』，我的老兄！」

「我不稀罕，」河鼠固執地說，「我不會跟你去的。我還是會像以往那樣，守著我的河流，在洞裏、在船上過我的日子。而且，鼴鼠會跟我一塊，他聽我的，對嗎，鼴鼠？」

「當然啦！」鼴鼠忠心耿耿地說，「我永遠聽你的，河鼠，你說得很對。但是，蟾蜍的想法似乎……似乎很有意思，對吧？」他有點依依不捨地說道。可憐的鼴鼠，他認為冒險的生活是新奇、刺激的，光憑這就夠吸引他的了！況且，他第一眼就愛上這輛淡黃色的馬車，還有車裏的各種小玩意兒。

河鼠察覺他的弦外之音，於是心裏動搖了。他不喜歡讓人失望，而且他又非常喜歡鼴鼠，願意為他做任何事情。蟾蜍全神貫注地盯著他們倆。

「先進屋裏吃午飯吧，」蟾蜍很是圓滑地說，「咱們邊吃邊商量，凡事不必匆忙地作出決定。當然囉，你們去不去我都不在乎，我只是想讓你們開心。『為別人的幸福而活！』就是我的座右銘。」

就像蟾蜍莊園裏應有盡有一樣，午飯當然是色香味俱全。此時蟾蜍已灑脫自如，他不理會河鼠，只顧著對經驗不足的鼴鼠高

談闊論。蟾蜍天生就能言善辯，又非常善於發揮自己的想像力，他把即將到來的旅遊說得繪聲繪影、五光十色；將一路上好玩的東西，說得讓鼴鼠神往不已，連坐都坐不住了。到後來，這三個夥伴似乎就這樣把出外旅行的事給定了下來。河鼠儘管心裏不樂意，但他的好心腸最後還是征服了心裏的反對。他不想讓兩位朋友失望，他們正在專心地做著旅行計劃，並且，把未來幾個星期裏每一天的活動都安排好了。

　　一切都準備好以後，得意洋洋的蟾蜍帶著他的夥伴來到養馬場，叫他們牽來那匹老灰馬。蟾蜍沒有事先徵求老馬的意願，就強迫他參加這次塵土飛揚的旅行，完成這個吃力的工作。老馬當然是一百個不情願，他顯然更喜歡留在馬場，因此河鼠和鼴鼠費了九牛二虎之力才捉住他。與此同時，蟾蜍往車上的櫃子裏塞滿了各種必需品，在車底下掛上了幾個飼料袋、幾包洋蔥、幾捆乾草和幾個籃子。他們終於制服了馬，並把他牽來套在馬車上。於是他們便出發了。三隻動物根據自己的愛好，有的走在馬車旁，有的坐在車上，大家高興地說著話。那是一個陽光燦爛的下午，他們的馬車揚起滾滾的塵煙，那情景讓他們十分得意。道路兩邊的果園裏，鳥兒從濃密的樹叢中探出頭來，高興地和他們打招呼；路上的行人向他們問好，有的還停下來稱讚他們漂亮的馬車；坐在自家門前樹籬邊上的野兔，舉起前爪說：「哎呀，多美呀！」

　　到了晚上，他們已然離家很遠了。這時的他們疲憊不堪，便在一塊遠離人煙的空地上停下車子，解開馬韁讓馬吃草，三個夥

伴坐在馬車旁的草地上吃起簡便的晚飯。蟾蜍滔滔不絕地說著自己今後的打算，明亮的星星對著他們眨眼睛，不知從何時悄悄升起的圓月也來和他們做伴，靜靜地聽著他們說話。後來，他們爬上了車上的小鋪。蟾蜍踢了踢自己的雙腿，睡意濃濃地說：「晚安，夥伴們！這才是一位紳士真正該過的日子！別再叨念你們那條河啦！」

「我不是在叨念我那條河，」耐心的河鼠答道，「「你知道我不是，蟾蜍。我是想念它——」他感傷地低喃道，「一直想念著它！」

鼴鼠把爪子從毯子下面伸了出來，在黑暗中摸了河鼠的爪子，並用力地捏了一下。「你要我做什麼我都聽你的，河鼠兄，」他壓低聲音說道，「我們明天就走——越早越好——回到我們在河邊的可愛老家去，怎麼樣？」

「不，我們要堅持到底。」河鼠輕聲答道，「謝謝你的好意，但我應該和蟾蜍在一起，直到旅行結束。我們把他一個人丟下太危險了。反正旅程很快就會結束的，他的熱情從來就沒有長久過。晚安！」

果然，這次旅行確實結束得比河鼠預料的還要早。

經過一整天令人興奮的旅行後，蟾蜍很快便沉睡了，第二天早上河鼠和鼴鼠費了很大勁兒也無法喚醒他。於是他們默默地幹起活來。河鼠餵了馬，生起了火，把前一晚的杯盤刷洗乾淨，開始準備早餐；鼴鼠則跑到最近的村子去買牛奶、雞蛋和各種東西——其實村子離他們很遠——當然囉，這些都是蟾蜍事先忘了

帶的物品。忙完這些事後，兩隻動物都筋疲力盡了。他們正坐著休息時，蟾蜍才興致勃勃地來到他們跟前，說他們現在的生活眞是輕鬆愉快極了，用不著去管各種瑣事，也不用做累人的家務。

那天，他們駕著馬車在荒野上到處漫遊，過得非常開心。到了晚上，他們同樣在一片開闊地上露營，與之前不同的是，河鼠和鼴鼠千方百計地讓蟾蜍做他本該做的事。結果，第二天早上該出發的時候，蟾蜍再也不稱讚荒野生活的美妙了，他只想再多睡一會兒，但河鼠和鼴鼠猛力地把他拉了起來。像前兩天一樣，他們還是走在荒野小道上，到了下午才走上公路，這是他們第一次走在公路上。就在這條公路上，一件誰也沒料到的災難迅速降臨了——這一場災難對他們此次出遊影響至深，而且對蟾蜍日後的生活有著決定性的影響。

他們慢悠悠地走在大馬路上，鼴鼠走在前面和馬說著話，原因是馬抱怨自己被所有人冷落，誰都沒有好好關心過他。蟾蜍和河鼠走在馬車的後面，一起說著話兒——正確地說，是蟾蜍說話，河鼠偶爾應聲：「是，沒錯、沒錯，那你怎麼跟他說呢？」其實他一直在想著別的事。這時，從他們身後傳來一種微弱的響聲，像是遠處蜜蜂的嗡嗡聲，彷彿正警示著前方。他們回頭一看，只見路上捲起一團塵煙，中間有一顆黑點正以驚人的速度向他們奔來，從煙塵中發出一種「刷——刷——」的響聲，活像一隻動物在痛苦呻吟。他們沒有把這些放在心上，繼續說著他們的話。然而，頃刻間，寧靜就被打破了。一陣猛烈的風和巨大的聲響使他們急忙跳進路邊的水溝裏，那東西向他們撲了過來！

「刷——刷——」的響聲震耳欲聾,慌亂中,他們終於看清那是一輛氣派到令人倒抽一口氣的汽車,汽車裏的駕駛員正全神貫注地緊握著方向盤。這個龐然大物從他們身邊飛馳而過,捲起一陣濃濃的灰塵,把他們團團圍住,使他們睜不開眼睛。很快地,汽車又變成了遠處的一個小黑點,越走越遠的嗡嗡聲,就此慢慢地消失了。

彼時,那匹灰色的老馬正一邊慢悠悠地邁步,一邊做夢,彷彿自己仍在寧靜舒適的馬場裏。因此面對這般意料之外的突發狀況,他猝不及防並且大亂陣腳。他一會向上高舉前蹄,一會向前猛烈俯衝,接著又逐步向後倒退。儘管鼴鼠拼命地拽著韁繩制止他失控的舉動,一面好聲好氣地安撫他、使他冷靜,仍舊徒勞無功。他執意向後退,硬生生地將大篷車往路邊的深溝裏推去。車身瞬間大力搖晃,隨之而來的即是一陣驚天動地的碎裂聲。這輛淡黃色的大篷車,與他們的驕傲和喜悅同在的高級馬車,就這樣側躺在深溝中,成了一堆支離破碎的殘骸。

河鼠氣得直跳腳,怒不可遏地說:「你們這群惡棍!」他握緊雙拳,破口大罵:「你們這群壞胚子、你們這群強盜,你們這群——你們這群——路霸!我要訴諸法律!我要舉發你們!我要把你們通通告上法院!」他的思鄉病頓時消失得無影無蹤,此時的他成為淡黃色船艦的船長,而敵方船隻正魯莽地橫衝直撞,將他的船艦強逼上淺灘。他一個勁兒地道出自己過去對蒸汽船船長說過的刻薄言詞,因為那些人總是把船駛得過份靠岸,掀起的水花經常淹濕他家客廳地毯的緣故。

蟾蜍傻楞楞地坐在漫天塵土的路中央，雙腿僵硬地向前伸直，目光定格在那輛汽車消失的方向。他呼吸急促但一臉平靜與滿足，並且每隔一段時間就嘟起雙唇，輕聲地發出「刷——刷——」的聲響。

鼴鼠忙著撫慰老灰馬，過了好一會才讓他的情緒緩和下來。接著他上前巡視那輛橫臥在深溝的大篷車，它的下場真是令人目不忍睹：不僅門窗全部碎裂，車軸更是彎得看不出原貌；其中一個輪子還從車體上脫落，原本在車內的沙丁魚罐頭亦散落各處。最慘的是賞鳥籠裏的鳥，他正可憐兮兮地不斷啜泣，哭求他們釋放自己。

河鼠上前協助鼴鼠，不過，即便他倆再努力也沒法扶起大篷車。「喂，蟾蜍！」他們齊聲喊道，「過來一起幫忙抬車，行嗎！」

蟾蜍悶不吭聲，一動也不動地坐在路中央，他們只好前去察看蟾蜍的狀況。他們發現蟾蜍坐在那一臉陶醉不已的模樣，雙眼緊盯著前方漫天的飛塵。嘴裏不時喃喃地發出「刷——刷——」的聲響。

河鼠雙手使勁地搖動蟾蜍的雙肩，厲聲問道：「蟾蜍！你到底要不要過來幫忙？」

「多麼璀璨耀眼又鼓舞人心的場面啊！」蟾蜍嘀咕著，身體卻一動也不動。「如此詩意的移動方式！這才是真正的旅遊！絕無僅有的旅遊！今天在這，明天就在那，從一座村莊開往下座村莊，從一座城鎮瞬移到另一座城鎮——永遠流轉在不同人的視野

第二章

之中！哦，幸福！哦，刷刷！哦，天啊！哦，我的天啊！」

「哦，不要再做蠢事了，蟾蜍！」鼹鼠無奈地喊道。

「我對這東西一無所知！」蟾蜍不斷地低聲囈語著，「我究竟虛擲了多少光陰？我作夢也想不到，世上有這般逸品的存在。但現在——我明白了，現在我完全開悟了！哦，從今往後，在我面前鋪展的，該是多麼光輝燦爛的美好前程！當我在道路上縱橫馳騁時，身後將揚起多少滾滾沙塵啊！我會毫不在意地將所有馬車推下深溝。哼，令人生厭的小馬車！哼，平凡無奇的馬車！哼，淡黃色的馬車！」

鼹鼠問河鼠：「我們該拿他如何是好？」

「一點辦法也沒有，」河鼠直接了當地說，「一直以來都是一點辦法也沒有，我認識他這麼久了，還不懂他嗎？他現在就是失心瘋。又著迷於新玩意了！他總是如此狂熱，這還只是第一階段呢。他將一連好幾天都是如此，就像一隻遊蕩在美夢裏的動物，在現實中完全派不上用場。別管他就是。我倆還是去看看該如何處理那輛大篷車吧！」

經過一番仔細的巡視後，他們認為，即使成功將大篷車扶正，它亦不敷使用。它的車軸殘破不堪，脫落的輪子也粉碎殆盡。

河鼠當機立斷，把老灰馬的韁繩繫在馬背上，一手牽著馬，一手提著鳥籠和裏頭早已歇斯底里的那隻鳥。「走吧！」河鼠冷冷地對鼹鼠說，「離這裏最近的城鎮少說也有五六英里遠，我們只能徒步前往了，所以得盡早動身才行。」

「那蟾蜍該怎麼辦？」他們正打算啓程時，鼴鼠焦急地問著，「我們不能讓他一個人神智不清地坐在路中央，置之不理。這非常危險。萬一有別的汽車駛來該如何是好？」

「哦，那個麻煩精，」河鼠氣急敗壞地說著，「我要和他斷絕關係！」

然而，他們才走沒多遠，身後就傳來急促的腳步聲。蟾蜍一把抓住他倆，一邊一爪，勾住他們的臂彎走著。他依舊上氣不接下氣，目光呆滯地直視空無一物的前方。

「你聽好了，蟾蜍！」河鼠嚴聲說道：「我們一到鎮上，你就直接往警局走去，去問問他們誰是那輛汽車的所有者，然後起訴他。接著，你得去鐵匠鋪或是修車鋪安排一下，讓他們把大篷車修好。雖然需要花費不少時間，不過它還不至於到完全無法修繕的地步。與此同時，我和鼴鼠將前往旅館找間舒適的客房住下，直到大篷車修復，也等到你的精神恢復爲止。」

「警察局？起訴？」蟾蜍發出囈語般的低語道，「讓我去起訴那幅喚醒我的絕世美景？修復大篷車？我已經和大篷車永別了！我再也不想見到它，也不想聽到有關它的隻字片語。河鼠！你絕對料想不到，我有多麼感激你此次應邀與我遠行。因爲你不來，我就沒辦法出發，那我也就永遠沒機會見到──那隻天鵝、那束光芒、那道閃電！我可能永遠也無法聽見那令人心醉神往的聲音，亦無法聞到那令人迷戀不已的香氣了！這一切多虧有你在，我的摯友！」

河鼠無奈地別過臉，「看到沒有？」他隔著蟾蜍的腦袋對鼴

鼠說：「他根本病入膏肓。算了吧，我放棄診治他──等我們到了城鎮，立刻前往火車站。走運的話，我們或許來得及搭上一列火車，今晚就能回到河岸。你看我以後還會不會跟這令人惱火的動物一同出遊玩樂，氣死我！」他氣憤地皺起鼻子，大力地發出哼聲，在這令人疲憊、乏味的旅途尾聲，他只與鼴鼠一人交談。

到達城鎮他們就直奔車站，把蟾蜍留在次等候車室，給了守門人兩便士後，就把蟾蜍全權交給他們嚴加看管。然後，他們把老灰馬寄放在一間旅館的馬廄裏，並說明怎麼處置馬車和車裏的所有物。終於，來了一列火車，緩緩地將他們載往距離蟾蜍莊園不遠的車站。他們護送醉生夢死，夢遊般的蟾蜍回家。他們將蟾蜍帶進家門，指示管家協助他用膳、更衣、就寢。緊接著，他倆就從船塢中划出自己的小船，順河而下，回到下游的家中。深夜裏，他們在自己面河的客廳裏坐下用餐。此刻的河鼠，無比地愜意與自在。

隔日的傍晚，鼴鼠很晚才起身，並且整日悠閒地在岸邊釣魚。而一直四處拜訪，並呼朋引伴到家中閒聊的河鼠，此時慢步地走向鼴鼠。「你聽見傳聞了嗎？」他說，「整個沿岸都在談論一件事。今早蟾蜍坐上早班的火車進城去，並且花了一大筆錢訂購一輛又大又昂貴的汽車。」

第三章　野林子

　　鼴鼠一直想結識獾。他從大家的談論中覺得，獾似乎是一個
很了不起的人物，雖然他很少露面，但卻無形地影響著這一帶的
每一個人。但每當鼴鼠跟河鼠提起自己的想法，河鼠都搪塞過去
了。「別急，」河鼠總是這樣說，「總有一天獾會出現在我們面
前的——他會的——到時候我再介紹你認識他，他可是最厚道的
人！不過，最好不要是你前去登門拜訪，而是在適當的時候，迎
面碰上他。」

　　「那你能不能邀請他來這兒——吃飯什麼的？」鼴鼠說。

　　「他不會來的，」河鼠答道，「獾討厭社交、邀約、吃飯，
諸如此類的事他都不喜歡。」

　　「那麼，我們能不能去拜訪他？」鼴鼠建議說。

　　「噢，我敢肯定他鐵定不歡迎我們，」河鼠十分警覺地說，
「他很害羞，你去拜訪他，他一定會覺得自己被冒犯了。即使我
和他熟識，我也從來不敢獨自去拜訪他。況且我們也去不了，那
根本不可能，因為他住在野林子的深處。」

　　「就算他住在野林子深處吧，」鼴鼠說，「但你跟我說過，

野林子沒什麼可怕的。」

「噢，我記得我講過，而且確實也沒什麼可怕的，」河鼠含糊其辭地答道，「但我覺得我們現在不能去那兒，現在還不是時候。那地方離這裏很遠，再說這個季節他不會待在家裏的。耐心地等吧，總有一天他會到這兒來的。」

聽河鼠這麼說，鼴鼠只好就此打住。但是獾始終沒有來。他們的快活日子一天天過去，送走了炎熱的夏天後，天氣漸漸變得寒冷，冰冷泥濘的道路使他們不得不待在家裏。窗外，暴漲的河水激烈地咆哮著，划船已是不可能的事。鼴鼠不由得想起了孤獨的灰獾，他在野林子深處的洞穴裏，獨自過著自己的生活。

在冬天，河鼠睡得很久，每天都是早睡晚起。在短暫的白天裏，他有時胡編幾句詩，有時做點家事。當然囉，經常有動物到家裏來，每當這時大家便沒完沒了地講起故事來，談論著夏天裏發生的一些事情。

現在回想起來，那是一段多麼美妙的時光啊！夏天裏發生的事，就像無數幅色彩繽紛的圖畫！河岸上盛大華麗的場面，一個接一個出現，它們就像舞臺上不斷變換的布景畫面。首先出現的是紫色馬鞭草，一簇簇茂密地生長在河邊，河水映出它們美麗的臉龐。緊接在後的是柔嫩的柳蘭，絢麗多姿，活像落日的晚霞。接著，紫中帶白的玻璃草慢悠悠地上場了。最後，在一個早上，羞怯的野薔薇邁著優雅的步伐，緩緩地走上舞臺。於是人們知道，六月在優美的弦樂伴隨下，終於來臨。人們還在等待著一個人：那是仙女們愛慕的牧羊人，是少女在窗前苦苦等待的騎士，

是能以一個吻喚醒沉睡的夏天，使它重新煥發生命和愛情的王子。當散發著芬芳香氣的野菊，穿著黃色緊身衣，溫文爾雅地走進隊伍裏，夏日的戲碼就此揭開了序幕。

　　那是一場多麼難忘的戲碼啊！雖然風雨在擊打著門口，但昏昏欲睡的動物們，此時正舒舒服服地躲在自己的洞穴裏，回味著令人神往的早晨：太陽還沒有露臉，濃濃的白霧籠罩在水面上；突然，有的動物跳進了河裏，有的在河岸上奔跑，趕走了清晨的寂靜；這時，太陽升起來了，大地、空氣、水都在變換著色彩，原來灰濛濛的一片變得金光燦爛，大地再度色彩斑斕。他們還記得，在炎熱的中午，自己在綠蔭下懶洋洋地打著盹兒，太陽透過樹葉間的縫隙照在他們的身上；到了午後，他們便在河裏划船、游泳、到塵土飛揚的小路去閒逛、到黃澄澄的玉米田去玩耍；然後是漫長、涼爽的夜晚，他們繼續講著沒完沒了的故事，或迎接一位又一位朋友的來訪，抑或是制定一個又一個關於未來的計劃。在短暫的冬日裏，圍在火爐旁，說著永遠也說不完的話兒。儘管如此，鼴鼠還是閒得發慌。一天下午，河鼠坐在火爐邊的沙發上，時而打著瞌睡，時而吟著不成韻的詩句。鼴鼠則下定決心，獨自到野林子去，他心想，說不定還能遇上獾先生。

　　那是一個寒冷陰沉的下午，天空像鉛一樣沉重，鼴鼠偷偷地走出溫暖的客廳來到曠野上。他腳下的地裸露著，周圍的樹木上一片葉子也沒有，他發覺自己從來沒有像這個冬日一樣，洞察到萬物的奧妙；大自然似乎脫下了自己的盛裝，正在酣睡。在枝繁葉茂的夏天，矮樹林、山谷、採石場以及其他隱密的地方，可都

是探險的好去處；如今，它們都悲慘地暴露自己的秘密，它們似乎在哀求鼴鼠不要看它們此時破敗的外表，它們多麼希望在鼴鼠面前只展示多姿多彩的面貌來迷惑他啊！它們此時的情形確實有點可憐，但這使鼴鼠感到快活，甚至興奮。他很高興，因為他喜歡脫掉華麗服裝、不加修飾的原野，他看到了它真實、純樸、壯實的一面。他不喜歡夏日裏熱情的三葉草，也不喜歡結著種子的禾草飛舞。繁茂的樹籬、波浪起伏的山毛櫸林和榆林，似乎都消逝了。鼴鼠興致勃勃地往野林子走去。對他來說，野林子就像是隱沒在沉寂的海洋中的黑色礁石，高傲而又險惡。

　　一踏入野林子，他並沒有感到驚慌。樹枝被他踩得沙沙作響，地上的木頭絆倒他，長在樹椿上的木耳，它浮誇的模樣活像在模仿那些他熟悉的漫畫人物；一切是那麼地有趣、那麼地令人激動。走著走著，他來到了光線昏暗的地方，這裏樹木密密麻麻，路兩邊的洞口，似乎在向他張開醜陋的嘴。

　　一切都靜悄悄的，暮色很快從四面八方向他襲來；陽光似乎像洪水一樣，漸漸地退去了。

　　這時，他看到了各式各樣的臉。

　　他轉頭往身後望去，看見一個模模糊糊的東西；他想那是一張臉，一張醜陋的楔形小臉，兩眼從洞裏盯著他看。只是當他轉身靠近時，那東西便不見了。

　　他加快了步伐，叮嚀自己不要胡思亂想，不然他會沒完沒了地想個不停。他走過了一個又一個的洞口，有人在看我嗎？——沒有呀！——有人嗎？分明有張著冷酷雙眼的小臉，從洞口裏瞪

著他看，然後又消失不見。他躊躇不前——然後又鼓起勇氣，繼續向前走。突然，他又看見了一張臉，似乎周圍的每一個洞口裏都藏有一張臉，這裏好幾百個洞口裏都有一張轉瞬即逝的臉，每一雙眼睛都不懷好意地盯著他，那些目光邪惡而又犀利。

他心裏想，要是能逃離陡坡上這些洞口，就不會再看到那些臉孔了。於是他急急地拐了一個彎，逃離小道，往林子裏人煙罕至的地方奔去。

這時，呼嘯聲響起來。

雖然這聲音是從他身後很遠的地方傳來，是一種隱隱約約的尖叫聲，但仍促使他加快步伐往前走。然後，那聲音又從他前方很遠的地方傳來，依然是隱隱約約的尖叫聲。他不禁猶豫地想往回走。就在他感到進退兩難之際，呼嘯聲突然在他的兩側同時響起，很快便傳遍了整個林子，使他不得不停下腳步。他們在防備著他的到來，他們到底是誰呢？鼴鼠手無寸鐵，孤零零的一個，沒有誰可以幫助他。此刻，夜幕已然降臨。

這時，傳來了啪嗒啪嗒的響聲。

最初他以為是落葉的聲音，因為那響聲非常微弱。漸漸地那響聲變得越來越有節奏，他心想，那一定是小腳踩在地面上發出的聲響，聽起來離他還很遠。但到底是從他的前方，還是身後傳來的呢？似乎先是一隻腳的聲音，接著是另一隻腳的聲音，然後是兩隻腳發出的響聲。腳步聲越來越多，他豎起耳朵聆聽，那腳步聲似乎正從四面八方向他圍攏過來。正當他站在那兒全神貫注地聆聽時，一隻野兔從樹叢中竄出來，朝他奔去。他停在那裏，

以爲野兔會放慢腳步，或從他身邊繞過去。出乎他的意料，那傢伙從他旁邊擦身而過，野兔板著臉，兩眼瞪著鼴鼠，「滾開！你這個笨蛋！滾開！」鼴鼠聽到他咬牙切齒地說道。野兔繞過一個樹樁，鑽進了一個地洞。

那腳步聲越來越大，變得像冰雹打在周圍厚厚的乾樹葉上的聲音。整個林子彷彿都在飛跑，追呀、趕呀，好像在圍捕什麼東西或著——什麼人似的？惶恐中，他也漫無目的地跑了起來，他不知道該往哪裏去。他一會兒撞到什麼東西、一會兒又摔倒在什麼東西上、一會兒掉在什麼東西上、一會兒急急地閃躲些什麼東西。最後，他躲進了一棵空心的老山毛欅樹裏，裏面雖然又深又黑，但終於有了一個藏身之處——也許可以平安無事了。但，誰又說得準呢？不管怎樣，他已經累得跑不動了，只好蜷伏在飄進樹洞裏的乾樹葉中，祈禱著自己能安然無恙。他躺在那裏喘著氣，渾身發抖，一面傾聽著外面的呼嘯聲和啪嗒聲。這時他終於明白，那正是住在田裏和樹籬下的小動物們，曾經在林子裏碰到過也被嚇壞過的東西；怪不得河鼠一心一意地不讓他到野林子裏來，原來他是怕鼴鼠被那東西嚇壞！

此時的河鼠正舒舒服服地坐在火爐邊打著瞌睡。那張剛寫了半首詩的紙片從他的膝蓋滑到地上，他的頭向後仰著，嘴巴張得大大的；這時他正夢見自己在綠草如茵的河岸上閒逛。突然，一根木炭在火中滑落，火爐發出的劈啪響聲和飛濺而出的火花，使他驚醒過來。他猛然想起剛剛做了一半的事。河鼠撿起那張掉在地上的紙片，看著那首沒寫完的詩，思考了片刻，然後轉過身

來，問鼴鼠是否能幫他想個好韻腳。

但鼴鼠不見了。

他試圖察聽鼴鼠的動靜，但屋裏悄然無聲。

接著，他喊了幾聲「鼴鼠老弟」也不見動靜，於是站起身走到客廳。

鼴鼠平時掛帽子的釘子上空空如也，他那雙經常放在傘架旁的高筒靴也不見了。

河鼠走出了屋子，在屋外泥濘的地面上仔細察看著，希望能找到鼴鼠的足跡。啊，這不是鼴鼠的鞋印嗎？那雙靴子是這個冬天新買的，鞋底的紋路清晰可辨。河鼠清楚地看到泥濘路面上的鞋印，逕直地通向野林子。

河鼠臉色凝重，站在地上沉思了一會兒。接著，他走回屋裏、繫上腰帶、插上兩把手槍、又從客廳的角落拿出一根粗木棍，步履敏捷地朝野林子走去。

當他來到林子邊時已是黃昏時分了，但他毫不猶豫地向林子深處走去。一路上，他焦急地左顧右盼，希望看到自己朋友的蹤影。與此同時，一些醜惡的小臉不時地從他兩邊的洞口裏探出來，但一見到這隻威武的動物腰上插著兩把手槍，手中握著一根粗大的木棒，這些可惡的小臉便馬上不見了；而他剛進林子時，清清楚楚地聽到的呼嘯聲和啪嗒聲也漸漸消失了，周圍的一切都悄無聲息。他雄赳赳地從林子的一頭走到另一頭，然後又折回來；這次他沒有走在道路上，而是走在野地裏，一邊不停地高喊：「鼴鼠、鼴鼠，你在哪兒？我是河鼠！」

　　他在林子裏搜索了一個多鐘頭，最後終於聽見了一聲很小的應答聲，這使他非常高興。順著應答聲尋去，他在黑暗中來到了一棵空心的老山毛櫸樹下，樹洞裏傳來微弱的聲音：「河鼠兄！真的是你嗎？」

　　河鼠爬進了樹洞，在裏面他見到了疲憊不堪、渾身發抖的鼴鼠。「噢，河鼠！」鼴鼠喊道，「你不知道我有多害怕啊！」

　　「哦，我知道的，」河鼠安慰他說，「鼴鼠，你真不該自己一個人跑出來的啊！我一直想辦法阻止你來這。我們這些住在河岸上的動物，平時是不會獨自到這兒來的。即使要來，也要結伴一起來，這樣才會平安無事。再說，到林子來之前得學會很多東西，我們都知道這些，而你還不瞭解。我指的是口令、標誌、特殊作用的諺語、要放在口袋裏的植物，還有必須背誦的口訣，以及能派上用場的逃脫術或作戰計劃。只要你懂了，這些都是很簡單的東西，但作為小動物你必須記住它們，要不然你會惹上麻煩的。當然啦，如果你是獾或水獺，那就另當別論了。」

　　「果敢的蟾蜍先生一定勇於獨自來這吧？」鼴鼠問道。

　　「蟾蜍那傢伙？」河鼠哈哈大笑地說，「給他一帽子的金幣，他也不會一個人到這兒來的。」

　　聽到河鼠開心的笑聲，看到他手中的木棒和發亮的手槍，鼴鼠感到十分欣慰。他不再發抖，膽子也慢慢大了起來，恢復以往的自在。

　　「好啦！現在，」過了一會兒，河鼠說道，「我們必須振作起來，趁現在天還亮著看得見路，趕緊回家。你知道，我們絕對

不能在這過夜,畢竟天氣太冷了。」

「親愛的河鼠兄,」可憐的鼴鼠說道,「真的非常抱歉,我實在是累壞了。真要回家,你得讓我多歇一會兒,好讓我喘口氣。」

「噢,好吧,」好心的河鼠說,「你休息吧。再說天也差不多全黑了,再過一會兒,月亮就會升起。」

於是鼴鼠鑽進乾樹葉裏,攤開四肢,不一會兒便睡著了;不過他睡得並不安穩,斷斷續續的。與此同時,河鼠用樹葉把自己蓋起來,使自己暖和一點;他耐心地躺著等待鼴鼠,一隻爪子握著一把手槍。

之後鼴鼠終於醒了過來,他精神好多了。於是,河鼠說:「我先到外面看一下,如果一切正常,那我們就馬上動身。」

他走到洞口把頭探了出去。接著,鼴鼠聽見他低聲自言自語:「哎呀!這下子可糟糕啦!」

「怎麼啦,河鼠兄?」鼴鼠問道。

「下雪了,」河鼠答道,「下得很大呢。」

鼴鼠走了過來,蹲在河鼠的身邊往外一看,只見那曾令他恐懼不已的林子已全然不一樣了;洞穴、凹地、水坑、陷阱和其他威脅著行人的地方,全不見了。地面似乎鋪上了一層潔白的地毯,白茫茫的,像美妙的仙境一般,精緻得令人不忍將自己的髒腳踩踏其上;空氣似乎彌漫著細細的粉末,落在面頰上,使人感到刺痛;潔白的地面映襯出黑黝黝的樹幹。

「哎呀,實在是沒辦法了,」河鼠沉思片刻後說道,「我想

我們還是趕快走，就當是碰碰運氣吧。但最糟的是，我不知道我們此刻的確切方位，這場雪使周圍的一切改變了面貌。」

確實是這樣，鼴鼠還真看不出這就是他曾走過的林子。但是他們還是勇敢地出發了。他們選擇了一條他們認為最合適的路線，肩並肩地走著。他們裝成一副興高采烈、無所畏懼的模樣，假作自己能在每一棵陌生且陰森、黯然的樹上，認出那些向他們打招呼的老朋友；又或者假裝自己能在這個分不清東西南北的冰雪世界裏，看見自己熟悉的道路。

過了一、兩個小時，他們已搞不清時間了，便停下腳步。走了這麼久，他們已是精疲力竭，心裏既沮喪又不知所措，於是坐在一棵倒下的樹幹上休息，一邊考慮下一步該怎麼辦。他們累得渾身痠痛，一路上的跌跌撞撞致使腿腳也碰傷了，甚至幾次掉進坑裏，全身都濕透了。地上的積雪越來越厚，每走一步都非常吃力。而且，樹木變得茂密更加難以分辨了。這林子似乎無邊無際，分辨不出東南西北，最糟的是，他們已找不到走出林子的路。

「我們可不能在這兒坐太久，」河鼠說，「我們得繼續往前走，然後再想點辦法。冷天總是沒好事，積雪很快會厚得讓我們難以趕路。」他仔細地看了看四周，認真地思考著。「嘿，」他接著說，「我想起來啦！在我們的前方有一條山谷，那裏都是地勢起伏不平的丘陵。我們就往那條山谷去，在那裏找一個地面乾燥、能避風雪的洞穴，然後好好地休息一下再走，畢竟我們倆都累壞啦！再說，雪也許會停，情況或許會有所好轉也說不定。」

　　於是他們又站起身，艱難地往山谷走去。來到山谷，他們四處尋找，希望發現一個乾爽的山洞或角落，以便躲避這刺骨的寒風和飄揚的大雪。他們正在搜尋河鼠提到的小山丘時，突然鼴鼠後腳一滑，撲倒在地上並尖叫起來。

　　「哎呀，我的腿！」他喊道，「噢，我可憐的大腿呀！」鼴鼠坐在雪地上說著，兩隻前爪抱起自己的後腿。

　　「可憐的鼴鼠！」河鼠心疼地說。

　　「你今天運氣似乎不佳啊。讓我看一下，唉！」他跪在地上察看鼴鼠的腿，一邊說道，「沒錯，你的腿被割傷了。我用我的手帕幫你包紮一下。」

　　「我一定是絆倒在樹枝或樹樁上了。」鼴鼠痛苦地說，「哎喲！哎喲！」

　　「這傷口邊緣非常整齊。」河鼠說著，又仔細地檢查了一下傷口，「這傷口絕對不是被樹枝或樹樁割傷的，看起來倒像是被什麼鋒利的鐵器割到的樣子。這就奇怪啦！」他想了一會兒，又看了看周圍的山坡。

　　「嘿，別管它是什麼刻的，」鼴鼠由於疼痛，說起話來連音都發不標準了，「不管是什麼割的，傷口都一樣疼。」

　　然而，河鼠用手帕給鼴鼠包好傷口後便丟下他，忙碌地在雪地裏刨起來。他手腳併用地不停地扒呀，挖呀，鼴鼠則在一邊不耐煩地等著，不時對他說：「別挖啦，河鼠！」

　　突然，河鼠喊道：「好哇！好哇！太好啦！」接著，在雪地裏興奮地手舞足蹈。

「你發現了什麼，河鼠兄？」鼴鼠叫道，兩隻前爪還抱著那條受了傷的腿。

「快過來看啊！」河鼠一邊跳著，一邊對他說。

鼴鼠一瘸一拐地走了過來，細心地看著。

「哎呀！」最後他慢慢地說，「我看出來啦。以前也見過同樣的東西，見過許多次呢！到底在哪見過這東西呢？噢，是一把鏟雪用的鐵鏟！那又怎麼樣？幹什麼為一把鏟子手舞足蹈？」

「難道你不明白這意味著什麼？你——你這個呆瓜！」河鼠不耐煩地叫道。

「我當然明白那是什麼意思。」鼴鼠答道，「這僅僅說明有個粗心愛忘事的傢伙，把自己的鏟子遺落在林子裏，這鏟子會絆倒每一個從這經過的人呢！要我說，這傢伙也太不小心了！等我回到家，一定要向——向什麼人投訴，等著瞧吧！」

「噢，天哪！」河鼠叫道，對鼴鼠的蠢笨感到非常失望，「哎，別吵了，快過來鏟雪！」說完自己便刨了起來，雪在他的四周飛舞著。

過了一會兒，他的辛勞終於獲得回報，一塊破舊的門口踏墊露了出來。

「看見了吧，我剛才跟你說了什麼？」河鼠如同大獲全勝般歡呼道。

「得了吧，河鼠！這東西根本就毫無意義，」鼴鼠十分坦率地答道。「嘿，」他接著說，「你似乎又能撿走別人扔掉的東西了，心裏一定很高興吧？如果你忍不住又要手舞足蹈的話，那就

跳吧，跳個夠吧！我們還有正經事要做呢！別把時間浪費在這些無用的東西上面。我們總不能拿腳踏墊當飯吃吧？總不能睡在踏墊下面吧？這踏墊總不能變成雪橇把我們拉回家去吧？你這討人厭的齧齒動物。」

「你——真——的——認——爲——」河鼠激動地大聲說道，「這塊踏墊什麼意思也沒有嗎？」

「得啦，河鼠！」鼴鼠很不高興地說，「我們還是別爲這種雞毛蒜皮的事爭吵了。有誰聽說過一塊踏墊有什麼特別的意思？不就是一塊踏墊嗎，難道還能有別的意思？」

「哎呀，你——你這愚蠢的動物。」河鼠非常生氣地答道，「一句話也不要說了，還是幹活吧。如果你今晚還想睡一個好覺，那就鏟雪吧！好好挖，還要留心看，特別是這座小山丘的兩側，這可是我們最後的機會啦！」

說著河鼠便衝向他們旁邊的一個雪堆，用他的木棒到處亂戳，接著便使勁地鏟起雪來。鼴鼠也急忙地鏟著，但他僅僅是爲了不再惹河鼠生氣才這麼做，在他看來，他的朋友已經糊塗了。

忙碌了大約十分鐘以後，河鼠的木棒碰觸到了什麼空心的東西。他用力地伸進一隻爪子，往裏面摸索，然後把鼴鼠叫過來幫忙。兩隻動物奮力挖呀，挖呀。最後他們的勞動成果終於清楚地展現在驚訝不已的鼴鼠面前。

在一個看起來像是雪堆的邊上有扇結實的小門，門板被漆成深綠色。門的旁邊有一個門鈴，門鈴下面釘著一塊銅牌，上面的字用方正的大寫字母刻成。藉著月光，他們看見上面的字是：

獾先生之宅

　　鼴鼠向後一倒，仰臥在雪地上，又驚又喜。「河鼠！」他不好意思地說，「你真神！你真的太偉大了。我全明白啦！從我倒下割傷腿的那一刻開始，你那聰明的腦袋就一直想弄清楚，並且一步步證實自己的想法。看著傷口，你那了不起的腦袋便想道：『鏟子！』於是你挖起雪來，找到了劃傷我腿的鏟子！你就此罷休了嗎？沒有。有些人到此就會非常滿足了，但你不是。你聰明的腦袋在想著，『只要我找到一塊踏墊，』你對自己說，『我的想法就會得到證實！』果不其然，你真的找到了踏墊。你真的太聰明了！我相信你能找到你想要的東西。『好了，』你又對自己說，『我似乎清楚地看見了一扇門。把它找出來就沒問題了』嘿，這種事情我在書上可看到過，但在生活中還真沒遇到過呢。你應當到一個能賞識並重用你的地方。和我們這些平凡的傢伙在一起可真是埋沒你。我要是有你這樣的腦袋，河鼠……」

　　「就算你沒有，」河鼠很客氣地打斷他的話，「我想你總不會就這樣坐在地上，喋喋不休地說一個晚上吧？快點起來，使盡全力拉動門邊的那個門鈴，我來捶門！」

　　河鼠用他的木棒猛敲門口，鼴鼠用力一躍，抓住了門鈴，他已兩腳離地，全身用力地擺著。他們聽到從很遠的地方傳來了低沉的鈴聲。

第四章　獾先生

　　河鼠和鼴鼠耐心地等著，一邊在雪地裏跺著腳，好讓雙腳不會凍著。似乎過了好久，他們才終於聽到屋裏有人拖著緩慢的腳步向門口走來。鼴鼠對河鼠說，那聲音很像是一個人穿著尺寸過大、後跟破損的大鞋發出的聲音。鼴鼠真聰明，讓他說對了。

　　接著，傳來拉門閂的聲音，門開了一條縫兒，僅夠探出長長的嘴巴和一雙睡眼惺忪的眼睛。「嘿，下一次還這樣的話，」是一個沙啞的聲音，帶著懷疑的口吻，「我可要生氣了。這次是誰在這樣的夜晚吵得人家不得安寧呀？說！」

　　「噢，獾呀，」河鼠喊道，「請讓我們進去吧。我是河鼠，還有我的朋友鼴鼠，我們在大雪中迷路啦。」

　　「啊，原來是河鼠，我可愛的小老弟！」獾用一種完全不一樣的聲音驚叫道，「你們快請進。唉，你們一定凍壞了。嘿，我從不會凍著！在晚上這種時候！在大雪中迷了路！而且還是在野林子裏！快進來吧！」

　　兩隻動物進屋心切，跌跌撞撞地爬了進去。大門砰的一聲在背後關上，兩個人都無比欣慰地鬆了一口氣。

　　獾穿著一件長長的睡袍，腳下那雙拖鞋的後跟確實已經磨得不成樣子了。他一隻爪子舉著黯淡的蠟燭。當他們敲門的時候，他也許正要上床睡覺呢。他慈祥地看著他倆，輕輕地拍了拍他們的頭。「今天晚上可不是小動物外出的好時候，」他關切地說道，「恐怕是又到哪裏去搞什麼惡作劇了吧，河鼠？不管怎樣，走，跟我到廚房去。那裏燒著一爐旺旺的火，吃的喝的要什麼有什麼。」

　　獾舉著蠟燭拖著鞋，走在他們的前面。河鼠和鼴鼠跟在後面，滿心期待地互相輕推著。他們走過了一條又長又暗又髒的通道，然後來到一間看起來像是大廳的房間，在那裏他們隱約看到幾條通往各處的通道，這些長長的通道顯得很神秘而且看不見盡頭。但是這間大廳也有幾個門口——都是用橡木做的，顯得很結實，讓人看了感到很舒服。獾猛地打開其中一個門，他們來到了燒著爐火、溫暖明亮的大廚房。

　　用紅磚鋪成的地板已經破損不堪。粗大的木頭在寬大的爐膛裏熊熊燃燒，兩邊的煙囱埋在牆壁裏，所以不會有濃煙倒灌進來。兩側擺放兩張面對面的高背長椅，坐在這兩張椅子上，一定相當舒適。房中央有一張放在支架上的簡樸長桌，桌子四周擺著長凳。在桌子的一端，獾吃剩的晚飯還擺在上面——他的晚飯很簡單但很充足，旁邊有一張扶手椅。在房子較遠的一頭，碗櫥裏擺著一排排潔淨的盤子；房頂的椽子下掛著火腿、一捆捆的乾草、幾袋洋蔥和幾籃子的雞蛋。這裏似乎是英雄們打了勝仗後舉行慶功宴的合適地方；在這裏，勞碌的收穫者們也可以圍著飯

桌，歡快地唱著慶祝豐收的歌曲；在這裏，兩、三個志趣相投的
朋友可以舒舒服服、心滿意足地坐著，一邊吃飯，一邊抽煙，一
邊聊天。破舊的紅磚地板微笑著仰望煙霧彌漫的天花板；裏著發
亮的長外套的高背椅興高采烈地互相看著；碗櫥裏的盤子對著架
子上的瓶瓶罐罐咧嘴大笑；壁爐裏的火苗閃爍不定，似乎在與每
樣物品玩鬧。

　　慈祥的獾先生讓他們坐在壁爐兩邊的高背椅上，好讓他們烤
火取暖，接著叫他們脫掉濕衣服和濕鞋子。然後，他給他們拿來
了睡袍和拖鞋，又端來熱水，親自為鼴鼠受傷的大腿敷藥，又用
藥膏把傷口包好，把一切都安排得妥當。在融融的火光裏，河鼠
和鼴鼠感到既溫暖又乾爽，他們伸著疲憊的雙腿，身後傳來獾先
生擺放盤子的叮噹聲，多悅耳的響聲啊！這兩隻動物受盡了風雪
之苦，現在已身處安全的避風港。對他們來說，剛剛逃離的寒風
凜冽、無路可走的野林子早已被他們拋到九霄雲外去了，而他們
所遭受的痛苦也像一場即將被遺忘的夢般，煙消雲散。

　　等到他們徹底暖和之後，獾先生把他們叫到飯桌旁，他剛才
一直忙著為他們準備晚飯呢。河鼠和鼴鼠早已感到饑腸轆轆，但
當他們看到晚飯擺在面前時，一時卻又不知從何處下手，因為所
有的食物都是那樣地誘人，不知道先吃了這道菜，別的食物會不
會被搶走。有很長一段時間他們誰也沒有說話。不過，當他們開
始開口說話時，又因嘴裏塞滿了食物而模糊不清。獾先生並不介
意，他也不在意他們一邊吃飯一邊把胳膊肘放在桌子上，大家同
時說話他也不在乎。由於他不出入社交場合，他認為這些都是無

關緊要的（當然我們知道，他這樣是不對的，他的眼界未免也太過狹隘了。因為這些事確實非常重要，只是要花很長的時間才能說明清楚。）他坐在桌子一端的扶手椅上，認真地聽著河鼠和鼴鼠講述他們的遭遇，不時還神色沉重地點點頭。他似乎對什麼事都不會大驚小怪，而且從沒說過一句類似「我早就跟你們說過」或「我一直都這麼認為」的話，也不說他們應該怎樣做，不應該怎樣做。鼴鼠對獾產生了親切感。

　　晚飯總算吃完了，他們的肚子撐得飽飽的。現在他們無憂無慮，再也用不著擔驚受怕。於是他們和獾先生一起圍坐在壁爐旁；河鼠和鼴鼠心想，吃飽喝足後，無拘無束地坐在火爐邊聊天熬夜，這是多麼愜意的事啊！他們聊了些尋常事後，獾先生高興地說：「好啦，跟我說說你們那一帶的情況吧。蟾蜍現在過得怎麼樣？」

　　「唉，一天不如一天哪。」河鼠心情沉重地說，鼴鼠則豎著耳朵坐在椅子上，舒舒服服地烤火。河鼠把腳翹過頭，竭力裝出一副很難過的樣子，「上週他又出了一次車禍，這一次撞得可慘啦。你知道他本來就不是開車的料，但偏要堅持自己開車。要是他雇用一個體面、穩重、訓練有素的司機，好好支薪，並把車交給司機駕駛，一切都會相安無事。但他偏不要，總覺得自己天生就是會開車，誰都沒他聰明，於是不幸的事就發生了。」

　　「幾次啦？」獾先生心情沉重地問。

　　「你是問撞過幾次車，還是買過幾次車？」河鼠問道，「唉，反正對蟾蜍來說都是一樣的，這已經是第七次了。你知道

他有間車庫嗎？嘿，那間車庫，這說來一點都不誇張，裏面全堆滿了汽車碎片，但沒一件比你的帽子大！那就是前六次車禍留下的東西，也是到目前為止所留下來的東西。」

「他已進過三次醫院了，」鼴鼠插話說，「至於他要付的罰款數目，說起來都讓人心驚膽跳。」

「是啊，但那只是麻煩的一部分，」河鼠接著說，「蟾蜍有錢，這我們都知道，但他終究不是百萬富翁呀。再說，他根本是一位無藥可救的惡劣駕駛，完全不把法律和秩序放在眼裏。他遲早會出事的，不是車毀人亡，就是傾家蕩產。獾！我們都是他的朋友，難道我們不應該為他做點什麼嗎？」

獾先生沉思了好一會兒。「你們聽我說！」他終於說話了，但語氣嚴肅，「你們知道我現在不能有所作為，對吧？」

他的兩位朋友點點頭，非常理解他的意思。按照動物的規矩，在漫長的冬季裏，任何動物都不能做出驚天動地的英勇行為來，即使是費點力氣的舉動也不行。大家都昏昏欲睡——有的確實已經睡著了。所有的動物都多少受到天氣的侷限；在度過了艱苦的日日夜夜之後，他們都已筋疲力盡，大家都在休息呢。

「那就對了！」獾先生接著說，「等冬天過後夜晚變短、當我半夜清醒感到煩躁，一心只盼黎明趕快到來，並且天未亮便要起床做事時，我就能夠——你們懂的！」

兩隻動物認真地點點頭，他們確實明白！

「嘿，到那時，」獾先生接著說，「我們——你，我，還有我們的朋友鼴鼠——會好好地教訓蟾蜍的。我們可不容忍他再做

出蠢事。我們一定要令他明白事理，必要的話，要讓他迫令就範。我們要把他變成理智的蟾蜍，我們要……你睡著啦，河鼠！」

「我沒睡！」河鼠突然驚醒過來說道。

「從吃過晚飯到現在，他已打了兩、三次瞌睡。」鼴鼠大笑著說。不知何故，他自己倒是很清醒，一點睡意也沒有。當然，因爲他天生就是一隻生活在地底的動物，獾先生的家剛好適合他，因此使他感到非常自在。而河鼠每晚都在微風習習的河岸邊上的臥室裏睡覺，這裏的環境自然使他感到壓抑難受，昏昏欲睡。

「嗯，我們都該上床睡覺了，」獾先生說著站起來，拿起昏暗的蠟燭，「跟我來，一起到你們的房間去。明天早上不用早起——早餐什麼時候吃都可以！」

他把他們帶到一間長方形的房子，看起來像臥室又像放雜物的閣樓。房子裏的一半空間堆滿了獾先生爲冬天準備的東西——一堆堆的蘋果、蘿蔔和馬鈴薯，以及一籃籃的花生和一罐罐的蜂蜜。但是房間裏擺放的兩張白色小床看起來舒適誘人，床上鋪的亞麻床單雖然粗糙卻很乾淨，而且還散發出薰衣草的芳香。河鼠和鼴鼠三、兩下便脫掉了身上的衣服，高高興興地鑽進了被窩。

遵照獾先生的吩咐，他們倆第二天早上很晚才到廚房吃早餐。廚房裏的火燒得正旺，兩隻小刺蝟正在飯桌旁的長凳上吃著用木碗盛的麥片粥。看到他們進來，兩隻刺蝟放下調羹，站了起來，恭敬地向他們點頭致意。

「坐下，坐下，」河鼠高興地說，「繼續吃你們的粥吧。你們這兩個小傢伙是從哪來的？我想一定是在大雪中迷路了吧？」

「是的，先生。」年紀較大的那隻刺蝟恭敬地說，「我和小比利正在尋找往學校的路——即使天氣如此寒冷，母親仍執意要我們上學去——於是我們便迷路了。先生，比利年紀小膽子也小，他嚇壞了，便大哭起來。後來我們無意中發現了獾先生家的後門，便冒昧地敲了門。先生，我們大家都知道獾先生是一個熱心的……」

「我知道。」河鼠一邊說一邊切下幾片燻肉，鼴鼠把幾個雞蛋放在一個平底鍋上。「外面的天氣怎麼樣？你不用這樣客氣地稱呼我『先生』。」他接著說道。

「噢，糟透啦，先生，雪積得好高了，」刺蝟說，「像你們這樣的紳士今天是不能出去的。」

「獾先生在哪兒？」鼴鼠問道，他正在火爐邊溫咖啡壺。

「主人進書房去了，先生。」刺蝟答道，「他交代說，他今天早上特別忙，任何情況下都不許打擾他。」

當然，在場的每個人都十分清楚這一句話的含意。事實如前面已經說過的，動物在度過半年非常活躍的生活後，後半年他就有點昏昏欲睡了，或者說進入睡眠狀態了。在後半年這段時間裏，如果有客人或者有事情要做，動物總不能以自己困倦而拒絕吧。所以這已是大家心照不宣的藉口了。事實上大家都知道，獾先生吃過豐盛的早餐後進去書房，舒舒服服地躺在扶手椅上，兩腳擱在另一張椅子上，臉上蓋著紅色的棉手帕。每年的這個時候

都是如此，都是用這種方式忙著呢。

　　這時前門的門鈴大作，叮咚叮咚地響了起來，河鼠正吃著奶油麵包片，滿臉油膩膩的。他叫小刺蝟比利去看看來者何人。客廳裏傳來很響的腳步聲，不一會刺蝟帶著水獺進來了。水獺撲在河鼠身上緊緊地抱著他，嘴裏親熱地問候著。

　　「走開！」河鼠喊著，嘴巴裏塞滿了食物。

　　「我早就猜到會在這兒找到你們。」水獺興高采烈地說，「今天早上我上河岸的時候，大家都慌了。他們說，河鼠整晚都沒回家，鼴鼠也沒回，一定是出了大事了。而且，大雪把你們的足跡都覆蓋住了。但我知道，人們遭遇困難時，多半會去找獾先生，就算沒找他，獾先生也會知道發生什麼事了。因此，我冒著風雪穿過林子，朝這裏奔來！哎呀，我剛才穿過雪地時，看見初升的太陽紅通通的，映照著黑色的樹幹，那景色美極了！林子裏靜悄悄的，不時從樹枝上撲通撲通掉下大塊大塊的雪，讓人不得不跳呀跑呀地閃躲。一夜之間不知從哪裏冒出了這麼多雪城堡、雪山洞，還有雪橋、雪梯田、雪城牆。要是沒事兒，我可以玩上幾個鐘頭呢。到處都可以見到被大雪壓斷的粗大樹枝，知更鳥在上面自以為是地跳個不停，好像這些樹枝是他們折斷似的。在頭頂，一行大雁飛翔在灰濛濛的高空上，幾隻烏鴉在樹上盤旋，他們在察看著什麼，然後又悻悻地飛回家去了。我沒有遇見可以打聽消息的動物。大約到了半路，我見到一隻坐在樹樁上的野兔，他正用兩隻爪子擦他那張傻乎乎的臉呢。我悄悄爬到他的身後，用前爪重重地拍了一下他的肩膀，他這下可嚇壞了，我只得又拍

了拍他的頭才使他回過神來。而我這才從他口中得知，昨天晚上有一個伙伴在野林子看見了鼴鼠。他說，他是和野兔們在地洞裏聊天時聽來的，還說河鼠先生的好朋友鼴鼠遇到了困難，說他迷了路，『他們』都出動了，正圍繞著他轉呢。『那你們為什麼沒有一個願意幫忙呢？』我問，『也許你們腦袋不管用，但畢竟人多勢眾，個個又壯又肥，而且你們的地道四通八達，至少可以把他拉進地洞好讓他安全、舒服一些。』『什麼，我們？』他說，『幫忙？我們這些野兔？』於是我又拍了拍他的頭，便丟下他走了。沒有別的辦法了。但無論如何，我瞭解了一些情況，而且，如果我有幸碰上『他們』當中的任何一個，我會知道更多的情況——或者是，讓他們知道。」

「你一點都不——呃——擔心嗎？」鼴鼠問道。一說起野林子，他又開始像昨天一樣害怕了起來。

「擔心？」水獺大笑，露出了兩排潔白、鋒利的牙齒，「該擔心的是那些膽敢對我無禮的傢伙。哎，鼴鼠，好傢伙，快煎幾片火腿給我。我都餓壞了，我還有話跟河鼠說呢，好久沒見到他了。」

於是好心的鼴鼠切了幾片火腿，讓兩隻刺蝟去煎，自己回到飯桌繼續吃早餐。而水獺和河鼠把頭湊得近近的，正喋喋不休、沒完沒了地說著話。

水獺吃完了一盤子的火腿，正要去多煎一點來。這時，獾先生進來了，他打著哈欠，關切地詢問大家的情況。「快到午飯時間了吧。」他對水獺說，「還是別吃了，等會兒和我們一塊吃午

飯吧？這麼冷的天，你一定很餓吧？」

「是啊！」水獺答道，一邊向鼴鼠擠眉弄眼，「看著這些貪吃的小刺蝟大口大口地吃著火腿，我都餓得難受了。」

小刺蝟呢，不過吃了點粥，還賣力地幫他們煎火腿，他們才感到餓呢。但是他們太膽小，沒敢說什麼，只得可憐地看著獾先生。

「嘿，你們兩個小傢伙快回家找媽媽吧，」獾先生和藹地說，「我會找人送你們回家。我敢肯定，你們今晚不會想在這吃晚餐的。」

說完，他給了他們每個人六便士，拍了拍他們的頭。兩隻小刺蝟畢恭畢敬地敬了禮，揮了揮帽子走了。

很快，他們又坐下來吃午飯了。鼴鼠發現自己的座位被安排在獾先生的旁邊。水獺和河鼠還在津津有味地聊著河岸的八卦，似乎什麼也不能分散他們的注意力。鼴鼠便藉機告訴獾先生，這裏是如何地舒適、如何地像家一樣溫馨。「一旦鑽進了地下，」他說，「我就覺得踏實多了，什麼事也不會有，誰也不會找你的麻煩。你完全可以自己作決定，用不著去請教誰，也用不著去管人家會怎麼說。地面上一切如常，你根本不用操心。要是你在地下待膩了，那就到地面去，那裏一切都在等著你呢。」

獾先生滿臉微笑地看著他。「我也這麼認為，」他答道，「只有在地下才能擁有安全感、寧靜與祥和。如果你有了新的想法，要住寬敞一點——挖一挖，刨一刨，就行啦！如果你覺得自己的房子太大了，堵掉一兩個洞就可以了！用不著去找建築工或

技工，更不用擔心別人隔著圍牆對你指指點點。最大的好處是，不用擔心天氣的變化無常。看看河鼠吧，洪水往上一漲，他就得搬家：租別人的房子住，既不舒適又不方便，房租還貴得嚇人。再說說蟾蜍，他的莊園我倒是沒有什麼可挑剔的，而且是這一帶最漂亮的房子。但假如發生了火災，蟾蜍會怎樣？假如瓦片被風刮掉，牆壁下陷或者龜裂，窗戶損壞……蟾蜍到哪兒去住呢？假如冷風鑽進屋子——我最討厭冷風鑽進屋子了——蟾蜍又該怎麼辦呢？要我說呀，戶外是閒逛和找食物的好地方，但最終還是要回到地底來住——這就是我對家的理解！」

　　鼴鼠對此深表贊同。於是獾先生更加喜歡了。「等吃完午飯，」他說，「我帶你去參觀一下我的小天地，我敢說你一定喜歡它。畢竟家應當建成什麼樣你很清楚。」

　　於是，吃過午飯後，河鼠和水獺圍坐在壁爐邊，熱烈地爭論關於鰻魚的事。獾先生點亮一個燈籠，叫鼴鼠跟在他的後面。穿過大廳後，他們便沿著一條主地道走著。搖曳的燈光映照出兩邊大大小小的房間，有的只有碗櫥那麼大，有的幾乎有蟾蜍的飯廳那麼寬敞、氣派。走過右邊的一條狹窄的通道，他們又進入了一條大的走廊，兩邊還是大大小小的房間。這裏有四通八達的地道、各種大小不一的房間、東西塞得滿滿的貯藏室，以及做工精巧的柱子、拱頂、路面等等，都讓鼴鼠驚歎不已。「獾先生，」他忍不住問道，「你到底花了多長的時間和多大的精力才做成這一切的？簡直讓人難以置信！」

　　「如果是我自己做的話，確實有點難以置信，」獾先生淡淡

地說，「但實際上我什麼也沒做，僅僅是清掃了一下我要用的通道和房間。這地下還有許多這樣的通道和房間，到處都是！我知道你不明白，我得給你解釋一下。嗯，很久以前，就在這野林子裏——樹木還未長成如此茂密的這裏——有一座城市，一座住滿人類的城市。唔，我們站的這個地方，就是他們曾經住的地方，他們在這裏散步、聊天、睡覺，做他們自己的事。這裏有他們的馬廄，還有他們歡宴的地方。他們就是從這裏騎馬出發，到外面去打仗或做生意。他們是一個強大的民族，很富有，又精通建築。他們要讓他們建造的房子永傳萬世，因爲他們相信自己的城市會萬代長存。」

「後來呢，後來發生什麼事？」鼴鼠問道。

「誰知道呢？」獾先生說道，「後來，來了許多人——他們在這兒住了一段時間，不僅讓這裏繁榮起來，還造了許多房子，之後他們又走了。人類就是這樣。但我們沒走。我聽說早在這個城市出現以前，這裏就住著很多獾。現在這裏又有很多獾了，我們是有耐性的動物，也許我們搬走過一段時間，但我們耐心地等待，後來我們回來了。將來也會永遠這樣。」

「那——那些人走了之後呢？」鼴鼠問道。

「他們走了之後，」獾先生接著說，「狂風不停地刮，大雨接連不斷地下，這樣持續了好幾年。也許是我們獾在發揮什麼作用吧——誰知道呢？這城市便慢慢地、慢慢地衰落了——從廢墟變爲平地直到最後消失。後來，漸漸地，地上的種子長出了許多樹苗，這些樹苗後來長成了森林，刺藤和蕨類植物也長出來了。

地上積了成堆的腐葉，冬天發大水的時候，溪流帶來的泥土便覆蓋在這一堆堆的腐葉上。天長日久，我們的家便形成了，於是我們搬了進來。在我們頭頂的地面上，也發生了同樣的事。動物們來了，喜歡上這裏，於是找到了自己的家，安頓了下來，在這裏繁衍生息。他們從不去管過去發生的事——現在也不管，他們太忙了。這地方也有一些小崗小丘什麼的，而且到處都有洞穴，但對動物來說這可是一大好處。他們也不去擔心將來會發生什麼事——將來也許那些人還會搬到這兒來住一段時間。現在野林子已經夠擁擠的了，住著各種各樣的動物，好心的、壞心眼的，還有對別人漠不關心的——我可沒有指名道姓喔。這個世界就需要各種各樣的動物。說到這裏，我想你對他們該有點瞭解了吧？」

「確實有些瞭解了。」鼴鼠有點顫抖地說道。

「好啦，好啦。」獾先生拍著他的肩膀說道，「你這是第一次見到他們。其實，他們並沒有多壞。我們都得生活，還要讓別人生活。明天我再給他們傳個話，我想你就不會再有麻煩了。在這一帶，我的朋友想上哪兒就上哪兒！」

當他們回到廚房時，發現河鼠焦躁不安地走來走去。地下的空氣使他感到既壓抑又心煩意亂，他似乎擔心如果再不回去守著那條河，它會消失的。於是他穿上外套，把手槍插進腰帶。「快，鼴鼠，」他一見到他們就焦急地說，「趁現在是白天，我們得趕緊走，我可不想在野林子裏再過一個晚上。」

「別著急，河鼠老弟，」水獺說道，「我會跟你一起走的，在這兒就算是蒙上眼睛我也認得路。再說了，如果遇上壞人，我

會幫你揍扁他的,你儘管放心!」

「你真的不必擔心,河鼠老弟。」獾先生溫和地說,「你也許沒想到,我的地道通得可遠啦!在林子的四周,都有我的換氣孔,雖然我不想讓大夥知道這事。如果你真的要走,我可以告訴你們一條捷徑。別擔心,還是坐下吧!」

儘管如此,河鼠還是急著要回去他那條老河去。於是獾先生又拿起燈籠,帶著他們走進一條潮濕又悶氣的地道。這地道穿過堅硬的岩石,彎彎曲曲地向下傾斜,有的是天然形成的,有的是鑿出來的。這條地道似乎有好幾英里長,他們都走累了。最後,他們透過洞口雜亂的野草,看到射進來的斑駁陽光。獾先生匆忙地跟他們道了一聲再見,把他們猛地推出洞口,然後用爬藤、樹枝和落葉蓋著洞口,把一切弄得不露一點破綻後,就鑽回了地洞。

他們發現自己正站在野林子的外邊。在他們身後的岩石上,錯綜複雜地交織著刺藤和樹根;在他們的前面是大片的田野,上面鑲嵌著一行行的樹籬,在白雪的映襯下顯得黑黝黝的;再往前看,就是他們熟悉的河流。冬日的太陽低低地掛在地平線上,照得滿天都紅通通的。水獺認得路,於是他走在前面帶路。他們沿著一條直線朝一道離他們很遠的柵欄走去。到了那裏,他們停下腳步往後一看,整片野林子被遼闊的潔白世界包圍著,顯得密不透風,陰森可怕。他們轉身飛快地朝自己的家奔去。去尋找溫暖、去看看他們熟悉的東西,聽一聽窗外的流水發出歡快的聲音,他們熟悉那條河,理解它的喜怒哀樂。他們永遠不會因為河

流而感到擔驚受怕。

　　鼴鼠匆匆地趕著路，他也在急切地盼望早點回到家裏，重新回到他所熟悉和喜歡的事物身邊。他清楚地認識到，自己是一隻離不開田地和樹籬的動物。他的天地是地裏的田埂、熱鬧的牧場、夜晚幽靜的小道和人們精心照料的花園；而別的動物熟悉大自然裏的衝突，能忍受各種嚴峻的考驗。所以他必須變得聰明，必須待在自己所能適應的天地，以他自己的方式去冒險、去度過他的一生。

第五章　可愛的家

　　一群綿羊擠成一團，亂哄哄地朝羊圈的圍欄擠去。他們昂著頭，靈巧的前蹄用力跺著地，鼻孔呼出熱氣，於是在擁擠的羊圈上便彌漫著薄薄的霧氣。河鼠和鼴鼠一路上談笑風生，情緒高漲，匆匆地從羊圈旁邊走過。他們和水獺在一片遼闊的高地上郊遊了一整天，從那裏發源的一些溪流匯集後流入他們那條老河流。冬日的太陽快要下山了，但他們還得走好長一段路。就在剛才，當他們無意中走過一塊犁過的田地時，聽到了羊的叫聲，便朝那走去。走過了羊圈，他們發現一條顯然很多人走過的小徑。走在這條路上他們感到舒服多了，而且使他們心中小小的疑問有了明確的答案：「對，沒錯，是回家的路！」

　　「我們好像快要到一個村子了。」鼴鼠有點疑惑地說。他放慢了腳步，因為那條小徑變得越來越大，現在他們走在一條鋪得很好的碎石路上。動物們不喜歡村子還有高速道路，雖然他們經常走高速道路，但他們都是自己決定走去哪，而不是被道路限制走去教堂、郵局或其他公共場所。

　　「噢，不要緊！」河鼠說道，「在這個季節，在這種時候男

女老少都待在家裏圍著火爐烤火，狗呀，貓呀什麼的都不會出門的。我們可以悄悄地穿過村子，不會出什麼問題的。如果你喜歡，還可以透過窗戶看看他們在屋裏都在做什麼。」

　　這是隆冬季節，夜晚很快便降臨了。他們輕輕地走在薄薄的積雪上，悄悄地進了小村莊。漆黑的街道上空蕩蕩的，只看見兩邊屋子的窗戶上透出一格格橙紅色燈光。大多數的花格窗都沒拉上窗簾，透過窗戶，他們看見有的屋子裏的人圍坐在茶桌邊，專心地做著手工藝品；有的屋子裏的人有說有笑，比手劃腳地做著手勢，那種優雅的表情和自然的動作，即便是訓練有素的演員也難以模仿出來——這種自然、優美的情景只有在不知道自己正在被觀察時，才會出現。河鼠和鼴鼠像看戲一樣，從一個窗戶到另一個窗戶著迷地看著。當他們看到貓得到撫愛，打瞌睡的小孩被抱上床，疲倦的男人伸著懶腰敲著煙斗時，眼睛都有點濕潤了；他們多希望自己是在家裏啊，但他們的家離這兒還遠著呢。

　　然而，其中最令他們好奇的，是從一個拉上了窗簾的窗戶中看到的情景——這個被窗簾圍上的小世界似乎把沉重的大自然關在外面，並且把它忘掉了。屋內緊靠著白色的窗簾，掛著一隻鳥籠，燈光把鳥籠的每一根鐵絲、棲枝及籠內的所有物品都清清楚楚地映在窗簾上，他們甚至可以看到鳥籠裏沒吃完的糖塊。鳥籠裏那隻毛茸茸的鳥站在中間那根棲枝上，頭埋進了羽毛裏。他離他們似乎非常近，他們似乎只要一伸爪，就可輕易地撫摸他一下；甚至連鳥的一根根羽毛都像是用鉛筆畫出來一樣，清晰地映在潔白的窗簾上。他們看見那隻昏昏欲睡的小傢伙心神不寧地挪

動著身子，不一會兒睜開了眼睛，然後抖了一下羽毛，把頭抬了起來。

接著，他們看見他張開小喙，疲憊地打著哈欠，看了看四周，然後把頭伸進了背部的羽毛裏，於是原來直豎的羽毛漸漸地收攏了起來。這時，一陣刺骨的寒風吹過，冷得他們縮起了脖子，幾滴冰冷的雨落在他們的背上，把他們從眼前的夢境中驚醒。此時，他們意識腳趾頭已凍僵了，腿累得酸痛，而他們自己的家離這兒還很遠，很遠。

走過了村子，道路兩邊的農舍突然不見了，黑暗中他們又聞到了田野上熟悉的芳香。他們重新振作起精神來，雖然離家還有很長的路，但這段路終究會走完的。到那時，只要聽到門閂的喀嚓一聲，生起暖烘烘的爐火，家那些格外熟悉的事物，會像盼望久別的親人一樣迎接他們的到來。他們堅定地邁著每一步，各自想著心事，沉默不語地走啊，走啊。鼴鼠心裏想的是一頓美好的晚餐；天色已經黑得伸手不見五指，而且對他來說這是一片陌生的曠野，因此他只好老老實實地跟在河鼠的後面，把一切交給他。河鼠則像平常一樣，他走在前面，離鼴鼠稍稍有一段距離；他聳起肩膀，眼睛盯著前方黯淡的筆直的路面。因此，當可憐的鼴鼠像觸電一樣突然感到一種召喚時，河鼠一點也沒注意到。

作為人類，我們早已喪失了那種非常微妙的感覺能力，甚至找不到合適的詞語來表達動物與周圍環境互相交流的情形。比如，我們只用「嗅」這個詞，來概括動物日日夜夜通過鼻孔的顫動所感受到的召喚、警告、煽動、拒絕等等各種微妙的資訊。鼴

鼠在黑暗裏感受到的正是這其中一種神秘、微妙的召喚，這種非常熟悉的召喚引發了他心裏的一陣陣震顫，儘管他一時還想不起那召喚究竟意味著什麼。他突然停下腳步，鼻子不停地往四周嗅著，千方百計想要確認那深深觸動他卻稍縱即逝的東西。過了一會兒，他又感覺到了那種召喚，隨之而來的是潮水般一擁而上的記憶。

家！那撫慰人心的召喚，那飄蕩在空氣中柔柔的氣息，那拖著他拉著他的無形小手都朝著同一個方向！哎呀，此時他的家一定就在不遠的附近，他的老家，就是他那天第一次見到那條河後匆匆忙忙離開、再也沒回過的老家！現在它正派它特有的哨兵和信使來攔住他，要把他帶回去。自從他在那個明媚的早晨離家出走以後，他就一直沉迷於他那充滿樂趣、驚奇和各種新鮮迷人經歷的新生活，把自己的老家一股腦兒拋在身後。啊，他想起來了，黑暗中的老家就清楚地在他的眼前！它確實顯得有點破舊、狹小，而且陳設簡陋；但那是他的家，他自己建造的家，他結束忙碌的一天，樂於返回的家。顯然，老家也很開心能與他相見，他離開後老家一直思念著他。

它希望他回來，而且正在通過他的鼻子這樣跟他說。老家有點哀怨，但沒有埋怨或責怪他的意思，它只是傷心地提醒他，它就在那兒，而且需要他。

老家對他如此清晰的召喚，他必須服從，馬上回老家去。「河鼠！」他高興又激動地喊道，「停下！回來！到我這兒來，快！」

「噢，快走吧，鼴鼠，別磨蹭了！」河鼠一邊回答，一邊繼續趕著路。

「請停一停，河鼠！」可憐的鼴鼠痛苦地哀求道，「你不明白！這是我的家，我的老家！我剛剛聞到了它的氣味，它就在附近，離這兒很近，因此我必須回去！必須回去！噢，回來，河鼠！求求你，快回來！」

這時，河鼠已經走到前面很遠的地方了，所以沒聽清楚鼴鼠在喊什麼，也沒有聽出他苦苦哀求的語氣。此刻，他滿腦子想的是天氣，因為他也聞到了某種東西——是一場可能即將來臨的大雪。

「鼴鼠，我們現在不能停下來，真的不能！」他喊道，「不管你現在發現了什麼，我們明天再說吧。現在我可不敢停下——太晚了，而且雪又快要降下了，我對回去的路也沒有把握！我需要你的鼻子來認路。鼴鼠，快點走吧，我的好夥伴！」河鼠說完，沒等鼴鼠答話，便匆匆地趕路了。

可憐的鼴鼠孤零零地站在路上，心都碎了。他清楚地知道，自己內心深處的悲傷情緒正急速翻湧，而淚水即將奪眶而出。然而，即使是在這樣嚴峻的考驗下，他對朋友的忠誠還是堅如磐石。他一刻也沒想過要拋棄自己的朋友。與此同時，老家還在苦苦地召喚著他，急切地要求他回去。他不敢久留在這種神奇的召喚之中。他狠下心來，低下頭繼續順從地跟隨在河鼠的後面，可是老家微弱的氣息襲向他的鼻子，責怪他喜新厭舊和冷酷無情。

他加快了步伐，趕上了對他情緒毫無覺察的河鼠。河鼠又在

興高采烈地說著回到家後要做的事情，說回家後要在客廳生起熊熊的爐火，還說要吃上一頓美好的晚飯。他一點也沒注意到自己夥伴的沉默和沉重的心情。就在他們往前走了很遠，正在通過路邊那片矮林的樹樁時，河鼠停下了腳步，關切地對鼴鼠說：「哎，鼴鼠老弟，你累壞了，看你一句話也不說，腳像灌了鉛一樣沉重。我們就在這兒坐下歇一歇。雪暫時還不會下，而且我們已經走了一大半的路了。」

鼴鼠滿臉愁容地坐在一棵樹樁上，努力控制住自己的情緒，因為這時他又感覺到老家的氣息向他襲來。他一直不想讓自己哭，不想被悲傷擊敗。但是空氣中一次次傳來老家的氣息，一次比一次強烈。最後鼴鼠終於忍不住了，不顧一切地大聲哭了起來，他知道一切都完了，他已經失去了本來可以找到的東西。

看到鼴鼠痛不欲生的嚎啕大哭，河鼠感到非常驚愕，好一會兒都不敢說話。最後他帶著同情的口氣，平靜地說：「怎麼了，老朋友？到底怎麼回事？告訴我你的心事，看看我能替你做些什麼。」

可憐的鼴鼠哭得胸口劇烈地起伏著，他想說話，但傷心得泣不成聲。「我知道那是一個……破舊、髒亂的小地方，」後來他一邊哭一邊斷斷續續地說，「比不上……你那個舒適的家……也比不上蟾蜍漂亮的府邸……更比不上獾先生的大房子……但那是我的小家……我喜歡它……我離開了它又把它忘了……當時我突然聞到了它的氣息……當時我在路上叫你，可你就是不聽，河鼠……我腦海裏突然浮現家中的一切……我需要家！……可是，

天哪！當時你硬是不回頭，河鼠……於是我不得不離開它，雖然我不停地聞到它的氣息……我想我的心都快要碎了。當時我們本來可以回去看一看，河鼠……只看一下……就在附近……但是你就是不回頭，河鼠，你硬是不回頭！天哪！……」

想起剛才的情景使他更加傷心，他又一次泣不成聲。

河鼠兩眼直直地看著他，默默無語，只是輕輕地拍他的肩膀。過了一會兒，他沉重地說：「我全明白了！我真是一頭蠢豬啊！我真該死啊！」

語畢，他靜靜地坐在那裏。等到鼴鼠暴風驟雨般的哭泣漸漸平息了下來，最後變成和風細雨般有節奏的吸鼻聲後，河鼠站了起來，語氣平淡地說：「好啦，我們還是繼續趕路吧，老朋友！」說完便重新上路，但卻是往回走他們剛才艱難地走過的路。

「你要往哪裏走呀，河鼠？」鼴鼠眨著淚水汪汪的雙眼，邊打嗝邊吃驚地大叫。

「我們要去找你那個家，老弟。」河鼠輕快地說，「你還是快走吧，要找到它可不容易，我需要你的鼻子探路。」

「噢，回來吧，河鼠，別去啦！」鼴鼠喊道，並站了起來，匆匆地追上了河鼠，「沒用的，聽我說！太晚了，天又這麼黑，那地方離這兒太遠了，馬上又要下雪了！而且……我本來不想讓你知道我怎麼想的……我只是一時衝動！想想河岸吧，還有你的晚飯！」

「暫時把河岸和晚飯拋到一旁吧！」河鼠真誠地說，「聽我

說，即使今晚不睡覺，我也要找到你的家。振作起來，老朋友，挽著我的手，我們很快就可以回到你的家了。」

麗鼠還在抽泣著，不停地哀求河鼠別去了，但河鼠什麼也不聽，拉著他的手便往回走。一路上河鼠興高采烈地說著許多有趣的事，試圖讓麗鼠高興起來，想讓原本漫長的路途變得短暫。終於，河鼠感到他們似乎已經走近剛才麗鼠被「攔截」的那一段路，便說道：「好了，別說話了。該做正事啦！好好發揮你鼻子的長處，一定要聚精會神。」

他們靜靜地走了一段路；突然，河鼠感覺到一股微弱的電流正透過麗鼠的身體，經由自己被挽著的手臂傳送過來。他立即鬆開麗鼠的手，往後退了一步，全神貫注地等待著。

那是他老家傳來的信號！

麗鼠一動也不動地站了一會兒，同時他抬起頭，鼻子微微地顫動，不停地感受著周圍的空氣。

接著，他飛快地向前跑——不對——停了一下——又往回嗅了一下，然後慢慢地滿懷信心地向前走。

河鼠激動不已，緊緊地跟在後面。麗鼠此時像夢遊似的，在微弱的星光下不斷用鼻子探尋著，走過一條乾涸的水溝，又穿過一道樹籬，最後來到一片空曠的田野。

突然，就在那個瞬間，麗鼠一聲不吭，毫無預警地跳進地洞。而河鼠對此早有準備，立即跟隨麗鼠那精準無比的嗅覺，一起鑽進地洞。

地洞又窄又悶，彌漫著濃濃的泥土味。河鼠覺得似乎走了很

久才走完通道，他終於可以站起來伸展一下四肢，抖一抖身子。鼴鼠劃了一根火柴，藉著火光，河鼠看見他們站在一塊空地上，到處都清掃得很乾淨，地上還鋪上了沙子。他們的面前便是鼴鼠家矮小的前門，門的一邊有門鈴，門上用粗體字寫著：「鼴鼠之宅」。

　　鼴鼠取下掛在牆壁釘子上的燈籠，把燈點上。河鼠看了看四周，發現他們站在房前的院子裏。門的一邊擺著一張座椅，另一邊放著一個壓路機。鼴鼠是一個愛清潔的動物，容不得別的動物把他院子裏的泥沙弄成一堆一堆的。牆上掛著好幾個鐵絲籃子，裏面裝著蕨類植物，籃子與籃子之間的支架上擺放著各種石膏塑像——有（義大利民族解放運動領袖）加里波底（Garibaldi），有幼兒時期的撒母耳，有英國女王維多利亞，還有一些當代義大利的英雄人物。院子的一邊有一條保齡球的球道，球道兩邊擺著長凳和小木桌，每張桌子上都留下圓圈的痕跡，表示上面曾經放過啤酒杯。院子中間有一個圓形的小池，裏面養有金魚，池塘周圍用海扇殼鑲嵌；池塘中間有一間非常別緻的房子，這房子的外表也鑲嵌著許多海扇殼，屋頂上有一隻大大的銀色玻璃球，球面上映出的東西都變形了，顯得特別好看。

　　看到這些熟悉的景物，鼴鼠高興得笑容滿面，他領著河鼠匆匆進門，點亮客廳的燈，朝四周望去。他看見屋裏的東西都積上了厚厚的灰塵，被他冷落了這麼久的家裏顯得毫無生氣，屋子不僅窄小，裏面的擺設又如此破舊——他突然癱坐在椅子上，雙手摀著臉。「噢，河鼠！」他沮喪地叫道，「我為什麼要這樣做？

我爲什麼要在這樣一個夜晚把你帶到這個醜陋、冰冷的小屋子？這個時候你本來已經回到河邊的家裏，坐在溫暖的爐火邊暖和你的身子，享受著你那些精緻的東西。」

河鼠對他的自責一點也不在意。他在屋子裏跑來跑去，打開房門，查看房間和碗櫥。他把各處的蠟燭跟電燈一一點亮。「這小屋子多麼別緻啊！」他高興地大聲說道，「設計得這樣講究！東西樣樣齊全，又擺放得這樣井井有條！我們一定會度過一個美好的夜晚。我們首先得升起一爐火，這由我來做——我總是知道在哪裏可以找到我要的東西。這麼說這就是客廳了？好舒適啊！牆上那些小床鋪是你自己設計嗎？太棒了！好，我這就去把柴火和煤拿來，你去拿撣子來——廚房飯桌的抽屜裏有一把——然後把東西打掃一下。快動手呀，老朋友！」

受到夥伴熱情的鼓舞，鼴鼠終於有所行動，他興致勃勃地清掃。而河鼠則跑上跑下地運送柴火，不一會兒，壁爐裏便燃起了熊熊烈火。他招呼鼴鼠過來烤火，暖暖身子。但是鼴鼠突然又變得愁眉苦臉，沮喪地倒在沙發上，把臉埋在撣子裏。

「河鼠，」他傷心地說道，「你的晚飯怎麼辦呢？你又餓又累，而我沒有什麼東西可吃——什麼都沒有——連麵包屑都沒有啊！」

「這點小事就把你難倒啊？」河鼠責怪地說，「嘿，我很肯定剛才自己在廚房碗櫥裏，清楚地看到一把開沙丁魚罐頭的開罐器，誰都知道這意味著周圍有沙丁魚罐頭。別洩氣，振作起來！走，跟我去找。」

　　於是，他們翻箱倒櫃地找起來，翻看了每一個櫃子和抽屜。他們希望能找到多一點東西，但結果並不十分令人滿意。他們找到了一罐沙丁魚，幾乎是一整盒的餅乾，還有一根用錫紙包的德國香腸。

　　「這夠我們飽餐一頓了！」河鼠說道，一面把東西擺在桌上，「我相信今晚有些動物會巴不得能和我們一起共進晚餐呢！」

　　「可是沒有麵包！」鼴鼠傷心地說道，「沒有奶油，也沒有……」

　　「沒有鵝肝醬，沒有香檳酒！」河鼠笑笑地接著說，「噢，我想起來了——通道盡頭的小門裏面是用來做什麼的？肯定是你家的地窖！這屋子裏最珍貴的東西肯定藏在裏面！你等一下。」

　　說完，他朝那個小門走去，不一會兒滿身灰塵地從地窖裏走出來，兩隻爪子各拿著一瓶啤酒，胳膊下還各夾著一瓶。「你似乎很會享受人生嘛，鼴鼠。」河鼠說道，「別否認了，這裏是我去過最愜意的地方。哎，你在哪兒買到那些畫的？掛上這些畫，這地方確實還真像個家呢，怪不得你這麼喜歡。鼴鼠，告訴我，你是如何把家布置成這樣的？」

　　河鼠一邊問，一邊忙著取來盤子和刀叉，把芥末放在蛋杯裏攪拌。鼴鼠此時情緒起伏還是有點大，起初還有點不好意思，說著說著便自然多了。他說道：這是如何設計的；那是經過怎樣一番考慮的；怎樣從姑姑那裏得到的意外之財，什麼經過討價還價買來的；那又是怎樣經過節衣縮食、辛辛苦苦攢錢買下來的。說

著說著，他的情緒漸漸恢復，忍不住過去撫摸那些擺設，還舉起了燈，滔滔不絕地誇耀這些東西的優點，忘了他們還沒吃晚飯這件事。河鼠這時已經餓慌了，但還是竭力掩飾著，他時而認真地點了點頭，時而皺著眉頭仔細地看著；而且只要有機會，還不時說「了不起」、「棒極了」這樣的話。

最後，河鼠終於成功地把話題引到吃飯上，當他正要拿起開沙丁魚罐頭的開罐器時，屋外的院子裏傳來了響聲……像是拖著小腳在沙礫上走路的聲音，夾雜著低沉的說話聲。他們斷斷續續地聽到：「哎，大家都排好隊……把燈籠舉高一點，湯米……先清一下嗓子……我說一、二、三之後誰都不許咳嗽……小比爾在哪兒？……哦，快過來，我們大家都在等……」

「是誰在說話？」河鼠停下手邊的事問道。

「我想一定是田鼠他們。」鼴鼠有點得意地答道，「每年的這個時候，他們都挨家挨戶地唱聖誕頌歌，都成了這一帶的風俗了。他們從未錯過我家——他們總是最後才到鼴鼠之宅來。以往他們來了，我都會給他們端上熱茶，手頭寬裕的時候，我還會做晚飯給他們吃。聽到他們唱歌又使我想起過去的美妙時光。」

「那我們出去看看吧！」河鼠叫道。他跳了起來，朝門口走去。

他們猛地打開門，眼前的景象既應景又美好。在燈光昏暗的燈籠下，八、九隻小田鼠排成半圓形站在院子裏；每隻田鼠的脖子上都圍上紅色羊毛圍巾，前爪插在口袋裏，小腳不停地在地上跺著取暖。一雙雙晶亮的小眼睛羞怯地互相看著，不好意思地笑

著，不時吸吸鼻子，扯扯袖子。當門打開時，那隻拿著燈籠、年紀稍長的田鼠正在發口令：「預備，一、二、三！」於是他們便尖聲地唱了起來。他們唱的是一首古老的頌歌，是他們的祖先們在結霜的休耕農地裏，或是被大雪圍繞的壁爐角落裏創作出來的，並且代代相傳。每當耶誕節來臨時，田鼠們就會站在泥濘的大街上，對著明亮的窗戶唱起這首頌歌。

聖誕頌歌

鄉親們，在這個冰天雪地的時節，
請打開你們的家門，
儘管風在颳，雪在下，
但請把我們迎到你們的火爐旁，
明天你們將會擁有歡樂！

我們站在冰冷的雪地裏，
忍著寒冷，跺著腳丫兒，
不遠千里為你們送上祝福——
你們在火旁，我們在街上——
願明天的歡樂屬於你們！

很久以前的一個深夜，
一顆星星引導我們前來，
賜予我們歡樂和祝福——
祝福明天和未來，
日日都幸福！

約瑟在雪地裏艱難跋涉——
望見了馬廄上空的一顆星；
瑪麗亞再也無法往前走——
走進了草棚，倒在褥草上！
明晨將有幸福降臨！

他們聽到天使的聲音：
「誰首先喊出聖誕快樂？
這一榮耀屬於動物，因為上帝降生在——
他們棲息的馬廄裏！
明天他們將滿載歡樂！」

　　歌聲戛然而止，歌手們羞答答地微笑著，左顧右盼地交換著眼色。緊接著沉默下來——但只持續短短的一會兒。突然，外面遠處叮噹的鐘聲順著他們剛剛走過的地洞傳過來，悅耳動聽。

「唱得非常好，孩子們！」河鼠開心地大聲說道，「你們大家都進屋裏來吧，到火爐邊坐坐，烤烤火，吃點熱東西！」

「對呀，進來吧，田鼠們，」鼴鼠急切地喊道，「就像以前一樣，進來後把門關上，把那張高背長椅挪到火爐邊。呃，你們稍等一會兒，我們要……噢，河鼠！」他不知所措地叫道，癱倒在椅子上，眼淚都快要流出來了，「我們該怎麼辦？我們拿什麼招待他們？」

「一切都交給我。」河鼠不慌不忙地說道，「嘿，這位提著燈籠的老弟，到這兒來一下，我想跟你說一下話。告訴我，晚上這個時候還有商店開門嗎？」

「當然有啦，先生，」拿著燈籠的田鼠恭敬地答道，「每年的這個時候，我們的商店是全天不打烊的呢。」

「那好！」河鼠說道，「你現在馬上就打著燈籠去商店，幫我買……」

這時，田鼠們嘀嘀咕咕地說起話來，鼴鼠只斷斷續續地聽到一些話：「買新鮮的，千萬當心！……不，那東西買一磅就足夠了……記住要買布根斯牌的，別的牌子我可不要……不，只買最好的……如果你在那兒買不到，到別的店試試……對，當然啦，要手工做的，罐裝的都不要……好啦，要盡力辦好啊！」最後，他聽見錢幣在爪子上傳遞的叮噹聲，看到河鼠把一隻大籃子交給那隻田鼠，田鼠提著燈籠，匆匆地買東西去了。

其餘的田鼠並排坐在長椅上，他們搖晃著小腿，心滿意足地烤著火，烤得長著凍瘡的腳直發癢。鼴鼠想引導他們輕鬆地對

談，卻一頭栽進他們的家族史。他們一一背誦自己無數弟弟們的大名，並提到弟弟們因為年紀太小，爸爸媽媽今年還不讓他們出來唱聖誕頌歌，但他們都盼望著能快點得到父母的同意。

這個時候河鼠仔細地看著一隻啤酒瓶上的商標。「我可以看出這是老伯頓牌，」他贊許地說道，「好個聰明的鼴鼠！這可是好貨啊！我們要把這些啤酒熱來喝！把東西拿來，鼴鼠，我把瓶塞打開。」

沒多久河鼠便把啤酒倒進了錫壺，然後把錫壺放到了火紅的爐膛裏。過了一會兒，每隻田鼠都啜飲著自己的熱啤酒。由於啤酒是熱的，喝一點就讓人受不了，因此他們都嗆得咳嗽起來；大家都笑著擦著眼睛，渾身發熱，似乎忘記了曾經忍受過的寒冷。

「這些小傢伙還會演戲呢。」鼴鼠對河鼠說，「他們會自己編故事，然後自己排練。而且演得還真不錯！去年他們演的那齣戲很精采。講的是一隻田鼠的故事：他在埃及巴巴里的海上被一個海盜抓住，海盜逼迫他在大木船上划槳，後來他逃回了家，但這時他的心上人已進修道院當修女。……嘿，你！我記得你有演出那齣戲。站起來背一段台詞給我們聽聽。」

被鼴鼠叫到的那隻田鼠站了起來，靦腆地咯咯笑著。他看了看大家，害羞得不知如何開口。他的夥伴們都在為他打氣，鼴鼠也哄著他，河鼠更是走向前抓住他的肩膀搖著，但怎麼樣也沒能讓這個怯場的演員開口。他們如同一群水手遵照皇家人道協會的規章，救助一位昏迷的溺水者般賣力。這時，門閂喀噠一聲，門開了，打著燈籠去買東西的田鼠回來了，沉甸甸的籃子使他走起

路來都搖搖晃晃的。

　　當滿籃子的東西被倒在桌面時，再也沒有人說什麼演戲的事了。在河鼠的指揮下，大家都動起手來，你做這樣我拿那樣。很快晚飯便準備好了。鼴鼠坐在主人的座位上，看到剛才還一無所有的桌面擺滿了各色各樣美味可口的食物，他覺得自己像是在做夢一樣。他的小朋友們毫不遲疑地吃了起來，個個都眉開眼笑，於是他也敞開肚子大口大口地吃了起來——他確實是餓壞了。他吃著像是變魔術得來的佳餚，心裏想著這次回家竟是如此地開心。他們一邊吃一邊說著往事，田鼠們跟鼴鼠說他們那一帶最近發生的事。他沒完沒了地問著，他們都盡力地回答他所提的問題。河鼠幾乎一句話也沒說，只是確定每位客人都吃飽喝足，讓鼴鼠不用操心任何事情。

　　最後，田鼠們嘰嘰嘎嘎地向主人道了謝，還說了許多節日祝福的話，口袋裏塞滿了帶給家中弟妹的紀念品，高高興興地回家去了。等到他們慢慢走遠，燈籠的燈光也漸漸消失後，鼴鼠和河鼠把門關上重新燒旺爐火，把椅子挪近，又溫了最後一杯睡覺前喝的啤酒，說起這一天來發生的事。後來，河鼠打了一個長長的呵欠說道：「鼴鼠老弟，我快要撐不住了，睏得難以形容。那邊那張是你的床鋪嗎？好，我睡這張床。這小屋子簡直是妙不可言！一切都這麼舒適方便！」

　　說完他爬上自己的床鋪，用毛毯把自己裹了起來，很快便呼呼入睡了。如同一片大麥，被迅速地收攏進割麥機的臂彎裏一樣。

　　鼴鼠也已困倦不堪了，恨不得倒頭便睡。很快他便枕著枕頭，心裏有說不盡的高興和滿足。他正要闔眼睡覺，但兩眼還是忍不住環顧一下火光中溫馨不已的房間；火爐上的火苗歡快地跳躍著，火光照在屋子裏他所熟悉的擺設上。直到現在他才意識到，這些東西早已成為他生命的一部分。它們不但對他毫無怨言，而且還露出親切的微笑，歡迎他的歸來。他此時的心情正是機靈的河鼠不聲不響地促成的。他很清楚這個家是多麼地簡樸和狹小，但他更清楚的是，這個家之於他的意義有多特殊。這是他人生的避風港啊！可即便如此，他一點也不想拋棄已展開的新生活，以及新生活給他帶來的廣闊天地；他不願放棄溫暖的陽光、清新的空氣和一切美妙的東西；他不想傻呼呼地待在家裏。即使他現在睡在地洞裏，外面的世界還是強烈地吸引著他，他知道必須回到那個更大的舞臺去。但是，想到自己擁有這個家，這個完全屬於自己的家，而這個家中的一切又是不論何時都歡迎他的歸來，他的心裏該是多麼地舒坦啊！

第六章　蟾蜍先生

這是初夏裏一個陽光明媚的早晨，像往年一樣，河裏漲滿了水，河水也歡快地流淌著。火熱的太陽似乎正在用一根根細絲把青草拔起，讓大地變得鬱鬱蔥蔥的。天剛蒙蒙亮，鼴鼠和河鼠起床了，又該是划船的季節了，他們正忙著船上的事情呢。他們給船刷上油漆，把船擦得亮亮的；然後縫補座墊，找回遺失的船鉤，忙東忙西。他們正在小客廳吃早餐，熱烈地商量著當天要做的事，這時傳來了重重的敲門聲。

「討厭！」河鼠說，他滿臉的蛋屑，「鼴鼠老弟，你吃完了，去看看是誰來了。」

鼴鼠走出去開門，河鼠聽見他驚叫了一聲。不一會兒，鼴鼠猛地打開客廳的門，正式地大聲通報：「獾先生大駕光臨！」

這確實是令人驚奇的事，獾先生居然會親自拜訪他們，他一向不輕易去拜訪別人。一般來說，如果你非常想見他，就得趁他在大清早或夜晚悄悄穿過樹籬時攔住他，或者去他的家裏找他，那可是一件非常不容易的事。

獾先生邁著沉重的腳步走進了客廳，然後站在那裏，神情嚴

肅地看著鼴鼠和河鼠。河鼠手中的湯匙滑到桌布去，他坐在椅子上，嘴巴張得大大的。

「時候到了！」獾先生鄭重其事地說道。

「什麼時候到了？」河鼠不安地問道，眼睛看了一下壁爐架上的鐘。

「你應該問『誰的時候到了』，」獾先生回答道，「是蟾蜍！教訓蟾蜍的時候到了！我跟你們說過，等冬天一過我一定教訓他，今天我就找他去！」

「對呀，是時候了！」鼴鼠高興地嚷道，「好哇，我記起來了！我們要把他教訓成一隻理智的蟾蜍！」

「今天早上，」獾先生接著說，一邊坐到一張扶手椅上，「又有一輛強大馬力的新汽車開往蟾蜍莊園，準備供他試用。這是我從可靠的管道獲得的消息。也許就在此刻，蟾蜍正忙著穿上他喜愛卻令眾人憎惡的奇裝異服，那身打扮使他從一隻相貌還算好看的蟾蜍，變成了任何正派的動物都討厭的傢伙。趁現在還來得及，我們得趕緊出門。你們倆馬上隨我一起去蟾蜍莊園，拯救蟾蜍的行動很快就要開始啦。」

「說得好！」河鼠跳起來大聲說道，「我們要拯救那個可憐又不幸的傢伙。我們要讓他徹底改變！他必須做一隻改邪歸正的蟾蜍，否則我們跟他斷絕來往！」

於是，在獾先生的率領下，他們動身去執行挽救蟾蜍的使命。當動物們結伴出行時，他們不是一窩蜂地散在路上，而是規規矩矩地排成一列，以防突然遇到危險，大家能夠互相照應。

　　他們來到了蟾蜍莊園的行車道。果然不出獾先生所料，屋前停著一輛嶄新的大汽車，車身的顏色是鮮豔的紅色（蟾蜍最喜愛的顏色）。他們走近門口時，門突然地打開了，蟾蜍先生戴著帽子、墨鏡，腳上穿著長筒橡膠靴，身上披著一件寬大的風衣。他大搖大擺地走下臺階，途中不時地拉了拉手上的長手套。

　　「你們好！朋友們！」他一見他們便高興地喊道，「你們來得正是時候，和我一起去……去兜風……去，呃……快活……」

　　他本來得意洋洋的口氣變得吞吞吐吐，話還沒說完卻不敢往下說了，因為這時他看到那些沉默的朋友們臉上嚴肅的表情。

　　獾先生大步走上臺階。「把他押進屋裏。」他厲聲地對兩個夥伴說道。於是，河鼠和鼴鼠把蟾蜍推進屋內，蟾蜍不停地掙扎著，口裏嚷個不停。獾先生走到負責開新車的司機跟前。

　　「恐怕今天你得回去了，」他說，「蟾蜍先生已經改變主意，他不需要這部車了。請相信這是最終的決定，你不必等他回心轉意了。」他說完就跟在河鼠他們身後走進屋裏，關上了門。

　　當他們四個都進了客廳，他對蟾蜍說：「現在你聽著，首先把你身上那些醜陋的衣服脫下！」

　　「不！」蟾蜍氣急敗壞地說，「你們如此無理地冒犯我是什麼意思？你們給我說清楚。」

　　「你們兩個，脫下他的衣服！」獾先生命令道。

　　蟾蜍拼命抗拒，又是踢又是罵，他們不得不把蟾蜍按在地上，才好把他身上的衣服脫下。河鼠坐在他的身上，鼴鼠則負責一件件地脫下他為坐車兜風穿上的花俏衣服，然後才讓他重新站

了起來。被脫下那身穿戴後，蟾蜍的怒氣似乎已消了大半。現在
他只是蟾蜍而已，不再是公路上製造危險的恐怖分子了。他難堪
地笑了笑，似乎已明白了這到底是怎麼回事。

「你明知遲早會是這樣的結果，蟾蜍，」獾先生厲聲地對他
說道，「你對我們的忠告充耳不聞，整天揮霍浪費你父親留下的
錢財；你開車魯莽，損壞財物，還敢和警察吵架，破壞我們在此
地區的名聲。自由自在當然很好，但是我們動物決不容許自己的
朋友毫無限制地幹蠢事、丟人現眼，而你做得已經夠過分的了。
聽著，在許多方面你還是個不錯的傢伙，因此我不想對你過於嚴
厲。我決定再次努力，試著讓你清醒過來。你跟我到吸煙室去談
談你的所作所為，一會兒等我們從房間出來後，看你會不會就此
悔悟。」

他緊緊地抓住蟾蜍的手，把他領進吸煙室，然後關上門。

「那樣做根本沒有用！」河鼠冷笑著說，「談心絕對改變不
了他，他一定會承諾一切，但之後仍舊我行我素。」

河鼠和鼴鼠舒服地坐在扶手椅上，耐心地等待著。他們聽見
門內傳來獾先生滔滔不絕地說話的嗡嗡聲，聲音時高時低，抑揚
頓挫。不久，獾先生的說教聲便不時被傷心的哭泣聲打斷，顯然
是蟾蜍發出的哭聲，他可是一個軟心腸、感情豐富的傢伙，讓他
改邪歸正最容易不過了——不過只是暫時的。

大約過了四十五分鐘，門開了，獾先生神色莊重地用爪子領
著垂頭喪氣的蟾蜍走了出來。蟾蜍兩腿顫抖著，不住地流著淚，
面頰布滿了皺紋，獾先生的話深深地感動了他。

「坐下，蟾蜍。」獾先生指著一張椅子慈祥地說。「朋友們，」他接著說，「我很高興地告訴你們，蟾蜍終於知錯了。他深深地為過去的錯誤感到悔恨，並就此鄭重向我承諾，他將痛下決心永遠和汽車一刀兩斷。」

「這可是非常好的消息。」鼴鼠認真地說。

「的確是好消息，」河鼠滿懷疑慮地說道，「只是，只是……」

他一邊說著，一邊盯著蟾蜍。此時的他，總覺得自己在蟾蜍那哀愴的雙眼裏，似乎隱約地看見了什麼東西正閃爍著。

「眼下只剩一件未完之事，」獾先生心滿意足地繼續說道，「蟾蜍，我要你當著朋友的面，鄭重地複述一次你剛才的話。首先，你要為你的過錯感到悔恨，並且承認你的行為十分愚蠢。」

經過一段長時間的沉默，蟾蜍絕望地左顧右盼，其他幾隻動物則默不作聲地等待著。最後，他終於開口了。

「不！」他有點賭氣地說，但口氣強硬，「我不後悔，我的所作所為一點也不愚蠢，相反地，光榮極了！」

「什麼？」獾先生驚駭不已地高聲嚷道，「你這個不知悔改的傢伙，剛才在裏面你不是跟我說……」

「是呀，是呀，在裏面，」蟾蜍不耐煩地說，「在裏面我什麼都會說的。你太懂得說話了，親愛的獾先生。你說得頭頭是道、感人肺腑，並且十分有說服力——在裏頭你說什麼，我都會聽從。但我一直思考著，並回想過去的所作所為，我覺得自己一點也沒錯、一點也不後悔。所以要說我錯了，一點道理也沒有，

對吧？」

「這麼說來，你不但不肯發誓，」獾先生說道，「還打算繼續玩汽車了？」

「我決不發誓！」蟾蜍十分堅決地答道，「相反地，我坦白告訴你們，要是眼前有一輛汽車，我會二話不說立刻把它開走。」

「我說得沒錯吧？」河鼠對鼴鼠說。

「那好吧，」獾先生站了起來，嚴厲地說，「既然你不聽我們好心勸說，我們就用強硬的辦法。我早料到有這一天。你不是常叫我們來這漂亮的宅邸和你住一段時間嗎？好，就這麼辦。我們要矯正好你的觀念後才會離開；你不悔改，我們決不走。你倆把他押到樓上，把他鎖在臥室裏，然後我們再商量下一步該怎麼做。」

「這都是爲你好，蟾蜍，」河鼠和善地說，他們把蟾蜍拖上樓，他使勁地掙扎著，「想想吧，要是你痛改前非，我們又可以像以前一樣去玩耍，那該有多開心啊！」

「一切都交給我們，蟾蜍，直到你大徹大悟爲止。」鼴鼠說道，「我們再也不能看著你像以前一樣，隨便揮霍錢財了。」

「也不會讓你再和警察頂嘴了，蟾蜍。」河鼠說道。他們把他推進了臥室。

「也不會讓你再受傷住院了，蟾蜍，免得你總是受那些女護士的擺布。」鼴鼠把門鎖上時對他說道。

他們走下樓梯時，蟾蜍透過鑰匙孔對他們破口大罵。接著，

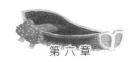

第六章

三個朋友一起商量對策。

「這可真是件苦差事啊。」獾先生歎氣說道，「我從來沒見過蟾蜍這樣頑固。但不管怎樣，我們要堅持到底，隨時守著他、輪流看著他，直到他放棄那些糊塗的想法。」

於是，他們安排好值班的順序。晚上他們輪流睡在蟾蜍的臥室裏，白天也輪流待在他的身邊。起初蟾蜍確實讓三個細心的看護頭痛不已。當老毛病一發作，他便把臥室裏的椅子排成汽車的模樣，蹲在最前面的那張椅子，彎下腰，兩眼直直地盯著前方，同時嘴裏發出粗魯恐怖的叫聲，直喊得聲嘶力竭。飆到最高速之後，他翻了一個大筋斗，趴在東倒西歪的椅子中間，顯然這會兒是心滿意足了。但是時間一久，這些痛苦的發作漸漸減少了，而他的朋友亦千方百計地把他的心思引領到別的事情上。然而，他似乎無法對其他東西提起任何興致，他明顯變得無精打采、鬱鬱寡歡。

一個晴朗的早晨，輪到河鼠值班了。他走上樓跟獾先生換班，獾先生看來有些坐立難安，並對他說自己要到林子裏去散散步，還得回去看看他的地洞。「蟾蜍還沒起床，」他走出門外對河鼠說，「沒能讓他承認些什麼，他只說『讓我安靜一會兒，我什麼都不要，也許我很快就會好的，不用為我擔心』等話。河鼠，你可要當心！當蟾蜍變得安靜順從，裝成一個聽話的學生時，那可是他耍陰謀的時候，肯定會鬧出什麼事來，我是瞭解他的。我現在必須走了。」

「今天過得好嗎，老朋友？」河鼠走近蟾蜍的床邊，和顏悅

097

色地問道。

過了好一會兒，他才聽到蟾蜍有氣無力地說：「非常感謝你的問候，親愛的河鼠！但先告訴我，你和聰明的鼴鼠還好嗎？」

「噢，我們都很好。」河鼠答道，接著漫不經心地補述，「鼴鼠和獾先生要到外面散心，直到午飯時間才回來，這樣我和你就可以快活一個早上了，我會盡力讓你高興起來的。快起床，好傢伙，這樣明媚的早上，怎能愁眉苦臉躺在床上呢！」

「好河鼠，」蟾蜍喃喃說道，「你真不瞭解我的情況啊，不知道我連起床也不想——也許永遠也起不來啦！別來煩我了，我不想成為朋友的負擔，我不想再給你們添麻煩了，我真的不想。」

「嘿，我也希望如此，」河鼠真心地說，「這段時間你讓我們操透了心，我很高興這一切就快要結束了。天氣多好呀，划船的季節又快到了！這對你太可惜了，蟾蜍！我不在乎你給我們帶來麻煩，但你確實讓我們錯過了很多東西。」

「恐怕你還是嫌我給你造成麻煩吧，」蟾蜍無精打采地說，「我可以理解，這是理所當然的事。你已經厭倦照顧我，我也不會再麻煩你了。我知道自己是一個討人厭的傢伙。」

「你的確是一個討人厭的傢伙，」河鼠說道，「但我告訴你，要是你決心做一隻理智的動物，我願意為你做任何事。」

「河鼠，如果可以，」蟾蜍喃喃地說，比以往顯得更加有氣無力，「我想求你——也許這是最後一次了——儘快地趕到村子裏去——也許有點遲了——把醫生叫來。算了，不必麻煩你了，

只是一點小毛病，就讓我這樣吧。」

「爲什麼要請醫生來？」河鼠問道，走前仔細地看著他。蟾蜍依然一動也不動地躺在那裏，說話的聲音更加微弱，態度也改變了許多。

「最近你一定發現——」蟾蜍喃喃地說，「不——你怎麼會發覺呢？那可麻煩得很，當然啦，明天你也許會對自己說：『噢，要是我早點注意到就好啦！要是我採取了什麼措施就好了。』算了啦，那是件麻煩事。別在意——就當我沒說吧。」

「好啦，老朋友，」河鼠有點驚慌地說，「如果你眞的需要請醫生，我當然會幫你把他叫來。但你還沒病到需要請醫生的地步，我們還是談點別的吧。」

「親愛的朋友，」蟾蜍苦笑地說，「『談』對這種病沒什麼用處——醫生也不見得能治好這種病。儘管如此，只要還有一點點希望，總該盡力爭取吧。順便說一下——你去請醫生的話——我眞的不想再給你添麻煩，我想起了你會經過他家門口的——你能同時把律師叫來嗎？這樣我會更省事。人生中總有一些時刻——也許我該說某個時刻——人必須面對不愉快的結局，花任何代價也於事無補！」

「律師！天哪，他一定病得不輕！」河鼠驚恐地想道。他匆匆忙忙離開了房間，當然他沒忘了把門鎖好。

走到屋外，他停下腳步認眞思考著。他的兩個朋友都出去了，沒有人可以和他商量。

「我最好還是小心一點，」他心裏尋思著，「我以前聽說過

蟾蜍無緣無故地以爲自己病了，但從沒聽他說過要請律師！如果他眞的沒病，醫生會罵他是頭老蠢驢，叫他別垂頭喪氣，那樣也好。我還是順他的意去把醫生請來，反正也用不了太多時間。」於是他出於好意，前往村裏請醫生去了。

蟾蜍一聽到鎖門聲便輕輕地從床上跳起來，然後走到窗戶旁，認眞地觀察著，直到看見河鼠消失在車道上。他高興得開懷大笑，順手抓起最漂亮的衣服飛快地穿上，又從牆邊桌子的抽屜裏取出錢，塞滿了幾個口袋。接著，他把一張張床單打結當成繩子，一端牢牢地繫在那個漂亮的都鐸式的窗櫺上。然後，他爬上窗臺，順著繩子滑到地面上，興沖沖地朝河鼠的相反方向走去，一邊愉快地吹著口哨。

當獾先生和鼴鼠終於回來時，河鼠正悶悶不樂地吃著午飯，可憐兮兮地說著事情的經過。實在太令人難以置信了。他早料到獾先生會說讓他難受的刻薄話，所以也就沒太計較，但讓他感到更難受的是，儘管鼴鼠盡可能地站在他這邊，也還是忍不住說：「你這次怎麼有點不中用啊，河鼠！連蟾蜍這樣的動物也能騙倒你啊！」

「他的確裝得太像了！」河鼠沮喪地說。

「是『你』太好騙了！」獾先生氣惱地回敬他，「現在說什麼都無濟於事了，顯然他已經溜掉了。最糟糕的是，他肯定會自以爲聰明過人，以致於做出什麼蠢事來也說不定。唯一值得慶幸的是，我們終於自由了，不用再浪費寶貴的時間守著他了。但我們最好還是在他家多待一些日子。蟾蜍也許隨時都會被送回

來——要嘛是躺在擔架上回來，要嘛是被警察押回來。」

獾先生口裏雖然這麼說，但他不僅不知道蟾蜍會出什麼事，也不知道他這一去結局會如何，更不知道什麼時候他才會平安回到這幢祖先留給他的莊園。

就在這時候，蟾蜍無拘無束、得意洋洋地快步走在公路上，離家已好幾英里了。一開始他專抄小路，穿過了一塊塊的田地，好幾次還改變路線，爲的是擺脫被獾先生等人追蹤。現在，他覺得已經沒有被抓回去的危險了，太陽對他露出燦爛的笑容，大自然歡唱讚美他的歌。他得意忘形地走在路上，腳步輕快，幾乎要跳起舞來了。

「我做得太漂亮了！」他高興得暗自發笑，「以智力鬥武力——智力占了上風——這是必然的結局。可憐的河鼠！哎呀，獾先生一回來他就慘囉！河鼠算是一個不錯的傢伙，他有許多可取之處，唯獨笨了一點，而且一點文化也沒有。有朝一日我定要好好教訓他，看看能不能把他調教成材。」

蟾蜍滿腦子裝的都是這些自高自大的想法。他昂首闊步地走在路上，沒多久便來到一個小鎮，看到大街上一家叫「紅雄獅」的飯館招牌在迎風招展。這時他才想起自己沒吃早餐，走了這麼遠的路，肚子餓得咕咕叫。他走進了餐館，點了一份可以迅速上菜的佳餚，坐在咖啡室裏吃了起來。

吃到一半的時候，大街上傳來一種非常熟悉的響聲，這響聲使他大吃一驚並且渾身顫抖。「突——突——」的響聲越來越近，他聽見汽車開到了旅館的院子裏，停了下來。蟾蜍不得不緊

抱著桌腳，這才控制住自己的衝動。不一會兒，汽車上的那幫人走進了咖啡室，他們個個都餓了，但還是眉飛色舞地說著整個上午開車兜風的快樂。蟾蜍聚精會神地聽了一會兒，最後他再也抑制不住了。他悄悄地溜了出去，在櫃檯結了帳。一出門便踮腳偷偷來到旅館的院子。「『看』一下也沒什麼吧！」他心裏想著。

汽車就停在院子中央，周圍無人看守，因為大家都在吃午飯。蟾蜍圍著汽車轉來轉去，一邊看一邊評頭論足，心裏盤算著。

他自言自語道：「不知道這種牌子的車是否容易發動？」

就在他還來不及弄清楚怎麼回事時，下一秒便發現自己早已握住啓動桿，並且發動起來。汽車發出熟悉的響聲，以往那種衝動又控制住他，全權支配了他整個身心。他覺得自己彷彿在做夢，他坐到駕駛座上拉動了操縱桿；在這場夢裏，他開著車在院子裏繞了一圈，然後駛出拱門。在夢中，什麼是非善惡和後果，似乎完全不存在似。他加快了車速，汽車在大街上狂奔，又風馳電掣般衝上公路，在曠野上飛馳著。此刻的他只知道他又變成蟾蜍了，那個威風凜凜、不可一世的蟾蜍，在公路上無法無天、橫衝直撞的霸主。在他面前一切都得讓路，否則就會被撞得粉身碎骨，一命嗚呼。蟾蜍一面駕著汽車飛快地奔馳，一面哼著歌，汽車也轟隆隆地和著他的歌聲。汽車不斷地奔馳，他也不知道要把車子開往何方，只知道先滿足自己的欲望，及時享受這段美妙的時光，並且毫不考慮這樣做的後果。

第六章

※ 法庭上 ※

「我認爲，」法院院長激動地說，「本案沒有什麼冤情，現在唯一的問題是，我們要怎樣才能讓站在被告席上這個屢教不改的惡棍、無可救藥的流氓，眞正清楚事情的嚴重性。讓我瞧瞧：被告的罪證非常明確，沒錯，他就是罪證確鑿。首先，他盜竊了一輛貴重的汽車；其次，他粗暴駕駛、危害公共安全；最後，他侮辱鄉村警察。書記官，請你說說，針對每一條罪狀，我們能判的最重刑罰是什麼？想當然耳，他不能享有減刑的權利，因爲他根本沒有這個資格。」

書記員用鋼筆搔了搔鼻子。「也許有些人認爲，」他說，「盜竊汽車是最嚴重的罪狀，確實如此。但毫無疑問，辱罵警察才更應加以重罰，確實應該如此。因此盜竊罪判一年徒刑，這算是情節輕微的；危險駕駛罪判三年徒刑，這還是從寬發落的；侮辱公務員罪——根據證人的證詞來判斷，這種侮辱十分惡劣——即使我們僅相信證詞的十分之一，我本身是不會相信多於十分之一的人——仍應判十五年徒刑。三罪併罰，依法判處有期徒刑十九年。

「太好了！」院長說。

「把刑期定爲二十年整，這樣似乎更好。」書記員最後說。

「這個建議很不錯！」院長贊許地說，「罪犯！提起精神，站直。本院判你有期徒刑二十年。請你注意，如果你下次再到本院，不管你犯的是什麼罪，本院都將嚴厲處置。」

　　宣判過後，那些表情冷峻的法警上前一把抓住可憐的蟾蜍，給他帶上鐐銬後，把他拖出法庭。蟾蜍高聲尖叫著，又是求情，又是抗議。當他被押著穿越市場時，那些幸災樂禍的群眾用現下流行的詞彙譏笑他，並向他投擲胡蘿蔔。如果僅僅是被通緝而已，那些人都會表示同情並願意提供幫助；但對於像蟾蜍這樣，已被法院判刑的罪犯，他們向來都是深惡痛絕。他被押著經過學校時，孩子們看到這樣穿戴整齊的紳士被判刑，送往監獄，他們天真的臉上露出興奮的神情。他被押著走過噹噹作響的吊橋，穿過布滿鐵釘的吊閘，走進古城堡陰森恐怖的拱門，只見城堡的尖塔高聳入雲。當他經過坐滿休息中的哨兵的警衛室時，哨兵們向他露出獰笑；走過值勤的哨兵身邊時，他們發出可怕的咳嗽聲，以此來表示對罪犯的輕蔑和厭惡。他走上年久失修的螺旋式樓梯，走過一些身披盔甲的士兵身邊，他們從頭盔裏向他投來可怕的目光。當他穿過院子時，警犬猛力掙扎著身上的皮帶，張牙舞爪，要向他撲過來。他還看到一些年老的看守，他們把兵器靠在牆上，一手拿著餡餅，一手拿著啤酒在那裏打瞌睡。就這樣，他被押著向前走著，走過兩個刑房——拉肢房和夾拇指房——走過一個通向絞架的拐彎處，最後來到了監獄中心最陰森的地牢門前。他們終於在這裏停下了腳步。一個非常年老的監獄看守坐在門邊，手裏撥弄著一大串鑰匙。

　　「喂！」法警對著他嚷道，一面脫下頭盔，一面擦拭額頭上的汗水，「快醒醒，你這個不中用的老東西。我們把這可惡的蟾蜍交給你了，他可是罪大惡極的罪犯，詭計多端，狡猾無比。你

第六章

千萬要好好看住他。老頭子，要是出了什麼差錯，當心你的腦
袋！」

　　老看守沉臉點了點頭，把那隻乾巴巴的手搭在可憐蟾蜍的肩
膀上。他用一把鏽跡斑斑的鑰匙把鎖打開，大門噹噹地打開了。
從此以後，蟾蜍就成了全英格蘭最牢固的城堡中，戒備最森嚴、
最偏僻的地牢中一個無依無靠的囚犯。

第七章　黎明前的笛聲

　　鷦鷯躲在河岸邊上的陰影中，嘰嘰喳喳地唱著歌。雖然已經過了晚上十點，天空中還殘留著落日的餘輝。短暫的仲夏夜正用涼快的手指驅散午後太陽所留下的酷熱。鼴鼠躺在河岸邊，悶熱的天氣使他難受地喘著氣——從日出到日落，天上一絲雲彩也沒有。鼴鼠等待著朋友的歸來。今天一整天他都在河上和一些夥伴玩耍，好讓河鼠能空出時間去赴水獺的邀約。剛才他回到家時發現屋裏一片漆黑，不見河鼠的蹤影，顯然他還在水獺家。鼴鼠覺得待在屋子裏太悶熱，便躺在河邊的草地上，回味著一整天所經歷的種種，心想這真是愉快的一天。

　　不一會兒，傳來河鼠穿越枯草地時的輕快腳步聲。「啊，終於可以涼快一會兒了。」他說。然後坐在地上，默默地盯著河面，一副心事重重。

　　「你一定在那裏吃過晚飯了吧？」過了一會兒鼴鼠問道。

　　「簡直無法推辭，」河鼠說，「不吃飯他們根本不讓我走。你知道他們一向很熱情。在我離開之前，他們一直盡力維持歡樂的氣氛。一整天我都感到很難受，雖然他們竭力不想讓我知道，

但我還是清楚知道發生什麼不幸的事。鼴鼠，我擔心他們遇到什麼麻煩了。小胖子又失蹤了，你一定知道他的父親該有多想念他，儘管他父親從不多談這件事。」

「什麼，是那孩子的事？」鼴鼠滿不在乎地說，「唉，就算是他失蹤了，用得著那麼擔心嗎？他總是東竄西竄，今天走失了，明天又冒出來。他就是喜歡冒險，但從來沒出過事。這一帶的人都認識和喜歡他，就像喜歡他的父親水獺一樣。說不定會有哪隻動物見了他，然後把他送回家來。哎，有一次我們不是在離他家好幾英里的地方找到他嗎？當時那小傢伙還一副興高采烈，若無其事的樣子！」

「你說得沒錯，不過這一次問題很嚴重。」河鼠沉重地說，「他已經失蹤了好幾天了，水獺們尋遍了每一個角落，但就是找不到他的蹤影，而且他們還問過附近的動物，但都沒有他的下落。雖然水獺什麼都沒說，但心裏肯定焦急萬分。我從他那裏得知，小胖子還不太會游泳。我看得出，他是擔心小胖子會不會在水壩那發生什麼危險。每年這個時候，那裏的水流很急，小孩特別愛到那裏玩耍。而那地方有……嗯，像是陷阱什麼的……這你是清楚的。水獺只有在緊急時刻才會替兒子擔心，然而，現在的他非常焦躁不安。我走的時候，他送我出來……說他想呼吸點新鮮空氣、活動一下身子。但我看得出不是那麼回事，便套了他的話，於是他終於向我坦承。原來他打算在淺灘守候一個晚上。你還記得那塊淺灘吧？那時候他們還沒在那裏造橋呢。」

「我記得一清二楚，」鼴鼠說，「但水獺為什麼要去那裏守

候呢？」

「唉，也許因爲那是水獺第一次教小胖子游泳的地方，」河鼠接著說，「小胖子便是在那個淺水、水下鋪著礫石的岬角學習怎麼游到岸邊的。水獺也在那教他釣魚，小胖子第一次釣到魚就在那，當時這小傢伙還很得意呢。那孩子喜歡去那兒。水獺心想他如果從某處玩耍回來後——可憐的小傢伙，但願他現在還活著——他可能會到他非常喜愛的淺灘去；或者他碰巧逛到淺灘，他一定會記起那些回憶，說不定會在那裏玩耍呢。因此，水獺每天晚上都到那兒去守候……想碰碰運氣，你知道，只是想碰碰運氣！」

他們沉默不語想著同一件事——憂心忡忡的水獺蜷曲著身子孤零零地守候在淺灘旁，整晚在那裏苦苦地等待——只是想碰一下運氣。

「好啦，好啦，」河鼠開口說，「我想我們也該上床睡覺了。」但他自己沒任何舉動。

「河鼠，」鼴鼠說，「如果我們不做點什麼，我還真睡不著……儘管我們似乎幫不上什麼忙，但要我因此毫無作爲，我也辦不到。我們把船拖出來，划著船到上游去。一個鐘頭後月亮就會出來了。到時候我們也盡力找找看……不管怎樣，總比躺在床上什麼事都不做來得有意義。」

「我也這麼想，」河鼠說，「今天晚上還真不是睡覺的時候，反正沒多久天就亮了。這樣吧，我們就一路划船搜索，也許還能向早起的人打聽小胖子的下落。」

他們把船拖出來，河鼠拿起船槳，小心地划著。天空隱隱約約地倒映在河中央一片狹窄、清澈的水面上，岸上高高低低的樹木昏暗地倒映在靠近岸邊的淺水上，不留神看的話，還以為是河岸呢。鼴鼠小心翼翼握好舵。夜很黑，到處空無一人，但隨處都能聽到各式各樣低低的聲音。這是那些晚上不睡覺、緊張忙碌的小動物們唱歌、聊天和走路的聲音，他們徹夜忙著自己的事情，等到太陽一出來，他們才會歇息。河水發出咕嚕的響聲，聽起來比白天更加清晰，彷彿就在耳邊。有時，背後突然傳來一陣清脆聲，似乎是在呼喚他們，把他們嚇了一跳。

地平線在天空的映襯下顯得清晰而粗獷。不久，在線條的某一段漸漸露出銀色的磷光，使得剛才明亮的地方暗了起來。最後，等待許久的大地迎接徐徐升起的月亮。很快，一輪明月便懸掛在空中，河鼠和鼴鼠又能看清周圍的一切——遼闊的草地和寂靜的花園。河流的兩岸展現在他們的眼前，一切光亮如白晝，再也沒有黑暗時的神秘和恐怖，但和白天的景象截然不同。他們往日所到之處，如今彷彿換裝向他們致意。似乎它們剛剛溜去什麼地方換上嶄新的衣服，又悄悄地跑回來，此刻正微笑著並羞澀地看著他們，想看看他們是否還能認出自己。

兩個好朋友把船繫到一棵柳樹上，走上這個靜謐的銀色世界。他們穿過一道道樹籬，鑽進空心的樹木，走進大大小小的地道、涵洞以及溝渠，仔細地搜尋。然後回到船上，繼續划著船往上游前進。月亮靜靜地掛在晴朗的高空，她也在盡力幫助他們，直到她下山的時候到了，才依依不捨地離他們而去。田野和河流

又籠罩在神秘中。

接著，夜色慢慢地發生著變化。地平線漸漸亮了起來，田野和樹木跟夜間時的樣貌截然不同，他們變得更加清晰明亮，籠罩著大地的神秘色澤漸漸消散了。一隻鳥突然發出一聲鳴叫後，一切又歸於寂靜。一陣微風徐徐吹來，蘆葦和蒲草發出沙沙的響聲。這時划船的是鼴鼠，他一面輕輕地划著槳，讓船慢慢前行，一面細心地看著兩岸。坐在船尾掌舵的河鼠突然坐直了身子，豎直了耳朵，全神貫注地聽著，於是鼴鼠好奇地看著他。

「那聲音消失了！」河鼠歎息著，重新坐回自己的座位，「多麼美妙、多麼新奇的聲音！可惜消失得太快了，還不如一開始就別讓我聽見。它激起我心中的渴望，令我痛苦萬分。我渴望再聽見那聲音，而且永遠地聽下去，除此之外的一切似乎變得不再重要。噢！那聲音又出現了！」他興奮地叫了起來。接著，他默不作聲，如癡如醉地聽了很長一段時間。

「那聲音就要遠去，即將消失不見了。」他突然說道，「噢，鼴鼠！那美妙的聲音！多麼歡快活潑，多麼優美動聽呀！眞像是遠處傳來的輕喚。我從沒想過世界上還有這樣優美的音樂！從這優美的音樂中我聽到了一種強烈的召喚。快點划呀，鼴鼠！那音樂一定是在召喚我們。」

鼴鼠感到十分驚訝，但還是照河鼠說的用力地划著船。「我什麼都沒聽到，」他說，「只聽見風吹得蘆葦、蒲草和柳枝沙沙作響。」

河鼠沒有答話，也許他根本沒聽到鼴鼠在說什麼。他神情癡

迷，又喜不自勝，全身都在顫抖。那神奇的聲音徹底征服了他，在它面前，他徹底成為一個無助但又快樂的嬰兒。

鼴鼠默默地划著船，不久他們來到了河流的一個分岔口，一道河水從這分岔出另一道靜止的支流。河鼠早已忘了掌舵，這時他把頭輕輕一擺，示意夥伴讓船駛進支流。天色越來越亮，現在他們已能看清河邊花朵的顏色。

「那聲音越來越清楚了，」河鼠高興地叫道，「現在你總算能聽見了吧！啊——終於聽到了——看來你聽到了！」

那悠揚的笛聲如同波濤向鼴鼠襲來，他屏息肅靜地聽著，聽得心醉神迷。他呆呆地站著，手中的槳也不知不覺地停了下來。他看見夥伴臉頰上的淚水，心領神會地點了點頭。他們在那裏停了好一會兒，河岸邊的紫色珍珠菜輕撫著他們。接著，那令人心醉的音樂彷彿急切地召喚著鼴鼠，他不知不覺地彎下身，划起槳來。天變得更亮了，鳥兒不像黎明到來時那樣唱歌了。除了那彷彿來自仙境的奇妙音樂，周圍的一切都寂然無聲。

他們的船向前划行，兩岸的青青草地非常地青翠欲滴。他們也從來沒有見過玫瑰如此鮮豔，柳蘭如此多姿，繡線菊如此芳香誘人。不一會兒，水壩的流水聲越來越清晰，他們意識到自己即將抵達終點，儘管他們不知道等待著他們的會是什麼，但肯定正等待著他們的到來。

展現在眼前的竟是一片寬廣的半圓形水面，巨大的水壩攔住了河水的去路，使這裏成為一個波光粼粼的湖：翻滾的漩渦使水面泛起無數泡沫，莊嚴而鎮定的轟隆聲蓋過其他聲音。一座小島

安詳地躺在湖中央被河岸擁抱著，柳樹、白樺和橙木環繞著島的四周。它矜持、羞澀又意味深長地把一切都藏在帷幕的後面，一直等到適當時機才會召喚那些受選者。

河鼠和鼴鼠緩慢但毫不遲疑地划著船，內心懷著一股莊嚴的期待，穿過那片滾滾翻騰的湖面，最後把船停靠在小島那長滿鮮花的邊上。他們默不作聲地上岸，走過一簇簇的花叢，穿過芬芳的草叢和矮樹叢，走過一塊平地，最後來到一片綠油油的草地；其四周長著山楂、野櫻桃和黑刺李等大自然的各種果樹。

「那音樂就是從這裏傳來的，我聽見的優美仙樂就是在此演奏的，」河鼠如夢囈般低聲地說，「如果我們能找到那位吹笛人，他肯定在這裏——在這個神聖的地方。」

就在這時，鼴鼠突然感受到一股強烈的威嚴感向他襲來，使他全身無力，只能將頭垂得低低的，而腳下似乎長了根似的。但那絕不是恐懼——事實上他心裏感到無比地平靜和快樂——那是一種將他徹底征服的威嚴。他知道，這意味著他們離那令人敬畏的存在相當靠近，雖然他仍未見到。他吃力地轉過身去找他的朋友，看見他誠惶誠恐地站在他的身邊，渾身劇烈地顫抖著。他們四周的樹枝上棲息著許多鳥兒，但他們卻悄無聲息。曙光變得越來越明亮了。

此刻那笛聲雖早已靜下，但那召喚仍然十分霸道且不容抗拒，要不是如此，鼴鼠是怎樣也不敢抬起雙眼向四周張望的。因為一旦以肉眼直視那深藏不露的東西，就算死神即刻降臨在他身上，他亦會甘之如飴，死不足惜。他渾身顫抖著，順從了那種召

喚，抬起了他卑微的頭。這時，周圍的一切都已清晰可見，大地
又披上了繽紛的色彩，萬物屏住呼吸。他兩眼緊盯著這位「朋友
和救世主」。他看見頭上兩隻向後伸展的角在陽光下閃閃發亮；
看見那雙安詳的雙眼間有一個剛毅的鷹勾鼻；看見那雙眼睛意興
豐饒地看著他們；看見那張滿是鬍鬚的嘴角牽起一絲笑意；看見
他寬闊的胸膛前橫著一隻肌肉突起的手臂，靈巧的手上還拿著剛
從嘴唇邊移開的排笛；看見那雙毛茸茸的腿悠閒地擱在草地上；
最後看見那圓胖的小水獺安靜地躺著，睡得正香。鼴鼠清清楚楚
地看見這一切。有好一會兒，他呼吸急促，激動不已。小胖子看
起來還活著，仍活著，他猜想著。

「河鼠！」他顫抖著低聲說，「你害怕嗎？」

「害怕？」河鼠喃喃地說道，兩眼流露著無以名狀的愛意，
「害怕他？噢，一點也不！但是……但是……噢，鼴鼠，我的確
有點害怕！」

於是兩隻動物跪在地上，低下頭頂禮膜拜起來。

突然，一輪金色的太陽躍出了地平線，陽光照在平靜的水面
上，折射進他們的眼睛，刺得他們睜不開眼。當他們又能看清東
西時，剛才所見一切已消失無蹤，鳥兒的鳴叫聲環繞四周，正歡
慶著黎明的到來。

當他們慢慢意識到，眼前所見眨眼間就要消逝，他們茫然地
凝望著對方，心裏感到莫名的惆悵。一陣變幻莫測的微風從水面
吹來，輕輕地搖動山楊樹，吹動了帶著露珠的玫瑰，輕撫著他們
的臉龐。隨著微風的撫摸，剛才的記憶也隨之消逝，這正是那位

慈祥的半人半神顯靈幫助他人後，最終賜予的最佳大禮。

　　他選擇讓他們遺忘，是爲了不讓這些可怕的記憶繼續留在他們的腦海裏，給他們的歡樂帶來陰影；爲了不讓這些難以釋懷的記憶破壞動物們日後的生活，並恢復他們以往的幸福快樂。鼴鼠揉了揉眼睛，盯著河鼠；河鼠困惑不解地看著他。鼴鼠問：「我沒聽清楚，河鼠，你剛才說什麼？」。

　　「我說，」河鼠慢慢地說，「這就是我們要找的地方，如果我們會在什麼地方找到他，那就是這裏。哎呀！看哪，他在那兒，那小傢伙！」他一邊高興地叫著，一邊朝睡得正香的小胖子跑去。

　　但是，有好一會兒鼴鼠呆站在那裏，陷入了沉思。他就像突然從美夢中醒來，竭力想在腦海搜尋夢中的情景，但什麼也沒找到，只是模糊地感到夢的美妙！後來，那種美妙的感覺也漸漸消失，他不得不接受美夢消散的痛苦並失落地清醒，接受這懲罰。於是，鼴鼠傷心地搖著頭，緊跟在河鼠的身後。

　　小胖子醒來後發出開心的吱吱聲，看到這兩位經常陪自己玩耍的父親友人，他高興得又蹦又跳。但沒過多久，他突然變得面無表情，一臉哀求似的四處尋找著什麼。就像一個在褓母懷裏熟睡後醒來的小孩，發現自己被孤零零地放在一個陌生的地方，心裏感到說不出的失望；於是從一個房間跑到另一個房間，翻箱倒櫃，到處尋找。小胖子不知疲憊地找遍了小島的每個角落，最後他失望不已地坐在地上，傷心地大哭起來。

　　鼴鼠連忙跑過去安慰他，而河鼠站在原地，滿心疑惑地凝視

著草地上那些深深的蹄印。

「一隻……大……動物……來過這裏。」他沉思著並喃喃自語，呆呆地站在那裏左思右想。

「河鼠，快過來呀！」鼴鼠喊道，「可憐的水獺還在淺灘邊苦苦地守候呢！」

小胖子很快便被哄住了，因為他們答應讓他坐河鼠先生的船在河上遊玩。然後，他們倆把他帶到水邊，抱他上船，讓他坐在他倆之間，離開這片靜止的水域。這時，太陽已升得很高，晒得他們暖洋洋的。鳥兒扯著嗓子縱情歡唱，兩岸的花兒向他們點頭微笑，但不知怎地，他們覺得此時的花兒不若剛才那般鮮豔多姿——他們不清楚究竟是在何處看見剛才那些花的。

到了主河道，他們掉過船頭朝上游划去，他們知道他們的朋友正在淺灘邊上孤零零地守候著。當他們靠近熟悉的淺灘時，鼴鼠把船划向岸邊。他們把小胖子抱上岸又把他放在拖船的小徑上，命令他快步前行，並輕拍他的背跟他告別。接著便把船划到河中央。他們一路照看著小傢伙神氣十足地蹣跚行走，接著看見他突然抬起嘴角然後歡叫著，並加快步伐向前跑去，因為他似乎認出了什麼。站在船上的他們，看見水獺從他耐心守候的淺灘上站起緊張又僵硬的身軀，蹦蹦跳跳地穿過柳樹林，接著衝上拖船的小徑，發出驚喜的叫聲。鼴鼠一隻手用力地划著槳，將船掉頭並順流而下，他們的搜尋終於愉快地結束了。

「我感到異常地疲憊，河鼠。」鼴鼠說，疲倦地靠在船槳上，讓船順水飄流，「你可能會說，那是因為我整晚沒睡，但熬

夜算得了什麼。每年的這個季節，每周有三、四晚都不睡覺呢。跟睡眠不足無關。我覺得自己好像經歷了激動人心卻又可怕的事情，而這段歷程終於結束了，但又似乎什麼也沒發生過。」

「非常驚人、非常壯觀和非常美妙的事情。」河鼠低聲地說，閉上眼睛，身子後靠在船上，「我的感受和你一樣，鼴鼠，簡直是疲憊不堪——但不是身體上的疲勞。好在我們還可以坐船順流回家。能再次感受到陽光灑在身上，彷彿要沁入骨髓似，這感覺真好！你聽，風把蘆葦吹得沙沙作響，多麼優美動聽啊！」

「就像遠處傳來的音樂。」鼴鼠說，疲倦地點點頭。

「我覺得，」河鼠彷彿在夢中喃喃地說道「像連續不斷且輕快的舞曲……還配有歌聲……時有時無……我有時能聽到歌聲……然後又變成了舞曲，接著只聽見蘆葦發出輕輕的沙沙聲。」

「你聽得比我清楚，」鼴鼠沮喪地說，「我聽不出歌聲來。」

「讓我認真聽聽，然後把歌詞告訴你，」河鼠輕聲地說，眼睛還閉著，「現在舞曲裏又摻有歌聲……聲音微弱但很清晰……『為了不使畏懼長駐在你們心頭……不使你們的快樂變成煩憂……當你們需要我時，我會在你們身邊……但你們將忘了我！』現在蘆葦接著唱出……『遺忘，遺忘！』蘆葦歎息著，歌聲慢慢消失了，又變成了蘆葦的沙沙聲。歌聲又回來了……

『為了不讓手腳紅腫綻裂……我把裝下的陷阱移開……當我把羅網撕開時，也許你們會瞥見我……你們一定要忘了我！』把

116

船划近一點，鼴鼠，讓船更靠近蘆葦！歌聲漸漸變弱，快聽不見了。

『我撫慰在林中流浪的小孩童……我幫助林中迷路的小羔羊……我撫平他們身上的創傷……囑咐他們忘卻一切！』再近點，鼴鼠，再近點！唉，沒用了！歌聲又變成了蘆葦的沙沙聲。」

「但那些歌詞是什麼意思呢？」鼴鼠迷惑不解地問。

「我也不知道，」河鼠簡單地說，「我只是把聽到的歌詞告訴你。啊，歌聲又回來了，這次更加清晰！這一次更加真實，簡單明瞭……感情豐富……完美無比……」

「嗯，那你說給我聽聽。」鼴鼠說。他耐心地等了幾分鐘，溫暖的太陽晒得他昏昏欲睡。

但他沒聽到任何回答。他看一下便明白是怎麼回事了。河鼠臉上掛著幸福的微笑，看似還在認真地傾聽，事實上早已疲倦地睡去。

第八章　蟾蜍歷險記（一）

　　蟾蜍被監禁在一個骯髒潮濕的地牢裏。他知道這座陰暗的中世紀城堡已經把他和外面陽光燦爛的世界，徹底地隔絕開來。不久前，不可一世的他還駕車縱情馳騁在平坦的碎石公路上——彷彿當時的他早已買下英格蘭所有的道路似。想到這些，他絕望地趴在地上，傷心的淚水奪眶而出。他心裏想：「一切都完了，至少蟾蜍的事業完蛋了，反正都是同一回事。多麼英俊瀟灑、惹人喜歡的蟾蜍，多麼富有而又好客的蟾蜍，多麼自由自在、無憂無慮又風度翩翩的蟾蜍啊！這樣的我，膽大妄為地偷竊那輛漂亮的汽車，又辱罵一大幫肥頭大耳、面紅耳赤的警察，最終依法鋃鐺入獄。我怎能指望自己還能逍遙法外！」想到這，他哽咽地說，「我是一個多麼愚蠢的傢伙啊！如今我必須在地牢裏忍受折磨，直到我的名字被認識我而感到自豪的人淡忘為止！噢！多麼睿智的獾先生！多麼機靈的河鼠！多麼理智的鼴鼠！你們的判斷是多麼正確，你們對世事是多麼清楚啊！噢，我這個不幸的、遭人鄙視的蟾蜍！」就這樣，他唉聲歎氣地度過了幾個星期，不肯吃飯，連點心也不吃。儘管那個臉色難看的老看守因為知道蟾蜍有

錢，經常向他暗示：只要給錢，許多好吃的東西——甚至是奢侈品——都可以弄進來。

那個老看守有一個女兒，性格開朗，心地善良。她經常和父親一起值勤，幫他做一些自己力所能及的工作。她特別喜愛動物，養有幾隻花斑老鼠和一隻活蹦亂跳的松鼠，還養了一隻金絲雀。白天，她把金絲雀的籠子掛在監獄高牆的釘子上，這使得那些喜歡飯後打盹的囚犯非常惱火；晚上，她把鳥籠放在客廳的桌子上，用椅罩裹起來。這個好心腸的姑娘很同情蟾蜍。一天，她對父親說：「爸爸！我不忍看著那隻可憐的動物整天悶悶不樂，一天天地消瘦下去！你把他交給我吧。你知道我有多麼喜歡小動物。我要餵他吃飯，還要讓他打起精神做各式各樣的事。」

她父親說，隨便她要怎樣都行。反正蟾蜍愁眉苦臉的模樣、不可一世的神態和一毛不拔的吝嗇，早讓他煩透了。於是，有天她便去執行感化蟾蜍的使命，她敲了下蟾蜍牢房的門。

「振作起來，蟾蜍，」她一進門便哄著他說，「快坐起來，擦掉眼淚，做一隻聽話的動物。你多少吃點東西啊，你看，我把我的飯菜也帶來給你了，還熱著呢。」

盤子裏盛的是捲心菜煎馬鈴薯，用另一個盤子蓋著，香味飄滿了狹小的牢房。蟾蜍愁容滿面地躺在地上，鼻子不斷地聞到捲心菜誘人的香味，有那麼一瞬間，他覺得生活也許並不像他所想得那麼空虛絕望。但他依然又哭又喊，兩腳亂踢亂蹬，怎麼勸也勸不聽。於是，聰明的姑娘暫時離開牢房，留下熱騰騰的菜香縈繞在房裏。蟾蜍在哭泣之餘，腦海裏浮現嶄新且激勵人心的想

法。他想起了騎士精神、詩歌、要做的事；沐浴在陽光下、和風
輕拂的遼闊草地及吃草的牛群；想起了茱園、筆直的花壇和被蜜
蜂團團圍住的金魚草；想起了蟾蜍莊園，餐桌上擺放碗碟時發出
的叮噹聲和準備吃飯時大家拖動椅子發出的響聲。窄小的牢房裏
似乎彌漫著玫瑰的芬芳。他也想起了他的朋友，他們一定能為他
做點什麼；想起了律師，他們本來很樂意為他辯護，自己當初沒
有請幾個律師真是愚蠢至極；最後他想起了自己是多麼地足智多
謀，只要肯動腦子，有什麼事他辦不到呢？想到這裏，他似乎又
恢復了往日的自信。

　　幾個小時以後，姑娘回來了，手裏捧著一個托盤，上面有一
杯冒著熱氣、香味濃郁的茶，還有滿碟子熱騰騰、抹了奶油的烤
麵包片。麵包片切得很厚，兩面都烤得金黃，上面的氣孔掛著金
黃的油珠，像是剛剛從蜂窩裏取下的蜂蜜。奶油麵包的香味彷彿
在和蟾蜍說話，談及溫暖的廚房、寒夜清晨的早餐；談及冬夜散
步歸來時穿著拖鞋、腳踩踏板，對著客廳那溫暖的爐火；談及貓
咪心滿意足的咕嚕聲，還有金絲雀昏昏欲睡時發出的嘰嘰聲。蟾
蜍終於又坐了起來，把眼淚擦乾，喝了一口茶，咬了一口麵包。
沒過多久，他便和姑娘無拘無束地聊了起來，說了很多關於自己
的事情；說到了以前住的大房子和他在家裏做的事，還吹噓自己
有多麼了不起，自己的朋友又如何地想念他。

　　看守的女兒看得出這種話題和香茶一樣，對他確實很有好
處，便鼓勵地繼續往下說。

　　「跟我說說蟾蜍莊園吧，」她說，「那地方聽起來真美

啊。」

「蟾蜍莊園，」蟾蜍得意洋洋地說，「是老成持重的紳士才有資格居住的邸宅，它舉世無雙。它始建於十四世紀，但如今它的現代化設備一應俱全，安裝有新穎的衛生設備。它離教堂、郵局和高爾夫球場只有五分鐘的路程，相當適合……」

「上帝保佑你，」姑娘大笑著說道，「我可不想要它，你還是說一說房子的具體情況吧。噢，等一下，我去幫你再端些茶和麵包來。」

說完，她走了出去，很快便端來滿滿一托盤的新鮮食物。蟾蜍的情緒已完全恢復，他一邊狼吞虎嚥地嚼著麵包，一邊滔滔不絕地跟她講起了遊艇停泊的地方、養魚池、有圍牆的古老菜園、豬圈、馬廄、鴿棚、雞舍、乳品儲藏室、洗衣坊、瓷器櫥、大櫥櫃（這是她聽得最津津有味的東西）。他還說到了宴會廳，說到他和別的動物聚會時的歡樂情景。接著，蟾蜍還高興地為動物們唱歌、講故事，大家都盡興而歸。於是她叫他說一說他的朋友，他便告訴她他們如何生活、平時做什麼事情來打發時光，這些她都聽得津津有味。當然，她沒有告訴蟾蜍她非常喜歡養小動物，因為她看得出那一定會讓他非常生氣。她幫他把水罐盛了水，又為他鋪好了地上的稻草，然後跟他道了晚安。蟾蜍又變成了往日那隻逍遙自在、得意洋洋的動物。他唱起了以往和朋友聚餐時唱的小調，把身子蜷起，縮在稻草裏。那天晚上，他睡得特別地香，做了許多美妙的夢。

從那以後，他們經常在一起談天說笑，以打發枯燥煩悶的日

子。老看守的女兒對蟾蜍越來越同情，在她看來，蟾蜍犯的只是一個小小的過錯，把這隻可憐的小動物關在監獄裏是極不公平的事。而自高自大的蟾蜍認為她之所以對他如此同情，一定是因為對他日久生情的緣故。只可惜他們的社會地位相差過於懸殊，儘管她是一個美麗的姑娘，而且明顯地對他相當傾心。

某天早上，姑娘顯得心事重重，蟾蜍問她話，她答得心不在焉；對蟾蜍妙趣橫生的言談和富於真知灼見的評論，她似乎並沒有像往常一樣表現出應有的興趣。

「蟾蜍，」她突然說道，「你聽我說，我有一個姑媽，她專門幫別人洗衣服的。」

「好啦，好啦，」蟾蜍優雅而親切地說，「不要緊，別再想這件事了，我也有幾個應該給別人洗衣服的姑媽。」

「求求你安靜一下，蟾蜍，」姑娘說，「你講得太多了，這是你最大的毛病。我正思索著，而你一直打斷我。我剛才提到我有一個專門幫別人洗衣服的姑媽，這座城堡裏囚犯的衣服都交由她來洗，你知道我們家就靠這個賺錢過日子。每星期一早上她會把要洗的衣服拿走，星期五傍晚把洗好的衣服送來。今天是星期四。聽著，我是這麼想的：你很有錢——至少你經常這樣跟我說——而她很窮。幾英鎊對你來說是不足掛齒的，對她來說卻是一大筆錢。我想，如果你好好待她，用你們動物的話來說，如果你給她一點錢，那我們就可以把事情辦妥。你換上她的服裝，扮成一個洗衣婦，然後逃出這座城堡。你們相貌上有許多相像的地方——特別是身材。」

「才不像呢，」蟾蜍十分生氣地說，「以我的角度來看，我的身段如此優美。」

「以我姑媽的角度來看，她的身段也很優美，」姑娘回答說，「不過，你想怎樣就怎樣吧，你這個自大、忘恩負義、醜陋不堪的傢伙，虧我還好心地同情你，想方設法幫助你！」

「好吧，好吧，妳說的都對，我真的非常感謝妳。」蟾蜍急忙說，「不過話又說回來了，妳總不能讓蟾蜍莊園的蟾蜍先生裝扮成一個洗衣婦到處亂跑吧！」

「那你就永遠關在這個地牢裏吧，」姑娘非常激動地說，「我看你是想坐著漂亮的四輪馬車離開監獄吧！」

誠實的蟾蜍一向勇於承認自己的錯誤。「妳是一個聰明善良的姑娘，」他說，「而我確實是一隻愚蠢、高傲的蟾蜍。那就拜託妳介紹我認識妳尊敬的姑媽吧！我相信我和妳那位優秀的女士可以把條件談妥，讓雙方都滿意的。」

第二天晚上，姑娘把她的姑媽帶進蟾蜍的地牢，她手裏拿著前一周他讓她洗的衣服，用毛巾包著。老太婆事先為這次見面做好了準備，當她看到蟾蜍特意擺放在桌子上的金幣，就知道交易即刻成立，不必再進行討價還價。蟾蜍的金幣換來的是一件印花布罩衣、一條圍裙、一條頭巾和一頂紅褐色的女帽。老太婆要求蟾蜍把她捆起來、嘴巴塞住，並扔在牆角。她解釋說，儘管這件事看起來有許多可疑之處，但她希望透過被綁住的場面，再加上她胡亂編造的故事，能夠讓她保住飯碗。

蟾蜍對她的建議感到非常高興。這使他能夠有模有樣地逃離

這個監獄，他那亡命之徒的名聲也絲毫不受影響。於是，他便動手幫助看守的女兒把她的姑媽捆起來，盡可能地使她看起來像無力反抗的受害者。

「輪到你了，蟾蜍。」姑娘說，「把外套和背心脫下，你太胖了。」

她一面大笑不止，一面給他穿上那件印花罩衣；幫他扣上鈕扣，把頭巾疊成洗衣婦們的樣子，然後把那頂紅褐色的帽子戴上，把帽帶繫在他的下巴。

「你看起來跟她一模一樣了，」她咯咯笑道，「不過，我敢肯定你從未看起來如此可敬。再見了，蟾蜍，祝你好運！沿著你來時的路一直走出去。如果有人和你說話也別擔憂，因為男人們都愛搭話，你就和他們開開玩笑，敷衍過去即可。但千萬記住你現在是一位寡婦，在這個世界上無依無靠，不能做出有失身分的事。」

蟾蜍膽顫心驚，盡力地邁著穩健的步伐，小心翼翼地開始了他那看起來非常愚蠢而危險的行動。但很快地他便驚喜地發現，一切都進行得非常順利。但想到身為一個有地位的紳士，現在竟然穿著女人的衣服逃獄，他覺得很難為情。穿著人人熟悉的印花布罩衣的矮胖洗衣婦，似乎是每道關卡的通行證。甚至當他猶豫不決，不知該朝哪個方向走的時候，下道關卡的看守也會給他指路。有個看守還大聲叫他快點走，免得他整夜守在門口，因為他急著下班回家喝茶。一路上，不時有人跟他開玩笑，他理應及時且恰當地答話，但這對他頗具危險性。因為蟾蜍的自尊心特別

強，他覺得這些玩笑粗俗不堪，一點也不幽默。然而，他控制住了自己的脾氣，好不容易才得體地和那些人應答著。這才讓他的話既符合洗衣婦的身分，又不損害他作爲一個有品位的人的形象。

他似乎覺得走了好幾個鐘頭，才來到了最後一個院了。他拒絕了最後一個警衛房的哨兵的盛情邀請，最後一個看守熱情地伸出雙臂，要和他擁抱告別，但他巧妙地躲開了。最後，監獄大門旁的小門在他身後關上了。他感到監獄外的清新空氣正輕拂著他的額頭，他知道自己終於自由了！

膽大妄爲的冒險就這樣輕而易舉地成功了，蟾蜍喜出望外。他快步朝燈火輝煌的鎮上走去，但一點也不知道自己下一步該做些什麼，不過有一件事他很清楚：那個洗衣婦在這一帶家喻戶曉且十分受歡迎，因此他必須趕緊離開這個地方。

他一邊想一邊往前走的時候，他的注意力被離鎮上不遠的紅綠燈吸引住了。他聽到了火車頭的噗哧聲和火車轉軌時發出的叮噹聲。「啊！」他想，「我的運氣眞好！此時此刻，我最想去的地方就是火車站，這樣，我就不必穿過鎮上，也不必爲了裝扮這個丟人現眼的老太婆而跟別人東拉西扯了。雖然那樣做非常管用，但有損我的自尊心。」

於是，他朝火車站走去，到那裏後看了一下時刻表，發現再過半個小時有一趟火車開往他家的方向。「運氣太好了！」蟾蜍激動地說。於是走到售票處，準備買火車票。

他把離蟾蜍莊園最近的車站名告訴售票員，然後下意識地把

手伸進背心口袋掏錢。但他身上穿的並不是背心，而是這件一直忠實地保護著他，而他又一直不當回事的印花布罩衣。他找不到錢。像是做噩夢一樣，有狡猾的東西把他的雙手絆住了，他使不上力，並且不斷地被它放肆嘲笑。排在他身後的旅客不耐煩地等著，有的七嘴八舌地幫他出主意，有的對他的做法說三道四。最後，他掙脫了身上的束縛——他甚至不知道是怎樣掙脫的，把手伸到了背心口袋應該在的地方，但發現那裏不但沒有錢，而且連裝錢的口袋都沒有，更糟糕的是他根本沒有穿背心！

他驚恐地想起自己的外套和背心都留在牢房裏，而且他的皮夾、錢、鑰匙、手錶、火柴、鉛筆盒也都丟在牢房裏。在蟾蜍看來，那是所有讓生活有價值的物品，能區分富有的高等動物和貧窮或不富有的低等動物：有錢的動物是萬物的主宰，沒錢的動物只能到處流浪，根本沒有競爭的條件。

痛苦之中，他竭力想矇混過關，便擺出往日他那既像鄉紳又像大學教師的模樣，說道：「聽我說！我忘了帶錢包了，請你把車票給我，明天我會把錢送來。我可是這一帶的名人。」

售票員盯著他的眼睛，又看了看他頭上那頂紅褐色的女帽，接著大笑起來。「如果妳經常玩這種把戲，」他說，「我相信妳很快就會出名。夫人，請不要站在窗口，妳會妨礙別人買票。」

站在他身後的一位老先生一直不停地推著他的手臂，最終把蟾蜍推到一邊；更過分的是，他竟然把蟾蜍稱做他太太，這是那天晚上最令蟾蜍氣憤的事。蟾蜍滿懷沮喪，火車還停在鐵軌上，而他只能沿著站臺毫無目的地走著，兩行眼淚撲簌簌地掉了下

來。眼看著快要安全回到家了，卻因為缺幾個錢，沒能買到火車票，還要受這些人的氣。想到這裏，他心裏感到難受極了。很快地他的逃跑將會被人察覺，就要展開對他的搜尋，他會再次被抓起來；人們會訓斥他，重新給他戴上鐐銬，再次把他投進監獄，讓他回到那種啃麵包、喝冷水、晚上睡在乾稻草上的生活；人們對他的監禁會更加嚴密，對他的處罰會更加嚴厲；噢，那姑娘該會怎樣譏諷他呢！他該怎麼辦啊？他的腿走起路來又不快，更不幸的是，別人很容易就能認出來。難道他不能擠在火車座位的下面？他曾經看過一些學童用這種方法，因為他們把父母給自己買票的錢花到別的更有趣的東西上了。他邊想邊走，不知不覺來到了火車頭的前面。一位身材魁梧的司機一手提著油罐一手拿著廢棉紗，正在細心地用油擦試、保養火車頭。

「喂，大嬸！」司機說，「看妳愁容滿面的樣子，一定是遇到什麼麻煩事了吧？」

「別提啦，先生！」蟾蜍說，又哭了起來，「我是一個不幸的窮洗衣婦，身上的錢全弄丟了，沒買到車票，可是我今晚無論如何必須趕回家，該怎麼辦我也不知道。噢，天啊，天啊！」

「那可真是一件很不幸的事，」司機若有所思地說，「丟了錢……回不了家……如果我沒說錯的話，家裏一定有小孩等著吧？」

「有好幾個呢，」蟾蜍傷心地哭泣著說，「他們肯定要挨餓……他們會玩火柴……會弄翻油燈，我可憐的小東西呀！……他們還會吵架，家裏會鬧得一塌糊塗。噢，天哪，天哪！」

「嗯，讓我想想，看我能不能幫妳的忙，」好心的司機說，「妳說妳是個洗衣婦，那正好。也許妳看出來了，我是開火車的，那可真是個又髒又累的工作。每天穿的襯衫都弄得髒兮兮的，我太太洗得都煩啦。妳回家後如果能幫我洗幾件襯衫，再幫我送來，我就讓妳坐在我的駕駛室，帶妳回家。這樣做雖然違反鐵路公司的規定，但在這種偏僻的地方，我們也不必那麼認真。」

聽司機這麼一說，蟾蜍的痛苦馬上煙消雲散。他滿心歡喜，立刻衝上駕駛室。當然囉，他這輩子一件衣服也沒洗過，想洗也不會洗，以後也不打算洗。不過，他想：等我平安回到蟾蜍莊園，有了錢，有了裝錢的口袋，我一定送一筆錢給這個司機，夠他洗好多多多的衣服；這樣做和幫他洗衣服是一樣的，甚至更好。

站長揮動小旗，示意可以開車。司機拉響汽笛作為回應，火車徐徐駛離車站。火車越開越快，蟾蜍看著鐵路兩旁的田野、樹木、樹籬、牛和馬匹從他身邊飛馳而去。想到自己離蟾蜍莊園越來越近；想到日夜都在思念他的朋友們；想到口袋裏叮噹作響的錢幣；想到柔軟舒適的床鋪；想到家裏的美味佳餚；想到他的朋友在聽他講述自己的歷險、吹噓自己如何聰明過人時對他的讚歎和欽佩，他情不自禁地在駕駛室裏又蹦又跳，又喊又唱。火車司機感到驚訝不已，他以前偶爾也見過洗衣婦，可是從來沒有見過這樣怪異的洗衣婦。

火車走了很長的路，當蟾蜍正在考慮自己回到家後要吃什麼

晚飯時，他看見司機把頭探出車外，認真地聽著，臉上露出疑惑不解的神情。接著，他看見司機爬上煤堆，從車頂往後張望。然後他回到自己的座位上，對蟾蜍說：「真奇怪，這是今天晚上往這個方向開的最後一班車，但我敢發誓，我聽到有一輛車正追在我們的後面。」

蟾蜍立即停止了剛才那種輕浮滑稽的表演。他臉色一沉，顯得十分沮喪；他感到背脊隱隱作痛，大腿也痛得不能站立。他不得不坐下來，竭力不去想可能發生的事情。

這時月光明亮，司機站在煤堆上，可以看清車後很遠的景物。突然，他叫了起來：「我看清楚啦！在這條鐵軌上，有一輛列車飛快地開來，好像是在追趕我們！」

可憐的蟾蜍驚恐地蹲縮在煤堆上，絞盡腦汁要想出點什麼辦法來，但怎麼也想不出來。

「他們快追上我們了！」司機喊道，「車上擠滿了很多古怪的人！有揮舞著長矛的監獄看守，有揮舞著警棍、戴著頭盔的警察，還有戴著禮帽、衣衫襤褸的傢伙。我從這裏都可以清楚地看出他們是便衣警察，他們都在揮動著手槍和手杖，整車人齊聲高喊：『停車！停車！停車！』」

這時，蟾蜍跪倒在煤上，兩隻爪子合握苦苦地哀求說：「救救我，救救我啊，好心的司機先生，我要向你坦承一切！我根本不是什麼窮洗衣婦！我也沒有孩子在家裏等著我！我是蟾蜍——聞名遐邇，擁有大筆財產的蟾蜍先生。我的敵人把我抓進陰暗的地牢，憑著過人的膽識和智慧，我逃了出來。如果那輛火車上的

第八章

人把我抓起來，我這可憐、不幸、無辜的蟾蜍又要再次被戴上鐐銬，回到那種啃麵包、喝冷水、晚上睡乾稻草的悲慘生活！」

司機神情嚴肅地往下盯著他說：「老實告訴我，你到底犯了什麼罪，為什麼會被送進監獄？」

「其實也沒什麼，」蟾蜍滿臉通紅，可憐兮兮地說，「我只是趁車主在吃午飯的時候借用了一下他的汽車，反正他們當下又用不到嘛！我真的沒有偷車的意思。但人們——特別是法官——對這種一時衝動的無意之舉看得非常嚴重。」

司機臉色陰沉地說：「我想你確實是一隻傷天害理的蟾蜍，按理我應當把你送交法院審判。但看到你走投無路，我不會扔下你不管。原因是：第一，我討厭汽車；再者，我開車時最討厭被警察擺布；第三，看到動物淚流滿臉總是使我感到特別難受。別哭喪著臉，振作起來！我會盡力幫你，我們還可以把他們甩掉！」

他們拼命地往鍋爐裏鏟煤，燒得鍋爐呼呼地響，火星四濺。火車飛也似的向前駛著，但後面那輛車還是漸漸地追了上來。司機用一團廢棉紗擦去額頭上的汗水，歎了一口氣說：「大事不妙了，蟾蜍。他們的火車頭後面沒帶車廂，而且跑得比我們的快。我們只剩下一個辦法了，那是你唯一的機會，所以你要仔細聽好。前面不遠有一條長長的隧道，隧道那頭是一片茂密的樹林。在穿過隧道的時候，我會讓火車頭全速行駛，而我們後面那輛自然不敢開得很快，因為他們害怕出事。過了隧道後我會關上氣門來個緊急剎車，在他們駛出隧道之前，你趕緊跳車躲進樹林裏，

不要被他們發現。然後我再繼續全速前進，讓他們來追我，他們愛追多久、多遠都行。現在作好準備，我一下令你就跳車！」

他們又往鍋爐裏加了很多煤，火車狂奔著衝進了隧道，火車轟隆隆地吼叫著，沒過多久，火車便駛出了隧道，行駛在清新的空氣和寧靜的月光中。鐵路兩旁的樹林黑漆漆的，這對蟾蜍非常有利。司機突然關掉了氣門，開始刹車。蟾蜍走到踏板上，當火車漸漸慢下來、徐徐行駛的時候，他聽見司機大聲喊道：「就是現在，跳車！」

蟾蜍跳下了車，從路堤上滾了下來。他站了起來，發現自己居然沒有受傷，於是連忙爬進樹林藏了起來。

他偷偷往鐵路上一看，只見他剛才坐的火車正在加速，然後飛駛起來，轉眼便不見了。接著，那輛追趕他們火車呼嘯著從隧道裏衝出。車上的人都在揮舞著各式各樣的武器，高喊著：「停車！停車！停車！」等他們的車開過去之後，蟾蜍開懷大笑起來——這是他進監獄以來，第一次如此開心地大笑。

但他的笑聲很快便停住了，因爲他意識到現在已是深夜，天又黑又冷，自己待在這片陌生的樹林裏，遠離朋友和家鄉，身無分文且沒有晚飯可吃。火車轟隆隆地駛過之後，周圍一片死寂，使他感到毛骨悚然。他不敢離開這片供他藏身的樹林，於是朝林子深處走去，心想離鐵路越遠越好。

被囚禁在監獄裏這麼長時間之後，他覺得這片樹林是如此地陌生並且不懷好意，似乎老是想嘲弄他。貓頭鷹在發出單調的鳴叫聲，這使他感到林子裏似乎到處是搜尋他的監獄看守，正在向

他圍攏過來。一隻貓頭鷹悄無聲息地朝他飛過來，翅膀擦了一下他的肩膀，他驚恐地跳了起來，以為那是一隻手。然後貓頭鷹像飛蛾一樣飛走了，嘴裏發出低沉的「呵呵」笑聲，蟾蜍覺得他的行為非常沒有格調。他還遇上一隻狐狸，他停下腳步，上上下下地打量著他，眼裏流露出一種挖苦的神色，嘴裏說道：「嘿，洗衣服！這個星期妳弄丟了我的一隻襪子和一個枕頭套！下次再發生這樣的事，我找妳算帳！」說完，趾高氣揚地走了，嘴裏還竊笑著。蟾蜍想找一塊石頭砸他但卻沒找到，這使他非常惱火。最後，饑寒交迫、疲憊不堪的蟾蜍躲進一棵空心樹，他設法用枯枝乾樹葉鋪了一張可以睡覺的床，便躺在上面呼呼地睡著了。

第九章　一起遠行

河鼠坐立不安，不知何故，他自己也不清楚為什麼。夏天的熱鬧景象依然沒有消退，雖然樹林裏有的樹木已染上了深深的黃褐色，花兒正在變紅，但是陽光依然燦爛、空氣依然溫暖、大地上的色彩依然斑斕，沒有一點寒冷即將到來的徵兆。果園和樹籬裏經常上演的大合唱越來越少，只留下少數幾個不知疲倦的演員偶爾在黃昏來臨時獻上一首曲子。知更鳥又開始神氣起來。空氣中有一種萬物在變化，大家都在辭別遠行的氣氛。布穀鳥早就停止了歌唱，而幾個月來一直扮演這幅風景畫裏部分角色的鳥兒們，多數早已不見了，這支隊伍的成員正一天天地減少。河鼠平日裏非常留意鳥兒的飛行方向，他發現他們都往南邊飛去了。晚上躺在床上時，他也能聽到鳥兒在夜空飛行時急切地拍打翅膀的聲音，知道他們在回應天命的召喚。

大自然的宏偉旅店和其他旅店一樣，也有自己的旺淡季節。隨著客人一個個地打點行裝、付帳、退房，在旅店的餐廳裏吃飯的客人一天比一天少。隨著一間一間的客房被關閉，一塊塊地毯被捲起，一個個服務員被辭退；那些留下來領養老金，並且一直

住到下一個旺季的房客，亦不得不受到這些遷移和告別的影響。看到別人熱烈地談論著遷移計劃、路線和新的住處，看到自己的夥伴一天天減少，不免會變得煩躁不安、情緒低落、愛發脾氣。為什麼如此地喜新厭舊？為什麼不像我們一樣安靜地留下來，一起快快樂樂地過日子？你們不知道這座旅店在淡季的時候是什麼樣子；不知道我們這些留下來，並看到旅店一年四季所有美景的人，究竟可以享受到怎樣的快樂。

那些遷移者總是說，你說的當然對，我們也很羨慕你們，也許將來我們會住上一整年；但現在我們已訂好計劃，車在門口等著我們呢，我們得走了！於是他們微笑著點點頭走了。我們想念他們，心裏感到很不是滋味。河鼠是一隻守著土地、自給自足的動物，不管誰走了，他都留下不走。儘管如此，他還是不由自主地注意著空中的變化，感受這種變化對他的影響有多深刻。

由於每天都有夥伴遷移，要靜下心來認真做事是非常困難的。河裏的水越來越少，露出了又密又高的燈蕊草。河鼠離開河邊，來到田野上，漫無目的地到處閒逛。他走過了牧場，鑽進了麥田。牧場上的草已經枯萎，塵土到處可見。田裏的小麥在和風的吹拂下，翻起了金色的波浪竊竊私語著。河鼠喜歡到麥田裏散步，徜徉在粗壯的麥稈叢中，他的頭頂上有片麥穗織成的金黃色的天空。這片閃閃發光的天空整天都歡快地跳舞，當微風吹過，它便不停地搖晃，然後把頭一甩，歡笑著恢復原樣。在這裏，他還有許多小朋友，組成自己的圈子整天都在忙著做自己的事。但只要客人一來，他們也會偷閒和客人聊天，互相交換消息。然

而，今天的情況大不相同。雖然田鼠和巢鼠依然對他彬彬有禮，但他們都在全神貫注地忙著自己的事。有些緊張地挖洞；有的三五成群地湊在一起，檢查著建造小居室的計劃和圖紙。這些房子必須建得漂亮，結構要緊湊，而且要靠近商店，這樣才便利。他們有的在把滿布灰塵的箱子和裝衣服的籃子拖出洞外，有的在緊張地收拾自己的東西。地上到處擺放著一堆堆、一捆捆的小麥、燕麥、大麥、山毛櫸堅果和各種乾果，這些都是即將運走的東西。

「河鼠老兄來啦！」他們一見到他便叫了起來，「過來幫一下忙，河鼠，別站在那裏閒著！」

「你們到底在玩什麼把戲？」河鼠十分嚴肅地說，「你們知道，現在還不是考慮過多住處的時候，還早著呢！」

「噢，是呀，這我們也清楚，」一隻田鼠很不好意思地解釋說，「但早點準備又不是壞事，對吧？趁那些可惡的機器還沒有隆隆地開到田地裏之前，我們真的必須運走這些家具、行李和貯存的食物。你知道，如今最好的房子早就被佔據，所以要是你遲了一步，多差的房子都得將就著住；而且在搬進新家前，還要好好地清理一下。當然，我們知道現在動手還是早了點，但我們只是剛剛開始呀。」

「嘿，別忙啦，」河鼠說，「今天天氣這麼好，我們去划划船，去樹籬邊上閒逛，在林子裏野炊，或者做點別的什麼，怎麼樣？」

「我想今天不行，謝謝你啦，」田鼠急忙回答，「也許改天

柳林中的風聲

吧，等到我們有空的時候……」

河鼠輕蔑地哼了一聲，轉身便走，但一隻腳絆到一個帽盒，摔倒在地上。他氣得顧不得面子，開口就罵了起來。

「要是大家都能多加小心，走路多留點神的話，」一隻田鼠口氣堅硬地說，「就不會傷到自己，也不會那麼難堪了。小心別碰到那只手提箱，河鼠！你最好還是找個地方坐一下。再過一、兩個小時，或許我們才有空和你聊天。」

「我想，在耶誕節來臨之前，你們是不會有什麼空閒的。」河鼠沒好氣地回敬道，然後走出了麥田。

他有點沮喪地回到他的河岸——這條忠於他的、不停地流淌著的古老河流永遠不會打點行李，永遠不會離他而去，也永遠不會住進過冬的房子。

他看見河邊的柳樹上停著一隻燕子，很快又有第二隻、第三隻燕子飛來。他們在柳枝上煩躁不安地跳來跳去，低聲地認真交談著。

「什麼，要走啦？」河鼠走過去說道，「為什麼這麼著急？真是荒唐極了。」

「噢，我們還沒有要遷徙，如果你是在問這個的話，」第一隻燕子回答說，「我們只是在制定計劃，作好安排。目前，我們正在討論今年該走哪條路線、在哪兒落腳等等，你明白的。這很好玩呀！」

「好玩？」河鼠說，「這就是我不明白的地方。如果你們不得不離開這個可愛的地方，離開想念你們的好朋友，離開你們已

138

習慣的舒適家園；我敢肯定，屆時你們將會毫不猶豫地離開，並接受隨之而來的各種麻煩和變化，好適應新環境。然後你們會安慰自己說，你們沒有過得不好。但在那樣的情況來臨之前，你們為什麼不能先好好商量，好好考慮自己是不是真的需要……」

「不，你當然不明白。」第二隻燕子說，「首先，我們心裏感到躁動不安，那是一種甜蜜的衝動。然後，一個又一個的回憶像信鴿般出現在我們的腦海。晚上，它們拍著翅膀飛進我們的夢裏；白天，它們和我們一起在空中翱翔。當那些早已被我們遺忘的氣味、聲音和地名，一樣一樣地重新回到我們的記憶裏召喚我們的時候，我們便急切地互相確認，交換看法，看看大家的感覺是否都是一樣。」

「難道你們今年就不能留下來嗎？」河鼠戀戀不捨地說，「我們會盡力讓你們感覺在家裏一樣。你們不知道，你們飛走後我們在這裏過得有多快活。」

「有一年，我曾經試圖『留下來』過，」第三隻燕子說，「當時我喜歡上了這地方，因此到該走的時候，我留了下來，讓別的燕子繼續往南飛。剛開始幾個星期我過得還真不錯，但後來……噢，那長夜真難熬啊！白天看不到太陽，空氣冷冰冰的，冷得我直發抖！而且到處都找不到一隻蟲子！噢，我這一步可是走錯了。我感到心灰意冷。於是，在一個風雨交加的寒夜，我乘著強勁的東風向內陸飛去。我飛越那些大山的山谷時遇上了大雪，我使盡全力才飛了過去。當我飛到蔚藍平靜的湖上，享受著溫暖的陽光，吃上第一隻肥美可口的蟲子，那種身處極樂世界般

的感覺使我終生難忘！過去就像一場噩夢，未來的每一天都是快樂的假日。一天又一天，我不斷地向南飛去，逍遙自在，愛留多久就留多久，因此我對來自南方的召喚可不敢怠慢！我已透過親身經歷嘗到教訓，我再也不敢違背自然法則了。」

「啊，是呀，南方的召喚，南方！」其他兩隻燕子也嘰嘰喳喳、十分神往地說，「南方美妙的歌聲、繽紛的色彩、明媚的陽光！噢，你們還記不記得……」他們滿懷深情地回憶著，忘了河鼠的存在。河鼠著迷地聽著他們的回憶，心裏湧起一種渴望。他知道，他心中那根一直處於休眠狀態的弦正在被撥動。這些即將南飛的鳥兒的議論，他們輕描淡寫的轉述，其實不足以喚醒他這種野性的新慾望，使他激動得久久不能平靜。但要是眞的能親身體驗一下南方溫暖的陽光、芬芳的氣味，他的心裏會有什麼感受呢？他閉上眼睛，讓自己縱情想像。他重新睜開眼睛時，看見河流似乎像鐵一般冰冷，綠色的田野顯得灰濛濛的，毫無生氣。於是，他那顆忠誠的心，似乎正爲了自己軟弱叛逆的一面哭喊著。

「那你們爲何還要再飛回來呢？」他羨慕地問燕子，「這個單調乏味的小地方哪裏吸引你們了？」

「在一定的季節來臨時，」第一隻燕子說，「我們同樣也會感到另外一種召喚。綠油油的草地、飄香的果園、昆蟲經常光顧的池塘、牧場上的牛羊、曝晒的乾草、藍天之下密密麻麻的農舍，所有這些難道不會召喚我們嗎？」

「你以爲，」第二隻燕子問，「你是唯一苦苦等待布穀鳥重新歌唱的動物嗎？」

「時候一到，」第三隻燕子說，「我們又會想念家鄉寧靜的河面上漂流的睡蓮。但是，今天這一切顯得那麼遙遠和渺茫。此時此刻，我們心裏渴望的是其他的東西。」

他們又嘰嘰喳喳地交談起來，這一次他們眉飛色舞地談論著碧藍的海洋、金色的沙灘和蜥蜴光顧的牆壁。

河鼠心神不寧地走開了。他爬上河流北岸上的那面斜坡，躺在那裏，向南望著遠處的丘陵。那些丘陵擋住了他的視線——丘陵的這一邊是他熟知的世界。以前，他根本不屑知道丘陵那一邊他不知的世界。但是，今天，當他遙望南方時，內心滋生了一種新的渴望；今天，那個看不見也無從知曉的世界對他來說，意味著真正的生活，意味著一切。低矮的丘陵上明亮的天空似乎充滿著希望。丘陵的這一邊現在才是真正的空白，而另一邊在他的心中則是繽紛多彩、熙熙攘攘的世界。那裏有碧波蕩漾、遼闊無邊的大海！有陽光燦爛的海灘！有橄欖樹掩映的白色別墅！有寧靜的港灣，港灣裏泊滿了大船，這些船即將駛往到處是美酒和香料的島嶼，駛往那些安詳地躺在大海懷抱裏的島嶼！

他再一次起身向河邊走去，但很快就改變了主意，朝塵土飛揚的小路邊走去。靠近小路的灌木樹籬又茂密又陰涼，他鑽進洞躺了下來，他能想像得出這條碎石鋪成的路通往那個神奇的世界，曾經在這條路上走過的遠行者，想像得出他們到遠方去找到的或沒找到的財富和冒險的樂趣。

突然，一陣腳步聲傳到他的耳朵。接著，他看見一個步履艱難的身影。看得出那是一隻老鼠，渾身灰塵。那遠行者走近他

時，出於禮貌向他行了一個具有異國風情的大禮，此人猶豫了一會，接著笑容滿面地離開小路，走到他的身邊坐下。他似乎顯得十分疲憊不堪，所以河鼠沒有立即跟他說話，讓他好好歇一會兒。河鼠知道這位遠行者在想什麼，他也知道，當動物們身心疲憊時，是多麼珍視無聲的陪伴。

這位遠行者樣子消瘦，卻顯得非常精悍。他的肩膀下垂，爪子又瘦又長，眼角布滿許多皺紋，勻稱的耳朵上戴著一對小小的金耳環。身上穿的那藍色的運動衣已經褪色，褲子布滿補丁和汗漬，隱隱約約看出是藍色的布料。他的行李捆在一塊藍色的棉手帕裏。

那老鼠休息了一會兒，歎了口氣，用鼻子嗅了嗅周圍的空氣，往四處張望。

「暖風吹來的是三葉草的芳香，」他說，「此時我們聽到的是身後乳牛啃食牧草和他們輕輕哈氣的聲音。遠處傳來農民們收割的聲音，那林子邊上的農舍升起了一縷縷藍色的炊煙。附近有小河流淌著，聽得見水鳥的叫聲。看你的體格就知道你是河上划船的好手。一切似乎都睡著了，又似乎在不停地發生著變化。朋友，你的生活一定充滿了樂趣。只要你身體強壯，能夠享受這一切，我敢肯定那是世界上最美妙的東西。」

「是的，這就是生活，我唯一的生活。」河鼠恍恍惚惚地答道，語氣裏少了他常有的自信。

「我不是那個意思，」那陌生的老鼠小心地說，「但無疑你的生活是最美妙的。我有這種生活的經歷，所以我知道。因為我

是剛離開那種生活來到這裏的，六個月以來我過的都是這種生活，所以我知道那是最美好的。我已腿腳痠痛，饑腸轆轆，但我還要繼續向南走，回應那種古老的召喚，回到過去那種生活中去——我屬於那種生活，怎麼也擺脫不了。」

「難道這一位也是要遷移的？」河鼠心裏想。「那你是從哪兒來的？」他問。他不敢問他要到哪裏去，因爲他似乎很清楚他要到哪裏去。

「從一個漂亮的小農場來的，」遠行者簡短地答道，「就是那個方向。」他朝北點了點頭，「那不重要。在那裏我要什麼有什麼——我期望從生活中得到的一切，我都擁有了，甚至更多。現在我來到這裏了！我同樣很開心來到這，眞的很高興終於來到了這！沿著這條路繼續往前走好好多多英里、好久的時間，就會越來越接近我的心之所向！」

他那雙明亮的眼睛緊緊盯著遠方的地平線，似乎在傾聽一種內陸所沒有的聲音，如同牧場和農莊迴盪的歡樂歌聲。

「你不是我們當中的一員，」河鼠說，「也不是耕地的，我猜想，你甚至不是這個國家的一員。」

「你說得對，」那老鼠說，「我是一隻以航海爲業的老鼠。我原先從君士坦丁堡啓航，雖然從某種意義上來說，我也不是那裏的人。朋友，你聽說過君士坦丁堡吧？那是一座美麗、古老而光榮的城市。你也許還聽說過挪威國王西格德，他率領一支六十艘船的船隊航行到君士坦丁堡。在那裏，他和他的手下騎馬經過的街道都裝飾著紫色和金色的天棚，以示對他們的熱烈歡迎。皇

帝和皇后來到他的船上，和他一起慶祝。當西格德回國時，他的許多手下留在君士坦丁堡，成了皇帝身邊的侍衛。我的祖先來自挪威，也留在當時西格德送給皇帝的船上。自此我們一直都以航海爲業，就也不足爲奇了。至於我本人，我出生的那座城市也算不上我的家，君士坦丁堡和倫敦之間的任何一個迷人的港口，都是我的家。我熟悉這些港口，它們也認得我。只要到了這些港口的任何一個碼頭和海濱，我就算是到了家。」

「我猜你一定到遠洋航行過，」河鼠興趣盎然地說，「一連幾個月見不著陸地，食物短缺，少量的飲水，每天只能以大海爲伴，所有這些你一定經歷過吧？」

「正好恰恰相反，」海鼠坦率地說，「你所描繪的生活根本不適合我。我從事的是沿海貿易，很少離開陸地。吸引我的是岸上的歡樂時光，就像航海一樣。哦，那些南部的海港！它們的氣味、夜晚的錨泊燈，多迷人啊！」

河鼠語帶懷疑地說：「唉，也許你選擇了某種更好的生活方式，如果你願意，跟我說說你在海岸上的生活吧。說說看，一隻有靈性的動物能從這種生活中獲得什麼，讓他可以坐在火爐旁盡情地回憶，並溫暖他的晚年呢？老實跟你說，我今天深刻地感覺自己的生活有些狹隘和封閉。」

「上一次航行把我帶到了這個國家，」海鼠說起了他的經歷，「原先我是滿懷希望要到內陸農場去的。這次的航行生活，是我歷次航行的一個實例，或者確切地說，是我那豐富多彩的生活的一個縮影。像往常一樣，我那次出海是由於家裏出了事，我

所在的那片海岸升起了風暴信標；於是我登上一艘小商船，從君士坦丁堡出發，跨過古老的海洋，前往希臘群島和地中海東岸。航海途中的每一朵浪花都讓我留下了永生難忘的回憶。那是一段光輝的黃金歲月與芬芳的迷人夜晚！我們的船到了一個又一個海港，每到一處都會遇到往日的朋友。烈日炎炎的白天，我們便睡在陰涼的廟宇或廢棄的水箱裏；晚上，我們在柔和的星光下飲酒歡歌！後來，我們轉往亞德里亞海航行，看到海岸有時呈琥珀色，有時呈玫瑰色，和藍寶石般的大海交相輝映。我們有時停留在陸地懷抱裏遼闊的港口，有時漫遊在歷史悠久的古城。終於在一個早上，當太陽莊嚴地升起時，我們的船沿著一條金色的水道駛進了威尼斯。噢，威尼斯可真是一座漂亮的城市，在那裏，海鼠可以逍遙自在地漫遊、歡樂！當夜幕降臨、兩腳走得痠痛之後，你可以坐在大運河邊，和朋友們盡情歡宴。這時，空中飄蕩著優美動聽的音樂，天上布滿了閃爍的星星，鳳尾船搖搖晃晃，燈光照耀著擦得光亮的鋼製船頭。這些船緊靠著，所以你可以踩著它們從河的這頭走到那頭。至於吃的東西——你喜歡吃牡蠣嗎？好啦，好啦，我現在還是不談這些好。」

　　他沉默了一會兒，河鼠聽得入了迷，也沉默了。恍惚中，河鼠彷彿看見自己漂在運河上，彷彿還聽到了迴盪在灰濛濛的、浪濤拍打屋牆間的嘹亮歌聲。

　　「後來，我們又繼續向南航行，」海鼠接著說，「沿著義大利海岸，最後到了西西里島的巴勒莫港。在那裏，我下了船，在岸上度過了一段長長的幸福時光。我從不在同艘船上待得太久，

因為那樣會使人變得心胸狹窄、產生偏見。而且，西西里島也是我的樂土之一。我認識那裏的每一個人，我喜歡他們的言談舉止。我在島上快樂地和朋友們度過數個星期。當我又感到煩躁不安時，我上了一艘駛往薩丁島和科西嘉島的商船。海上的清風和泡沫又拂在我的臉上，我感到高興極了。」

「但是待在——船艙？你們是這樣稱呼的嗎？你不覺得又悶又熱嗎？」河鼠問。

這位航海專家有所保留地朝他眨了眨眼睛，又非常坦白地說：「我可是老手，船長的房間是我最愛的地方。」

「不管怎麼說，那種生活太艱難了。」河鼠喃喃地說道，陷入了沉思。

「船員的生活就是這樣。」航海專家又眨了眨眼，嚴肅地說。

「我在科西嘉島登上了一艘把葡萄酒運到歐洲大陸的船，」海鼠接著說，「晚上，我們到了阿雅克肖。由於逆風，船停在了海上。大家用一根長繩子把酒桶一個個串起，然後放到海裏。水手們用小船拖著一長串的酒桶朝岸邊划去。他們一邊划船一邊唱歌，那串長長的酒桶漂在水上，活像排成一長列的海豚。到了岸上，已經有馬匹等著他們，那些馬把酒桶迅速拖上小鎮陡峭的街道，酒桶發出叮噹的響聲。等到最後一隻酒桶運到目的地，我們就和朋友一起上街喝酒、休息，一直玩到深夜。第二天早上，我走進一片橄欖樹林，在那裏休息了很長一段時間。我早已遊歷夠多的島嶼，也看夠了港口與船隻。所以我到農村悠閒地過著日

子,有時躺在農地看農夫耕作;有時我在高高的山坡上一邊伸展,一邊眺望遠處蔚藍的地中海。再後來,我從一個地方到另一地方,有時走路,有時坐船。我到了馬賽,在那兒遇到許多曾經同船的老朋友,參觀了許多遠洋巨輪,還和朋友們一起歡宴。那裏的牡蠣真是美味可口!唉,有時我做夢都夢見馬賽的牡蠣,醒過來後,傷心得直哭!」

「這倒提醒了我,」河鼠禮貌地說,「你剛才提到你肚子餓了,我本該早點開口的。先到我家吃午飯吧,我的家就在附近。現在已過了午飯時間,不過我很歡迎你到我家隨便吃點東西。」

「謝謝你的好意,對我像兄弟一樣,」海鼠說,「剛才我坐下來時,肚子就很餓了。當我無意中說起牡蠣時,肚子餓得咕咕叫。你能不能把午飯端到這兒來?除非迫不得已,我是不太喜歡鑽進地洞去的。如果我們在這兒吃飯,我還可以繼續跟你說我的航行以及我那愜意的生活——至少我覺得很愜意,而且看你聽得這麼專心,我猜你肯定喜歡這種生活。但如果我們進洞裏吃,我肯定會很快就睡著的。」

「這建議的確不錯。」河鼠說。於是他急忙回家。到了家裏,他拿出午餐籃,裝上簡單的飯食。當然,他沒有忘記陌生人的出身和喜好,所以特意裝上長條的法式麵包、一條蒜味香腸、一些乳酪,還有一瓶用草包著的、在南方的山地釀造的美酒。他提著飯籃,飛快地回到海鼠坐的地方。他們把籃子裏的飯菜取出來擺在路邊的草地上。海鼠對河鼠的品味和判斷力讚不絕口,河鼠高興得臉都紅了起來。

　　等到海鼠吃了點東西，饑餓稍有緩解後，他便繼續說起了他最近的一次航行。他的故事把他那位單純的聽眾帶往西班牙一個又一個的港口，然後又把他帶到葡萄牙的里斯本、波爾圖，還有法國的波爾多，讓他認識了迷人的康恩瓦爾港和德文港。最後，海鼠說起自己在海上歷盡風雨後，搭上一艘沿著英吉利海峽航行的船，向北來到他最後一個碼頭。他到那裏時，美妙溫暖的春天剛剛來臨。他深受鼓舞，便向內地奔去。他希望在那裏過過寧靜的鄉間生活，遠離他已經感到厭倦的大海波濤。

　　河鼠聽得如癡如醉，激動得渾身顫抖。他隨這位歷險家在海上到處神遊，走過風雨交加的港灣，穿過擁擠不堪的港口，順著洶湧的潮水駛過港口的淺灘，沿著蜿蜒的河道，來到河流拐彎處繁忙的小鎮。聽了海鼠講述的經歷，他遺憾地歎了口氣，他一點也不想聽海鼠說起內陸單調乏味的鄉下生活。

　　這時，他們吃完了午飯。我們的航海家精神又抖擻了起來，他的聲音更加洪亮，眼睛閃爍著光芒——就像海面燈塔上的明燈。他又倒上一杯暗紅色的南方釀造葡萄酒，一邊說著話，一邊靠近河鼠，兩眼緊緊地盯著他，河鼠被他深深地吸引住了。

　　海鼠那雙灰綠色的眼睛就像北方波濤翻滾的大海，不斷地變幻著顏色。杯裏紅寶石般的美酒彷彿就是南方的心臟，在為他這個有勇氣接受它的人跳動。海鼠眼裏那閃爍不定的灰色和酒杯中那固定不變的紅色，強烈地吸引住他，使他心醉神迷，癱軟無力。這兩道光亮之外的寧靜世界已變得暗淡無光，甚至不復存在。

　　海鼠滔滔不絕地講述著他的美妙經歷——像是在演講，又像是在唱歌——像是水手們把滴著水的鐵錨拖出水面時哼唱的曲子，像帆索在猛烈的東北風中發出的洪亮響聲，像是漁夫在杏黃色的晚霞中收網時哼唱的歌謠，又像是威尼斯的鳳尾船上傳出的吉他和曼陀林的琴聲。他的說話聲彷彿變成了風聲，開始時像低沉的哀鳴，很快變成了尖銳的呼嘯，繼而化為撕心裂肺的汽笛，最後變成滿滿的風帆上，音樂般優美動聽的響聲。如癡如醉的河鼠似乎聽到了所有聲音，還聽到饑餓的海鷗不安的鳴叫、海浪的轟鳴和海濱砂石的怒吼。這些聲音又變成海鼠的說話聲。河鼠懷著激動的心情，聽海鼠講述他在一個又一個海港的歷險，他經歷的一次次爭鬥、逃亡、聚會，他結交的一個又一個的朋友，他參加的一個又一個的海上壯舉。他曾經在許多島嶼上尋寶，在寧靜的海灣邊釣魚，有時在溫暖的白色沙灘上睡上整整一天。河鼠聽海鼠跟他說起深海捕魚的情景，說他們怎樣拖起幾英里長的漁網，漁網裏滿是銀白色的魚；還說了在漆黑的夜晚，巨輪在濃霧中出現時給他們帶來突如其來的危險；還講了他們到岸時的歡樂情景，港口燈火通明映照圓圓的海角，模糊地看到在碼頭上歡迎他們歸來的人群，然後他們的船拋了錨，他爬過陡峭狹窄的街道朝亮著溫馨燈光的家走去。

　　最後，他恍恍惚惚地覺得這位海上冒險家站了起來，但嘴裏還說著話，那雙灰綠色的眼睛還緊盯著他。

　　「好啦，」海鼠輕聲地說，「我又得上路了。我還要在塵土飛揚的道路上繼續向西南方走很多天，一直走到海邊那座我熟悉

的灰色小鎮。從昏暗的門廊向下望去，可以看見一列石階，上面覆蓋著一整片簇擁的粉色纈草，石階的盡頭直至一片波光粼粼的藍海。在舊海堤的繫船柱和繫船環上拴的小船，漆得像我童年時爬進爬出的小艇一樣艷麗。漲潮時鮭魚歡快地躍出水面，成群的鯖魚一邊跳躍一邊嬉鬧地游過碼頭與前灘。巨輪日夜不停地駛過窗前，航向泊船處或大海。所有航海國家的船隻遲早都會抵達那處，在那、在一定的時刻，我挑選的船也會在那裏停泊。我會耐心地一直等下去，直到最後。直到那艘等待著我、最適合我的船，蜿蜒地駛進水中央，它會載滿了貨物且船首朝向著港口。這時我將乘小艇或沿著錨鏈悄悄地攀上船去。然後在某日清晨，水手們的歌聲與腳步聲，以及船絞盤的叮噹聲和錨鏈的嘎吱嘎吱聲，將我從睡夢中喚醒。我們將拉起船首的三角帆以及前檣帆，此時海港邊的白色房屋，將緩慢地從我們身旁滑過，航海即刻啓程！當船向海角緩緩航行，她全身裹著的帆布，一到外海後便迎風飛揚，隨著碧波滾滾的浪淘聲，往南方航行！

你也跟我一起走吧，小兄弟。你知道的，光陰一去不復返，南方在等著你。趁現在還來得及，回應召喚，去冒險吧！你只需關上家門，然後無憂無慮地上路。走出你的舊生活，去擁抱新生活吧！將來有朝一日，等你飲完了海上歷險這杯香茶，如果你願意，你可以重新回到這裏，坐在寧靜的河邊，盡情地回憶一幕幕的往事。你會輕易地趕上我，因爲你還年輕而我已上了年紀，走路緩慢。在路上我會不停地回頭張望，我相信，我最終會見到你興沖沖地向我走來，臉上露出對南方的熱切渴望！」

海鼠的話音漸漸遠去，就像昆蟲響亮的叫聲一樣，迅速地歸於沉默。河鼠怔怔地癱軟在地上，最後他抬起頭，只看見遠處的路上一個小小的斑點。

他像個機械似的站了起來，悠然而又細心地把東西裝回籃子。他又如機械似回到家中，把幾樣必用的小東西和他喜愛的珍寶放進一個帆布旅行包，接著他像一個夢遊者一樣在屋裏踱著步，張開嘴仔細地聽著。他把帆布包甩上肩膀，又精心地為遠行挑選了一根粗粗的木棍。正當他不急不徐但又毫不猶豫地跨過門檻時，鼴鼠出現在他的面前。

「嘿，你要上哪兒去呀，河鼠？」鼴鼠抓住他的手臂，十分吃驚地問。

「和他們一起到南方去，」河鼠彷彿在夢囈一樣喃喃說道，看都沒看鼴鼠，「先到海邊，然後上船，到那些正在召喚我的海岸去！」

他堅定地邁開步伐，還是不疾不徐，但臉上露出固執的神情。鼴鼠此刻驚慌不已，他擋住了河鼠的去路，緊盯著他的眼睛。他發現，河鼠的雙眼目光呆滯，像是蒙上了一層飄忽不定的灰色條紋——這不是他朋友的眼睛，而是別的動物的眼睛！鼴鼠用力抓住他的雙臂，把他拖進屋，按倒在地上，又緊緊地抱著他不放。

河鼠不顧一切地掙扎了一會兒，但似乎很快便精疲力竭了。他閉著眼睛躺在地上，渾身發抖。接著，鼴鼠扶著他站了起來，讓他坐到椅子上。河鼠癱倒在椅子上，縮成一團，渾身劇烈地顫

抖著，然後便歇斯底里地嚎叫起來。鼴鼠把門緊緊閂上，把帆布包扔進抽屜鎖上。然後，他悄悄坐在他朋友身旁的桌子上，等待著他這奇怪的發作過去。漸漸地，河鼠便睡著了，只是睡得很不安穩，時而驚起，時而在夢中喃喃地說些鼴鼠聽不懂的古怪內容，然後便沉沉地昏睡過去。

鼴鼠心裏很焦急。他讓河鼠安靜地睡著，自己忙著做起家務。他回到客廳時天已黑了，河鼠還坐在椅子上。他已完全清醒，但他一言不發顯得無精打采，十分落寞。鼴鼠匆匆地看了他一眼，發現他那雙眼睛又像以往那樣灰綠、清澈，鼴鼠感到十分欣慰。他在河鼠的身邊坐下，不停地勸他，讓他把剛才發生的事說出來。

可憐的河鼠想盡辦法解釋著剛才的事。但他怎麼能冷靜地把自己在聽到海鼠的話後產生的聯想說出來呢？他怎麼能回憶起迴盪在他耳畔的大海的聲音呢？又怎麼能再現那位航海家說起的無數冒險經歷呢？那些神奇的歷險在他心中的誘惑已煙消雲散，此刻連他自己也無法解釋清楚幾小時前他想做的事。因此，他無法向鼴鼠說清楚自己這一天來的經歷也就不足為奇了。

對鼴鼠來說，有一點已很清楚：河鼠那陣歇斯底里的發作，或者說突發，現在已經過去了。雖然他受到了沉重的打擊，但終於清醒過來了。但是河鼠似乎對日常的事，換季所要做的、以往他也樂於做的事情都失去了興趣。

於是，鼴鼠漫不經心地把話題轉到正在進行的秋收上。他說到裝得像小山一樣的馬車和長長的馬車隊，說到越堆越高的乾草

堆，又圓又大的月亮，從點綴著一捆捆農作物的光禿禿田野上升起來。他還說到周圍正在變紅的蘋果、正在變成褐色的栗子，說到果醬、醃製的食品和釀製的甜酒。說著說著，他便說到隆冬時節舒適的居家生活和各樣的歡樂情景，說得娓娓動聽。

漸漸地河鼠坐直了身子，開始說起話來。他那雙黯淡無光的眼睛變得明亮起來，無精打采的神情也漸漸地消失。

這時，機靈的鼴鼠悄悄離開客廳。不一會兒，他拿著鉛筆和一些小紙片回來了。他把東西放在河鼠胳膊旁的桌面上。

「你很久沒有寫詩了，」他說，「今天晚上你不妨吟上幾句，別——呃，別顧慮太多。我知道，只要你寫點什麼，你就會感覺好多了——哪怕只寫上幾個韻腳也行。」

河鼠疲倦地推開紙片，但細心的鼴鼠趁機離開了客廳。過一會兒，他往門裏偷看時，發現河鼠聚精會神地伏在桌上，一會兒在紙上寫幾個字，一會兒咬著鉛筆，全然忘記周圍的一切。其實，他咬著鉛筆的時候比寫字的時候多很多，但鼴鼠非常高興，因為他知道，他的方法已經發揮了作用。

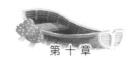

第十章　蟾蜍歷險記（二）

　　蟾蜍棲身的樹洞大門是朝東的，因此蟾蜍第二天早上很早便醒了過來。一部分原因是燦爛的陽光照在他的身上，另一部分原因是他的腳趾冷得難受。他昏沉地做著夢，夢見在一個寒冷的冬夜，自己睡在家裏那間漂亮的臥室──那間臥室有一個氣派的都鐸式窗戶──的床鋪上；天氣太冷了，床鋪上的床單、被子、毛毯、枕頭等等都起床了，咕咕噥噥地抱怨說，它們再也無法忍受這樣的嚴寒了，就邊說邊跑下樓到廚房旁的爐火去取暖了。蟾蜍光著腳跟在它們的後面，他在冰冷的石頭通道上走了好幾英里，和它們爭辯著，苦苦哀求它們別這麼狠心……要不是他曾經在牢房裏石板上的乾稻草堆睡過幾個星期，使他幾乎忘了蓋著厚厚的毯子那種舒服的感覺，他大概還會醒得更早。

　　他坐起來揉了雙眼，然後又搓了搓凍僵的腳趾。他睜開眼看了看四周，想尋找那熟悉的石牆和鐵窗，一時之間想不起自己身在何處。接著，他心裏「怦」地一跳，想起了一切──他的逃跑、他的奮鬥，以及在火車上的追趕。他想起了一件事，最棒的一件事：他自由了！

　　自由！光是這兩個字和它所包含的意義，就抵得上五十條毛毯。當他想到樹洞外那個充滿歡樂的世界，他從頭到腳都感到暖和的那個世界正焦急地等著他凱旋，它還會像他入獄前那樣，隨時都想討好他，願意為他效勞，和他做伴。他抖了抖身子，用手指梳理頭髮，把頭上的樹葉弄掉。梳妝完畢後，他大步走進早晨舒適的陽光裏。他雖然渾身發冷但充滿信心；雖然饑腸轆轆，但滿懷希望。昨天的一切恐懼已經被一個晚上的睡眠和令人鼓舞的陽光驅趕得無影無蹤。

　　在這個夏天的清晨，他擁有整個世界。他穿過了那片靜謐的、到處掛滿露珠的樹林，然後來到綠油油的田野。田野上只有他一個人，他愛做什麼都可以。他走上大路時，覺得那條路像一條迷路的狗，十分孤單且焦急地尋找夥伴。但是，蟾蜍要尋找的是一樣能說話的東西，可以清楚地為他指路的東西。如果你心情愉快、問心無愧、口袋裝著錢，如果沒有人到處搜尋你的蹤跡，要把你重新拖回監獄，那麼你根本不用在乎應該走哪一條路。但是，對講求實際的蟾蜍來說，走哪一條路事關重大。他知道，每一分鐘對他都很重要，但這條可惡的路卻默不作聲，他真想狠狠地踩它幾腳。

　　蟾蜍在這條笨拙無言的路上走了好一會兒，突然，路旁出現了一條小運河，小運河就像一個羞答答的小兄弟，牽著道路的手，在它的身邊信心十足地流淌著。但它對陌生人同樣是抱著緘默的態度。「真是討厭！」蟾蜍想道，「不過有一點是清楚的：它們倆肯定是從什麼地方來，又到什麼地方去。這是無庸置疑

156

的！」於是，他便沿著河邊耐心地走著。

在小河的拐彎處，一匹孤零零的馬邁著沉重的步子緩緩走來，低著頭，似乎正焦急地思忖著。馬脖子上繫著長長的韁繩，隨著他的步伐，韁繩的末端還滴著水珠。蟾蜍讓馬從他身邊走過，站在那裏，等待著命運對他的安排。

靜靜的河水在河道拐彎處歡快地打轉，一艘平底船徐徐地滑了過來，上了漆的甲板邊緣跟拖船的小徑平行，船上唯一的乘客是一位粗壯肥胖的婦女。她戴著一頂闊邊遮陽帽，一隻大手把著舵柄。

「今天早上天氣真好，夫人！」她的船趕上蟾蜍時，向他打聲招呼。

「是的，夫人！」蟾蜍走在她身旁拖船的小徑上，禮貌地答道，「對那些不像我這樣遇到麻煩的人來說，這的確是一個美妙的早晨。妳看，我那已經出嫁的女兒寄來一封十萬火急的信，叫我趕緊到她家去。於是我匆匆忙忙上路了，不知道她發生了什麼事，也不知道會發生什麼事，但心裏總擔心是什麼不幸的事。如果妳也是一個母親，我想妳會理解我的心情的，夫人。我丟下了家事——妳一定已經看出我是一個洗衣婦，夫人——小孩我也顧不上啦。我那群小孩簡直是世界上最淘氣、最難管的孩子，夫人。更糟糕的是，我的錢都弄丟了，還迷了路。我那已經出嫁的女兒到底出了什麼事，我簡直是連想都不敢想，夫人！」

「妳那出嫁了的女兒住在哪裏，夫人？」船上的女人問。

「她住在河邊，夫人，」蟾蜍答道，「離那幢叫做蟾蜍莊園

的漂亮房子不遠。也許妳聽說過那幢房子，就在附近這一帶的什麼地方。」

「蟾蜍莊園？嘿，我正要往那個方向去呢，」船上的女人說，「這條小運河在前面幾英里的地方和河流匯合，然後再往上游走不遠便是蟾蜍莊園。妳上我的船來吧，我帶妳去。」

她讓船靠近岸邊，蟾蜍不停地感謝，然後輕巧地跨上了船，心滿意足地坐下。「蟾蜍的運氣又來啦！」他想，「我總是能化險為夷！」

「妳說妳專門替人洗衣服，夫人？」船徐徐向前駛去，那女人很有禮貌地說，「那可是很不錯的職業，我這樣說應該沒有冒犯到妳吧？」

「這真是全世界最好的職業，」蟾蜍快活地說，「這一帶有身分的人都會來找我——即使給他們錢，他們也不會去找別人。我是很出名的。洗衣服我很在行，樣樣都親力親為，例如洗、漿、熨，有時還為高貴的紳士縫製參加社交活動穿的漂亮襯衣——一切都在我的監督下完成！」

「這麼說，這些活並不是妳一個人做的，夫人？」那女人恭敬地問。

「噢，我雇用許多女孩子幫忙。」蟾蜍輕鬆地說，「長年為我打工的就有二十幾個女孩子。女孩子，妳是知道的，夫人！個個都很難管教！」

「妳說得對，」那女人十分贊同地說，「但我相信妳能管好這些無所事事的女孩們！妳很喜歡洗衣服嗎？」

「非常喜歡，」蟾蜍說，「我簡直離不開這個工作。每當我把雙手伸進洗衣盆裏，內心就感到非常愉快。一切都那麼容易，一點也不費力！我可以肯定地告訴您，那才是真正的樂趣，夫人！」

「遇上妳真幸運！」那女人若有所思地說，「對我倆來說，今天的相遇可是再好不過的事！」

「妳這麼說是什麼意思？」蟾蜍緊張地問。

「唉，跟妳說吧，」那女人答道，「和妳一樣，我也喜歡洗衣服。而且不管我喜歡不喜歡，我都得洗自己的衣服，儘管我到處漂流。我丈夫是個不務正業的人，總是把船丟給我照料。我根本沒時間做自己的事。按理他現在該在船上，或是把舵，或是牽馬──好在這匹馬還懂得自己照顧自己。但他卻帶著狗出去了，說是到什麼地方去抓野兔回來做菜呢。他說他將在下一個水閘那裏和我碰面。唉，也許是那樣吧。我根本不相信他，因為只要他帶著那條比他還糟糕的狗出去，他的話從來就沒算數過。話又說回來了，我那些要洗的衣服該怎麼辦？」

「噢，別想洗衣服的事了。」蟾蜍說，他不喜歡這個話題，「還是想想妳丈夫即將拿回的野兔吧。那一定是一隻又肥又嫩的野兔。家裏有洋蔥嗎？」

「除了那些要洗的衣服，我什麼都不願想。」划船的女人說，「我真不明白，眼前明明擺著這樣一件樂趣無窮的差事，而妳還說什麼野兔。在船艙的角落裏有一大堆要洗的衣服。要是妳挑出一、兩件最需要洗的衣服──我用不著跟妳這樣有經驗的夫

人說是哪幾件，妳一眼就能看出來——然後我開船，妳把衣服放進洗衣盆裏洗。嘿，就像妳剛才說的，那對妳來說肯定是一種享受，也算是幫了我的大忙。妳一定可以輕易地從船上找到盆子、肥皂、爐灶上的水壺，還有木桶，妳就用它從運河裏取水吧。我想妳會洗得很開心的，這樣總比坐在這裏無所事事、打著哈欠看風景好得多吧？」

「妳還是讓我掌舵吧！」蟾蜍非常惶恐的說，「這樣妳就可以愛怎麼洗就怎麼洗。也許我洗不好妳的衣服，妳可能不會滿意。我比較擅長洗男人的衣服，那是我的特長。」

「讓妳掌舵？」那女人大笑著說，「要想掌好舵，還得接受一些訓練。況且掌舵太無聊了，我希望妳能快樂一些。不行，妳還是做妳喜歡的洗衣工作吧。我繼續掌舵，妳千萬不要辜負了我的一片好意！」

蟾蜍這下可是騎虎難下了。他看看這邊，又看看那邊，想溜之大吉。但船離岸太遠了，他根本無法跳到岸上。他只好鬱悶地聽天由命了。「如果我會洗衣服，」他絕望地想，「那麼連傻瓜都會洗了。」

他從船艙裏拿出盆子、肥皂和其他洗衣用的東西，又隨便地揀了幾件髒衣服。他一邊盡力回憶自己曾經透過窗戶看見人家洗衣的情景，一邊洗著衣服。

漫長的半個小時過去了。這期間蟾蜍的脾氣越變越壞，他費盡心機，但那些衣服就是不聽他的話。他試過哄它們，用巴掌抽打它們，又用拳頭猛打它們，但它們依舊只躺在洗衣盆裏對著他

笑，沒有絲毫的改變。它們似乎對自己骯髒的模樣感到十分滿意。有一、兩次他回過頭去緊張地看那女人，但她似乎專注地看著前方，聚精會神地掌著舵。他的背脊很疼，他看到自己的爪子皺巴巴的，這使他非常沮喪，因為他對自己的爪子一向都感到很自豪。他狠狠地低聲咒罵，這些罵人的話既不符合洗衣婦的身分，也不符合蟾蜍先生的身分。他手中的肥皂再次滑落，他都不知道掉了幾百次了。

一陣笑聲使他站了起來，他看了看四周。那女人向後斜著身子，毫無顧忌地哈哈大笑，直笑得眼淚都流了出來。

「我一直都在看著妳。」她上氣不接下氣地說，「看妳說話時得意洋洋、不可一世的樣子，我就知道妳是個冒牌貨。還敢說自己是個洗衣婦！我敢打賭，妳這輩子連一塊擦碗布都沒洗過！」

蟾蜍本來一直都忍著，現在他再也無法忍下去了，這口惡氣終於爆發了出來。

「妳這個粗鄙的肥婆娘！」他吼道，「居然也敢如此對上等人說話！洗衣婦？老實告訴妳吧，我是蟾蜍，遐邇聞名、受人尊敬、出身高貴的蟾蜍！不錯，我是碰到了一點麻煩事，但我決不接受被妳這樣的划船婆取笑！」

那女人走近他，緊緊盯著帽子底下的那張臉。「啊，原來是你！」她高聲嚷叫，「天哪！你這骯髒、可惡、噁心的蟾蜍！真沒想到你會坐在我這條乾淨的船上！這可是決不能容忍的事！」

她放下手中的舵柄，猛然伸出一隻長滿斑點的大手，一把抓

住蟾蜍的前腿，另一隻手緊緊地抓住他的後腿。接著，蟾蜍只覺得天翻地覆，船似乎在天空中飛行，風在他的耳邊呼嘯著。蟾蜍發現自己飛在空中不停地旋轉著。

最後，他撲通一聲掉進水中。他感到河水冰涼，但冰涼的河水並不能壓住他的傲氣，也沒有澆滅他心中燃燒的怒氣，他大叫地掙扎著浮上水面，抹去沾在臉上的浮萍，看到那胖女人在逐漸遠去的船尾看著他哈哈大笑。水嗆得他不停地咳嗽，但他還是嚷著要找她算帳。

他吃力地游向岸邊，但身上那件棉罩衣使他游得更加艱難。當他終於靠近岸邊時，發現河岸很陡，無人幫忙很難爬上去。他好不容易上了岸，休息一會兒，喘口氣。然後，他把濕漉漉的衣服挽在手上，拔腿就去追那條船。他怒氣衝天，一心想著要報仇。

當他追到船邊時，那女人還在哈哈大笑。「把你自己放進脫水機去絞一絞吧，洗衣婆！」她大聲喊道，「再用熨斗把臉熨一熨，把它熨成波浪形，那樣你就變成一隻相貌堂堂的蟾蜍了！」

蟾蜍沒有停下腳步回話，他要的是實實在在的報復，而不是廉價、空洞的口頭上的勝利，儘管他很想回罵一、兩句。他非常清楚自己的目的。他奮力追上那匹馬，解開拖船的繩子又把它狠狠地扔在地上，輕輕地躍上馬背，用力踢著馬的肚子使他飛奔起來。他騎著馬離開了拖船的小徑，沿著一條滿是車轍的小道，向曠野奔去。他回頭看了一下，看見那隻船已擱淺在運河的對岸，那女人發了瘋似的打著手勢，聲嘶力竭地喊道：「停下！停下！

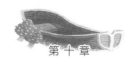

停下來！」

　　「這些話我聽得多啦！」蟾蜍大笑著說道，一邊奮力策馬向前飛奔。但這匹拖船的馬狂奔沒多久，很快地，他的速度便慢了下來，不一會兒便悠然地走著。但蟾蜍對此感到很滿意，因為他知道，不管怎麼說他還在走著，而那條船完全停在那裏。他覺得自己做了一件非常得意的事，因此心頭的怒火已消得差不多了。在陽光下悠閒地騎著馬，他感到心滿意足。他故意走一些偏僻的小路和人很少走的馬道，竭力忘記自己已經很久沒有像樣地吃頓飽飯的這件事。這時，運河已被他遠遠地拋在後面了。

　　他騎著馬走了幾英里路，炎熱的太陽晒得他昏昏欲睡。馬停了下來，低下頭吃起草來。突然，他從瞌睡中驚醒，好不容易才沒讓自己從馬背上掉下來。他看了看四周，發現自己來到了一片一望無際的開闊地，地上長滿了一塊一塊的荊棘和金雀花。離他不遠的地方，有一輛破破爛爛的吉普賽大篷車，一個男人坐在一隻倒在車旁的木桶上。他一面抽煙，一面望著遼闊的原野出神。他的旁邊燃著一堆火，火上吊著一只鐵鍋，正在咕嘟咕嘟地往外冒著熱氣。鐵鍋散發各種不同的濃郁氣味，繚繞地盤旋在空氣中，最後化為一股誘人的香味，就像是大自然的靈魂呈現在她的孩子面前，像位母神給他們母親般的安慰。蟾蜍從來沒有像現在如此飢餓過。早上他只是隱隱地感到有一點餓，此刻他感到自己的的確確是餓壞了，而且必須趕緊解決這個問題，要不然肯定會出事。他一面仔細地察看著那個吉普賽人，一面盤算著自己是不是他的對手，或者能不能用甜言蜜語哄騙他。蟾蜍坐了下來，一

163

面呼蚩呼蚩地嗅著，一面望著那吉普賽人。吉普賽人坐在那裏抽著煙，也在望著他。

不一會兒，那吉普賽人從嘴上取下煙斗，漫不經心地說：「想賣掉妳的馬嗎？」

蟾蜍聽了大吃一驚。他不知道吉普賽人非常喜歡買賣馬匹，他們決不放過任何一個做馬匹交易的機會；他也不知道吉普賽人的大篷車每天都要由馬匹拉著從一個地方走到另一個地方。他想都沒想過要把這匹馬換成現金。於是，那個吉普賽人的提議似乎使他非常想得到的兩樣東西——現金和一頓實實在在的早餐——變成唾手可得。

「什麼？」他說，「讓我賣掉這匹漂亮的駿馬？噢，不，根本不可能。把馬賣了，誰每個星期幫我把洗好的衣服送到顧客的家裏呢？況且，我這麼喜歡他，他也離不開我呀。」

「換一頭驢子用用吧，妳會喜歡的，」吉普賽人建議道，「有些人很喜歡驢呢。」

「你似乎沒有看出，」蟾蜍說，「我這匹好馬並不是你所能買得起的。第一，這是匹純種馬。部分是。不是你看的那個地方，是別的地方。第二，這匹馬曾經得過獎。那是以前的事了，但只要你懂馬，我想你肯定一眼就能看得出來。不行，我可不想把他賣掉。話雖這麼說，要是你真的想買，這樣漂亮的駿馬你能出多少錢？」

吉普賽人把馬從頭到尾仔細地打量一番，然後又同樣仔細地打量了一番蟾蜍，又轉過去看馬。「一條腿一先令。」他簡短地

說，然後轉身走開繼續抽著煙，兩眼出神地盯著前面的曠野。

「一先令一條腿？」蟾蜍嚷道，「你等等，我得好好算一下，看看那一共是多少錢。」

他下了馬，讓馬到一邊吃草，自己坐到吉普賽人的旁邊。接著用手指算了起來。最後他說：「一條腿一先令？那加起來剛好是四先令。噢，不行。這麼漂亮的駿馬就賣四先令，這價格我無論如何也不能接受。」

「好吧，」吉普賽人說，「我再給你加一點，五先令，這已經比這匹馬的實際價值多出了三先令六便士。我只能給這個價錢了！」

蟾蜍坐在那裏，沉思了很久。他已饑腸轆轆，又身無分文，離家又遠——他也不知道到底有多遠——而且，他的敵人也許還在別處搜尋他。在這種情況下，五先令應該是一筆不少的錢了，再說，一匹馬也值不了多少錢。況且，這匹馬根本不是他的，所以，能賣多少錢都划算！最後，他堅定地說：「聽我說，吉普賽人！我最後給你出個價。你給我六先令六便士，我們一手交錢一手交貨。除此之外，你還得讓我在你這兒吃一頓飽飯，當然，就吃你那鐵鍋裏香噴噴的東西吧。然後，我就把這匹活蹦亂跳的馬交給你，他身上那套漂亮的鞍具也免費送給你。如果覺得那樣不合算，趕緊說，我好騎馬走人。這附近有個人幾年來一直想買我的馬呢。」

那吉普賽人大聲地發起牢騷，他抱怨說，如果這樣做生意，用不了多久他就會血本無歸。但最後他還是從褲袋深處摸出一個

髒兮兮的帆布錢包，拿出六先令六便士，交到蟾蜍的爪子裏。然後他爬上大篷車，不一會兒，取來了一只大鐵盤、一副刀叉和一把湯匙。他撬起鐵鍋，把香味濃郁、熱氣騰騰的濃湯咕嚕咕嚕地倒進了盤子裏。這鍋東西是用山鷸鶉、野雞、家雞、野兔、家兔、雌孔雀、珍珠雞和其他的東西燉成的，因此，真的說得上是世界上最美味的濃湯。蟾蜍把熱呼呼的盤子放在大腿上，不停地吃著，激動得差點大哭起來。他吃完一盤又叫吉普賽人再盛一盤，那吉普賽人也讓他盡情地吃。這樣，蟾蜍吃得肚子都撐了。他想他這輩子還沒吃過這麼好吃的早餐呢。

　　蟾蜍一直吃到自己認為夠本了才站起來，向吉普賽人道別，又依依不捨地和他的馬告別。那吉普賽人對河岸很熟悉，他給蟾蜍指了路。於是，蟾蜍便興高采烈地起程了。毫無疑問，他和一個小時前的那隻蟾蜍已大不相同了。太陽照在他的身上，如今濕漉漉的衣服已差不多乾了，口袋裏又有錢了，而且離家、離朋友跟安全都越來越近了。最重要的是他吃了豐盛的一餐，既豐盛又熱騰騰的一餐，這使他覺得渾身是勁，無憂無慮而且信心十足。

　　他一邊興沖沖地往前走，一邊回想自己一次又一次的冒險活動和逃跑經過，似乎每當到了窮途末路的時候，他總能急中生智，轉危為安。想到這裏他更加高傲自大，「呵！呵！」他邊走邊想，下巴翹得高高的，「我是一隻多麼聰明的蟾蜍啊！全世界的動物就數我最聰明！我的敵人把我關進監獄，對我嚴加看管，夜以繼日地守著我的牢房。我憑著超人的膽量，硬是從守衛森嚴的監獄裏逃了出來。他們派了持槍的警察開著火車追趕我，我跳

下火車，一轉眼就溜進樹林裏躲起來。不幸的是，我被一個狠毒的肥婆扔進了運河。但那又有什麼？我游到岸邊，成功地奪走了她的馬。我還用那匹馬換來了滿口袋的金錢和一頓豐盛的早餐！呵！呵！我就是蟾蜍，英俊瀟灑、討人喜歡、無往而不勝的蟾蜍！」他趾高氣揚地走著，忍不住編了一首讚美自己的歌，聲嘶力竭地高唱著，儘管聽眾只有他自己。也許，再也沒有哪隻動物能編出如此自高自大的歌曲來了：

世界上豪傑輩出，
史書上寫得一清二楚，
但是他們的名氣
沒有一個比得上偉大的蟾蜍！
牛津大學的才子們，盡知天下的一切。
但是他們的學識，
沒有一個比得上聰明的蟾蜍。

諾亞方舟裏的動物們，
個個淚眼汪汪地哭喊。
是誰高喊「前面就是陸地」？
是有膽有識的蟾蜍。
行進在大路上的軍人，

　　　　　全體一致舉手敬禮。

　　是來了國王還是英國名將基欽納？

　　　　　不，是來了蟾蜍。

　　　　　　王后和侍女，

　　　　坐在窗下縫衣服。

　　她驚叫：「看，那俊美的男子是哪位？」

　　侍女們答道：「是聰明的蟾蜍。」

　　歌中諸如此類的歌詞還有許多，但都是些自我吹噓之辭，寫在這裏不甚合適。上面記下的僅是其中比較含蓄的幾節。

　　他邊唱邊走，邊走邊唱。他的高傲每時每刻都在膨脹，但是，很快他就要倒大楣了。

　　走了幾英里的鄉間小道，他來到了公路。沿著白色的公路一眼望去，他看見前方有一個小黑點離他越來越近，黑點也越來越大，最後變成一個他非常熟悉的東西。接著，一、兩聲喇叭聲傳入了他的耳朵，這熟悉不過的聲音使他興奮不已。

　　「這眞是太好了！」蟾蜍心情激動地說，「這才是眞正的生活，我終於又要回到朝思暮想的廣闊天地了！我要讓車上的那些兄弟停下車來，然後再給他們編一段動聽的故事。聽了我的故事，他們肯定會讓我上車。到了車上，我再給他們多講幾段。也許，要是運氣好的話，我最後會開著汽車回到蟾蜍莊園，讓獾先

169

生好好瞧瞧！」

　　他滿懷信心地走上公路，招呼汽車停下。汽車慢悠悠地開了過來，走近公路和小道的岔路口時便慢了下來。突然，他臉色變得蒼白，心跳加快，兩腿顫抖不已，不一會兒便痛苦不堪地癱倒在地。不幸的蟾蜍這回可真是罪有應得，因為他碰上的正是他在紅雄獅旅館院子裏偷走的那輛汽車！而他的一切不幸就是從那倒楣的一天開始的！車上坐的正是他在旅館的咖啡屋裏吃午飯時見到的那夥人！

　　他可憐兮兮地癱坐著，活像公路中間的一小堆垃圾，嘴裏絕望地喃喃自語：「這下完了！一切都完了！等待我的又是鐐銬！警察！監獄！又得啃冷麵包喝冷水啦！天哪，我好蠢啊！為什麼要在大白天裏在曠野上趾高氣揚地到處亂晃，唱著狂妄自大的歌曲，還滿不在乎地招呼別人停車？為什麼不躲起來，等到天黑再悄悄地走偏僻小道溜回家？噢，不幸的蟾蜍，誰來救救我啊！」

　　那輛可怕的汽車離他越來越近，最後他聽見車在他的面前停了下來。兩位先生從車上走下，他們圍著這堆顫抖不已的東西走了一圈，其中一位說：「噢，糟了！是一個可憐的東西——顯然是一個洗衣婦——暈倒在路的中央了！可憐的人，也許她是中暑暈倒的，也可能是因一整天都沒有吃東西。我們把她抬到車上，送她到附近的村子，那裏一定有認識她的人。」

　　他們把蟾蜍輕輕地抬進汽車，給他墊上柔軟的座墊，然後繼續上路。

　　蟾蜍聽到他們充滿同情的話語，便知道自己沒有被認出來。

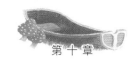

他的膽量又慢慢恢復了。他小心翼翼地先睜開一隻眼睛，然後又睜開另一隻。

「你們看，」一位先生說道，「她好點啦，清新的空氣使她甦醒過來了。您感覺怎麼樣，夫人？」

「非常感謝你們，先生，」蟾蜍用虛弱的聲音說，「我感到好多了！」那位先生接著說，「很好，好好坐著別動，還有，儘量不要說話。」

「好吧，」蟾蜍說，「我只是在想，我能不能坐在司機旁邊那個座位上？那樣我能呼吸到更多的清新空氣，然後就會很快好起來。」

「多聰明的太太！」那位先生說，「當然可以。」於是，他們又小心地扶著蟾蜍到司機旁邊的座位坐下。汽車繼續向前開著。

此刻蟾蜍差不多已恢復到原來的樣子。他坐直身子，東張西望，竭力地控制住心中燃起的渴望，但這長久以來的渴望是如此強烈，最後完全佔據了他。

「我就是命該如此啊！」他心裏想，「為什麼要克制？為什麼要跟自己過不去？」於是他把臉轉向身邊的司機。

「哎，先生，」他說，「我真希望你能讓我試著開一下汽車。我一直很認真觀察你開車，看起來似乎很容易，而且很有意思。我真想讓我的朋友知道，我也曾經開過汽車！」

司機聽了哈哈大笑，笑聲很大，旁邊的先生連忙追問發生了什麼事。司機把蟾蜍的想法告訴他後，他說道：「好啊，夫人！

妳的勇氣令我欽佩！讓她試一試吧，幫她一下，她不會給我們惹麻煩的。」

蟾蜍聽了樂不可支。他連忙爬到司機的座位上，兩手把住方向盤，假裝恭恭敬敬地聽著司機的指令。他發動了汽車，一開始開得很慢，而且小心翼翼，因為他自己也決心謹慎開車。

坐在後排的先生們熱烈地鼓起了掌。蟾蜍聽見他們說：「看她開得多好啊！真沒想到一個洗衣婦也能把車開得這麼好，這真是我有生以來第一次見到！」

蟾蜍加快了一點車速，接著他把車開得越來越快。

他聽見那些先生大聲警告道：「開慢一點！洗衣婦！」這讓他很不高興，漸漸地失去了理智。

司機試圖制止他，但被他用一隻手臂按在座位上，然後讓車子全速行駛起來。風呼呼地吹在他的臉上，馬達在隆隆地響著，車身在微微地顛簸，這一切使他那簡單的頭腦變得飄飄然起來。「洗衣婦！我才不是洗衣婦呢！」他不顧一切地叫道，「呵，呵！我是蟾蜍！是盜車賊，是越獄的囚犯，是總能死裏逃生的蟾蜍！坐著別動，讓我教教你們什麼才叫真正的開車，因為坐在你們面前的是赫赫有名、車術超群、無所畏懼的蟾蜍！」

車裏的人驚叫著站了起來，個個撲向蟾蜍。「抓住他！」他們喊道，「抓住蟾蜍！該死的偷車賊！偷我們車的就是他！把他綁起來，戴上鎖鏈，送到附近的警察局！打倒這個危險的亡命之徒！」

哎呀，可惜太晚啦！他們早就應該好好想一下，早就應該謹

慎一點，早就應該記得把車停下，而不是在車上進行這些危險行為。蟾蜍把方向盤猛地一拐，汽車衝過路邊低矮的樹籬，接著汽車高高彈起，衝進了旁邊的飲馬池，車輪把池塘的爛泥打得滿天亂飛。

蟾蜍感到自己被拋向空中，像燕子一樣劃了一道優美的弧線。他喜歡這種在空中飛翔的感覺。他享受高飛的感覺，還因此幻想著自己是否能持續飛行，直到他長出一雙翅膀，變成一隻蟾蜍鳥。突然，他背脊朝地，重重地掉落在一塊茂盛、鬆軟的草地上。當他坐起來時，只見池塘裏的汽車差不多被水淹沒了，司機和那幾位先生在水中掙扎著，他們身上的長外套使他們行動很不方便。

蟾蜍趕緊站起來，在曠野上拼命地奔跑著。他穿過樹籬，跳過水溝，走過田地，最後累得上氣不接下氣，不得不放慢腳步。當他稍微喘過氣來，能夠清楚地思考時，忍不住嗤嗤地笑起來，接著又哈哈地大笑起來，笑得他都彎了腰，不得不坐在樹籬下休息一會兒。「呵，呵！」他得意忘形地叫道，「我還是那隻無往不勝的蟾蜍！是誰成功地騙他們把我接上車的？是誰設法坐到汽車前排座位享受新鮮空氣的？是誰說服他們，讓他們看看我會不會開車的？是誰把他們全拋到飲馬池的？又是誰在空中快樂地飛翔，安然無恙地落到地上，然後不聲不響地溜掉的？當然是蟾蜍！那幾個心胸狹窄、吝嗇小氣、膽小怕事又愛兜風的傢伙，活該在池塘裏掙扎！啊哈，蟾蜍還是蟾蜍，聰明、偉大、善良的蟾蜍！」

接著，他又扯著喉嚨，大聲唱起歌來——

汽車飛馳在路上，

喇叭聲嘟嘟嘟。

要問是誰把車開進了池塘，

是聰明絕頂的蟾蜍先生。

「噢，我多麼聰明！多聰明啊多聰明，多麼聰……」

在他身後不遠的地方傳來一陣微弱的聲音，他連忙轉過頭去。哎呀！他心裏立刻又充滿了恐懼、痛苦、絕望！

離他大約兩塊地遠，穿著高筒鞋的司機和兩個魁梧壯實的鄉村警察正朝他奔來！

可憐的蟾蜍跳了起來，拔腿便跑，心臟都快跳出來了。「噢，天哪！」他一面氣喘吁吁地往前奔，一面氣急敗壞地嚷道，「我真是一頭蠢驢！一頭自以為是、不顧一切的蠢驢！尾巴又翹起來啦！為什麼要狂妄地嚷嚷，得意忘形地高歌！為什麼要坐在那兒透氣！唉，天哪！完啦！完啦！」

他又回頭一望，看見他們離他越來越近，他不禁嚇得大驚失色。他不顧一切地向前跑，一面不停地回頭張望，可是他們仍然一步步逼近。儘管他盡力奔跑，但畢竟是隻肥胖的動物，腿又短，所以追趕他的人很快就要追上了。他聽得見他們已在自己的身後了。他已經顧不上自己往哪個方向跑，只是盲目地、發瘋似

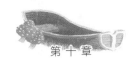

的跑著，一面不停地回頭看那些快要追上他的得意洋洋的敵人。
突然他腳下一個踏空，兩手在空中胡亂地抓了幾下，撲通一聲掉
進深水裏，水流很急，把他推著向前沖去。他根本無法抗拒那股
強大的力量。過了一會兒，他終於明白發生了什麼事，原來他在
盲目的逃亡中途，掉進了河裏。

　　他浮上水面，拼命想抓住靠近岸邊的蘆葦和燈心草。但由於
水流太急，他兩手抓到的東西很快便被扯斷了。「噢，天哪！」
可憐的蟾蜍驚恐萬分地叫道，「我再也不敢偷汽車了！我再也不
敢唱狂妄自大的歌曲了！」接著，他又被捲到水裏，又掙扎著浮
出水面。突然，他看見自己正在靠近河岸上一個黑黑的大洞口，
很快洞口就在他的頭頂上。當急流捲著他沖到那裏時，他伸出一
隻爪子，緊緊抓住了河岸。接著，他用力地慢慢爬出水面，終於
能夠把雙手擱在洞口邊上。他就這樣休息了幾分鐘，呼蚩呼蚩地
直喘著粗氣。經過水裏的一番掙扎，他已經精疲力竭了。

　　他一面沮喪地喘著粗氣，一面盯著眼前的黑洞，他看見洞的
深處有什麼明亮的東西閃爍著向他走來。當那東西靠近他時，在
他的周圍慢慢形成一張臉，一張他所熟悉的臉！

　　那是一張小巧褐色的臉，上面長著鬍鬚。

　　那是一張嚴肅的圓臉，上面長著一雙勻稱的耳朵和絲絨般的
茸毛。

　　原來是河鼠。

第十一章 「他淚如雨下」

　　河鼠伸出一隻潔淨的褐色小爪，緊緊地抓住蟾蜍的脖子，用力往上拽，於是渾身濕透的蟾蜍被慢慢地、穩穩地拖進洞，最後終於平安無事地站在河鼠家的客廳裏。當然啦！他現在全身布滿汙泥和雜草，而水珠亦不斷地往下淌，模樣相當狼狽。但是他仍像從前那般神采飛揚，非常開心，因為他知道自己又來到了朋友的家，此刻再也用不著東躲西藏。他現在可以脫掉那套有失身分、與他根本不相匹配的服裝了。

　　「噢，河鼠！」他大聲說道，「自從上次和你分開後，我遭遇的一切絕對令你無法想像！那種考驗和煎熬，我都咬牙關熬過了！我幾次死裏逃生、喬裝打扮、花言巧語地掩人耳目，每一次都是精心設計的，然後又成功地付諸實施！我進過監獄——當然後來逃了出來！被人扔進運河，但我游到了岸邊！我還偷了一匹馬，趁機賣了換來一大筆錢！他們都被我騙了——我要他們做什麼他們就做什麼！噢，毫無疑問，我是一隻聰明絕頂的蟾蜍。你想知道我剛才的壯舉嗎？我跟你說……」

　　「蟾蜍」，河鼠嚴肅而堅決地說，「你立刻上樓去，脫掉你

176

身上那件本來是哪個洗衣婦穿的舊棉罩衣,把自己徹底擦洗乾淨,穿上我的衣服,盡可能把自己打扮成一個紳士再下樓見我。我這輩子從沒見過像你這樣骯髒、邋遢、寒酸的傢伙!好了,別再辯了!快上樓去!等一下我還有話跟你說!」

蟾蜍本想停下腳步,與河鼠爭辯幾句。他在監獄裏已受夠了別人對他的指使,如今一隻河鼠也敢對他發號施令!他正要發作,但是,一眼瞥見自己在衣帽架上方的鏡子裏的模樣,看到破舊的紅褐色女帽歪歪扭扭地戴在頭上,還遮去了自己的一隻眼睛,他改變了主意,乖乖地快步走到樓上河鼠的更衣室裏。他把自己徹底地擦洗了一番,換上衣服,站在鏡子面前好長一段時間,得意洋洋地欣賞著自己的光輝形象,心裏想那些人居然錯把他當做洗衣婦,簡直是白癡!

蟾蜍走下樓時,河鼠已經把午飯擺到桌上,他見了非常高興,因為從那吉普賽人讓他吃一頓早餐到現在,他的冒險經歷耗掉了他大量的體力。他們一邊吃飯,蟾蜍一邊跟河鼠說起他那些冒險經歷,主要是吹噓自己如何聰明,緊要關頭自己頭腦如何清醒,陷入困境時自己又如何機靈。聽他的口氣,似乎他那番歷險是多麼豐富多彩,自己為此感到多麼自豪。但是,他說得越多,河鼠就變得越嚴肅、越沉默。

最後,蟾蜍吹噓夠了才停下來。屋內突然一片沉默。接著河鼠說:「聽著,蟾蜍。我不想再讓你遭受皮肉之苦,畢竟你已歷經了這麼多事。但是,說實在的,難道你不知道你把自己弄成了一頭多麼令人討厭的蠢驢了嗎?你剛剛說你被戴上手銬,坐過

牢，餓過肚子，被人追得魂不附體，又被人譏笑汙辱，還被一個
女人拋進水裏！難道這些你都覺得很好玩，很有趣嗎？這些都是
因爲你偷了別人汽車的緣故。你知道，自從你第一次看見汽車，
汽車只會讓你闖禍。你這傢伙就是這樣，只要看見一樣東西，不
到五分鐘就要把它弄到手。但你也不該去偷呀！如果你覺得不夠
刺激，那就當一個瘋子；如果你下定決心、如果你要改變，那就
宣布破產。爲什麼非要當一個罪犯呢？你究竟要到什麼時候才能
變得理智，爲朋友著想，爲朋友爭光？比方說吧，當我聽到動物
們在背後議論，說我的朋友是一個慣犯，你覺得我會好受嗎？」

　　蟾蜍的性格中有一點令人感到欣慰，那就是他是一隻心胸寬
大的動物，自己的好朋友如何數落他，他都不會介意。但無論別
人說得口乾舌燥，他都堅持自己的想法。所以，雖然河鼠苦口婆
心，蟾蜍心裏還是桀驁不馴地想道：「那確實好玩！好玩極
了！」還在心裏不停地模仿汽車的「嘟——嘟」、「突——突」
的響聲，以及其他類似沉悶的鼾聲或開啤酒瓶的聲音。但是，當
河鼠說完以後，他重重地歎了一口氣，非常謙卑地說：「你說得
很對，河鼠！你總是說得合情合理！是的，我明白了，自己曾經
眞的是一頭狂妄自大的蠢驢。但現在我要做一隻聽話的蟾蜍，再
也不會像以前那樣了。至於汽車，自從我上次開車掉進你家旁邊
的這條河裏，我就對汽車失去興趣了。事實是，當我抓住你家的
洞簷，吊在河上艱難地透氣的時候，我腦子裏突然產生一個念
頭——一個絕妙的主意——和汽船有關。哎！老朋友，別把臉拉
得這麼長，也別跺腳，以免弄翻了東西。那僅僅是一個想法而

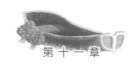

已,現在我們就不多談它啦。我們還是喝杯咖啡,抽支煙,好好聊聊。然後我還要一路閒逛回蟾蜍莊園去,換上自己的衣服,做我以往做的事。冒險的滋味我嘗夠了,我要過安安靜靜、規規矩矩的體面生活,好好打理自己的家產,讓它生息增值;平時抽空養花種草。我還會像從前一樣——就是像我變得煩燥不安、盡想幹蠢事之前那樣,朋友來了,我都會準備好飯好菜相待;我還要備一輛輕便馬車到鄉下閒逛。」

「一路閒逛回蟾蜍莊園去?」河鼠非常激動地嚷道,「看你在胡說些什麼?難道你真的沒聽說嗎?」

「聽說什麼?」蟾蜍說,臉色變得非常蒼白,「告訴我,河鼠!快!別擔心我受不了!我沒聽說什麼?」

「你是說,」河鼠用他的小拳頭猛力地擊著桌子,大聲吼著,「你完全沒聽說有關那些白鼬和黃鼠狼的事?」

「什麼,野林子裏那些盜賊?」蟾蜍渾身顫抖地喊道,「沒有,一點也沒聽說,他們做了什麼?」

「也沒聽說他們已經搶佔蟾蜍莊園的事?」河鼠接著說。

蟾蜍把雙手斜靠在桌子上,兩隻爪子托著下巴。眼睛裏湧出大顆大顆的淚珠,滴答滴答地掉落在桌子上。

過了一會,他喃喃地說:「你說吧,河鼠,把一切都告訴我。最難受的時刻已經過去了,我又變成了一隻真正的蟾蜍。說吧,我受得了。」

「自從你遭遇了……那……那……些麻煩事,」河鼠字斟句酌地慢慢說道,「我是說,當你……因為對……對……某種機器

產生了錯誤的想法，而在社會上……消失了一段時間之後……我想你明白我的意思……」

蟾蜍點了點頭。

「呃，可想而知，這一帶的動物便議論紛紛，」河鼠接著說，「不僅河岸上的動物議論，野林子裏的動物也議論。動物們爭執不下，分成兩派。就像往常一樣，住在河岸上的動物都支持你，為你辯護，說你受到了不公平的對待，還說如今天下再也無公正可言了。但是，野林子裏的動物說了許多壞話，說你罪有應得，還說這事該有個了斷。他們還非常狂妄自大，到處散布謠言說你這回完蛋了！你再也不會回來了，永遠也不會回來了！」

蟾蜍默默無言地又點了點頭。

「他們就是那種可惡的小畜生，」河鼠又接著說，「但是鼴鼠和獾先生都支持你，他們無論何時何地都堅稱你很快就會回來。雖然他們不知道你會怎麼樣回來，但堅信你一定會回來。」

蟾蜍重新坐直了身子，臉上露出一絲笑容。

「他們用歷史上的事實來證明自己的觀點，」河鼠繼續說，「說懲罰像你那樣的無禮行為貌似合法，但卻沒有一點法律依據，再說你又是有錢人家的後代。於是他們便把自己的東西搬進了蟾蜍莊園，住在裏面，每天打開門窗讓屋子通風，還把東西整理得井井有條，等待你回來。雖然他們猜不到會出什麼事，但還是提防著野林子裏的動物。下面我就說說那段最痛苦、最悲慘的經過吧。在一個漆黑的晚上，天黑得伸手不見五指，狂風大作，還下著傾盆大雨，一群全副武裝的黃鼠狼悄悄地沿著車道摸到了

你家的前門。與此同時，一群無法無天的雪貂從菜園摸進去，佔領了後院跟辦公室；另一群白鼬則侵占了溫室跟撞球間，守住了通向草坪的法式落地窗。

「鼴鼠和獾先生當時坐在吸煙室的火爐邊。他們正在聊天，對外面的情況毫無察覺，因為任何動物都不會在這樣的夜晚外出活動的。突然，那群嗜血成性的歹徒破門而入，從各個方向撲向他們倆。他們奮起抵抗，但又有什麼用呢？他們身上沒帶武器，又是遭到突擊，再說兩隻動物怎能敵得過數百隻瘋狂的動物？他倆講義氣、為朋友兩肋插刀，可是他們被那夥惡棍抓住還用木棍毒打，最後被趕到屋外的淒風冷雨中，還遭受惡毒的辱罵！」

聽到這裏已經麻木的蟾蜍突然暗自發笑，然後馬上又抑制自己，盡力裝出一副非常嚴肅的樣子。

「從那以後，那夥野林子強盜便一直盤踞在蟾蜍莊園。」河鼠接著說，「他們把整幢房子搞得烏煙瘴氣！我聽說他們白天也賴在床上，隨時都在吃吃喝喝。裏面的東西弄得一塌糊塗，慘不忍睹！他們吃你的食物，喝你的好酒，但卻說你的壞話，唱一些關於……關於監獄、法官、警察的下流歌曲，那儘是些惡毒攻擊你的歌，粗俗不堪。他們還到處揚言說他們將永遠住在那裏！」

「噢，他們膽敢這樣說！」蟾蜍說，然後站起來，拿起一根木棒，「我去教訓教訓他們！」

「沒有用的，蟾蜍！」河鼠在他的身後喊道，「你還是回來坐下，你這樣只會闖禍！」

但蟾蜍還是衝了出去，河鼠怎麼攔也攔不住。他肩上扛著木

棒，怒氣沖沖地奔跑在路上，很快便來到了他家的大門。突然，木柵欄後面閃出一隻拿著槍的雪貂。

「是誰啊？」雪貂尖聲問道。

「少說廢話！」蟾蜍氣沖沖地說「你竟敢這樣跟我說話，快給我滾出來，要不然我就……」

雪貂二話不說就端起槍來對準蟾蜍。蟾蜍連忙趴在地上，「乒！」一顆子彈從他的頭頂呼嘯而過。

驚慌失措的蟾蜍趕緊從地上爬了起來，拔腿便往回跑，耳邊傳來那隻雪貂的哈哈聲，接著又傳來其他雪貂怪腔怪調的笑聲。

他萬般沮喪地回到河鼠家，把剛才的經過告訴了河鼠。

「我不是告訴你了嗎？」河鼠說，「沒用的，他們到處安置了哨兵，屋裏個個都全副武裝。你必須耐心等待。」

然而，蟾蜍並不想就這樣善罷甘休。於是他拖出小船，划船逆水而上，來到了他家花園前面的河邊。

現在他能夠清楚地看見自己的家。他放下船槳，仔細地觀察起來。周圍的一切都顯得那樣寂靜，一個人影也不見。他看見整個蟾蜍莊園在晚霞中熠熠發光，三三兩兩的鴿子落在筆直的屋頂線上，花園裏開滿了嬌豔的花朵，通向遊艇停泊處的小河，還有那上面的木橋。這一切都是那樣安靜，彷彿荒蕪人煙，顯然是在等待著他的歸來。「可以先試一試停放遊艇的屋子。」他心裏想道。他小心翼翼地把船划到小河的入口，正要從橋上穿過，突然——「砰！」

一塊巨大的石頭從橋上滾了下來，撞破了船底。船進了水，

很快便沉沒了。蟾蜍在深水中拼命掙扎。他抬頭一看，只見兩隻白鼬斜靠在木橋的欄杆上，得意地看著他，嘴裏發出猙獰的笑聲：「下次再來就要你的腦袋，蟾蜍！」看到怒氣沖天的蟾蜍掙扎著游向岸邊，那兩隻白鼬哈哈大笑，笑得渾身發軟，東倒西歪，然後互相抱著對方。因為每隻都差點笑暈了！

蟾蜍疲憊不堪地回到河鼠家，又一次沮喪地把自己的經歷告訴河鼠。

「唉，我不是跟你說了嗎？」河鼠非常生氣地說，「哎呀，你看看，你都做了些什麼蠢事！把我那心愛的小船弄丟了！還把我借給你的這套漂亮西裝搞得一塌糊塗！說真的，你真是一個令人討厭的傢伙，我真不知道你能跟誰交上朋友！」

蟾蜍馬上意識到自己的輕舉妄動是多麼愚蠢，他向河鼠認錯，說自己太固執己見，損失了船又搞髒了西服。對此他表示誠懇的歉意。接著，他拉下面子說：「河鼠！我真是一隻剛愎自用、任性妄為的蟾蜍！從今以後，請你相信我，我一切都聽你的，沒有你的同意，我決不會再輕舉妄動！」每當這種時候，他的朋友往往被他這種低三下四的說辭所打動，他們也就不會對他說什麼。

「既然如此，」好心的河鼠說，怒氣已平靜下來，「那我給你的忠告是，先坐下來吃晚飯，時候不早了，晚飯很快就好。另外，你千萬要有耐心。在沒有見到鼴鼠和獾先生之前，我們是無能為力的。等見到他們，我們幾個再開個會、瞭解最新的情況、聽取他們的看法，共同研究如何對付這件棘手的事。」

「啊，是呀！鼴鼠和獾先生，」蟾蜍高興地說，「這兩個可愛的傢伙，他們情況怎樣？我都把他們給忘了！」

「虧你還有臉問！」河鼠責備他說，「就在你開著豪華汽車馳騁在公路上的時候，就在你騎著駿馬在曠野上奔馳的時候，就在你於草地上享用著美味早餐的時候；那兩隻忠心耿耿、可憐的動物，一直在野外餐風露宿，過著艱苦的生活，他們在看著你的房子。他們在房子周圍巡邏，密切地注視著白鼬和黃鼠狼的一舉一動，還設法要為你搶回財產。你不配有這樣正直、忠誠的朋友，蟾蜍，你真的不配。如果你還不加倍地珍惜這份友誼的話，有朝一日你一定會後悔的，到那時就太遲啦！」

「現在我懂了，我真是一隻不知好歹的畜生！」蟾蜍抽泣著，流下了痛苦的淚水，「讓我出去找他們吧！和他們一起在寒冷的黑夜裏忍饑挨餓、分擔他們的痛苦，努力證明……等一等，我聽到了盤子的叮噹聲了！晚飯終於做好了！太好啦！走，河鼠，讓我們飽餐一頓再說！」

河鼠想起，可憐的蟾蜍在監獄裏待了很長一段時間，很久沒吃上好飯菜了，因此應該好好體諒他。他隨蟾蜍坐到飯桌旁，熱情地勸他多吃點，把過去的損失彌補回來。

他們剛吃完飯，正要坐回沙發上，突然傳來重重的敲門聲。

蟾蜍緊張起來，但河鼠非常神秘地朝他點了點頭，朝門口走去，把門打開。獾先生走了進來。

他滿臉倦容，顯然是因為放棄家裏的舒服生活到戶外熬了好幾個夜晚的緣故。他的鞋子上滿是泥巴，蓬頭垢面，一副不修邊

幅的樣子。不過，就算獾先生最注重打扮的時候，也算不上英俊瀟灑。他神色莊重地走到蟾蜍的跟前，握住他的爪子說道：「歡迎回家，蟾蜍！天哪！我都說了什麼？是啊，家！這次回家可不像從前啦，不幸的蟾蜍！」說完轉過身子，背對著蟾蜍坐到桌旁，又向前挪了挪椅子，拿起一大塊餡餅吃了起來。

蟾蜍對獾先生這種嚴肅而又不祥的問候方式感到非常吃驚。但河鼠在他耳邊小聲說：「沒關係，不要在意，現在先不要跟他說話。當他急著要吃飯時，他總是這副情緒低落的樣子。半個小時以後他就是另外一副樣子了。」

於是，他們默默地看著獾先生吃飯。不一會兒，又傳來一聲輕輕的敲門聲。河鼠向蟾蜍點了點頭，走去開門，把鼴鼠迎了進來。鼴鼠也是一副幾天沒洗過澡、渾身髒兮兮的樣子，毛髮上還沾著幾片乾稻草。

「哎呀！蟾蜍兄回來了！」鼴鼠滿臉高興地叫道，「想不到你又回來啦！」接著在蟾蜍周圍跳來跳去，「我們做夢都沒想到你這麼快就回來了！哎，你一定是設法逃出來的，你這個聰明絕頂、足智多謀的蟾蜍！」

河鼠慌了，扯了扯蟾蜍的袖子，但是遲了，他已經變得驕傲自滿了。

「聰明！噢，得了吧！」他說，「在我的朋友看來，我並不聰明。我只不過是逃出了全英格蘭看守最森嚴的監獄，僅此而已！我爬上一列火車，逃脫了別人的追蹤，僅此而已！我喬裝打扮，在鄉間到處騙人，僅此而已！噢，我不聰明！我是一隻蠢

驢！我要跟你說說我的一兩段小小的冒險經歷，你自己再判斷看看！」

「好了，好了，」鼴鼠說道，一邊坐近飯桌，「我一邊吃飯，一邊聽你說好了。我從今早到現在一口飯也沒吃！噢，餓死我了！」說著坐了下來，大口大口地嚼起冷牛肉和酸菜來。

蟾蜍走到壁爐前，叉開兩腿，一隻爪子插進褲袋，摸出一把銀幣。「看吧！」他把銀幣遞給鼴鼠看，大聲叫道，「幾分鐘工夫就把這些弄到手了，不錯吧？你猜我是怎麼弄到的，鼴鼠？我偷了匹馬，然後賣了！」

「繼續說，蟾蜍。」鼴鼠興趣盎然地說。

「蟾蜍，請你安靜點！」河鼠說，「鼴鼠，你也別慫恿他了，你明知他是一個什麼樣的傢伙。如今蟾蜍回來了，你還是趕緊說說情況怎樣了，我們下一步該怎麼辦？」

「情況糟透了。」鼴鼠氣呼呼地說，「至於該怎麼辦，嘿，天知道！獾先生和我夜以繼日地在房子周圍轉來轉去，看見的還是老樣子，他們到處都設了崗哨，拿槍口對著我們，朝我們扔石頭。隨時都有一隻動物注視著我們的動向。而每當他們看見我們，哎呀！他們便發瘋似的對我們大笑！這是最讓我氣憤的！」

「形勢相當嚴峻，」河鼠沉思著說，「我想我很清楚蟾蜍應該做的事。要我說，他應該……」

「不，這不行！」鼴鼠嘴裏塞滿了食物，大聲嚷道，「決不能那樣！你不明白。他應該做的是，他應該……」

「嘿，無論如何我也不會照你們說的那樣去做的！」蟾蜍非

常激動地說。「我一點也不想聽從你們這些傢伙的指使！我們現在談論的是『我』的房子，我非常清楚該怎麼辦，告訴你們吧，我打算……」

這時，他們三個都在同時說話，個個都喊破了嗓子，聲音合起來簡直震耳欲聾。突然，傳來一個細細的、乾巴巴的聲音：「你們三個都給我住嘴！」屋子裏立即安靜了下來。

獾先生吃完了他的餡餅，從椅子上轉過身來，兩眼緊緊地瞪著他們。當獾先生看到他們已把注意力集中到他身上，而且顯然在等著他說話時，他卻轉過身去，伸手去抓桌上的乳酪。這位先生的高尚品性贏得了他們高度的尊敬，所以，在他吃完飯、揮掉膝蓋上的食物碎末之前，誰都沒有說話。蟾蜍一副坐立不安的樣子，但河鼠把他牢牢地按在椅子上。

獾先生做完自己的事情後從座位上站了起來，走到壁爐前沉思。最後，他說話了。

「蟾蜍！」他嚴厲地說，「你這個專門惹禍的傢伙！難道你對自己的所作所為不感到羞愧嗎？你想想，要是你的父親——我的老朋友現在還活著，知道了你的胡作非為，他會怎麼說？」

蟾蜍此刻正坐在沙發上，聽到這裏，他翹起兩腿，翻過身去，一頭撲在沙發上羞愧難當地哭了起來，直哭得渾身顫抖。

「好了，好了！」獾先生的口氣變得溫和起來，「別傷心，別哭了。過去的事就讓它過去吧，但你一定要痛改前非，重新做人。鼴鼠說得一點也沒錯，那些黃鼠狼到處都安置哨兵，他們設置的警戒是世界上最嚴密的。想硬攻是徒勞的，他們比我們強大

得多。」

「那一切全完了，」蟾蜍把臉埋在沙發坐墊裏，傷心地哭著，「我去報名從軍算了，再也不要見到我那可愛的蟾蜍莊園！」

「好了，不要洩氣，蟾蜍！」獾先生說，「要奪回一個地方，正面進攻並不是唯一的辦法。我的話還沒說完，來，告訴你們一個天大的秘密。」

蟾蜍慢慢坐直了身子，擦乾了眼淚。秘密對他來說總是有著無限的吸引力，因為他從來沒有能夠保守過一個秘密。平時他總是信誓旦旦地說不會把秘密洩露給別人，事後卻把秘密偷偷地告訴了別人，從而獲得一種心理上的刺激。

「有——一條——地下——通道，」獾先生鄭重其事地說，「從河岸這一帶一直通到蟾蜍莊園的中央。」

「算了，沒這回事啦，獾！」蟾蜍不屑一顧地說，「別人在酒館裏酒後瞎編的話你也相信。蟾蜍莊園裏裏外外的情況我了如指掌，根本沒那回事，我向你保證。」

「年輕人，」獾先生非常嚴肅地說，「你父親和我是最要好的朋友，他是一個可敬的人，是我認識的人當中最可敬的人。他生前跟我說了許多事，他發現了那條通道——當然不是他挖出來的，在他住進去之前存在好幾百年了。他對地道進行了修整和清理。因為他知道，有朝一日，要是發生了麻煩或危險，那會很有用的，他曾經帶我參觀過那條地道，還嚀囑我說：『不要讓我的兒子知道這事。他是個好孩子，可就是性格太浮躁、太變化無常

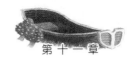

了，而且嘴巴又守不住。今後要是他真的陷入困境，這條地道對他會有好處的。到那個時候你再把這條秘密通道告訴他，不到時候，千萬別說。』」

河鼠和鼴鼠緊緊盯著蟾蜍，看他有什麼反應。起初蟾蜍悶悶不樂地緊繃著臉，但很快他便滿臉笑容，就像平時他得意時那樣。

「哎呀，哎呀，」他說，「也許我說太多話了。我這人就是有人緣——朋友們圍著我團團轉——我們在一起互相打趣逗樂，講些趣味無窮的故事——我的嘴巴就是有點喜歡說話，誰叫我有這麼好的口才呢？他們跟我說，我應該開一個叫什麼『沙龍』的東西——別管它叫什麼了。獾，繼續說。你說的這條地道對我們有什麼幫助？」

「最近我發現了一、兩件事，」獾先生繼續說，「我讓水獺裝扮成一個清潔工，肩上扛著掃帚、刷子去蟾蜍莊園的後門敲門，說要找份工作。他回來後說，明晚他們要舉行一個盛大的宴會，聽說是什麼人的生日——我想是黃鼠狼首領的生日——到時候所有的黃鼠狼都將聚集在餐廳，瘋狂地吃喝笑鬧。那樣的話，他們一定不會有什麼戒備的，身上也不會帶槍呀、劍呀、木棒這些武器的！」

「但他們還會像往常一樣安排崗哨。」河鼠說。

「一點也不錯，」獾先生說，「這正是我要說的。黃鼠狼們一定非常信任他們那些出色的哨兵。地道的作用就在這裏。那條有用的地道一直通到餐廳隔壁的備膳室！」

「啊！怪不得在備膳室裏有一塊嘎吱作響的木板！」蟾蜍說，「現在我終於明白了！」

「我們將神不知鬼不覺地爬進備膳室……」鼴鼠嚷道。

「拿著手槍、劍和木棒……」河鼠大叫道。

「然後給他們來個突擊！」獾先生說。

「再狠狠地揍他們，揍扁他們！」蟾蜍欣喜若狂地喊道。他興奮地在屋裏跑來跑去，在椅子上跳上跳下。

「好啦，」獾先生說，恢復了他平時那乾巴巴的語氣，「我們的方案就這麼定了，你們也不要再爭來吵去。時候不早了，你們一個個都立刻上床睡覺。明天早上我們再做些必要的準備工作。」

蟾蜍自然也乖乖地隨大家一起去睡覺了——他還不至於傻到違抗命令——雖然他感到自己激動得根本睡不著。但這一天他經歷了太多事，早已累壞；而且，和那漏風牢房的石頭地板上鋪的乾稻草比起來，河鼠家的床單和毛毯舒適多了，因此他躺下沒多久便鼾聲連天了。當然啦，他做了許許多多的夢，夢見自己正在奪路而逃時，路卻在他面前消失了；夢見運河在追他，還抓住了他；還有自己正在舉行晚宴時，一艘平底船載著他這一週要洗的衣服駛進了宴會廳；夢見自己獨自行走在秘密地道裏，但地道彎來拐去，還不斷地顫抖著，後來地道居然坐了起來；但不知怎麼地，最後他還是夢見自己安然無恙、得意洋洋地回到了蟾蜍莊園，所有的朋友都圍在他的周圍，個個都搶著對他說，他確實是一隻聰明絕頂的蟾蜍。

第二天早上，蟾蜍很晚才起床，他下樓時發現夥伴們早已吃過早飯。鼴鼠獨自溜去了什麼地方，誰也不知道。獾先生坐在扶手椅上看報紙，似乎一點也不關心今天晚上即將發生的事。另一方面，河鼠在屋裏跑來跑去，手裏拿著各式各樣的武器，又在地上把這些武器分成四小堆。他一邊跑，一邊激動得上氣不接下氣地說：「這把劍是給河鼠的，這把是給鼴鼠的，這把是給蟾蜍的，這把是給獾先生的！這支手槍是給河鼠的，這支是給鼴鼠的，這支是給蟾蜍的，這支是給獾先生的！」他分得有條有理，說得富有節奏，那四小堆東西漸漸變得越來越大。

「好啦，河鼠，」獾先生突然說，他停止了看報，抬起頭看著這個忙碌的小傢伙，「我不想責備你。但只要我們繞過那些帶槍的可惡白鼬，我敢保證，我們根本用不著這些劍呀槍呀什麼的。我們四個一旦進入了餐廳，嘿，用木棒在五分鐘之內就可以把他們都掃地出門。我一個人就可以把所有的事情解決，但是，我還是讓你們這些小傢伙也玩個痛快！」

「還是謹慎一點。」河鼠若有所思地說，一面用袖子擦了擦手槍的槍筒，還瞇著眼朝裏面看了一下。

蟾蜍吃完早餐後，揀起一根粗大的木棒，用力地揮舞著，向想像中的敵人猛打。「我要好好教訓你們！」他叫道，「誰教你們偷我的房子！誰教你們搶我的房子！」

「不要說『教你們』，蟾蜍，」河鼠聽後非常吃驚地說，「你那樣說不貼切。」

「你為什麼老是挑剔蟾蜍？」獾先生很不高興地問，「他那

樣說有什麼關係？我自己也常那樣說。如果我能那樣說，你也該能那樣說吧？」

「對不起，」河鼠恭敬地說，「我只是覺得應該說『叫他們』而不是『教他們』。」

「但我們不想叫他們，」獾先生應答道，「我們是想教他們——教訓他們，好好教訓他們！而且，我們就要那樣做啊！」

「噢，好吧，你們愛怎麼說就怎麼說吧。」河鼠說。他自己也被弄得糊塗，不一會兒，他獨自坐在角落裏，一邊不停地咕噥著：「教他們，叫他們，叫他們，教他們！」最後獾先生厲聲叫他閉嘴。

這時，鼴鼠蹦蹦跳跳地走了進來，顯然對自己感到非常得意。「我玩得可開心啦！」一進門他便說道，「我一個早上都在耍弄那些白鼬！」

「我想你沒闖出什麼禍吧，鼴鼠？」河鼠不放心地說。

「我想沒有吧！」鼴鼠十分自信地說，「今早我進廚房給蟾蜍熱早餐時，腦子裏突然產生一個念頭。我看見他昨天回家時穿的那件洗衣婦的舊罩衣掛在毛巾架上。於是我穿上那件衣服，還戴上那頂女帽，披上披巾，朝蟾蜍莊園走去。膽子夠大的吧？當然，那些持槍哨兵還在放哨。像往常一樣，他們問『來人是誰』和其他一些廢話。我非常恭敬地說：『早上好，先生們！今天要洗衣服嗎？』

「他們非常傲慢地看了我一眼，說道：『走開，洗衣婆！我們值勤時是不能幫妳拿衣服的。』我說：『其他時候呢？』呵，

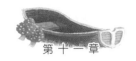

呵，呵！有意思吧，蟾蜍！」

「有意思！」蟾蜍不屑一顧地說。其實，他對鼴鼠的行動非常妒忌。要是他早點想到，要是他沒有睡懶覺，他自己也一定會那樣做的。

「有幾隻白鼬發火了，」鼴鼠接著說，「那位帶班的中士非常急促地對我說：『快點走開，女人，快走！我的人正在值勤呢，妳不要在這裏囉嗦！』『走開？』我說，『過不了多久，要走開的可就不是我嘍！』」

「噢，鼴鼠，你怎麼能那樣說？」河鼠吃驚地說。

獾先生放下手中的報紙。

「我看見他們豎直了耳朵，互相使著眼色，」鼴鼠接著說，「而那個中士卻對他們說：『別管她，她連自己在說什麼都不知道。』」

「『噢！我不知道？』我說，『嘿，老實跟你說吧，我女兒專為獾先生洗衣服，這樣你明白我知不知道自己在說什麼了吧？你很快就會明白了！就在今天晚上，一百隻嗜血成性的獾將從圍場向蟾蜍莊園進攻，他們都帶著來福槍；六船滿滿的老鼠，全都攜帶手槍和大彎刀，將在花園的岸邊登陸；另外，一群經過精選的蟾蜍——叫做什麼蟾蜍敢死隊，將猛攻果園。這幫蟾蜍見什麼搶什麼，高喊著不成功便成仁的口號，誓言要報仇雪恨。等到他們把你們都殺掉的時候，你們也就沒什麼衣服好讓我洗嘍。趁現在還有機會，你還不趕緊逃命！』說完我就走了，等他們看不見我時，我躲藏了起來。過了一會兒，我悄悄地沿著水溝爬了回

去，透過樹籬看看他們有什麼反應。他們一個個都驚恐萬分，連忙四處逃竄，互相撞在一起，每個人都在發號施令，但誰也不聽誰的。那個中士不停地派一隊隊的白鼬到各處去，接著又派別的白鼬去把他們叫回來。我聽見他們抱怨說：『這就是黃鼠狼的德性。他們就懂得待在宴會廳裏吃喝玩樂，而我們卻要在寒冷的黑夜站崗放哨，到頭來還要被嗜血的獾剁成碎片！』」

「噢，你真是蠢驢，鼴鼠！」蟾蜍叫道，「事情都被你搞砸了！」

「鼴鼠，」獾先生還是用他那種乾巴巴、平靜的語氣說，「我看得出你的一根手指頭，比一個全身肥胖的動物來得有智慧多。你做得非常出色，我很看好你，好鼴鼠！機靈的鼴鼠！」

蟾蜍簡直是妒忌死了！特別是他一輩子也弄不明白鼴鼠做的有什麼特別聰明的地方。所幸的是，他沒還來得及發脾氣，也沒來得及回應獾先生的挖苦，就傳來了吃午飯的鈴聲。午飯很簡單，但吃的都是些耐餓的食物：燻鹹肉、炒蠶豆、通心粉以及布丁。大家吃過飯後，獾先生坐到扶手椅上，說：「好啦，我們已經為今晚的行動作好了準備。今晚，等到我們把事情辦妥時，一定是深夜了。所以，我要趁這個機會小憩一會兒。」說完他用一塊手帕蓋住了自己的臉，很快便鼾聲如雷了。

閒不住的河鼠又焦急地繼續他的準備工作，在他那四小堆武器之間來回跑著，口裏念念有詞：「這條武裝帶是給我的，這是給鼴鼠的，這是給蟾蜍的，這是給獾先生的！」每加上一樣裝備，他嘴裏都要念上一遍，而他要加的裝備似乎沒完沒了。於

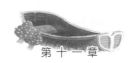

是，鼹鼠便挽著蟾蜍的手臂，拉他到屋外去，把他按在藤椅上，叫他從頭到尾講述他的冒險經歷，這當然是蟾蜍最樂意做的事啦。鼹鼠是一個忠實的聽眾，而蟾蜍呢，此時旁邊沒有誰會挑剔他的話，他就可以更自由地發揮了！確實，他說的大部分都屬於「要是我當時能想到的話，事情一定會怎樣怎樣，而不是真的能預期到之後發展」的這一類話。這些一般都是最吸引人的歷險，但為什麼不能認作是我們自己真正的經歷呢？而且，最不可能發生的事情，不是往往都會成真嗎？

第十二章　浪子回頭

　　天色漸漸暗了下來，河鼠激動而又神秘地把眾夥伴叫進客廳，讓他們站在各自的小堆武器的旁邊，然後一個個地把他們武裝起來，為即將到來的戰鬥作好準備。他每一件事都做得非常認真，因此花了很長一段時間。首先，每個人都要繫上武裝帶，在武裝帶的一邊要佩上劍，另一邊要插上彎刀，以保持平衡。每個人都要帶上兩支手槍、一根警棍、幾副手銬、一些繃帶和膠布、一個水壺和一個裝著三明治的盒子。獾先生爽朗地笑著說：「好啦，河鼠！這可是你自己想做的，對我也沒什麼壞處。不過我只要用這根木棒就夠了。」但河鼠說：「行行好吧，獾先生！我可不想讓你事後責備我，說我忘了什麼東西！」

　　一切準備就緒後，獾先生一隻爪子提著昏暗的燈籠，另一隻握著他那根粗大的木棒，說：「聽著，跟在我的身後！鼴鼠緊跟在我後面，因為我喜歡他，河鼠跟在鼴鼠後面，蟾蜍走在最後。安靜點，蟾蜍！別再嘮嘮叨叨的，要不然我會毫不客氣地把你送回來！」

　　蟾蜍本來很擔心會被排除在這次行動之外，因此，雖然他被

第十二章

安排在最不重要的位置，他也毫無怨言。於是大家出發了。獾先生領著他們沿著河岸走了一會兒，突然他一轉身鑽進了岸邊的一個洞裏。這個洞剛好在河水上面一點點。鼴鼠和河鼠看到獾先生鑽進了洞，也跟著鑽了進去。輪到蟾蜍進洞的時候，他不小心滑了一下，撲通一聲掉進了洞裏，還發出了驚恐的叫聲。他的朋友把他拖了起來，急忙幫他擦乾身子，擰乾衣服，安慰他幾句，又讓他站了起來。但獾先生非常生氣，並警告蟾蜍說，如果他再出什麼差錯，那他們一定會扔下他不管。

現在，他們終於進入了秘密地道，他們精心計劃的行動開始了！

地道低矮狹窄，昏暗潮濕。可憐的蟾蜍開始顫抖起來，一是因為害怕眼前將要發生的事，二是因為他全身濕透了。獾先生提著燈籠走在他前面很遠的地方，而他則落在後面的黑暗裏。這時，他聽到河鼠催促他：「快跟上，蟾蜍！」他不由得驚慌失措，生怕自己孤零零地落在黑暗裏。於是他拼命跟上，慌亂中撞倒了河鼠，河鼠撞倒在鼴鼠身上，而鼴鼠則倒在獾先生身上。一時間，一片混亂。獾先生還以為他們被敵人從身後偷襲呢。由於地方太窄，木棒和砍刀用不上，他拔出手槍，正準備朝蟾蜍開槍。當他明白怎麼回事時，氣憤極了，說道：「蟾蜍！你這個麻煩的傢伙，這回一定得留下！」

但蟾蜍抽抽噎噎地哭了起來，河鼠和鼴鼠也保證不會再讓他出事。最後，獾先生的怒氣平息了下來。四個傢伙又繼續向前進發，但這回是由河鼠殿後，他緊緊地抓住蟾蜍的肩膀。

他們慢慢地摸索前進，豎起耳朵注意動靜，爪子緊緊握著手槍。最後，獾先生說：「現在我們應該相當接近蟾蜍莊園了。」

突然，他們聽到似乎從某處傳來一陣低低的嘈雜聲，但那聲音明顯是來自他們的頭頂上，像是有人在高興地亂喊叫，用腳跺地板，用拳頭捶桌子。蟾蜍又變得驚恐萬分，但獾先生平靜地說：「一定是黃鼠狼們在胡鬧！」

地道向上傾斜著延伸，他們又摸索著往前走了一段。突然，那嘈雜聲又傳來了，這回聲音就在他們頭頂上，聽得非常清楚。「呼啦，呼——啦——呼——啦！」他們還聽到小腳跺地板的聲音和小拳頭捶在桌子上時玻璃杯的叮噹聲。「他們玩得很瘋啊！」獾先生說，「我們快走。」他們沿著地道匆匆前進，很快便來到了盡頭。他們發現，自己已經站在通向備膳室那塊活板門下面。

宴會廳裏的嘈雜聲如潮水一般，因此用不著擔心上面的人會聽到他們的響聲。獾先生說：「弟兄們，我們一起使勁！」於是，四個夥伴用肩膀猛力頂開了活板門。他們互相協助彼此爬上備膳室。現在，他們和宴會廳只隔一道門，敵人正在裏面狂歡作樂。

他們從地道出來時，宴會廳裏的喧鬧聲震耳欲聾。最後，歡叫聲和捶桌聲漸漸變弱，只聽見一個聲音道：「嘿，我不想耽誤你們太多時間，（一陣熱烈的掌聲）但在我回到座位之前，（一片歡呼聲）我想對我們好客的主人蟾蜍先生說一聲謝謝。我們都認識蟾蜍！（一陣哄堂大笑）好心的蟾蜍，謙虛的蟾蜍，誠實的

蟾蜍！（興奮的尖叫聲）」

「讓我進去把他殺了！」蟾蜍咬牙切齒地說。

「冷靜點！」獾先生說，一面使勁地拽住蟾蜍，「大家做好準備！」

「我來為大家唱一首歌。」又是那個聲音，「這是我特地為蟾蜍編的（熱烈的掌聲）。」

接著，黃鼠狼首領——說話的就是他——尖聲尖氣地唱了起來：

> 蟾蜍走在大街上，
>
> 膽大妄為地尋樂……

獾先生昂首挺胸，兩隻爪子緊緊地握住那根木棒，他朝夥伴們使了一個眼色，喊道：「時候到了！跟我來！」

門猛地被踢開了。

「哎呀！」

一時間，屋子裏一片尖叫、吱喳、嚎啕！

驚恐的黃鼠狼們急忙鑽到桌子底下，有的發瘋似的跳上窗戶！雪貂們慌亂地奔向壁爐，結果全都塞在煙囪裏！桌椅板凳東倒西歪，杯子碗碟乒乒乓乓地摔在地上。四勇士憤怒地衝進了宴會廳，黃鼠狼們嚇得魂飛魄散！力大無比的獾先生把他的大木棒揮舞得虎虎生風，他的鬍鬚都豎起來。冷酷無情的鼴鼠也揮舞著木棒！嘴裏喊著令人生畏的戰鬥口號：「我鼴鼠來了！天下無

敵的鼬鼠來了！」腰間掛著各個年代武器的河鼠也在拼命殺敵。自尊心受到傷害的蟾蜍激動不已，肚皮脹得比平時大了一倍。他跳往空中，嘴裏發出蟾蜍特有的，令黃鼠狼們和白鼬們聽了不寒而慄的怒吼聲。「蟾蜍爺爺來尋樂啦！」他嚷道，「殺死你們！」他直撲向黃鼠狼首領。雖然只有四人，但對驚恐萬狀的黃鼠狼們來說，大廳裏似乎到處都是揮舞著的木棒，朝他們猛撲的是灰色、黑色、褐色和黃色兇神惡煞般的動物。黃鼠狼們和白鼬們鬼哭狼嚎著四處逃竄，跳窗戶、鑽煙囪，個個都爭著逃離那些可怕的木棒。

戰鬥很快便結束了。四個朋友在客廳裏大步地走著，看到哪隻黃鼠狼冒出腦袋，就用力地敲上一棒。不到五分鐘，屋裏就被淨空了。透過破碎的玻璃窗，傳來黃鼠狼們從草坪上逃跑時伴隨的驚恐尖叫聲。地板上趴著十幾個投降了的敵人，鼬鼠正忙著給他們戴上手銬。廝殺得很累的獾先生正在挂著木棒休息，一面擦去額頭上的汗水。

「鼬鼠，」他說，「你這個最棒的傢伙！到屋外去照顧一下那些白鼬哨兵，看看他們都在做什麼。由於你的精彩表演，我想他們今晚不會給我們帶來什麼麻煩了！」

鼬鼠立即從窗戶跳了出去。獾先生吩咐另外兩個夥伴把一張桌子立直起來，從地上撿起刀叉碗碟，看能不能弄些吃的東西。「我確實想吃點東西了，」獾先生還是以他那種特有的語氣說道：「別拉長著臉呆站在那裏，蟾蜍！我們為你奪回了房子，還不找塊三明治來招待我們！」

　　蟾蜍的自尊心受到很大打擊，因為獾先生沒有對他說好聽的，卻誇獎了鼴鼠，說他在戰鬥中表現優異，是一個很出色的傢伙。蟾蜍本來對自己感到洋洋自得，覺得自己處置黃鼠狼首領的方式很帶勁，特別是他一棒就把黃鼠狼首領打得從桌子這頭飛過了那頭。蟾蜍雖然心裏不高興，但還是在屋子裏到處尋找起吃的東西來。河鼠也在找。不久，他們在玻璃盤裏找到了一些番石榴果凍，又找到了一隻冷雞，一根幾乎沒有動過的牛舌，一些甜點和不少的龍蝦沙拉。在備膳室裏，他們發現了一籃子的法式麵包捲，大量的奶酪、奶油和芹菜。他們正要坐下吃飯，這時鼴鼠抱著大捆的來福槍，咯咯笑著從窗戶爬了進來。

　　「一切都收拾完畢。」他報告說，「據我所知，那些白鼬早已膽戰心驚，一聽到宴會廳裏的尖叫聲，其中一些連忙扔下手中的槍，趕緊逃命；其他的站著沒動，但當黃鼠狼們從屋裏往他們那邊衝過去的時候，他們覺得自己被出賣了。於是白鼬們和黃鼠狼們扭打在一塊，黃鼠狼們掙扎著要逃竄，雙方互相拳打腳踢，打得難分難解，在地上滾來滾去，結果大多數都滾進了河裏！現在他們從不同方向溜走了。我撿回了他們扔下的槍。現在沒事了！」

　　「你做得很好，應該嘉獎！」獾先生說，嘴裏塞滿了雞肉和點心，「鼴鼠，我還有一件事要你去做，然後你再來和我們一起吃飯。我本來不想麻煩你，但我相信你能辦妥每件事，我希望我能對你們每個人都說這種話。我本想派河鼠去辦，但他是個浪漫的詩人。我要你把那些趴在地上的傢伙帶到樓上去，叫他們把臥

室打掃乾淨，整理得舒舒服服的。盯著他們把床底都打掃乾淨，鋪上乾淨的床單，換上乾淨的枕頭套，還要掀開被子的一角——我想你知道該怎樣做；然後在每個臥室裏放上一罐熱水，備好乾淨的毛巾和沒有用過的香皂。最後，如果你願意，就再狠狠地揍他們一頓，再從後門把他們轟出去。我再也不想見到他們了。事情辦完以後，再來吃點涼拌牛舌，味道好極了。我對你感到非常滿意，鼴鼠！」

　　好心的鼴鼠拿起一根木棒，讓他的俘虜排成一行，命令他們「齊步走」，把他們帶到了樓上。過了一會兒，他臉上帶著微笑回來了，說每個房間都已清理得整整潔潔。「我沒有揍他們。」他補充說，「我想，他們今晚挨的揍也夠多了。當我把道理跟他們說清楚後，他們都同意我的看法，說以後不會再找我們麻煩了。他們都很後悔，還爲自己的所作所爲感到抱歉，但那都是黃鼠狼首領和白鼬們作的孽；還說如果有機會，他們願意爲我們效勞，以彌補他們的過錯，我們儘管吩咐他們。因此，我給他們每人一個麵包捲，讓他們從後門出去，他們個個都飛也似的逃走了！」

　　接著，鼴鼠把椅子往桌邊挪了挪，大口大口地吃起牛舌來。這時蟾蜍已把對鼴鼠的妒忌放在一邊，擺出一副紳士的風度，誠懇地說：「親愛的鼴鼠，我對你今晚熱情的幫助表示衷心的感謝！對你今早的精彩表演表示欽佩！」獾先生聽了感到很滿意，說：「這才是好樣的蟾蜍！」於是，他們高高興興、心滿意足地吃完了晚飯，很快便鑽進了乾淨的被窩裏，安心地睡在祖傳的大

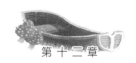

宅裏。這可是他們經過精心的策劃，靠著大無畏的勇氣和使用木棒奪回來的啊！

第二天早上，蟾蜍像往常一樣睡過了頭，非常難堪地走下樓吃早飯。他看到桌子上堆著許多蛋殼，只剩下一些又冷又硬的麵包屑，咖啡壺幾乎是空的，其他的什麼也沒留下。這使他很不高興，無論怎麼說，這可是他自己的家呀！透過餐廳的法式落地窗，他看見鼴鼠和河鼠正坐在草坪的籐椅上，時而哈哈大笑，時而把他們那粗短的腿踢向空中，他們顯然正在講著故事。獾先生坐在一張扶手椅上，專心地看著晨報。蟾蜍走進餐廳時，他只是朝他點了點頭。蟾蜍瞭解獾先生的脾氣，於是他坐了下來，盡所能做了一頓最好的早餐。他心裏不停地盤算著，什麼時候才和這三個傢伙算帳！當他將要吃完飯時，獾先生對他說：「對不起，蟾蜍，今天早上你還有重要的任務。你知道，我們真的應該立即舉行一個宴會，以慶祝這次勝利。大家都在看著你呢——其實這是規矩。」

「好啊！」蟾蜍馬上答應道，「我願意為你效勞。但是我不明白，為什麼非得在早上舉行宴會不可呢？不過，你放心，我不是為了自己的快樂而活，而是盡量滿足朋友們的需求，然後設法為大家安排妥當。我親愛的獾先生！」

「你別裝出一副蠢豬的樣子！」獾先生很生氣地說，「另外，說話的時候不要咕嚕地喝咖啡，那很不禮貌。我的意思是，宴會當然是在晚上舉行，但請柬必須馬上寫好分發。你得做好這件事。去，坐到那張桌子去——上面放著一疊疊的信箋，上頭都

印著藍色和金色的「蟾蜍莊園」字樣——寫好請束，並且發送給每個朋友。如果你專心做，我們午飯前就可以完成這件事。我也會幫忙，做我該做的工作。我將負責安排宴會。」

「什麼？」蟾蜍沮喪地嚷道，「這麼美妙的早晨，你卻叫我待在屋裏，寫那一大堆該死的請束！我還要去看看我的家產，把該處理的事情處理一下，到處閒逛，樂一樂！我決不寫請束！我會……再見……還是等一下！你看，親愛的獾先生，和別人的歡樂相比，我有什麼歡樂可言？你想叫我寫請束，那我就寫好啦！去吧，獾先生，去安排宴會事宜吧，你要怎麼安排就怎麼安排。然後到屋外去，和你那兩位年輕的朋友盡情說笑吧！忘記我的存在，忘記我的苦悶吧。為了友誼，我願意犧牲這個美妙的早晨！」

獾先生用懷疑的眼光看著他，但蟾蜍擺出一副真誠、開朗的樣子，很難看出他改變主意的背後有什麼不可告人的目的。於是，獾先生離開餐廳到廚房去了。門剛一關上，蟾蜍便匆匆來到寫字台邊。在剛才說話的時候，他的腦子裏就產生了一個絕妙的想法。他願意寫請束，但是他要把自己在這場戰鬥中的英勇表現寫上去，特別強調他是如何收拾黃鼠狼首領的；另外，他還要暗示他那一連串的冒險經歷，以及他創造的輝煌事績。在請束的扉頁上，他還準備附上宴會的即興節目。

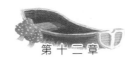

第十二章

節目表

演說………………………………………………蟾蜍
  （晚會期間蟾蜍還要發表另外幾個演說。）
致詞………………………………………………蟾蜍

內容提要

我們的監獄制度——舊英格蘭的水上交通——馬匹交易方法——私人財產；權利與義務——回歸自然——做一名典型的英格蘭鄉紳。

歌曲演唱………………………………………………蟾蜍
  （演唱者本人作詞作曲。）
其他歌曲………………………………………………蟾蜍
  （在晚會過程中由創作者本人演唱。）

這念頭使他非常得意，他很賣力地寫著。中午的時候，所有的信都寫完了。這時，下人向他報告說，門口來了一隻身材矮小、蓬頭垢面的黃鼠狼，誠惶誠恐地問他能為先生們做點什麼。蟾蜍大搖大擺地走了出去，發現那傢伙是前一天晚上被俘虜的一隻黃鼠狼，一副畢恭畢敬的樣子。蟾蜍拍了拍他的腦袋，把那捆請束塞到他的爪子裏，叮囑他以最快的速度把這些請束送到客人

205

手裏，還說如果今晚他願意再回來的話，也許會得到一先令的獎賞，也許不會。那可憐的黃鼠狼看起來一副感激涕零的樣子，急匆匆地執行任務去了。

獾先生、鼴鼠和河鼠在河邊盡情地玩了一個早上，此時興高采烈地回來吃午飯了。鼴鼠一個早上心裏都感到過意不去，他滿心疑惑地看著蟾蜍，以為他會悶悶不樂的。相反，蟾蜍歡天喜地、洋洋自得。鼴鼠便起了疑心，而河鼠和獾先生也意味深長地交換著眼色。

午飯一吃完，蟾蜍把兩隻爪子往口袋深深一插，不經意地說：「朋友們，你們想做什麼就做什麼吧，如果需要什麼儘管說！」然後便大搖大擺地朝花園走去。他想在花園裏認真考慮一下今晚的演說。這時，河鼠抓住了他的臂膀。

蟾蜍知道他想幹什麼，於是拼命掙脫，但當獾先生緊緊地抓住他的另一隻手臂時，他意識到事跡敗露了。兩隻動物押著蟾蜍走進了通向門廳的小吸煙室，關上門，然後把他按在椅子上。他們倆站在蟾蜍的面前，他默默地坐著，用懷疑的目光看著他們，顯得非常生氣。

「聽著，蟾蜍！」河鼠說，「是關於今天晚上宴會的事，很抱歉我得用這種口氣跟你說話。但我們想讓你知道，今晚既沒有什麼演說也沒有什麼歌曲演唱，你要弄清楚，在這個時候，我們可不想跟你爭辯，我們只想讓你知道該怎麼做。」

蟾蜍知道被算計了。他們瞭解他，看穿了他的一舉一動，因此搶先一步。他的如意算盤全完了。

「那我能不能只唱一首小曲子？」他可憐巴巴地哀求道。

「不行，一首曲子也不行！」河鼠堅決地回答，但他看到可憐的蟾蜍那不停顫抖著的嘴唇時，心裏感到很難過。「那對你一點好處也沒有，蟾蜍。你很清楚，那些歌曲全都是自我吹噓的東西，而你的演說也儘是些自吹自擂、粗俗誇耀的……」

「不實之辭。」獾先生用他特有的語氣插嘴道。

「我們這是為你好，蟾蜍，」河鼠接著說，「你知道你遲早都要痛改前非、重新做人，而現在開始重新做人是最好不過了，這是你一生中的轉捩點。我知道，我這樣說你不高興，但我也不好受呀。」

蟾蜍沉思了很久。最後，他抬起頭，從他的臉上可以看出剛才他在心裏經歷過一番劇烈的思想鬥爭。「你們說服了我，朋友們，」他有點前言不搭後語地說，「真的，我提的只是一個小小的要求……我只是想再放縱一個晚上，讓我再聽一次雷鳴般的掌聲……只有這種掌聲才能使我發揮最優秀的自我。沒錯，我知道你們說得對，我錯了。從今以後，我將變成一隻改頭換面的蟾蜍。朋友們，你們再也不用為我難為情了。但是，噢，天哪，這是一個多麼殘酷的世界呀！」

接著，他用手帕捂著臉，蹣跚地走出了房間。

「獾先生，」河鼠說，「我覺得這麼做很殘忍。不知道你心裏有什麼感覺？」

「噢，我理解，我理解，」獾先生心情沉重地說，「但我們必須這麼做。蟾蜍這傢伙必須在這裏住下來，必須守住他的家

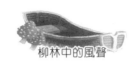
業，必須受到別人的尊敬，難道你願意讓他成爲大家的笑柄，讓白鼬們和黃鼠狼們譏諷取笑嗎？」

「當然不，」河鼠說，「說到黃鼠狼，也算我們走運，那隻小黃鼠狼要去分發請柬，正好被我們碰上。當時我想起你對我說的話，於是看了兩眼請柬，沒想到那上面的話簡直是丟人現眼。於是我把那些請柬全沒收了，現在勤快的鼴鼠正坐在那間藍色的臥室裏，書寫簡單扼要的請柬呢。」

舉行宴會的時間越來越近了。蟾蜍離開了獾先生和河鼠後不僅回到了自己的臥室，還坐在那裏神情憂鬱，思緒萬千。他用一隻爪子托著額頭，陷入了久久的沉思。漸漸地，他的表情變得舒展起來，臉上慢慢露出了微笑，接著又不好意思地咯咯笑了起來。最後，他站了起來，鎖上門，拉上窗簾，搬來房間所有的椅子圍成一個半圓，然後自己站在這些椅子的前面，肚皮明顯地鼓脹了起來。他鞠了一躬，乾咳兩下。接著，對著他想像中欣喜若狂的觀眾，他高聲地唱了起來：

蟾蜍最後的小曲

蟾蜍——回家了！
客廳裏一片恐慌，大廳裏一陣嚎叫，
牛棚裏哭聲不絕，馬廄裏叫聲震天，
蟾蜍——回來了！

蟾蜍——回來了！

窗戶被打碎，門被砸，

黃鼠狼聞風喪膽，

當蟾蜍——回到家——的時候！

咚咚咚！鑼鼓響！

號角嗚嗚響，士兵們歡呼，

大炮隆隆響，汽車喇叭嘟嘟叫，

因為——英雄——凱旋而歸！

高呼——萬歲！

讓每個人同聲高呼，

為令我們驕傲的蟾蜍歡呼，

因為這是他——偉大的——一天！

　　他高聲地唱著，歌聲裏充滿著激情。唱完一遍，他又從頭再唱一遍。

　　接著，他深深地歎了一口氣，這是一聲長長的、長長的歎息。

　　然後，他把髮梳放在水缸裏浸了浸，把自己的頭髮從中間分開，讓頭髮垂在臉頰兩邊，然後用梳子梳得平整光滑。梳理完畢，他打開門，悄悄地走下樓去接待客人。他知道，客人們一定

都聚在會客室裏。

　　他進屋時，所有的動物都歡呼起來。大家圍攏過來祝賀他，讚揚他的膽量、聰明和英勇戰鬥的精神，但蟾蜍只是微笑，喃喃說：「根本沒那回事」或者偶爾改口說：「恰恰相反」。水獺站在壁爐前的地毯上，正向一群朋友繪聲繪色地說，如果他在場的話，他會怎樣怎樣。見到蟾蜍，他嚷著走了過來，一隻手臂摟著蟾蜍的脖子，想帶著他繞著房子轉一圈。但蟾蜍沒有理會他這一套，掙開了水獺的手臂，輕輕地說：「是獾先生英明地策劃了這次戰鬥，鼴鼠和河鼠奮勇當先，我只是一名小兵，沒有做什麼。」動物們沒有料到他會如此謙虛，個個都驚訝不已。蟾蜍從一個客人走到另一個客人的面前，謙虛地回答大家的提問。他發現自己再次成為大家焦點。

　　獾先生把宴會安排得井井有條，宴會獲得了巨大的成功。動物們有說有笑，互相開著玩笑逗樂。但自始至終，蟾蜍都是低著頭坐在椅子上，輕聲地和坐在兩邊的動物謙虛地交談著。他不時地偷偷望一望獾先生和河鼠，他們總是互相地凝視，嘴巴張得大大的，蟾蜍便像獲得讚許似的暗自歡喜。天色越來越晚，一些年輕的動物低聲嘀咕著，說如今不像以往那樣好玩了；一些動物還敲著桌子高喊：「蟾蜍！說幾句！讓蟾蜍說幾句！唱歌！請蟾蜍唱一首！」但蟾蜍輕輕搖搖頭，舉起一隻爪子溫和地表示反對。他把美味食物夾給客人，跟他們聊天，關心地問候他們家裏那些尚未成年、還不能參加社交活動的成員，還讓他們知道，這次宴會是嚴格按傳統方式舉行的。

蟾蜍眞的變了！

這次宴會結束後，這四隻動物繼續過著自己的生活。他們的生活曾經被粗暴的內戰所破壞，但從那以後，他們都過著快樂、幸福的生活，從此不再受到干擾。蟾蜍和他的朋友們認眞商量後，挑選了一條漂亮的金項鏈，把它放在一個鑲著珍珠的首飾盒，附上一封感謝信送給了老看守的女兒。這封信寫得很謙虛，充滿了感激之情，連獾先生看了都感到滿意。火車司機也因所受的辛苦和麻煩得到了蟾蜍得體的酬謝。在獾先生的強烈要求下，蟾蜍經過一番周折找到了那位開船的婦女，並按價賠償了她的馬。但是蟾蜍對這一點很反感，他堅持認爲，是命運安排自己懲罰了那個手上長滿斑點的胖女人，誰讓她連一個體面的紳士都分辨不出呢！所幸賠償的總額並不算太高，而且根據當地估計員的計算，那個吉普賽人買馬出的價錢大致合理。

在漫長的夏夜，這幾位朋友常常到野林子去閒逛，因爲對他們來說，野林子已被成功地馴服了。進到野林子，那裏的居民對他們都很客氣，這使他們感到非常高興。母黃鼠狼們還把她們的孩子帶到洞口，用手指著他們的孩子說：「看，寶寶！那就是了不起的蟾蜍先生，走在他旁邊的是聰明勇敢的河鼠，他是位非常剽悍的戰士！那邊那位是鼎鼎有名的鼴鼠先生，就是你父親經常跟你說起的那位！」但是，當她們的孩子吵鬧不已的時候，她們會嚇唬他們，說如果不好好聽話，那隻可怕的灰獾就會來抓他們。這是對獾先生無端的誹謗，因爲雖然獾先生不喜歡社交，卻很喜歡孩子。但是母黃鼠狼這一招一直都很奏效。

I.
THE RIVER BANK

The Mole had been working very hard all the morning, spring-cleaning his little home. First with brooms, then with dusters; then on ladders and steps and chairs, with a brush and a pail of whitewash; till he had dust in his throat and eyes, and splashes of whitewash all over his black fur, and an aching back and weary arms. Spring was moving in the air above and in the earth below and around him, penetrating even his dark and lowly little house with its spirit of divine discontent and longing. It was small wonder, then, that he suddenly flung down his brush on the floor, said "Bother!" and "O blow!" and also "Hang spring-cleaning!" and bolted out of the house without even waiting to put on his coat. Something up above was calling him imperiously, and he made for the steep little tunnel which answered in his case to the gravelled carriage-drive owned by animals whose residences are nearer to the sun and air. So he scraped and scratched and scrabbled and scrooged and then he scrooged again and scrabbled and scratched and scraped, working busily with his little paws and muttering to himself, "Up we go! Up we go!" till at last, pop! his snout came out into the sunlight, and he found himself rolling in the warm grass of a great meadow.

"This is fine!" he said to himself. "This is better than whitewashing!" The sunshine struck hot on his fur, soft breezes caressed his heated brow, and after the seclusion of the cellarage he had lived in so long the carol of happy birds fell on his dulled hearing

almost like a shout. Jumping off all his four legs at once, in the joy of living and the delight of spring without its cleaning, he pursued his way across the meadow till he reached the hedge on the further side.

"Hold up!" said an elderly rabbit at the gap. "Sixpence for the privilege of passing by the private road!" He was bowled over in an instant by the impatient and contemptuous Mole, who trotted along the side of the hedge chaffing the other rabbits as they peeped hurriedly from their holes to see what the row was about. "Onion-sauce! Onion-sauce!" he remarked jeeringly, and was gone before they could think of a thoroughly satisfactory reply. Then they all started grumbling at each other. "How **stupid** you are! Why didn't you tell him——" "Well, why didn't **you** say——" "You might have reminded him——" and so on, in the usual way; but, of course, it was then much too late, as is always the case.

It all seemed too good to be true. Hither and thither through the meadows he rambled busily, along the hedgerows, across the copses, finding everywhere birds building, flowers budding, leaves thrusting—everything happy, and progressive, and occupied. And instead of having an uneasy conscience pricking him and whispering "whitewash!" he somehow could only feel how jolly it was to be the only idle dog among all these busy citizens. After all, the best part of a holiday is perhaps not so much to be resting yourself, as to see all the other fellows busy working.

He thought his happiness was complete when, as he meandered aimlessly along, suddenly he stood by the edge of a full-fed river. Never in his life had he seen a river before—this sleek, sinuous, full-bodied animal, chasing and chuckling, gripping things with a gurgle and leaving them with a laugh, to fling itself on fresh playmates that shook themselves free, and were caught and held again. All was a-shake and a-shiver—glints and gleams and sparkles, rustle and swirl,

chatter and bubble. The Mole was bewitched, entranced, fascinated. By the side of the river he trotted as one trots, when very small, by the side of a man who holds one spell-bound by exciting stories; and when tired at last, he sat on the bank, while the river still chattered on to him, a babbling procession of the best stories in the world, sent from the heart of the earth to be told at last to the insatiable sea.

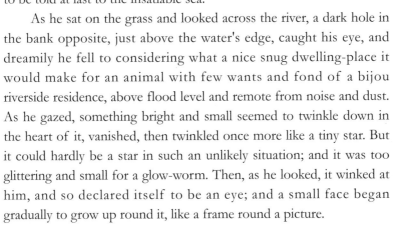

As he sat on the grass and looked across the river, a dark hole in the bank opposite, just above the water's edge, caught his eye, and dreamily he fell to considering what a nice snug dwelling-place it would make for an animal with few wants and fond of a bijou riverside residence, above flood level and remote from noise and dust. As he gazed, something bright and small seemed to twinkle down in the heart of it, vanished, then twinkled once more like a tiny star. But it could hardly be a star in such an unlikely situation; and it was too glittering and small for a glow-worm. Then, as he looked, it winked at him, and so declared itself to be an eye; and a small face began gradually to grow up round it, like a frame round a picture.

A brown little face, with whiskers.

A grave round face, with the same twinkle in its eye that had first attracted his notice.

Small neat ears and thick silky hair.

It was the Water Rat!

Then the two animals stood and regarded each other cautiously.

"Hullo, Mole!" said the Water Rat.

"Hullo, Rat!" said the Mole.

"Would you like to come over?" enquired the Rat presently.

"Oh, its all very well to **talk**," said the Mole, rather pettishly, he being new to a river and riverside life and its ways.

The Rat said nothing, but stooped and unfastened a rope and hauled on it; then lightly stepped into a little boat which the Mole had not observed. It was painted blue outside and white within, and was just the size for two animals; and the Mole's whole heart went out to it at once, even though he did not yet fully understand its uses.

The Rat sculled smartly across and made fast. Then he held up his forepaw as the Mole stepped gingerly down. "Lean on that!" he said. "Now then, step lively!" and the Mole to his surprise and rapture found himself actually seated in the stern of a real boat.

"This has been a wonderful day!" said he, as the Rat shoved off and took to the sculls again. "Do you know, I've never been in a boat before in all my life."

"What?" cried the Rat, open-mouthed: "Never been in a—you never—well I—what have you been doing, then?"

"Is it so nice as all that?" asked the Mole shyly, though he was quite prepared to believe it as he leant back in his seat and surveyed the cushions, the oars, the rowlocks, and all the fascinating fittings, and felt the boat sway lightly under him.

"Nice? It's the **only** thing," said the Water Rat solemnly, as he leant forward for his stroke. "Believe me, my young friend, there is **nothing**—absolute nothing—half so much worth doing as simply messing about in boats. Simply messing," he went on dreamily: "messing—about—in—boats; messing——"

"Look ahead, Rat!" cried the Mole suddenly.

It was too late. The boat struck the bank full tilt. The dreamer, the joyous oarsman, lay on his back at the bottom of the boat, his heels in the air.

"—about in boats—or **with** boats," the Rat went on composedly, picking himself up with a pleasant laugh. "In or out of 'em, it doesn't matter. Nothing seems really to matter, that's the charm of it. Whether you get away, or whether you don't; whether you arrive at your destination or whether you reach somewhere else, or whether you never get anywhere at all, you're always busy, and you never do anything in particular; and when you've done it there's always something else to do, and you can do it if you like, but you'd much better not. Look here! If you've really nothing else on hand this morning, supposing we drop down the river together, and have a long day of it?"

The Mole waggled his toes from sheer happiness, spread his chest with a sigh of full contentment, and leaned back blissfully into the soft cushions. "**What** a day I'm having!" he said. "Let us start at once!"

"Hold hard a minute, then!" said the Rat. He looped the painter through a ring in his landing-stage, climbed up into his hole above, and after a short interval reappeared staggering under a fat, wicker luncheon-basket.

"Shove that under your feet," he observed to the Mole, as he passed it down into the boat. Then he untied the painter and took the sculls again.

"What's inside it?" asked the Mole, wriggling with curiosity.

"There's cold chicken inside it," replied the Rat briefly; "coldtonguecoldhamcoldb eefpickledgherkinssaladfrenchrollscresssan dwichespottedmeatgingerbeerlemonades odawater——"

"O stop, stop," cried the Mole in ecstacies: "This is too much!"

"Do you really think so?" enquired the Rat seriously. "It's only what I always take on these little excursions; and the other animals are always telling me that I'm a mean beast and cut it **very** fine!"

The Mole never heard a word he was saying. Absorbed in the new life he was entering upon, intoxicated with the sparkle, the ripple, the scents and the sounds and the sunlight, he trailed a paw in the water and dreamed long waking dreams. The Water Rat, like the good little fellow he was, sculled steadily on and forebore to disturb him.

"I like your clothes awfully, old chap," he remarked after some half an hour or so had passed. "I'm going to get a black velvet smoking-suit myself some day, as soon as I can afford it."

"I beg your pardon," said the Mole, pulling himself together with an effort. "You must think me very rude; but all this is so new to me. So—this—is—a—River!"

"**The** River," corrected the Rat.

"And you really live by the river? What a jolly life!"

"By it and with it and on it and in it," said the Rat. "It's brother and sister to me, and aunts, and company, and food and drink, and (naturally) washing. It's my world, and I don't want any other. What it hasn't got is not worth having, and what it doesn't know is not worth knowing. Lord! the times we've had together! Whether in winter or summer, spring or autumn, it's always got its fun and its excitements. When the floods are on in February, and my cellars and basement are brimming with drink that's no good to me, and the brown water runs by my best bedroom window; or again when it all drops away and, shows patches of mud that smells like plum-cake, and the rushes and weed clog the channels, and I can potter about dry shod over most of the bed of it and find fresh food to eat, and things careless people have dropped out of boats!"

"But isn't it a bit dull at times?" the Mole ventured to ask. "Just you and the river, and no one else to pass a word with?"

"No one else to—well, I mustn't be hard on you," said the Rat with forbearance. "You're new to it, and of course you don't know. The bank is so crowded nowadays that many people are moving away altogether: O no, it isn't what it used to be, at all. Otters, kingfishers, dabchicks, moorhens, all of them about all day long and always wanting you to **do** something—as if a fellow had no business of his own to attend to!"

"What lies over **there?**" asked the Mole, waving a paw towards a background of woodland that darkly framed the water-meadows on one side of the river.

"That? O, that's just the Wild Wood," said the Rat shortly. "We don't go there very much, we river-bankers."

"Aren't they—aren't they very **nice** people in there?" said the Mole, a trifle nervously.

"W-e-ll," replied the Rat, "let me see. The squirrels are all right. **And** the rabbits—some of 'em, but rabbits are a mixed lot. And then there's Badger, of course. He lives right in the heart of it; wouldn't live anywhere else, either, if you paid him to do it. Dear old Badger! Nobody interferes with **him**. They'd better not," he added significantly.

"Why, who **should** interfere with him?" asked the Mole.

"Well, of course—there—are others," explained the Rat in a hesitating sort of way.

"Weasels—and stoats—and foxes—and so on. They're all right in a way—I'm very good friends with them—pass the time of day when we meet, and all that—but they break out sometimes, there's no denying it, and then—well, you can't really trust them, and that's the fact."

The Mole knew well that it is quite against animal-etiquette to dwell on possible trouble ahead, or even to allude to it; so he dropped the subject.

"And beyond the Wild Wood again?" he asked: "Where it's all blue and dim, and one sees what may be hills or perhaps they mayn't, and something like the smoke of towns, or is it only cloud-drift?"

"Beyond the Wild Wood comes the Wide World," said the Rat. "And that's something that doesn't matter, either to you or me. I've never been there, and I'm never going, nor you either, if you've got any sense at all. Don't ever refer to it again, please. Now then! Here's our backwater at last, where we're going to lunch."

Leaving the main stream, they now passed into what seemed at first sight like a little land-locked lake. Green turf sloped down to either edge, brown snaky tree-roots gleamed below the surface of the quiet water, while ahead of them the silvery shoulder and foamy tumble of a weir, arm-in-arm with a restless dripping mill-wheel, that held up in its turn a grey-gabled mill-house, filled the air with a soothing murmur of sound, dull and smothery, yet with little clear voices speaking up cheerfully out of it at intervals. It was so very beautiful that the Mole could only hold up both forepaws and gasp, "O my! O my! O my!"

The Rat brought the boat alongside the bank, made her fast, helped the still awkward Mole safely ashore, and swung out the luncheon-basket. The Mole begged as a favour to be allowed to unpack it all by himself; and the Rat was very pleased to indulge him, and to sprawl at full length on the grass and rest, while his excited friend shook out the table-cloth and spread it, took out all the mysterious packets one by one and arranged their contents in due order, still gasping, "O my! O my!" at each fresh revelation. When all was ready, the Rat said, "Now, pitch in, old fellow!" and the Mole was

indeed very glad to obey, for he had started his spring-cleaning at a very early hour that morning, as people **will** do, and had not paused for bite or sup; and he had been through a very great deal since that distant time which now seemed so many days ago.

"What are you looking at?" said the Rat presently, when the edge of their hunger was somewhat dulled, and the Mole's eyes were able to wander off the table-cloth a little.

"I am looking," said the Mole, "at a streak of bubbles that I see travelling along the surface of the water. That is a thing that strikes me as funny."

"Bubbles? Oho!" said the Rat, and chirruped cheerily in an inviting sort of way.

A broad glistening muzzle showed itself above the edge of the bank, and the Otter hauled himself out and shook the water from his coat.

"Greedy beggars!" he observed, making for the provender. "Why didn't you invite me, Ratty?"

"This was an impromptu affair," explained the Rat. "By the way—my friend Mr. Mole."

"Proud, I'm sure," said the Otter, and the two animals were friends forthwith.

"Such a rumpus everywhere!" continued the Otter. "All the world seems out on the river to-day. I came up this backwater to try and get a moment's peace, and then stumble upon you fellows!—At least—I beg pardon—I don't exactly mean that, you know."

There was a rustle behind them, proceeding from a hedge wherein last year's leaves still clung thick, and a stripy head, with high shoulders behind it, peered forth on them.

"Come on, old Badger!" shouted the Rat.

The Badger trotted forward a pace or two; then grunted, "H'm!

Company," and turned his back and disappeared from view.

"That's **just** the sort of fellow he is!" observed the disappointed Rat. "Simply hates Society! Now we shan't see any more of him to-day. Well, tell us, **who's** out on the river?"

"Toad's out, for one," replied the Otter. "In his brand-new wager-boat; new togs, new everything!"

The two animals looked at each other and laughed.

"Once, it was nothing but sailing," said the Rat, "Then he tired of that and took to punting. Nothing would please him but to punt all day and every day, and a nice mess he made of it. Last year it was house-boating, and we all had to go and stay with him in his house-boat, and pretend we liked it. He was going to spend the rest of his life in a house-boat. It's all the same, whatever he takes up; he gets tired of it, and starts on something fresh."

"Such a good fellow, too," remarked the Otter reflectively: "But no stability—especially in a boat!"

From where they sat they could get a glimpse of the main stream across the island that separated them; and just then a wager-boat flashed into view, the rower—a short, stout figure—splashing badly and rolling a good deal, but working his hardest. The Rat stood up and hailed him, but Toad—for it was he—shook his head and settled sternly to his work.

"He'll be out of the boat in a minute if he rolls like that," said the Rat, sitting down again.

"Of course he will," chuckled the Otter. "Did I ever tell you that good story about Toad and the lock-keeper? It happened this way. Toad...."

An errant May-fly swerved unsteadily athwart the current in the intoxicated fashion affected by young bloods of May-flies seeing life. A swirl of water and a "cloop!" and the May-fly was visible no more.

Neither was the Otter.

The Mole looked down. The voice was still in his ears, but the turf whereon he had sprawled was clearly vacant. Not an Otter to be seen, as far as the distant horizon.

But again there was a streak of bubbles on the surface of the river.

The Rat hummed a tune, and the Mole recollected that animal-etiquette forbade any sort of comment on the sudden disappearance of one's friends at any moment, for any reason or no reason whatever.

"Well, well," said the Rat, "I suppose we ought to be moving. I wonder which of us had better pack the luncheon-basket?" He did not speak as if he was frightfully eager for the treat.

"O, please let me," said the Mole. So, of course, the Rat let him.

Packing the basket was not quite such pleasant work as unpacking the basket. It never is. But the Mole was bent on enjoying everything, and although just when he had got the basket packed and strapped up tightly he saw a plate staring up at him from the grass, and when the job had been done again the Rat pointed out a fork which anybody ought to have seen, and last of all, behold! the mustard pot, which he had been sitting on without knowing it—still, somehow, the thing got finished at last, without much loss of temper.

The afternoon sun was getting low as the Rat sculled gently homewards in a dreamy mood, murmuring poetry-things over to himself, and not paying much attention to Mole. But the Mole was very full of lunch, and self-satisfaction, and pride, and already quite at home in a boat (so he thought) and was getting a bit restless besides: and presently he said, "Ratty! Please, **I** want to row, now!"

The Rat shook his head with a smile. "Not yet, my young friend," he said—"wait till you've had a few lessons. It's not so easy as it looks."

The Mole was quiet for a minute or two. But he began to feel more and more jealous of Rat, sculling so strongly and so easily along, and his pride began to whisper that he could do it every bit as well. He jumped up and seized the sculls, so suddenly, that the Rat, who was gazing out over the water and saying more poetry-things to himself, was taken by surprise and fell backwards off his seat with his legs in the air for the second time, while the triumphant Mole took his place and grabbed the sculls with entire confidence.

"Stop it, you **silly** ass!" cried the Rat, from the bottom of the boat. "You can't do it! You'll have us over!"

The Mole flung his sculls back with a flourish, and made a great dig at the water. He missed the surface altogether, his legs flew up above his head, and he found himself lying on the top of the prostrate Rat. Greatly alarmed, he made a grab at the side of the boat, and the next moment—Sploosh!

Over went the boat, and he found himself struggling in the river.

O my, how cold the water was, and O, how **very** wet it felt. How it sang in his ears as he went down, down, down! How bright and welcome the sun looked as he rose to the surface coughing and spluttering! How black was his despair when he felt himself sinking again! Then a firm paw gripped him by the back of his neck. It was the Rat, and he was evidently laughing—the Mole could **feel** him laughing, right down his arm and through his paw, and so into his— the Mole's—neck.

The Rat got hold of a scull and shoved it under the Mole's arm; then he did the same by the other side of him and, swimming behind, propelled the helpless animal to shore, hauled him out, and set him down on the bank, a squashy, pulpy lump of misery.

When the Rat had rubbed him down a bit, and wrung some of the wet out of him, he said, "Now, then, old fellow! Trot up and down

the towing-path as hard as you can, till you're warm and dry again, while I dive for the luncheon-basket."

So the dismal Mole, wet without and ashamed within, trotted about till he was fairly dry, while the Rat plunged into the water again, recovered the boat, righted her and made her fast, fetched his floating property to shore by degrees, and finally dived successfully for the luncheon-basket and struggled to land with it.

When all was ready for a start once more, the Mole, limp and dejected, took his seat in the stern of the boat; and as they set off, he said in a low voice, broken with emotion, "Ratty, my generous friend! I am very sorry indeed for my foolish and ungrateful conduct. My heart quite fails me when I think how I might have lost that beautiful luncheon-basket. Indeed, I have been a complete ass, and I know it. Will you overlook it this once and forgive me, and let things go on as before?"

"That's all right, bless you!" responded the Rat cheerily. "What's a little wet to a Water Rat? I'm more in the water than out of it most days. Don't you think any more about it; and, look here! I really think you had better come and stop with me for a little time. It's very plain and rough, you know—not like Toad's house at all—but you haven't seen that yet; still, I can make you comfortable. And I'll teach you to row, and to swim, and you'll soon be as handy on the water as any of us."

The Mole was so touched by his kind manner of speaking that he could find no voice to answer him; and he had to brush away a tear or two with the back of his paw. But the Rat kindly looked in another direction, and presently the Mole's spirits revived again, and he was even able to give some straight back-talk to a couple of moorhens who were sniggering to each other about his bedraggled appearance.

When they got home, the Rat made a bright fire in the parlour,

and planted the Mole in an arm-chair in front of it, having fetched down a dressing-gown and slippers for him, and told him river stories till supper-time. Very thrilling stories they were, too, to an earth-dwelling animal like Mole. Stories about weirs, and sudden floods, and leaping pike, and steamers that flung hard bottles—at least bottles were certainly flung, and **from** steamers, so presumably **by** them; and about herons, and how particular they were whom they spoke to; and about adventures down drains, and night-fishings with Otter, or excursions far a-field with Badger. Supper was a most cheerful meal; but very shortly afterwards a terribly sleepy Mole had to be escorted upstairs by his considerate host, to the best bedroom, where he soon laid his head on his pillow in great peace and contentment, knowing that his new-found friend the River was lapping the sill of his window.

This day was only the first of many similar ones for the emancipated Mole, each of them longer and full of interest as the ripening summer moved onward. He learnt to swim and to row, and entered into the joy of running water; and with his ear to the reed-stems he caught, at intervals, something of what the wind went whispering so constantly among them.

II.
THE OPEN ROAD

"Ratty," said the Mole suddenly, one bright summer morning, "if you please, I want to ask you a favour."

The Rat was sitting on the river bank, singing a little song. He had just composed it himself, so he was very taken up with it, and would not pay proper attention to Mole or anything else. Since early morning he had been swimming in the river, in company with his friends the ducks. And when the ducks stood on their heads suddenly, as ducks will, he would dive down and tickle their necks, just under where their chins would be if ducks had chins, till they were forced to come to the surface again in a hurry, spluttering and angry and shaking their feathers at him, for it is impossible to say quite **all** you feel when your head is under water. At last they implored him to go away and attend to his own affairs and leave them to mind theirs. So the Rat went away, and sat on the river bank in the sun, and made up a song about them, which he called

"DUCKS' DITTY."

All along the backwater,
Through the rushes tall,
Ducks are a-dabbling,
Up tails all!
Ducks' tails, drakes' tails,
Yellow feet a-quiver,
Yellow bills all out of sight
Busy in the river!

Slushy green undergrowth
Where the roach swim—
Here we keep our larder,
Cool and full and dim.

Everyone for what he likes!
We like to be
Heads down, tails up,
Dabbling free!

High in the blue above
Swifts whirl and call—
We are down a-dabbling
Uptails all!

"I don't know that I think so **very** much of that little song, Rat," observed the Mole cautiously. He was no poet himself and didn't care who knew it; and he had a candid nature.

"Nor don't the ducks neither," replied the Rat cheerfully. "They say, ʻ**Why** can't fellows be allowed to do what they like **when** they like and **as** they like, instead of other fellows sitting on banks and watching them all the time and making remarks and poetry and things about them? What **nonsense** it all is!' That's what the ducks say."

"So it is, so it is," said the Mole, with great heartiness.

"No, it isn't!" cried the Rat indignantly.

"Well then, it isn't, it isn't," replied the Mole soothingly. "But what I wanted to ask you was, won't you take me to call on Mr. Toad? I've heard so much about him, and I do so want to make his acquaintance."

"Why, certainly," said the good-natured Rat, jumping to his feet and dismissing poetry from his mind for the day. "Get the boat out, and we'll paddle up there at once. It's never the wrong time to call on Toad. Early or late he's always the same fellow. Always good-tempered, always glad to see you, always sorry when you go!"

"He must be a very nice animal," observed the Mole, as he got into the boat and took the sculls, while the Rat settled himself comfortably in the stern.

"He is indeed the best of animals," replied Rat. "So simple, so good-natured, and so affectionate. Perhaps he's not very clever—we can't all be geniuses; and it may be that he is both boastful and conceited. But he has got some great qualities, has Toady."

Rounding a bend in the river, they came in sight of a handsome, dignified old house of mellowed red brick, with well-kept lawns reaching down to the water's edge.

"There's Toad Hall," said the Rat; "and that creek on the left, where the notice-board says, 'Private. No landing allowed,' leads to his boat-house, where we'll leave the boat. The stables are over there to the right. That's the banqueting-hall you're looking at now—very old, that is. Toad is rather rich, you know, and this is really one of the nicest houses in these parts, though we never admit as much to Toad."

They glided up the creek, and the Mole shipped his sculls as they passed into the shadow of a large boat-house. Here they saw many handsome boats, slung from the cross beams or hauled up on a slip, but none in the water; and the place had an unused and a deserted air.

The Rat looked around him. "I understand," said he. "Boating is played out. He's tired of it, and done with it. I wonder what new fad he has taken up now? Come along and let's look him up. We shall hear all about it quite soon enough."

They disembarked, and strolled across the gay flower-decked lawns in search of Toad, whom they presently happened upon resting in a wicker garden-chair, with a pre-occupied expression of face, and a large map spread out on his knees.

"Hooray!" he cried, jumping up on seeing them, "this is splendid!" He shook the paws of both of them warmly, never waiting for an introduction to the Mole. "How **kind** of you!" he went on, dancing round them. "I was just going to send a boat down the river for you, Ratty, with strict orders that you were to be fetched up here at once, whatever you were doing. I want you badly—both of you. Now what will you take? Come inside and have something! You don't know how lucky it is, your turning up just now!"

"Let's sit quiet a bit, Toady!" said the Rat, throwing himself into an easy chair, while the Mole took another by the side of him and made some civil remark about Toad's "delightful residence."

"Finest house on the whole river," cried Toad boisterously. "Or

anywhere else, for that matter," he could not help adding.

Here the Rat nudged the Mole. Unfortunately the Toad saw him do it, and turned very red. There was a moment's painful silence. Then Toad burst out laughing. "All right, Ratty," he said. "It's only my way, you know. And it's not such a very bad house, is it? You know you rather like it yourself. Now, look here. Let's be sensible. You are the very animals I wanted. You've got to help me. It's most important!"

"It's about your rowing, I suppose," said the Rat, with an innocent air. "You're getting on fairly well, though you splash a good bit still. With a great deal of patience, and any quantity of coaching, you may——"

"O, pooh! boating!" interrupted the Toad, in great disgust. "Silly boyish amusement. I've given that up **long** ago. Sheer waste of time, that's what it is. It makes me downright sorry to see you fellows, who ought to know better, spending all your energies in that aimless manner. No, I've discovered the real thing, the only genuine occupation for a life time. I propose to devote the remainder of mine to it, and can only regret the wasted years that lie behind me, squandered in trivialities. Come with me, dear Ratty, and your amiable friend also, if he will be so very good, just as far as the stable-yard, and you shall see what you shall see!"

He led the way to the stable-yard accordingly, the Rat following with a most mistrustful expression; and there, drawn out of the coach house into the open, they saw a gipsy caravan, shining with newness, painted a canary-yellow picked out with green, and red wheels.

"There you are!" cried the Toad, straddling and expanding himself. "There's real life for you, embodied in that little cart. The open road, the dusty highway, the heath, the common, the hedgerows, the rolling downs! Camps, villages, towns, cities! Here to-day, up and off to somewhere else to-morrow! Travel, change, interest, excitement!

The whole world before you, and a horizon that's always changing! And mind! this is the very finest cart of its sort that was ever built, without any exception. Come inside and look at the arrangements. Planned 'em all myself, I did!"

The Mole was tremendously interested and excited, and followed him eagerly up the steps and into the interior of the caravan. The Rat only snorted and thrust his hands deep into his pockets, remaining where he was.

It was indeed very compact and comfortable. Little sleeping bunks—a little table that folded up against the wall—a cooking-stove, lockers, bookshelves, a bird-cage with a bird in it; and pots, pans, jugs and kettles of every size and variety.

"All complete!" said the Toad triumphantly, pulling open a locker. "You see—biscuits, potted lobster, sardines—everything you can possibly want. Soda-water here—baccy there—letter-paper, bacon, jam, cards and dominoes—you'll find," he continued, as they descended the steps again, "you'll find that nothing what ever has been forgotten, when we make our start this afternoon."

"I beg your pardon," said the Rat slowly, as he chewed a straw, "but did I overhear you say something about 'we,' and 'start,' and 'this afternoon?'"

"Now, you dear good old Ratty," said Toad, imploringly, "don't begin talking in that stiff and sniffy sort of way, because you know you've **got** to come. I can't possibly manage without you, so please consider it settled, and don't argue—it's the one thing I can't stand. You surely don't mean to stick to your dull fusty old river all your life, and just live in a hole in a bank, and **boat?** I want to show you the world! I'm going to make an **animal** of you, my boy!"

"I don't care," said the Rat, doggedly. "I'm not coming, and that's flat. And I **am** going to stick to my old river, **and** live in a hole, **and**

boat, as I've always done. And what's more, Mole's going to stick to me and do as I do, aren't you, Mole?"

"Of course I am," said the Mole, loyally. "I'll always stick to you, Rat, and what you say is to be—has got to be. All the same, it sounds as if it might have been—well, rather fun, you know!" he added, wistfully. Poor Mole! The Life Adventurous was so new a thing to him, and so thrilling; and this fresh aspect of it was so tempting; and he had fallen in love at first sight with the canary-coloured cart and all its little fitments.

The Rat saw what was passing in his mind, and wavered. He hated disappointing people, and he was fond of the Mole, and would do almost anything to oblige him. Toad was watching both of them closely.

"Come along in, and have some lunch," he said, diplomatically, "and we'll talk it over. We needn't decide anything in a hurry. Of course, I don't really care. I only want to give pleasure to you fellows. 'Live for others!' That's my motto in life."

During luncheon—which was excellent, of course, as everything at Toad Hall always was—the Toad simply let himself go. Disregarding the Rat, he proceeded to play upon the inexperienced Mole as on a harp. Naturally a voluble animal, and always mastered by his imagination, he painted the prospects of the trip and the joys of the open life and the roadside in such glowing colours that the Mole could hardly sit in his chair for excitement. Somehow, it soon seemed taken for granted by all three of them that the trip was a settled thing; and the Rat, though still unconvinced in his mind, allowed his good-nature to over-ride his personal objections. He could not bear to disappoint his two friends, who were already deep in schemes and anticipations, planning out each day's separate occupation for several weeks ahead.

When they were quite ready, the now triumphant Toad led his companions to the paddock and set them to capture the old grey horse, who, without having been consulted, and to his own extreme annoyance, had been told off by Toad for the dustiest job in this dusty expedition. He frankly preferred the paddock, and took a deal of catching. Meantime Toad packed the lockers still tighter with necessaries, and hung nosebags, nets of onions, bundles of hay, and baskets from the bottom of the cart. At last the horse was caught and harnessed, and they set off, all talking at once, each animal either trudging by the side of the cart or sitting on the shaft, as the humour took him. It was a golden afternoon. The smell of the dust they kicked up was rich and satisfying; out of thick orchards on either side the road, birds called and whistled to them cheerily; good-natured wayfarers, passing them, gave them "Good-day," or stopped to say nice things about their beautiful cart; and rabbits, sitting at their front doors in the hedgerows, held up their fore-paws, and said, "O my! O my! O my!"

Late in the evening, tired and happy and miles from home, they drew up on a remote common far from habitations, turned the horse loose to graze, and ate their simple supper sitting on the grass by the side of the cart. Toad talked big about all he was going to do in the days to come, while stars grew fuller and larger all around them, and a yellow moon, appearing suddenly and silently from nowhere in particular, came to keep them company and listen to their talk. At last they turned in to their little bunks in the cart; and Toad, kicking out his legs, sleepily said, "Well, good night, you fellows! This is the real life for a gentleman! Talk about your old river!"

"I **don't** talk about my river," replied the patient Rat. "You **know** I don't, Toad. But I **think** about it," he added pathetically, in a lower tone: "I think about it—all the time!"

The Mole reached out from under his blanket, felt for the Rat's paw in the darkness, and gave it a squeeze. "I'll do whatever you like, Ratty," he whispered. "Shall we run away to-morrow morning, quite early—**very** early—and go back to our dear old hole on the river?"

"No, no, we'll see it out," whispered back the Rat. "Thanks awfully, but I ought to stick by Toad till this trip is ended. It wouldn't be safe for him to be left to himself. It won't take very long. His fads never do. Good night!"

The end was indeed nearer than even the Rat suspected.

After so much open air and excitement the Toad slept very soundly, and no amount of shaking could rouse him out of bed next morning. So the Mole and Rat turned to, quietly and manfully, and while the Rat saw to the horse, and lit a fire, and cleaned last night's cups and platters, and got things ready for breakfast, the Mole trudged off to the nearest village, a long way off, for milk and eggs and various necessaries the Toad had, of course, forgotten to provide. The hard work had all been done, and the two animals were resting, thoroughly exhausted, by the time Toad appeared on the scene, fresh and gay, remarking what a pleasant easy life it was they were all leading now, after the cares and worries and fatigues of housekeeping at home.

They had a pleasant ramble that day over grassy downs and along narrow by-lanes, and camped as before, on a common, only this time the two guests took care that Toad should do his fair share of work. In consequence, when the time came for starting next morning, Toad was by no means so rapturous about the simplicity of the primitive life, and indeed attempted to resume his place in his bunk, whence he was hauled by force. Their way lay, as before, across country by narrow lanes, and it was not till the afternoon that they came out on the high-road, their first high-road; and there disaster, fleet and unforeseen, sprang out on them—disaster momentous indeed to their

expedition, but simply overwhelming in its effect on the after-career of Toad.

They were strolling along the high-road easily, the Mole by the horse's head, talking to him, since the horse had complained that he was being frightfully left out of it, and nobody considered him in the least; the Toad and the Water Rat walking behind the cart talking together—at least Toad was talking, and Rat was saying at intervals, "Yes, precisely; and what did **you** say to **him?**"—and thinking all the time of something very different, when far behind them they heard a faint warning hum; like the drone of a distant bee. Glancing back, they saw a small cloud of dust, with a dark centre of energy, advancing on them at incredible speed, while from out the dust a faint "Poop-poop!" wailed like an uneasy animal in pain. Hardly regarding it, they turned to resume their conversation, when in an instant (as it seemed) the peaceful scene was changed, and with a blast of wind and a whirl of sound that made them jump for the nearest ditch, It was on them! The "Poop-poop" rang with a brazen shout in their ears, they had a moment's glimpse of an interior of glittering plate-glass and rich morocco, and the magnificent motor-car, immense, breath-snatching, passionate, with its pilot tense and hugging his wheel, possessed all earth and air for the fraction of a second, flung an enveloping cloud of dust that blinded and enwrapped them utterly, and then dwindled to a speck in the far distance, changed back into a droning bee once more.

The old grey horse, dreaming, as he plodded along, of his quiet paddock, in a new raw situation such as this simply abandoned himself to his natural emotions. Rearing, plunging, backing steadily, in spite of all the Mole's efforts at his head, and all the Mole's lively language directed at his better feelings, he drove the cart backwards towards the deep ditch at the side of the road. It wavered an instant—

then there was a heartrending crash—and the canary-coloured cart, their pride and their joy, lay on its side in the ditch, an irredeemable wreck.

The Rat danced up and down in the road, simply transported with passion. "You villains!" he shouted, shaking both fists, "You scoundrels, you highwaymen, you—you—roadhogs!—I'll have the law of you! I'll report you! I'll take you through all the Courts!" His home-sickness had quite slipped away from him, and for the moment he was the skipper of the canary-coloured vessel driven on a shoal by the reckless jockeying of rival mariners, and he was trying to recollect all the fine and biting things he used to say to masters of steam-launches when their wash, as they drove too near the bank, used to flood his parlour-carpet at home.

Toad sat straight down in the middle of the dusty road, his legs stretched out before him, and stared fixedly in the direction of the disappearing motor-car. He breathed short, his face wore a placid satisfied expression, and at intervals he faintly murmured "Poop-poop!"

The Mole was busy trying to quiet the horse, which he succeeded in doing after a time. Then he went to look at the cart, on its side in the ditch. It was indeed a sorry sight. Panels and windows smashed, axles hopelessly bent, one wheel off, sardine-tins scattered over the wide world, and the bird in the bird-cage sobbing pitifully and calling to be let out.

The Rat came to help him, but their united efforts were not sufficient to right the cart. "Hi! Toad!" they cried. "Come and bear a hand, can't you!"

The Toad never answered a word, or budged from his seat in the road; so they went to see what was the matter with him. They found him in a sort of a trance, a happy smile on his face, his eyes still fixed

on the dusty wake of their destroyer. At intervals he was still heard to murmur "Poop-poop!"

The Rat shook him by the shoulder. "Are you coming to help us, Toad?" he demanded sternly.

"Glorious, stirring sight!" murmured Toad, never offering to move. "The poetry of motion! The **real** way to travel! The **only** way to travel! Here to-day—in next week to-morrow! Villages skipped, towns and cities jumped—always somebody else's horizon! O bliss! O poop-poop! O my! O my!"

"O **stop** being an ass, Toad!" cried the Mole despairingly.

"And to think I never **knew!**" went on the Toad in a dreamy monotone. "All those wasted years that lie behind me, I never knew, never even **dreamt!** But **now**—but now that I know, now that I fully realise! O what a flowery track lies spread before me, henceforth! What dust-clouds shall spring up behind me as I speed on my reckless way! What carts I shall fling carelessly into the ditch in the wake of my magnificent onset! Horrid little carts—common carts—canary-coloured carts!"

"What are we to do with him?" asked the Mole of the Water Rat.

"Nothing at all," replied the Rat firmly. "Because there is really nothing to be done. You see, I know him from of old. He is now possessed. He has got a new craze, and it always takes him that way, in its first stage. He'll continue like that for days now, like an animal walking in a happy dream, quite useless for all practical purposes. Never mind him. Let's go and see what there is to be done about the cart."

A careful inspection showed them that, even if they succeeded in righting it by themselves, the cart would travel no longer. The axles were in a hopeless state, and the missing wheel was shattered into pieces.

The Rat knotted the horse's reins over his back and took him by the head, carrying the bird cage and its hysterical occupant in the other hand. "Come on!" he said grimly to the Mole. "It's five or six miles to the nearest town, and we shall just have to walk it. The sooner we make a start the better."

"But what about Toad?" asked the Mole anxiously, as they set off together. "We can't leave him here, sitting in the middle of the road by himself, in the distracted state he's in! It's not safe. Supposing another Thing were to come along?"

"O, **bother** Toad," said the Rat savagely; "I've done with him!"

They had not proceeded very far on their way, however, when there was a pattering of feet behind them, and Toad caught them up and thrust a paw inside the elbow of each of them; still breathing short and staring into vacancy.

"Now, look here, Toad!" said the Rat sharply: "as soon as we get to the town, you'll have to go straight to the police-station, and see if they know anything about that motor-car and who it belongs to, and lodge a complaint against it. And then you'll have to go to a blacksmith's or a wheelwright's and arrange for the cart to be fetched and mended and put to rights. It'll take time, but it's not quite a hopeless smash. Meanwhile, the Mole and I will go to an inn and find comfortable rooms where we can stay till the cart's ready, and till your nerves have recovered their shock."

"Police-station! Complaint!" murmured Toad dreamily. "Me **complain** of that beautiful, that heavenly vision that has been vouchsafed me! **Mend** the **cart!** I've done with carts for ever. I never want to see the cart, or to hear of it, again. O, Ratty! You can't think how obliged I am to you for consenting to come on this trip! I wouldn't have gone without you, and then I might never have seen that—that swan, that sunbeam, that thunderbolt! I might never have

heard that entrancing sound, or smelt that bewitching smell! I owe it all to you, my best of friends!"

The Rat turned from him in despair. "You see what it is?" he said to the Mole, addressing him across Toad's head: "He's quite hopeless. I give it up—when we get to the town we'll go to the railway station, and with luck we may pick up a train there that'll get us back to riverbank to-night. And if ever you catch me going a-pleasuring with this provoking animal again!"—He snorted, and during the rest of that weary trudge addressed his remarks exclusively to Mole.

On reaching the town they went straight to the station and deposited Toad in the second-class waiting-room, giving a porter twopence to keep a strict eye on him. They then left the horse at an inn stable, and gave what directions they could about the cart and its contents. Eventually, a slow train having landed them at a station not very far from Toad Hall, they escorted the spell-bound, sleep-walking Toad to his door, put him inside it, and instructed his housekeeper to feed him, undress him, and put him to bed. Then they got out their boat from the boat-house, sculled down the river home, and at a very late hour sat down to supper in their own cosy riverside parlour, to the Rat's great joy and contentment.

The following evening the Mole, who had risen late and taken things very easy all day, was sitting on the bank fishing, when the Rat, who had been looking up his friends and gossiping, came strolling along to find him. "Heard the news?" he said. "There's nothing else being talked about, all along the river bank. Toad went up to Town by an early train this morning. And he has ordered a large and very expensive motor-car."

III.
THE WILD WOOD

The Mole had long wanted to make the acquaintance of the Badger. He seemed, by all accounts, to be such an important personage and, though rarely visible, to make his unseen influence felt by everybody about the place. But whenever the Mole mentioned his wish to the Water Rat he always found himself put off. "It's all right," the Rat would say. "Badger'll turn up some day or other—he's always turning up—and then I'll introduce you. The best of fellows! But you must not only take him **as** you find him, but **when** you find him."

"Couldn't you ask him here dinner or something?" said the Mole.

"He wouldn't come," replied the Rat simply. "Badger hates Society, and invitations, and dinner, and all that sort of thing."

"Well, then, supposing we go and call on **him?**" suggested the Mole.

"O, I'm sure he wouldn't like that at **all,**" said the Rat, quite alarmed. "He's so very shy, he'd be sure to be offended. I've never even ventured to call on him at his own home myself, though I know him so well. Besides, we can't. It's quite out of the question, because he lives in the very middle of the Wild Wood."

"Well, supposing he does," said the Mole. "You told me the Wild Wood was all right, you know."

"O, I know, I know, so it is," replied the Rat evasively. "But I think we won't go there just now. Not **just** yet. It's a long way, and he wouldn't be at home at this time of year anyhow, and he'll be coming along some day, if you'll wait quietly."

The Mole had to be content with this. But the Badger never came

along, and every day brought its amusements, and it was not till summer was long over, and cold and frost and miry ways kept them much indoors, and the swollen river raced past outside their windows with a speed that mocked at boating of any sort or kind, that he found his thoughts dwelling again with much persistence on the solitary grey Badger, who lived his own life by himself, in his hole in the middle of the Wild

Wood.

In the winter time the Rat slept a great deal, retiring early and rising late. During his short day he sometimes scribbled poetry or did other small domestic jobs about the house; and, of course, there were always animals dropping in for a chat, and consequently there was a good deal of story-telling and comparing notes on the past summer and all its doings.

Such a rich chapter it had been, when one came to look back on it all! With illustrations so numerous and so very highly coloured! The pageant of the river bank had marched steadily along, unfolding itself in scene-pictures that succeeded each other in stately procession. Purple loosestrife arrived early, shaking luxuriant tangled locks along the edge of the mirror whence its own face laughed back at it. Willow-herb, tender and wistful, like a pink sunset cloud, was not slow to follow. Comfrey, the purple hand-in-hand with the white, crept forth to take its place in the line; and at last one morning the diffident and delaying dog-rose stepped delicately on the stage, and one knew, as if string-music had announced it in stately chords that strayed into a gavotte, that June at last was here. One member of the company was still awaited; the shepherd-boy for the nymphs to woo, the knight for whom the ladies waited at the window, the prince that was to kiss the sleeping summer back to life and love. But when meadow-sweet, debonair and odorous in amber jerkin, moved graciously to his place

in the group, then the play was ready to begin.

And what a play it had been! Drowsy animals, snug in their holes while wind and rain were battering at their doors, recalled still keen mornings, an hour before sunrise, when the white mist, as yet undispersed, clung closely along the surface of the water; then the shock of the early plunge, the scamper along the bank, and the radiant transformation of earth, air, and water, when suddenly the sun was with them again, and grey was gold and colour was born and sprang out of the earth once more. They recalled the languorous siesta of hot mid-day, deep in green undergrowth, the sun striking through in tiny golden shafts and spots; the boating and bathing of the afternoon, the rambles along dusty lanes and through yellow cornfields; and the long, cool evening at last, when so many threads were gathered up, so many friendships rounded, and so many adventures planned for the morrow. There was plenty to talk about on those short winter days when the animals found themselves round the fire; still, the Mole had a good deal of spare time on his hands, and so one afternoon, when the Rat in his arm-chair before the blaze was alternately dozing and trying over rhymes that wouldn't fit, he formed the resolution to go out by himself and explore the Wild Wood, and perhaps strike up an acquaintance with

Mr. Badger.

It was a cold still afternoon with a hard steely sky overhead, when he slipped out of the warm parlour into the open air. The country lay bare and entirely leafless around him, and he thought that he had never seen so far and so intimately into the insides of things as on that winter day when Nature was deep in her annual slumber and seemed to have kicked the clothes off. Copses, dells, quarries and all hidden places, which had been mysterious mines for exploration in leafy summer, now exposed themselves and their secrets pathetically, and

seemed to ask him to overlook their shabby poverty for a while, till they could riot in rich masquerade as before, and trick and entice him with the old deceptions. It was pitiful in a way, and yet cheering—even exhilarating. He was glad that he liked the country undecorated, hard, and stripped of its finery. He had got down to the bare bones of it, and they were fine and strong and simple. He did not want the warm clover and the play of seeding grasses; the screens of quickset, the billowy drapery of beech and elm seemed best away; and with great cheerfulness of spirit he pushed on towards the Wild Wood, which lay before him low and threatening, like a black reef in some still southern sea.

There was nothing to alarm him at first entry. Twigs crackled under his feet, logs tripped him, funguses on stumps resembled caricatures, and startled him for the moment by their likeness to something familiar and far away; but that was all fun, and exciting. It led him on, and he penetrated to where the light was less, and trees crouched nearer and nearer, and holes made ugly mouths at him on either side.

Everything was very still now. The dusk advanced on him steadily, rapidly, gathering in behind and before; and the light seemed to be draining away like flood-water.

Then the faces began.

It was over his shoulder, and indistinctly, that he first thought he saw a face; a little evil wedge-shaped face, looking out at him from a hole. When he turned and confronted it, the thing had vanished.

He quickened his pace, telling himself cheerfully not to begin imagining things, or there would be simply no end to it. He passed another hole, and another, and another; and then—yes!—no!—yes! certainly a little narrow face, with hard eyes, had flashed up for an instant from a hole, and was gone. He hesitated—braced himself up

for an effort and strode on. Then suddenly, and as if it had been so all the time, every hole, far and near, and there were hundreds of them, seemed to possess its face, coming and going rapidly, all fixing on him glances of malice and hatred: all hard-eyed and evil and sharp.

If he could only get away from the holes in the banks, he thought, there would be no more faces. He swung off the path and plunged into the untrodden places of the wood.

Then the whistling began.

Very faint and shrill it was, and far behind him, when first he heard it; but somehow it made him hurry forward. Then, still very faint and shrill, it sounded far ahead of him, and made him hesitate and want to go back. As he halted in indecision it broke out on either side, and seemed to be caught up and passed on throughout the whole length of the wood to its farthest limit. They were up and alert and ready, evidently, whoever they were! And he—he was alone, and unarmed, and far from any help; and the night was closing in.

Then the pattering began.

He thought it was only falling leaves at first, so slight and delicate was the sound of it. Then as it grew it took a regular rhythm, and he knew it for nothing else but the pat-pat-pat of little feet still a very long way off. Was it in front or behind? It seemed to be first one, and then the other, then both. It grew and it multiplied, till from every quarter as he listened anxiously, leaning this way and that, it seemed to be closing in on him. As he stood still to hearken, a rabbit came running hard towards him through the trees. He waited, expecting it to slacken pace, or to swerve from him into a different course. Instead, the animal almost brushed him as it dashed past, his face set and hard, his eyes staring. "Get out of this, you fool, get out!" the Mole heard him mutter as he swung round a stump and disappeared down a friendly burrow.

The pattering increased till it sounded like sudden hail on the dry leaf-carpet spread around him. The whole wood seemed running now, running hard, hunting, chasing, closing in round something or—somebody? In panic, he began to run too, aimlessly, he knew not whither. He ran up against things, he fell over things and  into things, he darted under things and dodged round things. At last he took refuge in the deep dark hollow of an old beech tree, which offered shelter, concealment—perhaps even safety, but who could tell? Anyhow, he was too tired to run any further, and could only snuggle down into the dry leaves which had drifted into the hollow and hope he was safe for a time. And as he lay there panting and trembling, and listened to the whistlings and the patterings outside, he knew it at last, in all its fullness, that dread thing which other little dwellers in field and hedgerow had encountered here, and known as their darkest moment—that thing which the Rat had vainly tried to shield him from—the Terror of the Wild Wood!

Meantime the Rat, warm and comfortable, dozed by his fireside. His paper of half-finished verses slipped from his knee, his head fell back, his mouth opened, and he wandered by the verdant banks of dream-rivers. Then a coal slipped, the fire crackled and sent up a spurt of flame, and he woke with a start. Remembering what he had been engaged upon, he reached down to the floor for his verses, pored over

them for a minute, and then looked round for the Mole to ask him if he knew a good rhyme for something or other.

But the Mole was not there.

He listened for a time. The house seemed very quiet.

Then he called "Moly!" several times, and, receiving no answer, got up and went out into the hall.

The Mole's cap was missing from its accustomed peg. His goloshes, which always lay by the umbrella-stand, were also gone.

The Rat left the house, and carefully examined the muddy surface of the ground outside, hoping to find the Mole's tracks. There they were, sure enough. The goloshes were new, just bought for the winter, and the pimples on their soles were fresh and sharp. He could see the imprints of them in the mud, running along straight and purposeful, leading direct to the Wild Wood.

The Rat looked very grave, and stood in deep thought for a minute or two. Then he re-entered the house, strapped a belt round his waist, shoved a brace of pistols into it, took up a stout cudgel that stood in a corner of the hall, and set off for the Wild Wood at a smart pace.

It was already getting towards dusk when he reached the first fringe of trees and plunged without hesitation into the wood, looking anxiously on either side for any sign of his friend. Here and there wicked little faces popped out of holes, but vanished immediately at sight of the valorous animal, his pistols, and the great ugly cudgel in his grasp; and the whistling and pattering, which he had heard quite plainly on his first entry, died away and ceased, and all was very still. He made his way manfully through the length of the wood, to its furthest edge; then, forsaking all paths, he set himself to traverse it, laboriously working over the whole ground, and all the time calling out cheerfully, "Moly, Moly, Moly! Where are you? It's me—it's old

Rat!"

He had patiently hunted through the wood for an hour or more, when at last to his joy he heard a little answering cry. Guiding himself by the sound, he made his way through the gathering darkness to the foot of an old beech tree, with a hole in it, and from out of the hole came a feeble voice, saying "Ratty! Is that really you?"

The Rat crept into the hollow, and there he found the Mole, exhausted and still trembling. "O Rat!" he cried, "I've been so frightened, you can't think!"

"O, I quite understand," said the Rat soothingly. "You shouldn't really have gone and done it, Mole. I did my best to keep you from it. We river-bankers, we hardly ever come here by ourselves. If we have to come, we come in couples, at least; then we're generally all right. Besides, there are a hundred things one has to know, which we understand all about and you don't, as yet. I mean passwords, and signs, and sayings which have power and effect, and plants you carry in your pocket, and verses you repeat, and dodges and tricks you practise; all simple enough when you know them, but they've got to be known if you're small, or you'll find yourself in trouble. Of course if you were Badger or Otter, it would be quite another matter."

"Surely the brave Mr. Toad wouldn't mind coming here by himself, would he?" inquired the Mole.

"Old Toad?" said the Rat, laughing heartily. "He wouldn't show his face here alone, not for a whole hatful of golden guineas, Toad wouldn't."

The Mole was greatly cheered by the sound of the Rat's careless laughter, as well as by the sight of his stick and his gleaming pistols, and he stopped shivering and began to feel bolder and more himself again.

"Now then," said the Rat presently, "we really must pull ourselves

together and make a start for home while there's still a little light left. It will never do to spend the night here, you understand. Too cold, for one thing."

"Dear Ratty," said the poor Mole, "I'm dreadfully sorry, but I'm simply dead beat and that's a solid fact. You **must** let me rest here a while longer, and get my strength back, if I'm to get home at all."

"O, all right," said the good-natured Rat, "rest away. It's pretty nearly pitch dark now, anyhow; and there ought to be a bit of a moon later."

So the Mole got well into the dry leaves and stretched himself out, and presently dropped off into sleep, though of a broken and troubled sort; while the Rat covered himself up, too, as best he might, for warmth, and lay patiently waiting, with a pistol in his paw.

When at last the Mole woke up, much refreshed and in his usual spirits, the Rat said, "Now then! I'll just take a look outside and see if everything's quiet, and then we really must be off."

He went to the entrance of their retreat and put his head out. Then the Mole heard him saying quietly to himself, "Hullo! hullo! here—is—a—go!"

"What's up, Ratty?" asked the Mole.

"**Snow** is up," replied the Rat briefly; "or rather, **down**. It's snowing hard."

The Mole came and crouched beside him, and, looking out, saw the wood that had been so dreadful to him in quite a changed aspect. Holes, hollows, pools, pitfalls, and other black menaces to the wayfarer were vanishing fast, and a gleaming carpet of faery was springing up everywhere, that looked too delicate to be trodden upon by rough feet. A fine powder filled the air and caressed the cheek with a tingle in its touch, and the black boles of the trees showed up in a light that seemed to come from below.

"Well, well, it can't be helped," said the Rat, after pondering. "We must make a start, and take our chance, I suppose. The worst of it is, I don't exactly know where we are. And now this snow makes everything look so very different."

It did indeed. The Mole would not have known that it was the same wood. However, they set out bravely, and took the line that seemed most promising, holding on to each other and pretending with invincible cheerfulness that they recognized an old friend in every fresh tree that grimly and silently greeted them, or saw openings, gaps, or paths with a familiar turn in them, in the monotony of white space and black tree-trunks that refused to vary.

An hour or two later—they had lost all count of time—they pulled up, dispirited, weary, and hopelessly at sea, and sat down on a fallen tree-trunk to recover their breath and consider what was to be done. They were aching with fatigue and bruised with tumbles; they had fallen into several holes and got wet through; the snow was getting so deep that they could hardly drag their little legs through it, and the trees were thicker and more like each other than ever. There seemed to be no end to this wood, and no beginning, and no difference in it, and, worst of all, no way out.

"We can't sit here very long," said the Rat. "We shall have to make another push for it, and do something or other. The cold is too awful for anything, and the snow will soon be too deep for us to wade through." He peered about him and considered. "Look here," he went on, "this is what occurs to me. There's a sort of dell down here in front of us, where the ground seems all hilly and humpy and hummocky. We'll make our way down into that, and try and find some sort of shelter, a cave or hole with a dry floor to it, out of the snow and the wind, and there we'll have a good rest before we try again, for we're both of us pretty dead beat. Besides, the snow may leave off, or

something may turn up."

So once more they got on their feet, and struggled down into the dell, where they hunted about for a cave or some corner that was dry and a protection from the keen wind and the whirling snow. They were investigating one of the hummocky bits the Rat had spoken of, when suddenly the Mole tripped up and fell forward on his face with a squeal.

"O my leg!" he cried. "O my poor shin!" and he sat up on the snow and nursed his leg in both his front paws.

"Poor old Mole!" said the Rat kindly.

"You don't seem to be having much luck to-day, do you? Let's have a look at the leg. Yes," he went on, going down on his knees to look, "you've cut your shin, sure enough. Wait till I get at my handkerchief, and I'll tie it up for you."

"I must have tripped over a hidden branch or a stump," said the Mole miserably. "O, my! O, my!"

"It's a very clean cut," said the Rat, examining it again attentively. "That was never done by a branch or a stump. Looks as if it was made by a sharp edge of something in metal. Funny!" He pondered awhile, and examined the humps and slopes that surrounded them.

"Well, never mind what done it," said the Mole, forgetting his grammar in his pain. "It hurts just the same, whatever done it."

But the Rat, after carefully tying up the leg with his handkerchief, had left him and was busy scraping in the snow. He scratched and shovelled and explored, all four legs working busily, while the Mole waited impatiently, remarking at intervals, "O, **come** on, Rat!"

Suddenly the Rat cried "Hooray!" and then "Hooray-oo-ray-oo-ray-oo-ray!" and fell to executing a feeble jig in the snow.

"What **have** you found, Ratty?" asked the Mole, still nursing his leg.

"Come and see!" said the delighted Rat, as he jigged on.

The Mole hobbled up to the spot and had a good look.

"Well," he said at last, slowly, "I SEE it right enough. Seen the same sort of thing before, lots of times. Familiar object, I call it. A door-scraper! Well, what of it? Why dance jigs around a door-scraper?"

"But don't you see what it **means**, you—you dull-witted animal?" cried the Rat impatiently.

"Of course I see what it means," replied the Mole. "It simply means that some VERY careless and forgetful person has left his door-scraper lying about in the middle of the Wild Wood, **just** where it's **sure** to trip **everybody** up. Very thoughtless of him, I call it. When I get home I shall go and complain about it to—to somebody or other, see if I don't!"

"O, dear! O, dear!" cried the Rat, in despair at his obtuseness. "Here, stop arguing and come and scrape!" And he set to work again and made the snow fly in all directions around him.

After some further toil his efforts were rewarded, and a very shabby door-mat lay exposed to view.

"There, what did I tell you?" exclaimed the Rat in great triumph.

"Absolutely nothing whatever," replied the Mole, with perfect truthfulness. "Well now," he went on, "you seem to have found another piece of domestic litter, done for and thrown away, and I suppose you're perfectly happy. Better go ahead and dance your jig round that if you've got to, and get it over, and then perhaps we can go on and not waste any more time over rubbish-heaps. Can we EAT a doormat? or sleep under a door-mat? Or sit on a door-mat and sledge home over the snow on it, you exasperating rodent?"

"Do—you—mean—to—say," cried the excited Rat, "that this door-mat doesn't **tell** you anything?"

"Really, Rat," said the Mole, quite pettishly, "I think we'd had enough of this folly. Who ever heard of a door-mat **telling** anyone anything? They simply don't do it. They are not that sort at all. Door-mats know their place."

"Now look here, you—you thick-headed beast," replied the Rat, really angry, "this must stop. Not another word, but scrape—scrape and scratch and dig and hunt round, especially on the sides of the hummocks, if you want to sleep dry and warm to-night, for it's our last chance!"

The Rat attacked a snow-bank beside them with ardour, probing with his cudgel everywhere and then digging with fury; and the Mole scraped busily too, more to oblige the Rat than for any other reason, for his opinion was that his friend was getting light-headed.

Some ten minutes' hard work, and the point of the Rat's cudgel struck something that sounded hollow. He worked till he could get a paw through and feel; then called the Mole to come and help him. Hard at it went the two animals, till at last the result of their labours stood full in view of the astonished and hitherto incredulous Mole.

In the side of what had seemed to be a snow-bank stood a solid-looking little door, painted a dark green. An iron bell-pull hung by the side, and below it, on a small brass plate, neatly engraved in square capital letters, they could read by the aid of moonlight

MR. BADGER.

The Mole fell backwards on the snow from sheer surprise and delight. "Rat!" he cried in penitence, "you're a wonder! A real wonder, that's what you are. I see it all now! You argued it out, step by step, in that wise head of yours, from the very moment that I fell and cut my shin, and you looked at the cut, and at once your majestic mind said to

itself, 'Door-scraper!' And then you turned to and found the very door-scraper that done it! Did you stop there? No. Some people would have been quite satisfied; but not you. Your intellect went on working. 'Let me only just find a door-mat,' says you to yourself, 'and my theory is proved!' And of course you found your door-mat. You're so clever, I believe you could find anything you liked. 'Now,' says you, 'that door exists, as plain as if I saw it. There's nothing else remains to be done but to find it!' Well, I've read about that sort of thing in books, but I've never come across it before in real life. You ought to go where you'll be properly appreciated. You're simply wasted here, among us fellows. If I only had your head, Ratty——"

"But as you haven't," interrupted the Rat, rather unkindly, "I suppose you're going to sit on the snow all night and **talk?** Get up at once and hang on to that bell-pull you see there, and ring hard, as hard as you can, while I hammer!"

While the Rat attacked the door with his stick, the Mole sprang up at the bell-pull, clutched it and swung there, both feet well off the ground, and from quite a long way off they could faintly hear a deep-toned bell respond.

IV.

MR. BADGER

THEY waited patiently for what seemed a very long time, stamping in the snow to keep their feet warm. At last they heard the sound of slow shuffling footsteps approaching the door from the inside. It seemed, as the Mole remarked to the Rat, like some one walking in carpet slippers that were too large for him and down at heel; which was intelligent of Mole, because that was exactly what it was.

There was the noise of a bolt shot back, and the door opened a few inches, enough to show a long snout and a pair of sleepy blinking eyes.

"Now, the **very** next time this happens," said a gruff and suspicious voice, "I shall be exceedingly angry. Who is it **this** time, disturbing people on such a night? Speak up!"

"Oh, Badger," cried the Rat, "let us in, please. It's me, Rat, and my friend Mole, and we've lost our way in the snow."

"What, Ratty, my dear little man!" exclaimed the Badger, in quite a different voice. "Come along in, both of you, at once. Why, you must be perished. Well I never! Lost in the snow! And in the Wild Wood, too, and at this time of night! But come in with you."

The two animals tumbled over each other in their eagerness to get inside, and heard the door shut behind them with great joy and

relief.

The Badger, who wore a long dressing-gown, and whose slippers were indeed very down at heel, carried a flat candlestick in his paw and had probably been on his way to bed when their summons sounded. He looked kindly down on them and patted both their heads. "This is not the sort of night for small animals to be out," he said paternally. "I'm afraid you've been up to some of your pranks again, Ratty. But come along; come into the kitchen. There's a first-rate fire there, and supper and

everything."

He shuffled on in front of them, carrying the light, and they followed him, nudging each other in an anticipating sort of way, down a long, gloomy, and, to tell the truth, decidedly shabby passage, into a sort of a central hall; out of which they could dimly see other long tunnel-like passages branching, passages mysterious and without apparent end. But there were doors in the hall as well—stout oaken comfortable-looking doors. One of these the Badger flung open, and at once they found themselves in all the glow and warmth of a large fire-lit kitchen.

The floor was well-worn red brick, and on the wide hearth burnt a fire of logs, between two attractive chimney-corners tucked away in the wall, well out of any suspicion of draught. A couple of high-backed settles, facing each other on either side of the fire, gave further sitting accommodations for the sociably disposed. In the middle of the room stood a long table of plain boards placed on trestles, with benches down each side. At one end of it, where an arm-chair stood pushed back, were spread the remains of the Badger's plain but ample supper. Rows of spotless plates winked from the shelves of the dresser at the far end of the room, and from the rafters overhead hung hams, bundles of dried herbs, nets of onions, and baskets of

eggs. It seemed a place where heroes could fitly feast after victory, where weary harvesters could line up in scores along the table and keep their Harvest Home with mirth and song, or where two or three friends of simple tastes could sit about as they pleased and eat and smoke and talk in comfort and contentment. The ruddy brick floor smiled up at the smoky ceiling; the oaken settles, shiny with long wear, exchanged cheerful glances with each other; plates on the dresser grinned at pots on the shelf, and the merry firelight flickered and played over everything without distinction.

The kindly Badger thrust them down on a settle to toast themselves at the fire, and bade them remove their wet coats and boots. Then he fetched them dressing-gowns and slippers, and himself bathed the Mole's shin with warm water and mended the cut with sticking-plaster till the whole thing was just as good as new, if not better. In the embracing light and warmth, warm and dry at last, with weary legs propped up in front of them, and a suggestive clink of plates being arranged on the table behind, it seemed to the storm-driven animals, now in safe anchorage, that the cold and trackless Wild Wood just left outside was miles and miles away, and all that they had suffered in it a half-forgotten dream.

When at last they were thoroughly toasted, the Badger summoned them to the table, where he had been busy laying a repast. They had felt pretty hungry before, but when they actually saw at last the supper that was spread for them, really it seemed only a question of what they should attack first where all was so attractive, and whether the other things would obligingly wait for them till they had time to give them attention. Conversation was impossible for a long time; and when it was slowly resumed, it was that regrettable sort of conversation that results from talking with your mouth full. The Badger did not mind that sort of thing at all, nor did he take any

notice of elbows on the table, or everybody speaking at once. As he did not go into Society himself, he had got an idea that these things belonged to the things that didn't really matter. (We know of course that he was wrong, and took too narrow a view; because they do matter very much, though it would take too long to explain why.) He sat in his arm-chair at the head of the table, and nodded gravely at intervals as the animals told their story; and he did not seem surprised or shocked at anything, and he never said, "I told you so," or, "Just what I always said," or remarked that they ought to have done so-and-so, or ought not to have done something else. The Mole began to feel very friendly towards him.

When supper was really finished at last, and each animal felt that his skin was now as tight as was decently safe, and that by this time he didn't care a hang for anybody or anything, they gathered round the glowing embers of the great wood fire, and thought how jolly it was to be sitting up **so** late, and **so** independent, and **so** full; and after they had chatted for a time about things in general, the Badger said heartily, "Now then! tell us the news from your part of the world. How's old Toad going on?"

"Oh, from bad to worse," said the Rat gravely, while the Mole, cocked up on a settle and basking in the firelight, his heels higher than his head, tried to look properly mournful. "Another smash-up only last week, and a bad one. You see, he will insist on driving himself, and he's hopelessly incapable. If he'd only employ a decent, steady, well-trained animal, pay him good wages, and leave everything to him, he'd get on all right. But no; he's convinced he's a heaven-born driver, and nobody can teach him anything; and all the rest follows."

"How many has he had?" inquired the Badger gloomily.

"Smashes, or machines?" asked the Rat. "Oh, well, after all, it's the same thing—with Toad. This is the seventh. As for the others—

you know that coach-house of his? Well, it's piled up—literally piled up to the roof—with fragments of motor-cars, none of them bigger than your hat! That accounts for the other six—so far as they can be accounted for."

"He's been in hospital three times," put in the Mole; "and as for the fines he's had to pay, it's simply awful to think of."

"Yes, and that's part of the trouble," continued the Rat. "Toad's rich, we all know; but he's not a millionaire. And he's a hopelessly bad driver, and quite regardless of law and order. Killed or ruined—it's got to be one of the two things, sooner or later. Badger! we're his friends—oughtn't we to do something?"

The Badger went through a bit of hard thinking. "Now look here!" he said at last, rather severely; "of course you know I can't do anything **now?**"

His two friends assented, quite understanding his point. No animal, according to the rules of animal-etiquette, is ever expected to do anything strenuous, or heroic, or even moderately active during the off-season of winter. All are sleepy—some actually asleep. All are weather-bound, more or less; and all are resting from arduous days and nights, during which every muscle in them has been severely tested, and every energy kept at full stretch.

"Very well then!" continued the Badger. "**But**, when once the year has really turned, and the nights are shorter, and halfway through them one rouses and feels fidgety and wanting to be up and doing by sunrise, if not before—**you** know!——"

Both animals nodded gravely. **They** knew!

"Well, **then,**" went on the Badger, "we—that is, you and me and our friend the Mole here—we'll take Toad seriously in hand. We'll stand no nonsense whatever. We'll bring him back to reason, by force if need be. We'll **make** him be a sensible Toad. We'll—you're asleep,

Rat!"

"Not me!" said the Rat, waking up with a jerk.

"He's been asleep two or three times since supper," said the Mole, laughing. He himself was feeling quite wakeful and even lively, though he didn't know why. The reason was, of course, that he being naturally an underground animal by birth and breeding, the situation of Badger's house exactly suited him and made him feel at home; while the Rat, who slept every night in a bedroom the windows of which opened on a breezy river, naturally felt the atmosphere still and oppressive.

"Well, it's time we were all in bed," said the Badger, getting up and fetching flat candlesticks. "Come along, you two, and I'll show you your quarters. And take your time tomorrow morning—breakfast at any hour you please!"

He conducted the two animals to a long room that seemed half bedchamber and half loft. The Badger's winter stores, which indeed were visible everywhere, took up half the room—piles of apples, turnips, and potatoes, baskets full of nuts, and jars of honey; but the two little white beds on the remainder of the floor looked soft and inviting, and the linen on them, though coarse, was clean and smelt beautifully of lavender; and the Mole and the Water Rat, shaking off their garments in some thirty seconds, tumbled in between the sheets in great joy and contentment.

In accordance with the kindly Badger's injunctions, the two tired animals came down to breakfast very late next morning, and found a bright fire burning in the kitchen, and two young hedgehogs sitting on a bench at the table, eating oatmeal porridge out of wooden bowls. The hedgehogs dropped their spoons, rose to their feet, and ducked their heads respectfully as the two entered.

"There, sit down, sit down," said the Rat pleasantly, "and go on

with your porridge. Where have you youngsters come from? Lost your way in the snow, I suppose?"

"Yes, please, sir," said the elder of the two hedgehogs respectfully. "Me and little Billy here, we was trying to find our way to school—mother **would** have us go, was the weather ever so—and of course we lost ourselves, sir, and Billy he got frightened and took and cried, being young and faint-hearted. And at last we happened up against Mr. Badger's back door, and made so bold as to knock, sir, for Mr. Badger he's a kind-hearted gentleman, as everyone knows——"

"I understand," said the Rat, cutting himself some rashers from a side of bacon, while the Mole dropped some eggs into a saucepan. "And what's the weather like outside? You needn't 'sir' me quite so much?" he added.

"O, terrible bad, sir, terrible deep the snow is," said the hedgehog. "No getting out for the likes of you gentlemen to-day."

"Where's Mr. Badger?" inquired the Mole, as he warmed the coffee-pot before the fire.

"The master's gone into his study, sir," replied the hedgehog, "and he said as how he was going to be particular busy this morning, and on no account was he to be disturbed."

This explanation, of course, was thoroughly understood by every one present. The fact is, as already set forth, when you live a life of intense activity for six months in the year, and of comparative or actual somnolence for the other six, during the latter period you cannot be continually pleading sleepiness when there are people about or things to be done. The excuse gets monotonous. The animals well knew that Badger, having eaten a hearty breakfast, had retired to his study and settled himself in an arm-chair with his legs up on another and a red cotton handkerchief over his face, and was being "busy" in the usual way at this time of the year.

The front-door bell clanged loudly, and the Rat, who was very greasy with buttered toast, sent Billy, the smaller hedgehog, to see who it might be. There was a sound of much stamping in the hall, and presently Billy returned in front of the Otter, who threw himself on the Rat with an embrace and a shout of affectionate greeting.

"Get off!" spluttered the Rat, with his mouth full.

"Thought I should find you here all right," said the Otter cheerfully. "They were all in a great state of alarm along River Bank when I arrived this morning. Rat never been home all night—nor Mole either—something dreadful must have happened, they said; and the snow had covered up all your tracks, of course. But I knew that when people were in any fix they mostly went to Badger, or else Badger got to know of it somehow, so I came straight off here, through the Wild Wood and the snow! My! it was fine, coming through the snow as the red sun was rising and showing against the black tree-trunks! As you went along in the stillness, every now and then masses of snow slid off the branches suddenly with a flop! making you jump and run for cover. Snow-castles and snow-caverns had sprung up out of nowhere in the night—and snow bridges, terraces, ramparts—I could have stayed and played with them for hours. Here and there great branches had been torn away by the sheer weight of the snow, and robins perched and hopped on them in their perky conceited way, just as if they had done it themselves. A ragged string of wild geese passed overhead, high on the grey sky, and a few rooks whirled over the trees, inspected, and flapped off homewards with a disgusted expression; but I met no sensible being to ask the news of. About halfway across I came on a rabbit sitting on a stump, cleaning his silly face with his paws. He was a pretty scared animal when I crept up behind him and placed a heavy forepaw on his shoulder. I had to cuff his head once or twice to get any sense out of

it at all. At last I managed to extract from him that Mole had been seen in the Wild Wood last night by one of them. It was the talk of the burrows, he said, how Mole, Mr. Rat's particular friend, was in a bad fix; how he had lost his way, and 'They' were up and out hunting, and were chivvying him round and round. 'Then why didn't any of you **do** something?' I asked. 'You mayn't be blest with brains, but there are hundreds and hundreds of you, big, stout fellows, as fat as butter, and your burrows running in all directions, and you could have taken him in and made him safe and comfortable, or tried to, at all events.' 'What, **us**?' he merely said: 'do something? us rabbits?' So I cuffed him again and left him. There was nothing else to be done. At any rate, I had learnt something; and if I had had the luck to meet any of 'Them' I'd have learnt something more—or **they** would."

"Weren't you at all—er—nervous?" asked the Mole, some of yesterday's terror coming back to him at the mention of the Wild Wood.

"Nervous?" The Otter showed a gleaming set of strong white teeth as he laughed. "I'd give 'em nerves if any of them tried anything on with me. Here, Mole, fry me some slices of ham, like the good little chap you are. I'm frightfully hungry, and I've got any amount to say to Ratty here. Haven't seen him for an age."

So the good-natured Mole, having cut some slices of ham, set the hedgehogs to fry it, and returned to his own breakfast, while the Otter and the Rat, their heads together, eagerly talked river-shop, which is long shop and talk that is endless, running on like the babbling river itself.

A plate of fried ham had just been cleared and sent back for more, when the Badger entered, yawning and rubbing his eyes, and greeted them all in his quiet, simple way, with kind enquiries for every one. "It must be getting on for luncheon time," he remarked to the

Otter. "Better stop and have it with us. You must be hungry, this cold morning."

"Rather!" replied the Otter, winking at the Mole. "The sight of these greedy young hedgehogs stuffing themselves with fried ham makes me feel positively famished."

The hedgehogs, who were just beginning to feel hungry again after their porridge, and after working so hard at their frying, looked timidly up at Mr. Badger, but were too shy to say anything.

"Here, you two youngsters be off home to your mother," said the Badger kindly. "I'll send some one with you to show you the way. You won't want any dinner to-day, I'll be bound."

He gave them sixpence apiece and a pat on the head, and they went off with much respectful swinging of caps and touching of forelocks.

Presently they all sat down to luncheon together. The Mole found himself placed next to Mr. Badger, and, as the other two were still deep in river-gossip from which nothing could divert them, he took the opportunity to tell Badger how comfortable and home-like it all felt to him. "Once well underground," he said, "you know exactly where you are. Nothing can happen to you, and nothing can get at you. You're entirely your own master, and you don't have to consult anybody or mind what they say. Things go on all the same overhead, and you let 'em, and don't bother about 'em. When you want to, up you go, and there the things are, waiting for you."

The Badger simply beamed on him. "That's exactly what I say," he replied. "There's no security, or peace and tranquillity, except underground. And then, if your ideas get larger and you want to expand—why, a dig and a scrape, and there you are! If you feel your house is a bit too big, you stop up a hole or two, and there you are again! No builders, no tradesmen, no remarks passed on you by

fellows looking over your wall, and, above all, no **weather**. Look at Rat, now. A couple of feet of flood water, and he's got to move into hired lodgings; uncomfortable, inconveniently situated, and horribly expensive. Take Toad. I say nothing against Toad Hall; quite the best house in these parts, **as** a house. But supposing a fire breaks out—where's Toad? Supposing tiles are blown off, or walls sink or crack, or windows get broken—where's Toad? Supposing the rooms are draughty—I **hate** a draught myself—where's Toad? No, up and out of doors is good enough to roam about and get one's living in; but underground to come back to at last—that's my idea of **home!**"

The Mole assented heartily; and the Badger in consequence got very friendly with him. "When lunch is over," he said, "I'll take you all round this little place of mine. I can see you'll appreciate it. You understand what domestic architecture ought to be, you do."

After luncheon, accordingly, when the other two had settled themselves into the chimney-corner and had started a heated argument on the subject of **eels**, the Badger lighted a lantern and bade the Mole follow him. Crossing the hall, they passed down one of the principal tunnels, and the wavering light of the lantern gave glimpses on either side of rooms both large and small, some mere cupboards, others nearly as broad and imposing as Toad's dining-hall. A narrow passage at right angles led them into another corridor, and here the same thing was repeated. The Mole was staggered at the size, the extent, the ramifications of it all; at the length of the dim passages, the solid vaultings of the crammed store-chambers, the masonry everywhere, the pillars, the arches, the pavements. "How on earth, Badger," he said at last, "did you ever find time and strength to do all this? It's astonishing!"

"It **would** be astonishing indeed," said the Badger simply, "if I **had** done it. But as a matter of fact I did none of it—only cleaned

out the passages and chambers, as far as I had need of them. There's lots more of it, all round about. I see you don't understand, and I must explain it to you. Well, very long ago, on the spot where the Wild Wood waves now, before ever it had planted itself and grown up to what it now is, there was a city—a city of people, you know. Here, where we are standing, they lived, and walked, and talked, and slept, and carried on their business. Here they stabled their horses and feasted, from here they rode out to fight or drove out to trade. They were a powerful people, and rich, and great builders. They built to last, for they thought their city would last for ever."

"But what has become of them all?" asked the Mole.

"Who can tell?" said the Badger. "People come—they stay for a while, they flourish, they build—and they go. It is their way. But we remain. There were badgers here, I've been told, long before that same city ever came to be. And now there are badgers here again. We are an enduring lot, and we may move out for a time, but we wait, and are patient, and back we come. And so it will ever be."

"Well, and when they went at last, those people?" said the Mole.

"When they went," continued the Badger, "the strong winds and persistent rains took the matter in hand, patiently, ceaselessly, year after year. Perhaps we badgers too, in our small way, helped a little— who knows? It was all down, down, down, gradually—ruin and levelling and disappearance. Then it was all up, up, up, gradually, as seeds grew to saplings, and saplings to forest trees, and bramble and fern came creeping in to help. Leaf-mould rose and obliterated, streams in their winter freshets brought sand and soil to clog and to cover, and in course of time our home was ready for us again, and we moved in. Up above us, on the surface, the same thing happened. Animals arrived, liked the look of the place, took up their quarters, settled down, spread, and flourished. They didn't bother themselves

about the past—they never do; they're too busy. The place was a bit humpy and hillocky, naturally, and full of holes; but that was rather an advantage. And they don't bother about the future, either—the future when perhaps the people will move in again—for a time—as may very well be. The Wild Wood is pretty well populated by now; with all the usual lot, good, bad, and indifferent—I name no names. It takes all sorts to make a world. But I fancy you know something about them yourself by this time."

"I do indeed," said the Mole, with a slight shiver.

"Well, well," said the Badger, patting him on the shoulder, "it was your first experience of them, you see. They're not so bad really; and we must all live and let live. But I'll pass the word around to-morrow, and I think you'll have no further trouble. Any friend of **mine** walks where he likes in this country, or I'll know the reason why!"

When they got back to the kitchen again, they found the Rat walking up and down, very restless. The underground atmosphere was oppressing him and getting on his nerves, and he seemed really to be afraid that the river would run away if he wasn't there to look after it. So he had his overcoat on, and his pistols thrust into his belt again. "Come along, Mole," he said anxiously, as soon as he caught sight of them. "We must get off while it's daylight. Don't want to spend another night in the Wild Wood again."

"It'll be all right, my fine fellow," said the Otter. "I'm coming along with you, and I know every path blindfold; and if there's a head that needs to be punched, you can confidently rely upon me to punch it."

"You really needn't fret, Ratty," added the Badger placidly. "My passages run further than you think, and I've bolt-holes to the edge of the wood in several directions, though I don't care for everybody to know about them. When you really have to go, you shall leave by one

of my short cuts. Meantime, make yourself easy, and sit down again."

The Rat was nevertheless still anxious to be off and attend to his river, so the Badger, taking up his lantern again, led the way along a damp and airless tunnel that wound and dipped, part vaulted, part hewn through solid rock, for a weary distance that seemed to be miles. At last daylight began to show itself confusedly through tangled growth overhanging the mouth of the passage; and the Badger, bidding them a hasty good-bye, pushed them hurriedly through the opening, made everything look as natural as possible again, with creepers, brushwood, and dead leaves, and retreated.

They found themselves standing on the very edge of the Wild Wood. Rocks and brambles and tree-roots behind them, confusedly heaped and tangled; in front, a great space of quiet fields, hemmed by lines of hedges black on the snow, and, far ahead, a glint of the familiar old river, while the wintry sun hung red and low on the horizon. The Otter, as knowing all the paths, took charge of the party, and they trailed out on a bee-line for a distant stile. Pausing there a moment and looking back, they saw the whole mass of the Wild Wood, dense, menacing, compact, grimly set in vast white surroundings; simultaneously they turned and made swiftly for home, for firelight and the familiar things it played on, for the voice, sounding cheerily outside their window, of the river that they knew and trusted in all its moods, that never made them afraid with any amazement.

As he hurried along, eagerly anticipating the moment when he would be at home again among the things he knew and liked, the Mole saw clearly that he was an animal of tilled field and hedge-row, linked to the ploughed furrow, the frequented pasture, the lane of evening lingerings, the cultivated garden-plot. For others the asperities, the stubborn endurance, or the clash of actual conflict, that went with

Nature in the rough; he must be wise, must keep to the pleasant places in which his lines were laid and which held adventure enough, in their way, to last for a lifetime.

V.

DULCE DOMUM

The sheep ran huddling together against the hurdles, blowing out thin nostrils and stamping with delicate fore-feet, their heads thrown back and a light steam rising from the crowded sheep-pen into the frosty air, as the two animals hastened by in high spirits, with much chatter and laughter. They were returning across country after a long day's outing with Otter, hunting and exploring on the wide uplands where certain streams tributary to their own River had their first small beginnings; and the shades of the short winter day were closing in on them, and they had still some distance to go. Plodding at random across the plough, they had heard the sheep and had made for them; and now, leading from the sheep-pen, they found a beaten track that made walking a lighter business, and responded, moreover, to that small inquiring something which all animals carry inside them, saying unmistakably, "Yes, quite right; **this** leads home!"

"It looks as if we were coming to a village," said the Mole somewhat dubiously, slackening his pace, as the track, that had in time become a path and then had developed into a lane, now handed them over to the charge of a well-metalled road. The animals did not hold with villages, and their own highways, thickly frequented as they were, took an independent course, regardless of church, post office, or public-house.

"Oh, never mind!" said the Rat. "At this season of the year they're all safe indoors by this time, sitting round the fire; men,

women, and children, dogs and cats and all. We shall slip through all right, without any bother or unpleasantness, and we can have a look at them through their windows if you like, and see what they're doing."

The rapid nightfall of mid-December had quite beset the little village as they approached it on soft feet over a first thin fall of powdery snow. Little was visible but squares of a dusky orange-red on either side of the street, where the firelight or lamplight of each cottage overflowed through the casements into the dark world without. Most of the low latticed windows were innocent of blinds, and to the lookers-in from outside, the inmates, gathered round the tea-table, absorbed in handiwork, or talking with laughter and gesture, had each that happy grace which is the last thing the skilled actor shall capture—the natural grace which goes with perfect unconsciousness of observation. Moving at will from one theatre to another, the two spectators, so far from home themselves, had something of wistfulness in their eyes as they watched a cat being stroked, a sleepy child picked up and huddled off to bed, or a tired man stretch and knock out his pipe on the end of a smouldering log.

But it was from one little window, with its blind drawn down, a mere blank transparency on the night, that the sense of home and the little curtained world within walls—the larger stressful world of outside Nature shut out and forgotten—most pulsated. Close against the white blind hung a bird-cage, clearly silhouetted, every wire, perch, and appurtenance distinct and recognisable, even to yesterday's dull-edged lump of sugar. On the middle perch the fluffy occupant, head tucked well into feathers, seemed so near to them as to be easily stroked, had they tried; even the delicate tips of his plumped-out plumage pencilled plainly on the illuminated screen. As they looked, the sleepy little fellow stirred uneasily, woke, shook himself, and raised his head. They could see the gape of his tiny beak as he yawned in a

bored sort of way, looked round, and then settled his head into his back again, while the ruffled feathers gradually subsided into perfect stillness. Then a gust of bitter wind took them in the back of the neck, a small sting of frozen sleet on the skin woke them as from a dream, and they knew their toes to be cold and their legs tired, and their own home distant a weary way.

Once beyond the village, where the cottages ceased abruptly, on either side of the road they could smell through the darkness the friendly fields again; and they braced themselves for the last long stretch, the home stretch, the stretch that we know is bound to end, some time, in the rattle of the door-latch, the sudden firelight, and the sight of familiar things greeting us as long-absent travellers from far over-sea. They plodded along steadily and silently, each of them thinking his own thoughts. The Mole's ran a good deal on supper, as it was pitch-dark, and it was all a strange country for him as far as he knew, and he was following obediently in the wake of the Rat, leaving the guidance entirely to him. As for the Rat, he was walking a little way ahead, as his habit was, his shoulders humped, his eyes fixed on the straight grey road in front of him; so he did not notice poor Mole when suddenly the summons reached him, and took him like an electric shock.

We others, who have long lost the more subtle of the physical senses, have not even proper terms to express an animal's inter-communications with his surroundings, living or otherwise, and have only the word "smell," for instance, to include the whole range of delicate thrills which murmur in the nose of the animal night and day, summoning, warning, inciting, repelling. It was one of these mysterious fairy calls from out the void that suddenly reached Mole in the darkness, making him tingle through and through with its very familiar appeal, even while yet he could not clearly remember what it

was. He stopped dead in his tracks, his nose searching hither and thither in its efforts to recapture the fine filament, the telegraphic current, that had so strongly moved him. A moment, and he had caught it again; and with it this time came recollection in fullest flood.

Home! That was what they meant, those caressing appeals, those soft touches wafted through the air, those invisible little hands pulling and tugging, all one way! Why, it must be quite close by him at that moment, his old home that he had hurriedly forsaken and never sought again, that day when he first found the river! And now it was sending out its scouts and its messengers to capture him and bring him in. Since his escape on that bright morning he had hardly given it a thought, so absorbed had he been in his new life, in all its pleasures, its surprises, its fresh and captivating experiences. Now, with a rush of old memories, how clearly it stood up before him, in the darkness! Shabby indeed, and small and poorly furnished, and yet his, the home he had made for himself, the home he had been so happy to get back to after his day's work. And the home had been happy with him, too, evidently, and was missing him, and wanted him back, and was telling him so, through his nose, sorrowfully, reproachfully, but with no bitterness or anger; only with plaintive reminder that it was there, and wanted him.

The call was clear, the summons was plain. He must obey it instantly, and go. "Ratty!" he called, full of joyful excitement, "hold on! Come back! I want you, quick!"

"Oh, **come** along, Mole, do!" replied the Rat cheerfully, still plodding along.

"**Please** stop, Ratty!" pleaded the poor Mole, in anguish of heart. "You don't understand! It's my home, my old home! I've just come across the smell of it, and it's close by here, really quite close. And I **must** go to it, I must, I must! Oh, come back, Ratty! Please,

please come back!"

The Rat was by this time very far ahead, too far to hear clearly what the Mole was calling, too far to catch the sharp note of painful appeal in his voice. And he was much taken up with the weather, for he too could smell something—something suspiciously like approaching snow.

"Mole, we mustn't stop now, really!" he called back. "We'll come for it to-morrow, whatever it is you've found. But I daren't stop now—it's late, and the snow's coming on again, and I'm not sure of the way! And I want your nose, Mole, so come on quick, there's a good fellow!" And the Rat pressed forward on his way without waiting for an answer.

Poor Mole stood alone in the road, his heart torn asunder, and a big sob gathering, gathering, somewhere low down inside him, to leap up to the surface presently, he knew, in passionate escape. But even under such a test as this his loyalty to his friend stood firm. Never for a moment did he dream of abandoning him. Meanwhile, the wafts from his old home pleaded, whispered, conjured, and finally claimed him imperiously. He dared not tarry longer within their magic circle. With a wrench that tore his very heartstrings he set his face down the road and followed submissively in the track of the Rat, while faint, thin little smells, still dogging his retreating nose, reproached him for his new friendship and his callous forgetfulness.

With an effort he caught up to the unsuspecting Rat, who began chattering cheerfully about what they would do when they got back, and how jolly a fire of logs in the parlour would be, and what a supper he meant to eat; never noticing his companion's silence and distressful state of mind. At last, however, when they had gone some considerable way further, and were passing some tree-stumps at the edge of a copse that bordered the road, he stopped and said kindly,

"Look here, Mole old chap, you seem dead tired. No talk left in you, and your feet dragging like lead. We'll sit down here for a minute and rest. The snow has held off so far, and the best part of our journey is over."

The Mole subsided forlornly on a tree-stump and tried to control himself, for he felt it surely coming. The sob he had fought with so long refused to be beaten. Up and up, it forced its way to the air, and then another, and another, and others thick and fast; till poor Mole at last gave up the struggle, and cried freely and helplessly and openly, now that he knew it was all over and he had lost what he could hardly be said to have found.

The Rat, astonished and dismayed at the violence of Mole's paroxysm of grief, did not dare to speak for a while. At last he said, very quietly and sympathetically, "What is it, old fellow? Whatever can be the matter? Tell us your trouble, and let me see what I can do."

Poor Mole found it difficult to get any words out between the upheavals of his chest that followed one upon another so quickly and held back speech and choked it as it came. "I know it's a—shabby, dingy little place," he sobbed forth at last, brokenly: "not like—your cosy quarters—or Toad's beautiful hall—or Badger's great house—but it was my own little home—and I was fond of it—and I went away and forgot all about it—and then I smelt it suddenly—on the road, when I called and you wouldn't listen, Rat—and everything came back to me with a rush—and I **wanted** it!—O dear, O dear!—and when you **wouldn't** turn back, Ratty—and I had to leave it, though I was smelling it all the time—I thought my heart would break.—We might have just gone and had one look at it, Ratty—only one look—it was close by—but you wouldn't turn back, Ratty, you wouldn't turn back! O dear, O dear!"

Recollection brought fresh waves of sorrow, and sobs again took

full charge of him, preventing further speech.

The Rat stared straight in front of him, saying nothing, only patting Mole gently on the shoulder. After a time he muttered gloomily, "I see it all now! What a **pig** I have been! A pig—that's me! Just a pig—a plain pig!"

He waited till Mole's sobs became gradually less stormy and more rhythmical; he waited till at last sniffs were frequent and sobs only intermittent. Then he rose from his seat, and, remarking carelessly, "Well, now we'd really better be getting on, old chap!" set off up the road again, over the toilsome way they had come.

"Wherever are you (hic) going to (hic), Ratty?" cried the tearful Mole, looking up in alarm.

"We're going to find that home of yours, old fellow," replied the Rat pleasantly; "so you had better come along, for it will take some finding, and we shall want your nose."

"Oh, come back, Ratty, do!" cried the Mole, getting up and hurrying after him. "It's no good, I tell you! It's too late, and too dark, and the place is too far off, and the snow's coming! And—and I never meant to let you know I was feeling that way about it—it was all an accident and a mistake! And think of River Bank, and your supper!"

"Hang River Bank, and supper too!" said the Rat heartily. "I tell you, I'm going to find this place now, if I stay out all night. So cheer up, old chap, and take my arm, and we'll very soon be back there again."

Still snuffling, pleading, and reluctant, Mole suffered himself to be dragged back along the road by his imperious companion, who by a flow of cheerful talk and anecdote endeavoured to beguile his spirits back and make the weary way seem shorter. When at last it seemed to the Rat that they must be nearing that part of the road where the Mole had been "held up," he said, "Now, no more talking. Business!

Use your nose, and give your mind to it."

They moved on in silence for some little way, when suddenly the Rat was conscious, through his arm that was linked in Mole's, of a faint sort of electric thrill that was passing down that animal's body. Instantly he disengaged himself, fell back a pace, and waited, all attention.

The signals were coming through!

Mole stood a moment rigid, while his uplifted nose, quivering slightly, felt the air.

Then a short, quick run forward—a fault—a check—a try back; and then a slow, steady, confident advance.

The Rat, much excited, kept close to his heels as the Mole, with something of the air of a sleep-walker, crossed a dry ditch, scrambled through a hedge, and nosed his way over a field open and trackless and bare in the faint starlight.

Suddenly, without giving warning, he dived; but the Rat was on the alert, and promptly followed him down the tunnel to which his unerring nose had faithfully led him.

It was close and airless, and the earthy smell was strong, and it seemed a long time to Rat ere the passage ended and he could stand erect and stretch and shake himself. The Mole struck a match, and by its light the Rat saw that they were standing in an open space, neatly swept and sanded underfoot, and directly facing them was Mole's little front door, with "Mole End" painted, in Gothic lettering, over the bell-pull at the side.

Mole reached down a lantern from a nail on the wall and lit it... and the Rat, looking round him, saw that they were in a sort of fore-court. A garden-seat stood on one side of the door, and on the other a roller; for the Mole, who was a tidy animal when at home, could not stand having his ground kicked up by other animals into little runs

that ended in earth-heaps. On the walls hung wire baskets with ferns in them, alternating with brackets carrying plaster statuary—Garibaldi, and the infant Samuel, and Queen Victoria, and other heroes of modern Italy. Down on one side of the forecourt ran a skittle-alley, with benches along it and little wooden tables marked with rings that hinted at beer-mugs. In the middle was a small round pond containing gold-fish and surrounded by a cockle-shell border. Out of the centre of the pond rose a fanciful erection clothed in more cockle-shells and topped by a large silvered glass ball that reflected everything all wrong and had a very pleasing effect.

Mole's face-beamed at the sight of all these objects so dear to him, and he hurried Rat through the door, lit a lamp in the hall, and took one glance round his old home. He saw the dust lying thick on everything, saw the cheerless, deserted look of the long-neglected house, and its narrow, meagre dimensions, its worn and shabby contents—and collapsed again on a hall-chair, his nose to his paws. "O Ratty!" he cried dismally, "why ever did I do it? Why did I bring you to this poor, cold little place, on a night like this, when you might have been at River Bank by this time, toasting your toes before a blazing fire, with all your own nice things about you!"

The Rat paid no heed to his doleful self-reproaches. He was running here and there, opening doors, inspecting rooms and cupboards, and lighting lamps and candles and sticking them, up everywhere. "What a capital little house this is!" he called out cheerily. "So compact! So well planned! Everything here and everything in its place! We'll make a jolly night of it. The first thing we want is a good fire; I'll see to that—I always know where to find things. So this is the parlour? Splendid! Your own idea, those little sleeping-bunks in the wall? Capital! Now, I'll fetch the wood and the coals, and you get a duster, Mole—you'll find one in the drawer of the kitchen table—and

try and smarten things up a bit. Bustle about, old chap!"

Encouraged by his inspiriting companion, the Mole roused himself and dusted and polished with energy and heartiness, while the Rat, running to and fro with armfuls of fuel, soon had a cheerful blaze roaring up the chimney. He hailed the Mole to come and warm himself; but Mole promptly had another fit of the blues, dropping down on a couch in dark despair and burying his face in his duster. "Rat," he moaned, "how about your supper, you poor, cold, hungry, weary animal? I've nothing to give you—nothing—not a crumb!"

"What a fellow you are for giving in!" said the Rat reproachfully. "Why, only just now I saw a sardine-opener on the kitchen dresser, quite distinctly; and everybody knows that means there are sardines about somewhere in the neighbourhood. Rouse yourself! pull yourself together, and come with me and forage."

They went and foraged accordingly, hunting through every cupboard and turning out every drawer. The result was not so very depressing after all, though of course it might have been better; a tin of sardines—a box of captain's biscuits, nearly full—and a German sausage encased in silver paper.

"There's a banquet for you!" observed the Rat, as he arranged the table. "I know some animals who would give their ears to be sitting down to supper with us to-night!"

"No bread!" groaned the Mole dolorously; "no butter, no——"

"No **pâté de foie gras**, no champagne!" continued the Rat, grinning. "And that reminds me—what's that little door at the end of the passage? Your cellar, of course! Every luxury in this house! Just you wait a minute."

He made for the cellar-door, and presently reappeared, somewhat dusty, with a bottle of beer in each paw and another under each arm, "Self-indulgent beggar you seem to be, Mole," he observed.

"Deny yourself nothing. This is really the jolliest little place I ever was in. Now, wherever did you pick up those prints? Make the place look so home-like, they do. No wonder you're so fond of it, Mole. Tell us all about it, and how you came to make it what it is."

Then, while the Rat busied himself fetching plates, and knives and forks, and mustard which he mixed in an egg-cup, the Mole, his bosom still heaving with the stress of his recent emotion, related—somewhat shyly at first, but with more freedom as he warmed to his subject—how this was planned, and how that was thought out, and how this was got through a windfall from an aunt, and that was a wonderful find and a bargain, and this other thing was bought out of laborious savings and a certain amount of "going without." His spirits finally quite restored, he must needs go and caress his possessions, and take a lamp and show off their points to his visitor and expatiate on them, quite forgetful of the supper they both so much needed; Rat, who was desperately hungry but strove to conceal it, nodding seriously, examining with a puckered brow, and saying, "wonderful," and "most remarkable," at intervals, when the chance for an observation was given him.

At last the Rat succeeded in decoying him to the table, and had just got seriously to work with the sardine-opener when sounds were heard from the fore-court without—sounds like the scuffling of small feet in the gravel and a confused murmur of tiny voices, while broken sentences reached them—"Now, all in a line—hold the lantern up a bit, Tommy—clear your throats first—no coughing after I say one, two, three.—Where's young Bill?—Here, come on, do, we're all a-waiting——"

"What's up?" inquired the Rat, pausing in his labours.

"I think it must be the field-mice," replied the Mole, with a touch of pride in his manner. "They go round carol-singing regularly at this

time of the year. They're quite an institution in these parts. And they never pass me over—they come to Mole End last of all; and I used to give them hot drinks, and supper too sometimes, when I could afford it. It will be like old times to hear them again."

"Let's have a look at them!" cried the Rat, jumping up and running to the door.

It was a pretty sight, and a seasonable one, that met their eyes when they flung the door open. In the fore-court, lit by the dim rays of a horn lantern, some eight or ten little fieldmice stood in a semicircle, red worsted comforters round their throats, their fore-paws thrust deep into their pockets, their feet jigging for warmth. With bright beady eyes they glanced shyly at each other, sniggering a little, sniffing and applying coat-sleeves a good deal. As the door opened, one of the elder ones that carried the lantern was just saying, "Now then, one, two, three!" and forthwith their shrill little voices uprose on the air, singing one of the old-time carols that their forefathers composed in fields that were fallow and held by frost, or when snowbound in chimney corners, and handed down to be sung in the miry street to lamp-lit windows at Yule-time.

CAROL

Villagers all, this frosty tide,
Let your doors swing open wide,
Though wind may follow, and snow beside,
Yet draw us in by your fire to bide;
Joy shall be yours in the morning!

Here we stand in the cold and the sleet,
Blowing fingers and stamping feet,
Come from far away you to greet—
You by the fire and we in the street—
Bidding you joy in the morning!

For ere one half of the night was gone,
Sudden a star has led us on,
Raining bliss and benison—
Bliss to-morrow and more anon,
Joy for every morning!

Goodman Joseph toiled through the snow—
Saw the star o'er a stable low;

Mary she might not further go—

Welcome thatch, and litter below!

Joy was hers in the morning!

And then they heard the angels tell

"Who were the first to cry **Nowell**?

Animals all, as it befell,

In the stable where they did dwell!

Joy shall be theirs in the morning!"

The voices ceased, the singers, bashful but smiling, exchanged sidelong glances, and silence succeeded—but for a moment only. Then, from up above and far away, down the tunnel they had so lately travelled was borne to their ears in a faint musical hum the sound of distant bells ringing a joyful and clangorous peal.

"Very well sung, boys!" cried the Rat heartily. "And now come along in, all of you, and warm yourselves by the fire, and have something hot!"

"Yes, come along, field-mice," cried the Mole eagerly. "This is quite like old times! Shut the door after you. Pull up that settle to the fire. Now, you just wait a minute, while we—O, Ratty!" he cried in despair, plumping down on a seat, with tears impending. "Whatever are we doing? We've nothing to give them!"

"You leave all that to me," said the masterful Rat. "Here, you with the lantern! Come over this way. I want to talk to you. Now, tell me, are there any shops open at this hour of the night?"

"Why, certainly, sir," replied the field-mouse respectfully. "At this

time of the year our shops keep open to all sorts of hours."

"Then look here!" said the Rat. "You go off at once, you and your lantern, and you get me——"

Here much muttered conversation ensued, and the Mole only heard bits of it, such as—"Fresh, mind!—no, a pound of that will do—see you get Buggins's, for I won't have any other—no, only the best—if you can't get it there, try somewhere else—yes, of course, home-made, no tinned stuff—well then, do the best you can!" Finally, there was a chink of coin passing from paw to paw, the field-mouse was provided with an ample basket for his purchases, and off he hurried, he and his lantern.

The rest of the field-mice, perched in a row on the settle, their small legs swinging, gave themselves up to enjoyment of the fire, and toasted their chilblains till they tingled; while the Mole, failing to draw them into easy conversation, plunged into family history and made each of them recite the names of his numerous brothers, who were too young, it appeared, to be allowed to go out a-carolling this year, but looked forward very shortly to winning the parental consent.

The Rat, meanwhile, was busy examining the label on one of the beer-bottles. "I perceive this to be Old Burton," he remarked approvingly. "**Sensible** Mole! The very thing! Now we shall be able to mull some ale! Get the things ready, Mole, while I draw the corks."

It did not take long to prepare the brew and thrust the tin heater well into the red heart of the fire; and soon every field-mouse was sipping and coughing and choking (for a little mulled ale goes a long way) and wiping his eyes and laughing and forgetting he had ever been cold in all his life.

"They act plays too, these fellows," the Mole explained to the Rat. "Make them up all by themselves, and act them afterwards. And very well they do it, too! They gave us a capital one last year, about a

field-mouse who was captured at sea by a Barbary corsair, and made to row in a galley; and when he escaped and got home again, his lady-love had gone into a convent. Here, **you!** You were in it, I remember. Get up and recite a bit."

The field-mouse addressed got up on his legs, giggled shyly, looked round the room, and remained absolutely tongue-tied. His comrades cheered him on, Mole coaxed and encouraged him, and the Rat went so far as to take him by the shoulders and shake him; but nothing could overcome his stage-fright. They were all busily engaged on him like watermen applying the Royal Humane Society's regulations to a case of long submersion, when the latch clicked, the door opened, and the field-mouse with the lantern reappeared, staggering under the weight of his basket.

There was no more talk of play-acting once the very real and solid contents of the basket had been tumbled out on the table. Under the generalship of Rat, everybody was set to do something or to fetch something. In a very few minutes supper was ready, and Mole, as he took the head of the table in a sort of a dream, saw a lately barren board set thick with savoury comforts; saw his little friends' faces brighten and beam as they fell to without delay; and then let himself loose—for he was famished indeed—on the provender so magically provided, thinking what a happy home-coming this had turned out, after all. As they ate, they talked of old times, and the field-mice gave him the local gossip up to date, and answered as well as they could the hundred questions he had to ask them. The Rat said little or nothing, only taking care that each guest had what he wanted, and plenty of it, and that Mole had no trouble or anxiety about anything.

They clattered off at last, very grateful and showering wishes of the season, with their jacket pockets stuffed with remembrances for the small brothers and sisters at home. When the door had closed on

the last of them and the chink of the lanterns had died away, Mole and Rat kicked the fire up, drew their chairs in, brewed themselves a last nightcap of mulled ale, and discussed the events of the long day. At last the Rat, with a tremendous yawn, said, "Mole, old chap, I'm ready to drop. Sleepy is simply not the word. That your own bunk over on that side? Very well, then, I'll take this. What a ripping little house this is! Everything so handy!"

He clambered into his bunk and rolled himself well up in the blankets, and slumber gathered him forthwith, as a swathe of barley is folded into the arms of the reaping machine.

The weary Mole also was glad to turn in without delay, and soon had his head on his pillow, in great joy and contentment. But ere he closed his eyes he let them wander round his old room, mellow in the glow of the firelight that played or rested on familiar and friendly things which had long been unconsciously a part of him, and now smilingly received him back, without rancour. He was now in just the frame of mind that the tactful Rat had quietly worked to bring about in him. He saw clearly how plain and simple—how narrow, even—it all was; but clearly, too, how much it all meant to him, and the special value of some such anchorage in one's existence. He did not at all want to abandon the new life and its splendid spaces, to turn his back on sun and air and all they offered him and creep home and stay there; the upper world was all too strong, it called to him still, even down there, and he knew he must return to the larger stage. But it was good to think he had this to come back to; this place which was all his own, these things which were so glad to see him again and could always be counted upon for the same simple welcome.

VI.

MR. TOAD

It was a bright morning in the early part of summer; the river had resumed its wonted banks and its accustomed pace, and a hot sun seemed to be pulling everything green and bushy and spiky up out of the earth towards him, as if by strings. The Mole and the Water Rat had been up since dawn, very busy on matters connected with boats and the opening of the boating season; painting and varnishing, mending paddles, repairing cushions, hunting for missing boat-hooks, and so on; and were finishing breakfast in their little parlour and eagerly discussing their plans for the day, when a heavy knock sounded at the door.

"Bother!" said the Rat, all over egg. "See who it is, Mole, like a good chap, since you've finished."

The Mole went to attend the summons, and the Rat heard him utter a cry of surprise. Then he flung the parlour door open, and announced with much importance, "Mr. Badger!"

This was a wonderful thing, indeed, that the Badger should pay a formal call on them, or indeed on anybody. He generally had to be caught, if you wanted him badly, as he slipped quietly along a hedgerow of an early morning or a late evening, or else hunted up in his own house in the middle of the Wood, which was a serious undertaking.

The Badger strode heavily into the room, and stood looking at the two animals with an expression full of seriousness. The Rat let his egg-spoon fall on the table-cloth, and sat open-mouthed.

"The hour has come!" said the Badger at last with great solemnity.

"What hour?" asked the Rat uneasily, glancing at the clock on the mantelpiece.

"**Whose** hour, you should rather say," replied the Badger. "Why, Toad's hour! The hour of Toad! I said I would take him in hand as soon as the winter was well over, and I'm going to take him in hand to-day!"

"Toad's hour, of course!" cried the Mole delightedly. "Hooray! I remember now! **We'll** teach him to be a sensible Toad!"

"This very morning," continued the Badger, taking an arm-chair, "as I learnt last night from a trustworthy source, another new and exceptionally powerful motor-car will arrive at Toad Hall on approval or return. At this very moment, perhaps, Toad is busy arraying himself in those singularly hideous habiliments so dear to him, which transform him from a (comparatively) good-looking Toad into an Object which throws any decent-minded animal that comes across it into a violent fit. We must be up and doing, ere it is too late. You two animals will accompany me instantly to Toad Hall, and the work of rescue shall be accomplished."

"Right you are!" cried the Rat, starting up. "We'll rescue the poor unhappy animal! We'll convert him! He'll be the most converted Toad that ever was before we've done with him!"

They set off up the road on their mission of mercy, Badger leading the way. Animals when in company walk in a proper and sensible manner, in single file, instead of sprawling all across the road and being of no use or support to each other in case of sudden trouble or danger.

They reached the carriage-drive of Toad Hall to find, as the Badger had anticipated, a shiny new motor-car, of great size, painted a

bright red (Toad's favourite colour), standing in front of the house. As they neared the door it was flung open, and Mr. Toad, arrayed in goggles, cap, gaiters, and enormous overcoat, came swaggering down the steps, drawing on his gauntleted gloves.

"Hullo! come on, you fellows!" he cried cheerfully on catching sight of them. "You're just in time to come with me for a jolly—to come for a jolly—for a—er—jolly——"

His hearty accents faltered and fell away as he noticed the stern unbending look on the countenances of his silent friends, and his invitation remained unfinished.

The Badger strode up the steps. "Take him inside," he said sternly to his companions. Then, as Toad was hustled through the door, struggling and protesting, he turned to the **chauffeur** in charge of the new motor-car.

"I'm afraid you won't be wanted to-day," he said. "Mr. Toad has changed his mind. He will not require the car. Please understand that this is final. You needn't wait." Then he followed the others inside and shut the door.

"Now then!" he said to the Toad, when the four of them stood together in the Hall, "first of all, take those ridiculous things off!"

"Shan't!" replied Toad, with great spirit. "What is the meaning of this gross outrage? I demand an instant explanation."

"Take them off him, then, you two," ordered the Badger briefly.

They had to lay Toad out on the floor, kicking and calling all sorts of names, before they could get to work properly. Then the Rat sat on him, and the Mole got his motor-clothes off him bit by bit, and they stood him up on his legs again. A good deal of his blustering spirit seemed to have evaporated with the removal of his fine panoply. Now that he was merely Toad, and no longer the Terror of the Highway, he giggled feebly and looked from one to the other

appealingly, seeming quite to understand the situation.

"You knew it must come to this, sooner or later, Toad," the Badger explained severely.

You've disregarded all the warnings we've given you, you've gone on squandering the money your father left you, and you're getting us animals a bad name in the district by your furious driving and your smashes and your rows with the police. Independence is all very well, but we animals never allow our friends to make fools of themselves beyond a certain limit; and that limit you've reached. Now, you're a good fellow in many respects, and I don't want to be too hard on you. I'll make one more effort to bring you to reason. You will come with me into the smoking-room, and there you will hear some facts about yourself; and we'll see whether you come out of that room the same Toad that you went in."

He took Toad firmly by the arm, led him into the smoking-room, and closed the door behind them.

"**That's** no good!" said the Rat contemptuously. "**Talking** to Toad'll never cure him. He'll **say** anything."

They made themselves comfortable in armchairs and waited patiently. Through the closed door they could just hear the long continuous drone of the Badger's voice, rising and falling in waves of oratory; and presently they noticed that the sermon began to be punctuated at intervals by long-drawn sobs, evidently proceeding from the bosom of Toad, who was a soft-hearted and affectionate fellow, very easily converted—for the time being—to any point of view.

After some three-quarters of an hour the door opened, and the Badger reappeared, solemnly leading by the paw a very limp and dejected Toad. His skin hung baggily about him, his legs wobbled, and his cheeks were furrowed by the tears so plentifully called forth by the Badger's moving discourse.

"Sit down there, Toad," said the Badger kindly, pointing to a chair. "My friends," he went on, "I am pleased to inform you that Toad has at last seen the error of his ways. He is truly sorry for his misguided conduct in the past, and he has undertaken to give up motor-cars entirely and for ever. I have his solemn promise to that effect."

"That is very good news," said the Mole gravely.

"Very good news indeed," observed the Rat dubiously, "if only—**if** only— —"

He was looking very hard at Toad as he said this, and could not help thinking he perceived something vaguely resembling a twinkle in that animal's still sorrowful eye.

"There's only one thing more to be done," continued the gratified Badger. "Toad, I want you solemnly to repeat, before your friends here, what you fully admitted to me in the smoking-room just now. First, you are sorry for what you've done, and you see the folly of it all?"

There was a long, long pause. Toad looked desperately this way and that, while the other animals waited in grave silence. At last he spoke.

"No!" he said, a little sullenly, but stoutly; "I'm **not** sorry. And it wasn't folly at all! It was simply glorious!"

"What?" cried the Badger, greatly scandalised. "You backsliding animal, didn't you tell me just now, in there— —"

"Oh, yes, yes, in **there**," said Toad impatiently. "I'd have said anything in **there**. You're so eloquent, dear Badger, and so moving, and so convincing, and put all your points so frightfully well—you can do what you like with me in **there**, and you know it. But I've been searching my mind since, and going over things in it, and I find that I'm not a bit sorry or repentant really, so it's no earthly good saying I

am; now, is it?"

"Then you don't promise," said the Badger, "never to touch a motor-car again?"

"Certainly not!" replied Toad emphatically. "On the contrary, I faithfully promise that the very first motor-car I see, poop-poop! Off I go in it!"

"Told you so, didn't I?" observed the Rat to the Mole.

"Very well, then," said the Badger firmly, rising to his feet. "Since you won't yield to persuasion, we'll try what force can do. I feared it would come to this all along. You've often asked us three to come and stay with you, Toad, in this handsome house of yours; well, now we're going to. When we've converted you to a proper point of view we may quit, but not before. Take him upstairs, you two, and lock him up in his bedroom, while we arrange matters between ourselves."

"It's for your own good, Toady, you know," said the Rat kindly, as Toad, kicking and struggling, was hauled up the stairs by his two faithful friends. "Think what fun we shall all have together, just as we used to, when you've quite got over this—this painful attack of yours!"

"We'll take great care of everything for you till you're well, Toad," said the Mole; "and we'll see your money isn't wasted, as it has been."

"No more of those regrettable incidents with the police, Toad," said the Rat, as they thrust him into his bedroom.

"And no more weeks in hospital, being ordered about by female nurses, Toad," added the Mole, turning the key on him.

They descended the stair, Toad shouting abuse at them through the keyhole; and the three friends then met in conference on the situation.

"It's going to be a tedious business," said the Badger, sighing.

"I've never seen Toad so determined. However, we will see it out. He must never be left an instant unguarded. We shall have to take it in turns to be with him, till the poison has worked itself out of his system."

They arranged watches accordingly. Each animal took it in turns to sleep in Toad's room at night, and they divided the day up between them. At first Toad was undoubtedly very trying to his careful guardians. When his violent paroxysms possessed him he would arrange bedroom chairs in rude resemblance of a motor-car and would crouch on the foremost of them, bent forward and staring fixedly ahead, making uncouth and ghastly noises, till the climax was reached, when, turning a complete somersault, he would lie prostrate amidst the ruins of the chairs, apparently completely satisfied for the moment. As time passed, however, these painful seizures grew gradually less frequent, and his friends strove to divert his mind into fresh channels. But his interest in other matters did not seem to revive, and he grew apparently languid and depressed.

One fine morning the Rat, whose turn it was to go on duty, went upstairs to relieve Badger, whom he found fidgeting to be off and stretch his legs in a long ramble round his wood and down his earths and burrows. "Toad's still in bed," he told the Rat, outside the door. "Can't get much out of him, except, 'O leave him alone, he wants nothing, perhaps he'll be better presently, it may pass off in time, don't be unduly anxious,' and so on. Now, you look out, Rat! When Toad's quiet and submissive and playing at being the hero of a Sunday-school prize, then he's at his artfullest. There's sure to be something up. I know him. Well, now, I must be off."

"How are you to-day, old chap?" inquired the Rat cheerfully, as he approached Toad's bedside.

He had to wait some minutes for an answer. At last a feeble

voice replied, "Thank you so much, dear Ratty! So good of you to inquire! But first tell me how you are yourself, and the excellent Mole?"

"O, **we're** all right," replied the Rat. "Mole," he added incautiously, "is going out for a run round with Badger. They'll be out till luncheon time, so you and I will spend a pleasant morning together, and I'll do my best to amuse you. Now jump up, there's a good fellow, and don't lie moping there on a fine morning like this!"

"Dear, kind Rat," murmured Toad, "how little you realise my condition, and how very far I am from 'jumping up' now—if ever! But do not trouble about me. I hate being a burden to my friends, and I do not expect to be one much longer. Indeed, I almost hope not."

"Well, I hope not, too," said the Rat heartily. "You've been a fine bother to us all this time, and I'm glad to hear it's going to stop. And in weather like this, and the boating season just beginning! It's too bad of you, Toad! It isn't the trouble we mind, but you're making us miss such an awful lot."

"I'm afraid it **is** the trouble you mind, though," replied the Toad languidly. "I can quite understand it. It's natural enough. You're tired of bothering about me. I mustn't ask you to do anything further. I'm a nuisance, I know."

"You are, indeed," said the Rat. "But I tell you, I'd take any trouble on earth for you, if only you'd be a sensible animal."

"If I thought that, Ratty," murmured Toad, more feebly than ever, "then I would beg you—for the last time, probably—to step round to the village as quickly as possible—even now it may be too late—and fetch the doctor. But don't you bother. It's only a trouble, and perhaps we may as well let things take their course."

"Why, what do you want a doctor for?" inquired the Rat, coming closer and examining him. He certainly lay very still and flat, and his

voice was weaker and his manner much changed.

"Surely you have noticed of late——" murmured Toad. "But, no—why should you? Noticing things is only a trouble. To-morrow, indeed, you may be saying to yourself, 'O, if only I had noticed sooner! If only I had done something!' But no; it's a trouble. Never mind—forget that I asked."

"Look here, old man," said the Rat, beginning to get rather alarmed, "of course I'll fetch a doctor to you, if you really think you want him. But you can hardly be bad enough for that yet. Let's talk about something else."

"I fear, dear friend," said Toad, with a sad smile, "that 'talk' can do little in a case like this—or doctors either, for that matter; still, one must grasp at the slightest straw. And, by the way—while you are about it—I **hate** to give you additional trouble, but I happen to remember that you will pass the door—would you mind at the same time asking the lawyer to step up? It would be a convenience to me, and there are moments—perhaps I should say there is **a** moment— when one must face disagreeable tasks, at whatever cost to exhausted nature!"

"A lawyer! O, he must be really bad!" the affrighted Rat said to himself, as he hurried from the room, not forgetting, however, to lock the door carefully behind him.

Outside, he stopped to consider. The other two were far away, and he had no one to consult.

"It's best to be on the safe side," he said, on reflection. "I've known Toad fancy himself frightfully bad before, without the slightest reason; but I've never heard him ask for a lawyer! If there's nothing really the matter, the doctor will tell him he's an old ass, and cheer him up; and that will be something gained. I'd better humour him and go; it won't take very long." So he ran off to the village on his errand of

mercy.

The Toad, who had hopped lightly out of bed as soon as he heard the key turned in the lock, watched him eagerly from the window till he disappeared down the carriage-drive. Then, laughing heartily, he dressed as quickly as possible in the smartest suit he could lay hands on at the moment, filled his pockets with cash which he took from a small drawer in the dressing-table, and next, knotting the sheets from his bed together and tying one end of the improvised rope round the central mullion of the handsome Tudor window which formed such a feature of his bedroom, he scrambled out, slid lightly to the ground, and, taking the opposite direction to the Rat, marched off lightheartedly, whistling a merry tune.

It was a gloomy luncheon for Rat when the Badger and the Mole at length returned, and he had to face them at table with his pitiful and unconvincing story. The Badger's caustic, not to say brutal, remarks may be imagined, and therefore passed over; but it was painful to the Rat that even the Mole, though he took his friend's side as far as possible, could not help saying, "You've been a bit of a duffer this time, Ratty! Toad, too, of all animals!"

"He did it awfully well," said the crestfallen Rat.

"He did **you** awfully well!" rejoined the Badger hotly. "However, talking won't mend matters. He's got clear away for the time, that's certain; and the worst of it is, he'll be so conceited with what he'll think is his cleverness that he may commit any folly. One comfort is, we're free now, and needn't waste any more of our precious time doing sentry-go. But we'd better continue to sleep at Toad Hall for a while longer. Toad may be brought back at any moment—on a stretcher, or between two policemen."

So spoke the Badger, not knowing what the future held in store, or how much water, and of how turbid a character, was to run under

bridges before Toad should sit at ease again in his ancestral Hall.

Meanwhile, Toad, gay and irresponsible, was walking briskly along the high road, some miles from home. At first he had taken by-paths, and crossed many fields, and changed his course several times, in case of pursuit; but now, feeling by this time safe from recapture, and the sun smiling brightly on him, and all Nature joining in a chorus of approval to the song of self-praise that his own heart was singing to him, he almost danced along the road in his satisfaction and conceit.

"Smart piece of work that!" he remarked to himself chuckling. "Brain against brute force—and brain came out on the top—as it's bound to do. Poor old Ratty! My! won't he catch it when the Badger gets back! A worthy fellow, Ratty, with many good qualities, but very little intelligence and absolutely no education. I must take him in hand some day, and see if I can make something of him."

Filled full of conceited thoughts such as these he strode along, his head in the air, till he reached a little town, where the sign of "The Red Lion," swinging across the road halfway down the main street, reminded him that he had not breakfasted that day, and that he was exceedingly hungry after his long walk. He marched into the Inn, ordered the best luncheon that could be provided at so short a notice, and sat down to eat it in the coffee-room.

He was about half-way through his meal when an only too familiar sound, approaching down the street, made him start and fall a-trembling all over. The poop-poop! drew nearer and nearer, the car could be heard to turn into the inn-yard and come to a stop, and Toad had to hold on to the leg of the table to conceal his over-mastering emotion. Presently the party entered the coffee-room, hungry, talkative, and gay, voluble on their experiences of the morning and the merits of the chariot that had brought them along so well. Toad

listened eagerly, all ears, for a time; at last he could stand it no longer. He slipped out of the room quietly, paid his bill at the bar, and as soon as he got outside sauntered round quietly to the inn-yard. "There cannot be any harm," he said to himself, "in my only just **looking** at it!"

The car stood in the middle of the yard, quite unattended, the stable-helps and other hangers-on being all at their dinner. Toad walked slowly round it, inspecting, criticising, musing deeply.

"I wonder," he said to himself presently, "I wonder if this sort of car **starts** easily?"

Next moment, hardly knowing how it came about, he found he had hold of the handle and was turning it. As the familiar sound broke forth, the old passion seized on Toad and completely mastered him, body and soul. As if in a dream he found himself, somehow, seated in the driver's seat; as if in a dream, he pulled the lever and swung the car round the yard and out through the archway; and, as if in a dream, all sense of right and wrong, all fear of obvious consequences, seemed temporarily suspended. He increased his pace, and as the car devoured the street and leapt forth on the high road through the open country, he was only conscious that he was Toad once more, Toad at his best and highest, Toad the terror, the traffic-queller, the Lord of the lone trail, before whom all must give way or be smitten into nothingness and everlasting night. He chanted as he flew, and the car responded with sonorous drone; the miles were eaten up under him as he sped he knew not whither, fulfilling his instincts, living his hour, reckless of what might come to him.

"To my mind," observed the Chairman of the Bench of Magistrates cheerfully, "the **only** difficulty that presents itself in this otherwise very clear case is, how we can possibly make it sufficiently hot for the incorrigible rogue and hardened ruffian whom we see

cowering in the dock before us. Let me see: he has been found guilty, on the clearest evidence, first, of stealing a valuable motor-car; secondly, of driving to the public danger; and, thirdly, of gross impertinence to the rural police. Mr. Clerk, will you tell us, please, what is the very stiffest penalty we can impose for each of these offences? Without, of course, giving the prisoner the benefit of any doubt, because there isn't any."

The Clerk scratched his nose with his pen. "Some people would consider," he observed, "that stealing the motor-car was the worst offence; and so it is. But cheeking the police undoubtedly carries the severest penalty; and so it ought. Supposing you were to say twelve months for the theft, which is mild; and three years for the furious driving, which is lenient; and fifteen years for the cheek, which was pretty bad sort of cheek, judging by what we've heard from the witness-box, even if you only believe one-tenth part of what you heard, and I never believe more myself—those figures, if added together correctly, tot up to nineteen years——"

"First-rate!" said the Chairman.

"—So you had better make it a round twenty years and be on the safe side," concluded the Clerk.

"An excellent suggestion!" said the Chairman approvingly. "Prisoner! Pull yourself together and try and stand up straight. It's going to be twenty years for you this time. And mind, if you appear before us again, upon any charge whatever, we shall have to deal with you very seriously!"

Then the brutal minions of the law fell upon the hapless Toad; loaded him with chains, and dragged him from the Court House, shrieking, praying, protesting; across the marketplace, where the playful populace, always as severe upon detected crime as they are sympathetic and helpful when one is merely "wanted," assailed him

with jeers, carrots, and popular catch-words; past hooting school children, their innocent faces lit up with the pleasure they ever derive from the sight of a gentleman in difficulties; across the hollow-sounding drawbridge, below the spiky portcullis, under the frowning archway of the grim old castle, whose ancient towers soared high overhead; past guardrooms full of grinning soldiery off duty, past sentries who coughed in a horrid, sarcastic way, because that is as much as a sentry on his post dare do to show his contempt and abhorrence of crime; up time-worn winding stairs, past men-at-arms in casquet and corselet of steel, darting threatening looks through their vizards; across courtyards, where mastiffs strained at their leash and pawed the air to get at him; past ancient warders, their halberds leant against the wall, dozing over a pasty and a flagon of brown ale; on and on, past the rack-chamber and the thumbscrew-room, past the turning that led to the private scaffold, till they reached the door of the grimmest dungeon that lay in the heart of the innermost keep. There at last they paused, where an ancient gaoler sat fingering a bunch of mighty keys.

"Oddsbodikins!" said the sergeant of police, taking off his helmet and wiping his forehead. "Rouse thee, old loon, and take over from us this vile Toad, a criminal of deepest guilt and matchless artfulness and resource. Watch and ward him with all thy skill; and mark thee well, greybeard, should aught untoward befall, thy old head shall answer for his—and a murrain on both of them!"

The gaoler nodded grimly, laying his withered hand on the shoulder of the miserable Toad. The rusty key creaked in the lock, the great door clanged behind them; and Toad was a helpless prisoner in the remotest dungeon of the best-guarded keep of the stoutest castle in all the length and breadth of Merry England.

VII.
THE PIPER AT THE GATES OF DAWN

The Willow-Wren was twittering his thin little song, hidden himself in the dark selvedge of the river bank. Though it was past ten o'clock at night, the sky still clung to and retained some lingering skirts of light from the departed day; and the sullen heats of the torrid afternoon broke up and rolled away at the dispersing touch of the cool fingers of the short midsummer night. Mole lay stretched on the bank, still panting from the stress of the fierce day that had been cloudless from dawn to late sunset, and waited for his friend to return. He had been on the river with some companions, leaving the Water Rat free to keep a engagement of long standing with Otter; and he had come back to find the house dark and deserted, and no sign of Rat, who was doubtless keeping it up late with his old comrade. It was still too hot to think of staying indoors, so he lay on some cool dock-leaves, and thought over the past day and its doings, and how very good they all had been.

The Rat's light footfall was presently heard approaching over the parched grass. "O, the blessed coolness!" he said, and sat down, gazing thoughtfully into the river, silent and pre-occupied.

"You stayed to supper, of course?" said the Mole presently.

"Simply had to," said the Rat. "They wouldn't hear of my going before. You know how kind they always are. And they made things as jolly for me as ever they could, right up to the moment I left. But I felt a brute all the time, as it was clear to me they were very unhappy,

though they tried to hide it. Mole, I'm afraid they're in trouble. Little Portly is missing again; and you know what a lot his father thinks of him, though he never says much about it."

"What, that child?" said the Mole lightly. "Well, suppose he is; why worry about it? He's always straying off and getting lost, and turning up again; he's so adventurous. But no harm ever happens to him. Everybody hereabouts knows him and likes him, just as they do old Otter, and you may be sure some animal or other will come across him and bring him back again all right. Why, we've found him ourselves, miles from home, and quite self-possessed and cheerful!"

"Yes; but this time it's more serious," said the Rat gravely. "He's been missing for some days now, and the Otters have hunted everywhere, high and low, without finding the slightest trace. And they've asked every animal, too, for miles around, and no one knows anything about him. Otter's evidently more anxious than he'll admit. I got out of him that young Portly hasn't learnt to swim very well yet, and I can see he's thinking of the weir. There's a lot of water coming down still, considering the time of the year, and the place always had a fascination for the child. And then there are—well, traps and things—**you** know. Otter's not the fellow to be nervous about any son of his before it's time. And now he **is** nervous. When I left, he came out with me—said he wanted some air, and talked about stretching his legs. But I could see it wasn't that, so I drew him out and pumped him, and got it all from him at last. He was going to spend the night watching by the ford. You know the place where the old ford used to be, in by-gone days before they built the bridge?"

"I know it well," said the Mole. "But why should Otter choose to watch there?"

"Well, it seems that it was there he gave Portly his first swimming-lesson," continued the Rat. "From that shallow, gravelly

spit near the bank. And it was there he used to teach him fishing, and there young Portly caught his first fish, of which he was so very proud. The child loved the spot, and Otter thinks that if he came wandering back from wherever he is—if he **is** anywhere by this time, poor little chap—he might make for the ford he was so fond of; or if he came across it he'd remember it well, and stop there and play, perhaps. So Otter goes there every night and watches—on the chance, you know, just on the chance!"

They were silent for a time, both thinking of the same thing—the lonely, heart-sore animal, crouched by the ford, watching and waiting, the long night through—on the chance.

"Well, well," said the Rat presently, "I suppose we ought to be thinking about turning in." But he never offered to move.

"Rat," said the Mole, "I simply can't go and turn in, and go to sleep, and **do** nothing, even though there doesn't seem to be anything to be done. We'll get the boat out, and paddle up stream. The moon will be up in an hour or so, and then we will search as well as we can—anyhow, it will be better than going to bed and doing **nothing**."

"Just what I was thinking myself," said the Rat. "It's not the sort of night for bed anyhow; and daybreak is not so very far off, and then we may pick up some news of him from early risers as we go along."

They got the boat out, and the Rat took the sculls, paddling with caution. Out in midstream, there was a clear, narrow track that faintly reflected the sky; but wherever shadows fell on the water from bank, bush, or tree, they were as solid to all appearance as the banks themselves, and the Mole had to steer with judgment accordingly. Dark and deserted as it was, the night was full of small noises, song and chatter and rustling, telling of the busy little population who were up and about, plying their trades and vocations through the night till sunshine should fall on them at last and send them off to their well-

earned repose. The water's own noises, too, were more apparent than by day, its gurglings and "cloops" more unexpected and near at hand; and constantly they started at what seemed a sudden clear call from an actual articulate voice.

The line of the horizon was clear and hard against the sky, and in one particular quarter it showed black against a silvery climbing phosphorescence that grew and grew. At last, over the rim of the waiting earth the moon lifted with slow majesty till it swung clear of the horizon and rode off, free of moorings; and once more they began to see surfaces—meadows wide-spread, and quiet gardens, and the river itself from bank to bank, all softly disclosed, all washed clean of mystery and terror, all radiant again as by day, but with a difference that was tremendous. Their old haunts greeted them again in other raiment, as if they had slipped away and put on this pure new apparel and come quietly back, smiling as they shyly waited to see if they would be recognised again under it.

Fastening their boat to a willow, the friends landed in this silent, silver kingdom, and patiently explored the hedges, the hollow trees, the runnels and their little culverts, the ditches and dry water-ways. Embarking again and crossing over, they worked their way up the stream in this manner, while the moon, serene and detached in a cloudless sky, did what she could, though so far off, to help them in their quest; till her hour came and she sank earthwards reluctantly, and left them, and mystery once more held field and river.

Then a change began slowly to declare itself. The horizon became clearer, field and tree came more into sight, and somehow with a different look; the mystery began to drop away from them. A bird piped suddenly, and was still; and a light breeze sprang up and set the reeds and bulrushes rustling. Rat, who was in the stern of the boat, while Mole sculled, sat up suddenly and listened with a

passionate intentness. Mole, who with gentle strokes was just keeping the boat moving while he scanned the banks with care, looked at him with curiosity.

"It's gone!" sighed the Rat, sinking back in his seat again. "So beautiful and strange and new. Since it was to end so soon, I almost wish I had never heard it. For it has roused a longing in me that is pain, and nothing seems worth while but just to hear that sound once more and go on listening to it for ever. No! There it is again!" he cried, alert once more. Entranced, he was silent for a long space, spellbound.

"Now it passes on and I begin to lose it," he said presently. "O Mole! the beauty of it! The merry bubble and joy, the thin, clear, happy call of the distant piping! Such music I never dreamed of, and the call in it is stronger even than the music is sweet! Row on, Mole, row! For the music and the call must be for us."

The Mole, greatly wondering, obeyed. "I hear nothing myself," he said, "but the wind playing in the reeds and rushes and osiers."

The Rat never answered, if indeed he heard. Rapt, transported, trembling, he was possessed in all his senses by this new divine thing that caught up his helpless soul and swung and dandled it, a powerless but happy infant in a strong sustaining grasp.

In silence Mole rowed steadily, and soon they came to a point where the river divided, a long backwater branching off to one side. With a slight movement of his head Rat, who had long dropped the rudder-lines, directed the rower to take the backwater. The creeping tide of light gained and gained, and now they could see the colour of the flowers that gemmed the water's edge.

"Clearer and nearer still," cried the Rat joyously. "Now you must surely hear it! Ah—at last—I see you do!"

Breathless and transfixed the Mole stopped rowing as the liquid run of that glad piping broke on him like a wave, caught him up, and

possessed him utterly. He saw the tears on his comrade's cheeks, and bowed his head and understood. For a space they hung there, brushed by the purple loose-strife that fringed the bank; then the clear imperious summons that marched hand-in-hand with the intoxicating melody imposed its will on Mole, and mechanically he bent to his oars again. And the light grew steadily stronger, but no birds sang as they were wont to do at the approach of dawn; and but for the heavenly music all was marvellously still.

On either side of them, as they glided onwards, the rich meadow-grass seemed that morning of a freshness and a greenness unsurpassable. Never had they noticed the roses so vivid, the willow-herb so riotous, the meadow-sweet so odorous and pervading. Then the murmur of the approaching weir began to hold the air, and they felt a consciousness that they were nearing the end, whatever it might be, that surely awaited their expedition.

A wide half-circle of foam and glinting lights and shining shoulders of green water, the great weir closed the backwater from bank to bank, troubled all the quiet surface with twirling eddies and floating foam-streaks, and deadened all other sounds with its solemn and soothing rumble. In midmost of the stream, embraced in the weir's shimmering arm-spread, a small island lay anchored, fringed close with willow and silver birch and alder. Reserved, shy, but full of significance, it hid whatever it might hold behind a veil, keeping it till the hour should come, and, with the hour, those who were called and chosen.

Slowly, but with no doubt or hesitation whatever, and in something of a solemn expectancy, the two animals passed through the broken tumultuous water and moored their boat at the flowery margin of the island. In silence they landed, and pushed through the blossom and scented herbage and undergrowth that led up to the level

ground, till they stood on a little lawn of a marvellous green, set round with Nature's own orchard-trees—crab-apple, wild cherry, and sloe.

"This is the place of my song-dream, the place the music played to me," whispered the Rat, as if in a trance. "Here, in this holy place, here if anywhere, surely we shall find Him!"

Then suddenly the Mole felt a great Awe fall upon him, an awe that turned his muscles to water, bowed his head, and rooted his feet to the ground. It was no panic terror—indeed he felt wonderfully at peace and happy—but it was an awe that smote and held him and, without seeing, he knew it could only mean that some august Presence was very, very near. With difficulty he turned to look for his friend and saw him at his side cowed, stricken, and trembling violently. And still there was utter silence in the populous bird-haunted branches around them; and still the light grew and grew.

Perhaps he would never have dared to raise his eyes, but that, though the piping was now hushed, the call and the summons seemed still dominant and imperious. He might not refuse, were Death himself waiting to strike him instantly, once he had looked with mortal eye on things rightly kept hidden. Trembling he obeyed, and raised his humble head; and then, in that utter clearness of the imminent dawn, while Nature, flushed with fullness of incredible colour, seemed to hold her breath for the event, he looked in the very eyes of the Friend and Helper; saw the backward sweep of the curved horns, gleaming in the growing daylight; saw the stern, hooked nose between the kindly eyes that were looking down on them humourously, while the bearded mouth broke into a half-smile at the corners; saw the rippling muscles on the arm that lay across the broad chest, the long supple hand still holding the pan-pipes only just fallen away from the parted lips; saw the splendid curves of the shaggy limbs disposed in majestic ease on

the sward; saw, last of all, nestling between his very hooves, sleeping soundly in entire peace and contentment, the little, round, podgy, childish form of the baby otter. All this he saw, for one moment breathless and intense, vivid on the morning sky; and still, as he looked, he lived; and still, as he lived, he wondered.

"Rat!" he found breath to whisper, shaking. "Are you afraid?"

"Afraid?" murmured the Rat, his eyes shining with unutterable love. "Afraid! Of **Him?** O, never, never! And yet—and yet—O, Mole, I am afraid!"

Then the two animals, crouching to the earth, bowed their heads and did worship.

Sudden and magnificent, the sun's broad golden disc showed itself over the horizon facing them; and the first rays, shooting across the level water-meadows, took the animals full in the eyes and dazzled them. When they were able to look once more, the Vision had vanished, and the air was full of the carol of birds that hailed the dawn.

As they stared blankly in dumb misery deepening as they slowly realised all they had seen and all they had lost, a capricious little

breeze, dancing up from the surface of the water, tossed the aspens, shook the dewy roses and blew lightly and caressingly in their faces; and with its soft touch came instant oblivion. For this is the last best gift that the kindly demi-god is careful to bestow on those to whom he has revealed himself in their helping: the gift of forgetfulness. Lest the awful remembrance should remain and grow, and overshadow mirth and pleasure, and the great haunting memory should spoil all the after-lives of little animals helped out of difficulties, in order that they should be happy and lighthearted as before.

Mole rubbed his eyes and stared at Rat, who was looking about him in a puzzled sort of way. "I beg your pardon; what did you say, Rat?" he asked.

"I think I was only remarking," said Rat slowly, "that this was the right sort of place, and that here, if anywhere, we should find him. And look! Why, there he is, the little fellow!" And with a cry of delight he ran towards the slumbering Portly.

But Mole stood still a moment, held in thought. As one wakened suddenly from a beautiful dream, who struggles to recall it, and can re-capture nothing but a dim sense of the beauty of it, the beauty! Till that, too, fades away in its turn, and the dreamer bitterly accepts the hard, cold waking and all its penalties; so Mole, after struggling with his memory for a brief space, shook his head sadly and followed the Rat.

Portly woke up with a joyous squeak, and wriggled with pleasure at the sight of his father's friends, who had played with him so often in past days. In a moment, however, his face grew blank, and he fell to hunting round in a circle with pleading whine. As a child that has fallen happily asleep in its nurse's arms, and wakes to find itself alone and laid in a strange place, and searches corners and cupboards, and runs from room to room, despair growing silently in its heart, even so

Portly searched the island and searched, dogged and unwearying, till at last the black moment came for giving it up, and sitting down and crying bitterly.

The Mole ran quickly to comfort the little animal; but Rat, lingering, looked long and doubtfully at certain hoof-marks deep in the sward.

"Some—great—animal—has been here," he murmured slowly and thoughtfully;and stood musing, musing; his mind strangely stirred.

"Come along, Rat!" called the Mole. "Think of poor Otter, waiting up there by the ford!"

Portly had soon been comforted by the promise of a treat—a jaunt on the river in Mr. Rat's real boat; and the two animals conducted him to the water's side, placed him securely between them in the bottom of the boat, and paddled off down the backwater. The sun was fully up by now, and hot on them, birds sang lustily and without restraint, and flowers smiled and nodded from either bank, but somehow—so thought the animals—with less of richness and blaze of colour than they seemed to remember seeing quite recently somewhere—they wondered where.

The main river reached again, they turned the boat's head upstream, towards the point where they knew their friend was keeping his lonely vigil. As they drew near the familiar ford, the Mole took the boat in to the bank, and they lifted Portly out and set him on his legs on the tow-path, gave him his marching orders and a friendly farewell pat on the back, and shoved out into mid-stream. They watched the little animal as he waddled along the path contentedly and with importance; watched him till they saw his muzzle suddenly lift and his waddle break into a clumsy amble as he quickened his pace with shrill whines and wriggles of recognition. Looking up the river, they could see Otter start up, tense and rigid, from out of the shallows where he

crouched in dumb patience, and could hear his amazed and joyous bark as he bounded up through the osiers on to the path. Then the Mole, with a strong pull on one oar, swung the boat round and let the full stream bear them down again whither it would, their quest now happily ended.

"I feel strangely tired, Rat," said the Mole, leaning wearily over his oars as the boat drifted. "It's being up all night, you'll say, perhaps; but that's nothing. We do as much half the nights of the week, at this time of the year. No; I feel as if I had been through something very exciting and rather terrible, and it was just over; and yet nothing particular has happened."

"Or something very surprising and splendid and beautiful," murmured the Rat, leaning back and closing his eyes. "I feel just as you do, Mole; simply dead tired, though not body tired. It's lucky we've got the stream with us, to take us home. Isn't it jolly to feel the sun again, soaking into one's bones! And hark to the wind playing in the reeds!"

"It's like music—far away music," said the Mole nodding drowsily.

"So I was thinking," murmured the Rat, dreamful and languid. "Dance-music—the lilting sort that runs on without a stop—but with words in it, too—it passes into words and out of them again—I catch them at intervals—then it is dance-music once more, and then nothing but the reeds' soft thin whispering."

"You hear better than I," said the Mole sadly. "I cannot catch the words."

"Let me try and give you them," said the Rat softly, his eyes still closed. "Now it is turning into words again—faint but clear—**Lest the awe should dwell—And turn your frolic to fret—You shall look on my power at the helping hour—But then you shall**

forget! Now the reeds take it up—**forget, forget**, they sigh, and it dies away in a rustle and a whisper. Then the voice returns—

"**Lest limbs be reddened and rent—I spring the trap that is set—As I loose the snare you may glimpse me there—For surely you shall forget!** Row nearer, Mole, nearer to the reeds! It is hard to catch, and grows each minute fainter.

"**Helper and healer, I cheer—Small waifs in the woodland wet—Strays I find in it, wounds I bind in it—Bidding them all forget!** Nearer, Mole, nearer! No, it is no good; the song has died away into reed-talk."

"But what do the words mean?" asked the wondering Mole.

"That I do not know," said the Rat simply. "I passed them on to you as they reached me. Ah! now they return again, and this time full and clear! This time, at last, it is the real, the unmistakable thing, simple—passionate—perfect——"

"Well, let's have it, then," said the Mole, after he had waited patiently for a few minutes, half-dozing in the hot sun.

But no answer came. He looked, and understood the silence. With a smile of much happiness on his face, and something of a listening look still lingering there, the weary Rat was fast asleep.

VIII.

TOAD'S ADVENTURES

When Toad found himself immured in a dank and noisome dungeon, and knew that all the grim darkness of a medieval fortress lay between him and the outer world of sunshine and well-metalled high roads where he had lately been so happy, disporting himself as if he had bought up every road in England, he flung himself at full length on the floor, and shed bitter tears, and abandoned himself to dark despair. "This is the end of everything" (he said), "at least it is the end of the career of Toad, which is the same thing; the popular and handsome Toad, the rich and hospitable Toad, the Toad so free and careless and debonair! How can I hope to be ever set at large again" (he said), "who have been imprisoned so justly for stealing so handsome a motor-car in such an audacious manner, and for such lurid and imaginative cheek, bestowed upon such a number of fat, red-faced policemen!" (Here his sobs choked him.) "Stupid animal that I was" (he said), "now I must languish in this dungeon, till people who were proud to say they knew me, have forgotten the very name of Toad! O wise old Badger!" (he said), "O clever, intelligent Rat and sensible Mole! What sound judgments, what a knowledge of men and matters you possess! O unhappy and forsaken Toad!" With lamentations such as these he passed his days and nights for several weeks, refusing his meals or intermediate light refreshments, though the grim and ancient gaoler, knowing that Toad's pockets were well lined, frequently pointed out that many comforts, and indeed luxuries,

could by arrangement be sent in—at a price—from outside.

Now the gaoler had a daughter, a pleasant wench and good-hearted, who assisted her father in the lighter duties of his post. She was particularly fond of animals, and, besides her canary, whose cage hung on a nail in the massive wall of the keep by day, to the great annoyance of prisoners who relished an after-dinner nap, and was

shrouded in an antimacassar on the parlour table at night, she kept several piebald mice and a restless revolving squirrel. This kind-hearted girl, pitying the misery of Toad, said to her father one day, "Father! I can't bear to see that poor beast so unhappy, and getting so thin! You let me have the managing of him. You know how fond of animals I am. I'll make him eat from my hand, and sit up, and do all sorts of things."

Her father replied that she could do what she liked with him. He was tired of Toad, and his sulks and his airs and his meanness. So that day she went on her errand of mercy, and knocked at the door of Toad's cell.

"Now, cheer up, Toad," she said, coaxingly, on entering, "and sit up and dry your eyes and be a sensible animal. And do try and eat a bit of dinner. See, I've brought you some of mine, hot from the oven!"

It was bubble-and-squeak, between two plates, and its fragrance filled the narrow cell. The penetrating smell of cabbage reached the nose of Toad as he lay prostrate in his misery on the floor, and gave him the idea for a moment that perhaps life was not such a blank and desperate thing as he had imagined. But still he wailed, and kicked with his legs, and refused to be comforted. So the wise girl retired for the time, but, of course, a good deal of the smell of hot cabbage remained behind, as it will do, and Toad, between his sobs, sniffed and reflected, and gradually began to think new and inspiring thoughts: of

chivalry, and poetry, and deeds still to be done; of broad meadows, and cattle browsing in them, raked by sun and wind; of kitchen-gardens, and straight herb-borders, and warm snap-dragon beset by bees; and of the comforting clink of dishes set down on the table at Toad Hall, and the scrape of chair-legs on the floor as every one pulled himself close up to his work. The air of the narrow cell took a rosy tinge; he began to think of his friends, and how they would surely be able to do something; of lawyers, and how they would have enjoyed his case, and what an ass he had been not to get in a few; and lastly, he thought of his own great cleverness and resource, and all that he was capable of if he only gave his great mind to it; and the cure was almost complete.

When the girl returned, some hours later, she carried a tray, with a cup of fragrant tea steaming on it; and a plate piled up with very hot buttered toast, cut thick, very brown on both sides, with the butter running through the holes in it in great golden drops, like honey from the honeycomb. The smell of that buttered toast simply talked to Toad, and with no uncertain voice; talked of warm kitchens, of breakfasts on bright frosty mornings, of cosy parlour firesides on winter evenings, when one's ramble was over and slippered feet were propped on the fender; of the purring of contented cats, and the twitter of sleepy canaries. Toad sat up on end once more, dried his eyes, sipped his tea and munched his toast, and soon began talking freely about himself, and the house he lived in, and his doings there, and how important he was, and what a lot his friends thought of him.

The gaoler's daughter saw that the topic was doing him as much good as the tea, as indeed it was, and encouraged him to go on.

"Tell me about Toad Hall," said she. "It sounds beautiful."

"Toad Hall," said the Toad proudly, "is an eligible self-contained gentleman's residence very unique; dating in part from the fourteenth

century, but replete with every modern convenience. Up-to-date sanitation. Five minutes from church, post-office, and golf-links, Suitable for——"

"Bless the animal," said the girl, laughing, "I don't want to **take** it. Tell me something real about it. But first wait till I fetch you some more tea and toast."

She tripped away, and presently returned with a fresh trayful; and Toad, pitching into the toast with avidity, his spirits quite restored to their usual level, told her about the boathouse, and the fish-pond, and the old walled kitchen-garden; and about the pig-styes, and the stables, and the pigeon-house, and the hen-house; and about the dairy, and the wash-house, and the china-cupboards, and the linen-presses (she liked that bit especially); and about the banqueting-hall, and the fun they had there when the other animals were gathered round the table and Toad was at his best, singing songs, telling stories, carrying on generally. Then she wanted to know about his animal-friends, and was very interested in all he had to tell her about them and how they lived, and what they did to pass their time. Of course, she did not say she was fond of animals as **pets**, because she had the sense to see that Toad would be extremely offended. When she said good night, having filled his water-jug and shaken up his straw for him, Toad was very much the same sanguine, self-satisfied animal that he had been of old. He sang a little song or two, of the sort he used to sing at his dinner-parties, curled himself up in the straw, and had an excellent night's rest and the pleasantest of dreams.

They had many interesting talks together, after that, as the dreary days went on; and the gaoler's daughter grew very sorry for Toad, and thought it a great shame that a poor little animal should be locked up in prison for what seemed to her a very trivial offence. Toad, of course, in his vanity, thought that her interest in him proceeded from a

growing tenderness; and he could not help half-regretting that the social gulf between them was so very wide, for she was a comely lass, and evidently admired him very much.

One morning the girl was very thoughtful, and answered at random, and did not seem to Toad to be paying proper attention to his witty sayings and sparkling comments.

"Toad," she said presently, "just listen, please. I have an aunt who is a washerwoman."

"There, there," said Toad, graciously and affably, "never mind; think no more about it. **I** have several aunts who **ought** to be washerwomen."

"Do be quiet a minute, Toad," said the girl. "You talk too much, that's your chief fault, and I'm trying to think, and you hurt my head. As I said, I have an aunt who is a washerwoman; she does the washing for all the prisoners in this castle—we try to keep any paying business of that sort in the family, you understand. She takes out the washing on Monday morning, and brings it in on Friday evening. This is a Thursday. Now, this is what occurs to me: you're very rich—at least you're always telling me so—and she's very poor. A few pounds wouldn't make any difference to you, and it would mean a lot to her. Now, I think if she were properly approached—squared, I believe is the word you animals use—you could come to some arrangement by which she would let you have her dress and bonnet and so on, and you could escape from the castle as the official washerwoman. You're very alike in many respects—particularly about the figure."

"We're **not**," said the Toad in a huff. "I have a very elegant figure—for what I am."

"So has my aunt," replied the girl, "for what **she** is. But have it your own way. You horrid, proud, ungrateful animal, when I'm sorry for you, and trying to help you!"

"Yes, yes, that's all right; thank you very much indeed," said the Toad hurriedly. "But look here! you wouldn't surely have Mr. Toad of Toad Hall, going about the country disguised as a washerwoman!"

"Then you can stop here as a Toad," replied the girl with much spirit. "I suppose you want to go off in a coach-and-four!"

Honest Toad was always ready to admit himself in the wrong. "You are a good, kind, clever girl," he said, "and I am indeed a proud and a stupid toad. Introduce me to your worthy aunt, if you will be so kind, and I have no doubt that the excellent lady and I will be able to arrange terms satisfactory to both parties."

Next evening the girl ushered her aunt into Toad's cell, bearing his week's washing pinned up in a towel. The old lady had been prepared beforehand for the interview, and the sight of certain gold sovereigns that Toad had thoughtfully placed on the table in full view practically completed the matter and left little further to discuss. In return for his cash, Toad received a cotton print gown, an apron, a shawl, and a rusty black bonnet; the only stipulation the old lady made being that she should be gagged and bound and dumped down in a corner. By this not very convincing artifice, she explained, aided by picturesque fiction which she could supply herself, she hoped to retain her situation, in spite of the suspicious appearance of things.

Toad was delighted with the suggestion. It would enable him to leave the prison in some style, and with his reputation for being a desperate and dangerous fellow untarnished; and he readily helped the gaoler's daughter to make her aunt appear as much as possible the victim of circumstances over which she had no control.

"Now it's your turn, Toad," said the girl. "Take off that coat and waistcoat of yours; you're fat enough as it is."

Shaking with laughter, she proceeded to "hook-and-eye" him into the cotton print gown, arranged the shawl with a professional fold,

and tied the strings of the rusty bonnet under his chin.

"You're the very image of her," she giggled, "only I'm sure you never looked half so respectable in all your life before. Now, good-bye, Toad, and good luck. Go straight down the way you came up; and if any one says anything to you, as they probably will, being but men, you can chaff back a bit, of course, but remember you're a widow woman, quite alone in the world, with a character to lose."

With a quaking heart, but as firm a footstep as he could command, Toad set forth cautiously on what seemed to be a most hare-brained and hazardous undertaking; but he was soon agreeably surprised to find how easy everything was made for him, and a little humbled at the thought that both his popularity, and the sex that seemed to inspire it, were really another's. The washerwoman's squat figure in its familiar cotton print seemed a passport for every barred door and grim gateway; even when he hesitated, uncertain as to the right turning to take, he found himself helped out of his difficulty by the warder at the next gate, anxious to be off to his tea, summoning him to come along sharp and not keep him waiting there all night. The chaff and the humourous sallies to which he was subjected, and to which, of course, he had to provide prompt and effective reply, formed, indeed, his chief danger; for Toad was an animal with a strong sense of his own dignity, and the chaff was mostly (he thought) poor and clumsy, and the humour of the sallies entirely lacking. However, he kept his temper, though with great difficulty, suited his retorts to his company and his supposed character, and did his best not to overstep the limits of good taste.

It seemed hours before he crossed the last courtyard, rejected the pressing invitations from the last guardroom, and dodged the outspread arms of the last warder, pleading with simulated passion for just one farewell embrace. But at last he heard the wicket-gate in the

great outer door click behind him, felt the fresh air of the outer world upon his anxious brow, and knew that he was free!

Dizzy with the easy success of his daring exploit, he walked quickly towards the lights of the town, not knowing in the least what he should do next, only quite certain of one thing, that he must remove himself as quickly as possible from the neighbourhood where the lady he was forced to represent was so well-known and so popular a character.

As he walked along, considering, his attention was caught by some red and green lights a little way off, to one side of the town, and the sound of the puffing and snorting of engines and the banging of shunted trucks fell on his ear. "Aha!" he thought, "this is a piece of luck! A railway station is the thing I want most in the whole world at this moment; and what's more, I needn't go through the town to get it, and shan't have to support this humiliating character by repartees which, though thoroughly effective, do not assist one's sense of self-respect."

He made his way to the station accordingly, consulted a time-table, and found that a train, bound more or less in the direction of his home, was due to start in half-an-hour. "More luck!" said Toad, his spirits rising rapidly, and went off to the booking-office to buy his ticket.

He gave the name of the station that he knew to be nearest to the village of which Toad Hall was the principal feature, and mechanically put his fingers, in search of the necessary money, where his waistcoat pocket should have been. But here the cotton gown, which had nobly stood by him so far, and which he had basely forgotten, intervened, and frustrated his efforts. In a sort of nightmare he struggled with the strange uncanny thing that seemed to hold his hands, turn all muscular strivings to water, and laugh at him

all the time; while other travellers, forming up in a line behind, waited with impatience, making suggestions of more or less value and comments of more or less stringency and point. At last—somehow—he never rightly understood how—he burst the barriers, attained the goal, arrived at where all waistcoat pockets are eternally situated, and found—not only no money, but no pocket to hold it, and no waistcoat to hold the pocket!

To his horror he recollected that he had left both coat and waistcoat behind him in his cell, and with them his pocket-book, money, keys, watch, matches, pencil-case—all that makes life worth living, all that distinguishes the many-pocketed animal, the lord of creation, from the inferior one-pocketed or no-pocketed productions that hop or trip about permissively, unequipped for the real contest.

In his misery he made one desperate effort to carry the thing off, and, with a return to his fine old manner—a blend of the Squire and the College Don—he said, "Look here! I find I've left my purse behind. Just give me that ticket, will you, and I'll send the money on to-morrow? I'm well-known in these parts."

The clerk stared at him and the rusty black bonnet a moment, and then laughed. "I should think you were pretty well known in these parts," he said, "if you've tried this game on often. Here, stand away from the window, please, madam; you're obstructing the other passengers!"

An old gentleman who had been prodding him in the back for some moments here thrust him away, and, what was worse, addressed him as his good woman, which angered Toad more than anything that had occurred that evening.

Baffled and full of despair, he wandered blindly down the platform where the train was standing, and tears trickled down each side of his nose. It was hard, he thought, to be within sight of safety

and almost of home, and to be baulked by the want of a few wretched shillings and by the pettifogging mistrustfulness of paid officials. Very soon his escape would be discovered, the hunt would be up, he would be caught, reviled, loaded with chains, dragged back again to prison and bread-and-water and straw; his guards and penalties would be doubled; and O, what sarcastic remarks the girl would make! What was to be done? He was not swift of foot; his figure was unfortunately recognisable. Could he not squeeze under the seat of a carriage? He had seen this method adopted by schoolboys, when the journey-money provided by thoughtful parents had been diverted to other and better ends. As he pondered, he found himself opposite the engine, which was being oiled, wiped, and generally caressed by its affectionate driver, a burly man with an oil-can in one hand and a lump of cotton-waste in the other.

"Hullo, mother!" said the engine-driver, "what's the trouble? You don't look particularly cheerful."

"O, sir!" said Toad, crying afresh, "I am a poor unhappy washerwoman, and I've lost all my money, and can't pay for a ticket, and I **must** get home to-night somehow, and whatever I am to do I don't know. O dear, O dear!"

"That's a bad business, indeed," said the engine-driver reflectively. "Lost your money—and can't get home—and got some kids, too, waiting for you, I dare say?"

"Any amount of 'em," sobbed Toad. "And they'll be hungry—and playing with matches—and upsetting lamps, the little innocents!—and quarrelling, and going on generally. O dear, O dear!"

"Well, I'll tell you what I'll do," said the good engine-driver. "You're a washerwoman to your trade, says you. Very well, that's that. And I'm an engine-driver, as you well may see, and there's no denying it's terribly dirty work. Uses up a power of shirts, it does, till my

missus is fair tired of washing of 'em. If you'll wash a few shirts for me when you get home, and send 'em along, I'll give you a ride on my engine. It's against the Company's regulations, but we're not so very particular in these out-of-the-way parts."

The Toad's misery turned into rapture as he eagerly scrambled up into the cab of the engine. Of course, he had never washed a shirt in his life, and couldn't if he tried and, anyhow, he wasn't going to begin; but he thought: "When I get safely home to Toad Hall, and have money again, and pockets to put it in, I will send the engine-driver enough to pay for quite a quantity of washing, and that will be the same thing, or better."

The guard waved his welcome flag, the engine-driver whistled in cheerful response, and the train moved out of the station. As the speed increased, and the Toad could see on either side of him real fields, and trees, and hedges, and cows, and horses, all flying past him, and as he thought how every minute was bringing him nearer to Toad Hall, and sympathetic friends, and money to chink in his pocket, and a soft bed to sleep in, and good things to eat, and praise and admiration at the recital of his adventures and his surpassing cleverness, he began to skip up and down and shout and sing snatches of song, to the great astonishment of the engine-driver, who had come across washerwomen before, at long intervals, but never one at all like this.

They had covered many and many a mile, and Toad was already considering what he would have for supper as soon as he got home, when he noticed that the engine-driver, with a puzzled expression on his face, was leaning over the side of the engine and listening hard. Then he saw him climb on to the coals and gaze out over the top of the train; then he returned and said to Toad: "It's very strange; we're the last train running in this direction to-night, yet I could be sworn that I heard another following us!"

Toad ceased his frivolous antics at once. He became grave and depressed, and a dull pain in the lower part of his spine, communicating itself to his legs, made him want to sit down and try desperately not to think of all the possibilities.

By this time the moon was shining brightly, and the engine-driver, steadying himself on the coal, could command a view of the line behind them for a long distance.

Presently he called out, "I can see it clearly now! It is an engine, on our rails, coming along at a great pace! It looks as if we were being pursued!"

The miserable Toad, crouching in the coal-dust, tried hard to think of something to do, with dismal want of success.

"They are gaining on us fast!" cried the engine-driver. And the engine is crowded with the queerest lot of people! Men like ancient warders, waving halberds; policemen in their helmets, waving truncheons; and shabbily dressed men in pot-hats, obvious and unmistakable plain-clothes detectives even at this distance, waving revolvers and walking-sticks; all waving, and all shouting the same thing— 'Stop, stop, stop!'"

Then Toad fell on his knees among the coals and, raising his clasped paws in supplication, cried, "Save me, only save me, dear kind Mr. Engine-driver, and I will confess everything! I am not the simple washerwoman I seem to be! I have no children waiting for me, innocent or otherwise! I am a toad—the well-known and popular Mr. Toad, a landed proprietor; I have just escaped, by my great daring and cleverness, from a loathsome dungeon into which my enemies had flung me; and if those fellows on that engine recapture me, it will be chains and bread-and-water and straw and misery once more for poor, unhappy, innocent Toad!"

The engine-driver looked down upon him very sternly, and said,

"Now tell the truth; what were you put in prison for?"

"It was nothing very much," said poor Toad, colouring deeply. "I only borrowed a motorcar while the owners were at lunch; they had no need of it at the time. I didn't mean to steal it, really; but people—especially magistrates—take such harsh views of thoughtless and high-spirited actions."

The engine-driver looked very grave and said, "I fear that you have been indeed a wicked toad, and by rights I ought to give you up to offended justice. But you are evidently in sore trouble and distress, so I will not desert you. I don't hold with motor-cars, for one thing; and I don't hold with being ordered about by policemen when I'm on my own engine, for another. And the sight of an animal in tears always makes me feel queer and softhearted. So cheer up, Toad! I'll do my best, and we may beat them yet!"

They piled on more coals, shovelling furiously; the furnace roared, the sparks flew, the engine leapt and swung but still their pursuers slowly gained. The engine-driver, with a sigh, wiped his brow with a handful of cotton-waste, and said, "I'm afraid it's no good, Toad. You see, they are running light, and they have the better engine. There's just one thing left for us to do, and it's your only chance, so attend very carefully to what I tell you. A short way ahead of us is a long tunnel, and on the other side of that the line passes through a thick wood. Now, I will put on all the speed I can while we are running through the tunnel, but the other fellows will slow down a bit, naturally, for fear of an accident. When we are through, I will shut off steam and put on brakes as hard as I can, and the moment it's safe to do so you must jump and hide in the wood, before they get through the tunnel and see you. Then I will go full speed ahead again, and they can chase me if they like, for as long as they like, and as far as they like. Now mind and be ready to jump when I tell you!"

They piled on more coals, and the train shot into the tunnel, and the engine rushed and roared and rattled, till at last they shot out at the other end into fresh air and the peaceful moonlight, and saw the wood lying dark and helpful upon either side of the line. The driver shut off steam and put on brakes, the Toad got down on the step, and as the train slowed down to almost a walking pace he heard the driver call out, "Now, jump!"

Toad jumped, rolled down a short embankment, picked himself up unhurt, scrambled into the wood and hid.

Peeping out, he saw his train get up speed again and disappear at a great pace. Then out of the tunnel burst the pursuing engine, roaring and whistling, her motley crew waving their various weapons and shouting, "Stop! stop! stop!" When they were past, the Toad had a hearty laugh—for the first time since he was thrown into prison.

But he soon stopped laughing when he came to consider that it was now very late and dark and cold, and he was in an unknown wood, with no money and no chance of supper, and still far from friends and home; and the dead silence of everything, after the roar and rattle of the train, was something of a shock. He dared not leave the shelter of the trees, so he struck into the wood, with the idea of leaving the railway as far as possible behind him.

After so many weeks within walls, he found the wood strange and unfriendly and inclined, he thought, to make fun of him. Nightjars, sounding their mechanical rattle, made him think that the wood was full of searching warders, closing in on him. An owl, swooping noiselessly towards him, brushed his shoulder with its wing, making him jump with the horrid certainty that it was a hand; then flitted off, moth-like, laughing its low ho! ho! ho; which Toad thought in very poor taste. Once he met a fox, who stopped, looked him up and down in a sarcastic sort of way, and said, "Hullo, washerwoman! Half a pair

of socks and a pillow-case short this week! Mind it doesn't occur again!" and swaggered off, sniggering. Toad looked about for a stone to throw at him, but could not succeed in finding one, which vexed him more than anything. At last, cold, hungry, and tired out, he sought the shelter of a hollow tree, where with branches and dead leaves he made himself as comfortable a bed as he could, and slept soundly till the morning.

IX.
WAYFARERS ALL

The Water Rat was restless, and he did not exactly know why. To all appearance the summer's pomp was still at fullest height, and although in the tilled acres green had given way to gold, though rowans were reddening, and the woods were dashed here and there with a tawny fierceness, yet light and warmth and colour were still present in undiminished measure, clean of any chilly premonitions of the passing year. But the constant chorus of the orchards and hedges had shrunk to a casual evensong from a few yet unwearied performers; the robin was beginning to assert himself once more; and there was a feeling in the air of change and departure. The cuckoo, of course, had long been silent; but many another feathered friend, for months a part of the familiar landscape and its small society, was missing too and it seemed that the ranks thinned steadily day by day. Rat, ever observant of all winged movement, saw that it was taking daily a southing tendency; and even as he lay in bed at night he thought he could make out, passing in the darkness overhead, the beat and quiver of impatient pinions, obedient to the peremptory call.

Nature's Grand Hotel has its Season, like the others. As the guests one by one pack, pay, and depart, and the seats at the **table-d'hôte** shrink pitifully at each succeeding meal; as suites of rooms are closed, carpets taken up, and waiters sent away; those boarders who are staying on, **en pension**, until the next year's full re-opening, cannot help being somewhat affected by all these flittings and farewells, this eager discussion of plans, routes, and fresh quarters, this

daily shrinkage in the stream of comradeship. One gets unsettled, depressed, and inclined to be querulous. Why this craving for change? Why not stay on quietly here, like us, and be jolly? You don't know this hotel out of the season, and what fun we have among ourselves, we fellows who remain and see the whole interesting year out. All very true, no doubt the others always reply; we quite envy you—and some other year perhaps—but just now we have engagements—and there's the bus at the door—our time is up! So they depart, with a smile and a nod, and we miss them, and feel resentful. The Rat was a self-sufficing sort of animal, rooted to the land, and, whoever went, he stayed; still, he could not help noticing what was in the air, and feeling some of its influence in his bones.

It was difficult to settle down to anything seriously, with all this flitting going on. Leaving the water-side, where rushes stood thick and tall in a stream that was becoming sluggish and low, he wandered country-wards, crossed a field or two of pasturage already looking dusty and parched, and thrust into the great sea of wheat, yellow, wavy, and murmurous, full of quiet motion and small whisperings. Here he often loved to wander, through the forest of stiff strong stalks that carried their own golden

sky away over his head—a sky that was always dancing, shimmering, softly talking; or swaying strongly to the passing wind and recovering itself with a toss and a merry laugh. Here, too, he had many small friends, a society complete in itself, leading full and busy lives, but always with a spare moment to gossip, and exchange news with a visitor. Today, however, though they were civil enough, the field-mice and harvest-mice seemed preoccupied. Many were digging and tunnelling busily; others, gathered together in small groups, examined plans and drawings of small flats, stated to be desirable and compact, and situated conveniently near the Stores. Some were hauling out dusty trunks and dress-baskets, others were already elbow-deep packing their belongings; while everywhere piles and bundles of wheat, oats, barley, beech-mast and nuts, lay about ready for transport.

"Here's old Ratty!" they cried as soon as they saw him. "Come and bear a hand, Rat, and don't stand about idle!"

"What sort of games are you up to?" said the Water Rat severely. "You know it isn't time to be thinking of winter quarters yet, by a long way!"

"O yes, we know that," explained a field-mouse rather shamefacedly; "but it's always as well to be in good time, isn't it? We really **must** get all the furniture and baggage and stores moved out of this before those horrid machines begin clicking round the fields; and then, you know, the best flats get picked up so quickly nowadays, and if you're late you have to put up with **anything**; and they want such a lot of doing up, too, before they're fit to move into. Of course, we're early, we know that; but we're only just making a start."

"O, bother **starts**," said the Rat. "It's a splendid day. Come for a row, or a stroll along the hedges, or a picnic in the woods, or something."

"Well, I **think** not **to-day**, thank you," replied the field-mouse hurriedly. "Perhaps some **other** day—when we've more **time**——"

The Rat, with a snort of contempt, swung round to go, tripped over a hat-box, and fell, with undignified remarks.

"If people would be more careful," said a field-mouse rather stiffly, "and look where they're going, people wouldn't hurt themselves—and forget themselves. Mind that hold-all, Rat! You'd better sit down somewhere. In an hour or two we may be more free to attend to you."

"You won't be ʻfree' as you call it much this side of Christmas, I can see that," retorted the Rat grumpily, as he picked his way out of the field.

He returned somewhat despondently to his river again—his faithful, steady-going old river, which never packed up, flitted, or went into winter quarters.

In the osiers which fringed the bank he spied a swallow sitting. Presently it was joined by another, and then by a third; and the birds, fidgeting restlessly on their bough, talked together earnestly and low.

"What, **already**," said the Rat, strolling up to them. "What's the hurry? I call it simply ridiculous."

"O, we're not off yet, if that's what you mean," replied the first swallow. "We're only making plans and arranging things. Talking it over, you know—what route we're taking this year, and where we'll stop, and so on. That's half the fun!"

"Fun?" said the Rat; "now that's just what I don't understand. If you've **got** to leave this pleasant place, and your friends who will miss you, and your snug homes that you've just settled into, why, when the hour strikes I've no doubt you'll go bravely, and face all the trouble and discomfort and change and newness, and make believe that you're not very unhappy. But to want to talk about it, or even think about it,

till you really need——"

"No, you don't understand, naturally," said the second swallow. "First, we feel it stirring within us, a sweet unrest; then back come the recollections one by one, like homing pigeons. They flutter through our dreams at night, they fly with us in our wheelings and circlings by day. We hunger to inquire of each other, to compare notes and assure ourselves that it was all really true, as one by one the scents and sounds and names of long-forgotten places come gradually back and beckon to us."

"Couldn't you stop on for just this year?" suggested the Water Rat, wistfully. "We'll all do our best to make you feel at home. You've no idea what good times we have here, while you are far away."

"I tried 'stopping on' one year," said the third swallow. "I had grown so fond of the place that when the time came I hung back and let the others go on without me. For a few weeks it was all well enough, but afterwards, O the weary length of the nights! The shivering, sunless days! The air so clammy and chill, and not an insect in an acre of it! No, it was no good; my courage broke down, and one cold, stormy night I took wing, flying well inland on account of the strong easterly gales. It was snowing hard as I beat through the passes of the great mountains, and I had a stiff fight to win through; but never shall I forget the blissful feeling of the hot sun again on my back as I sped down to the lakes that lay so blue and placid below me, and the taste of my first fat insect! The past was like a bad dream; the future was all happy holiday as I moved southwards week by week, easily, lazily, lingering as long as I dared, but always heeding the call! No, I had had my warning; never again did I think of disobedience."

"Ah, yes, the call of the South, of the South!" twittered the other two dreamily. "Its songs its hues, its radiant air! O, do you remember——" and, forgetting the Rat, they slid into passionate

reminiscence, while he listened fascinated, and his heart burned within him. In himself, too, he knew that it was vibrating at last, that chord hitherto dormant and unsuspected. The mere chatter of these southern-bound birds, their pale and second-hand reports, had yet power to awaken this wild new sensation and thrill him through and through with it; what would one moment of the real thing work in him—one passionate touch of the real southern sun, one waft of the authentic odor? With closed eyes he dared to dream a moment in full abandonment, and when he looked again the river seemed steely and chill, the green fields grey and lightless. Then his loyal heart seemed to cry out on his weaker self for its treachery.

"Why do you ever come back, then, at all?" he demanded of the swallows jealously. "What do you find to attract you in this poor drab little country?"

"And do you think," said the first swallow, "that the other call is not for us too, in its due season? The call of lush meadow-grass, wet orchards, warm, insect-haunted ponds, of browsing cattle, of haymaking, and all the farm-buildings clustering round the House of the perfect Eaves?"

"Do you suppose," asked the second one, that you are the only living thing that craves with a hungry longing to hear the cuckoo's note again?"

"In due time," said the third, "we shall be home-sick once more for quiet water-lilies swaying on the surface of an English stream. But to-day all that seems pale and thin and very far away. Just now our blood dances to other music."

They fell a-twittering among themselves once more, and this time their intoxicating babble was of violet seas, tawny sands, and lizard-haunted walls.

Restlessly the Rat wandered off once more, climbed the slope

that rose gently from the north bank of the river, and lay looking out towards the great ring of Downs that barred his vision further southwards—his simple horizon hitherto, his Mountains of the Moon, his limit behind which lay nothing he had cared to see or to know. To-day, to him gazing South with a new-born need stirring in his heart, the clear sky over their long low outline seemed to pulsate with promise; to-day, the unseen was everything, the unknown the only real fact of life. On this side of the hills was now the real blank, on the other lay the crowded and coloured panorama that his inner eye was seeing so clearly. What seas lay beyond, green, leaping, and crested! What sun-bathed coasts, along which the white villas glittered against the olive woods! What quiet harbours, thronged with gallant shipping bound for purple islands of wine and spice, islands set low in languorous waters!

He rose and descended river-wards once more; then changed his mind and sought the side of the dusty lane. There, lying half-buried in the thick, cool under-hedge tangle that bordered it, he could muse on the metalled road and all the wondrous world that it led to; on all the wayfarers, too, that might have trodden it, and the fortunes and adventures they had gone to seek or found unseeking—out there, beyond—beyond!

Footsteps fell on his ear, and the figure of one that walked somewhat wearily came into view; and he saw that it was a Rat, and a very dusty one. The wayfarer, as he reached him, saluted with a gesture of courtesy that had something foreign about it—hesitated a moment—then with a pleasant smile turned from the track and sat down by his side in the cool herbage. He seemed tired, and the Rat let him rest unquestioned, understanding something of what was in his thoughts; knowing, too, the value all animals attach at times to mere silent companionship, when the weary muscles slacken and the mind

marks time.

The wayfarer was lean and keen-featured, and somewhat bowed at the shoulders; his paws were thin and long, his eyes much wrinkled at the corners, and he wore small gold ear rings in his neatly-set well-shaped ears. His knitted jersey was of a faded blue, his breeches, patched and stained, were based on a blue foundation, and his small belongings that he carried were tied up in a blue cotton handkerchief.

When he had rested awhile the stranger sighed, snuffed the air, and looked about him.

"That was clover, that warm whiff on the breeze," he remarked; "and those are cows we hear cropping the grass behind us and blowing softly between mouthfuls. There is a sound of distant reapers, and yonder rises a blue line of cottage smoke against the woodland. The river runs somewhere close by, for I hear the call of a moorhen, and I see by your build that you're a freshwater mariner. Everything seems asleep, and yet going on all the time. It is a goodly life that you lead, friend; no doubt the best in the world, if only you are strong enough to lead it!"

"Yes, it's **the** life, the only life, to live," responded the Water Rat dreamily, and without his usual whole-hearted conviction.

"I did not say exactly that," replied the stranger cautiously; "but no doubt it's the best. I've tried it, and I know. And because I've just tried it—six months of it—and know it's the best, here am I, footsore and hungry, tramping away from it, tramping southward, following the old call, back to the old life, **the** life which is mine and which will not let me go."

"Is this, then, yet another of them?" mused the Rat. "And where have you just come from?" he asked. He hardly dared to ask where he was bound for; he seemed to know the answer only too well.

"Nice little farm," replied the wayfarer, briefly. "Upalong in that

direction"—he nodded northwards. "Never mind about it. I had everything I could want—everything I had any right to expect of life, and more; and here I am! Glad to be here all the same, though, glad to be here! So many miles further on the road, so many hours nearer to my heart's desire!"

His shining eyes held fast to the horizon, and he seemed to be listening for some sound that was wanting from that inland acreage, vocal as it was with the cheerful music of pasturage and farmyard.

"You are not one of **us**," said the Water Rat, "nor yet a farmer; nor even, I should judge, of this country."

"Right," replied the stranger. "I'm a seafaring rat, I am, and the port I originally hail from is Constantinople, though I'm a sort of a foreigner there too, in a manner of speaking. You will have heard of Constantinople, friend? A fair city, and an ancient and glorious one. And you may have heard, too, of Sigurd, King of Norway, and how he sailed thither with sixty ships, and how he and his men rode up through streets all canopied in their honour with purple and gold; and how the Emperor and Empress came down and banqueted with him on board his ship. When Sigurd returned home, many of his Northmen remained behind and entered the Emperor's body-guard, and my ancestor, a Norwegian born, stayed behind too, with the ships that Sigurd gave the Emperor. Seafarers we have ever been, and no wonder; as for me, the city of my birth is no more my home than any pleasant port between there and the London River. I know them all, and they know me. Set me down on any of their quays or foreshores, and I am home again."

"I suppose you go great voyages," said the Water Rat with growing interest. "Months and months out of sight of land, and provisions running short, and allowanced as to water, and your mind communing with the mighty ocean, and all that sort of thing?"

"By no means," said the Sea Rat frankly. "Such a life as you describe would not suit me at all. I'm in the coasting trade, and rarely out of sight of land. It's the jolly times on shore that appeal to me, as much as any seafaring. O, those southern seaports! The smell of them, the riding-lights at night, the glamour!"

"Well, perhaps you have chosen the better way," said the Water Rat, but rather doubtfully. "Tell me something of your coasting, then, if you have a mind to, and what sort of harvest an animal of spirit might hope to bring home from it to warm his latter days with gallant memories by the fireside; for my life, I confess to you, feels to me to-day somewhat narrow and circumscribed."

"My last voyage," began the Sea Rat, "that landed me eventually in this country, bound with high hopes for my inland farm, will serve as a good example of any of them, and, indeed, as an epitome of my highly-coloured life. Family troubles, as usual, began it. The domestic storm-cone was hoisted, and I shipped myself on board a small trading vessel bound from Constantinople, by classic seas whose every wave throbs with a deathless memory, to the Grecian Islands and the Levant. Those were golden days and balmy nights! In and out of harbour all the time—old friends everywhere—sleeping in some cool temple or ruined cistern during the heat of the day—feasting and song after sundown, under great stars set in a velvet sky! Thence we turned and coasted up the Adriatic, its shores swimming in an atmosphere of amber, rose, and aquamarine; we lay in wide land-locked harbours, we roamed through ancient and noble cities, until at last one morning, as the sun rose royally behind us, we rode into Venice down a path of gold. O, Venice is a fine city, wherein a rat can wander at his ease and take his pleasure! Or, when weary of wandering, can sit at the edge of the Grand Canal at night, feasting with his friends, when the air is full of music and the sky full of stars,

and the lights flash and shimmer on the polished steel prows of the swaying gondolas, packed so that you could walk across the canal on them from side to side! And then the food—do you like shellfish? Well, well, we won't linger over that now."

He was silent for a time; and the Water Rat, silent too and enthralled, floated on dream-canals and heard a phantom song pealing high between vaporous grey wave-lapped walls.

"Southwards we sailed again at last," continued the Sea Rat, "coasting down the Italian shore, till finally we made Palermo, and there I quitted for a long, happy spell on shore. I never stick too long to one ship; one gets narrow-minded and prejudiced. Besides, Sicily is one of my happy hunting-grounds. I know everybody there, and their ways just suit me. I spent many jolly weeks in the island, staying with friends up country. When I grew restless again I took advantage of a ship that was trading to Sardinia and Corsica; and very glad I was to feel the fresh breeze and the sea-spray in my face once more."

"But isn't it very hot and stuffy, down in the—hold, I think you call it?" asked the Water Rat.

The seafarer looked at him with the suspicion of a wink. "I'm an old hand," he remarked with much simplicity. "The captain's cabin's good enough for me."

"It's a hard life, by all accounts," murmured the Rat, sunk in deep thought.

"For the crew it is," replied the seafarer gravely, again with the ghost of a wink.

"From Corsica," he went on, "I made use of a ship that was taking wine to the mainland. We made Alassio in the evening, lay to, hauled up our wine-casks, and hove them overboard, tied one to the other by a long line. Then the crew took to the boats and rowed shorewards, singing as they went, and drawing after them the long

bobbing procession of casks, like a mile of porpoises. On the sands they had horses waiting, which dragged the casks up the steep street of the little town with a fine rush and clatter and scramble. When the last cask was in, we went and refreshed and rested, and sat late into the night, drinking with our friends, and next morning I took to the great olive-woods for a spell and a rest. For now I had done with islands for the time, and ports and shipping were plentiful; so I led a lazy life among the peasants, lying and watching them work, or stretched high on the hillside with the blue Mediterranean far below me. And so at length, by easy stages, and partly on foot, partly by sea, to Marseilles, and the meeting of old shipmates, and the visiting of great ocean-bound vessels, and feasting once more. Talk of shell-fish! Why, sometimes I dream of the shell-fish of Marseilles, and wake up crying!"

"That reminds me," said the polite Water Rat; "you happened to mention that you were hungry, and I ought to have spoken earlier. Of course, you will stop and take your midday meal with me? My hole is close by; it is some time past noon, and you are very welcome to whatever there is."

"Now I call that kind and brotherly of you," said the Sea Rat. "I was indeed hungry when I sat down, and ever since I inadvertently happened to mention shell-fish, my pangs have been extreme. But couldn't you fetch it along out here? I am none too fond of going under hatches, unless I'm obliged to; and then, while we eat, I could tell you more concerning my voyages and the pleasant life I lead—at least, it is very pleasant to me, and by your attention I judge it commends itself to you; whereas if we go indoors it is a hundred to one that I shall presently fall asleep."

"That is indeed an excellent suggestion," said the Water Rat, and hurried off home. There he got out the luncheon-basket and packed a

simple meal, in which, remembering the stranger's origin and preferences, he took care to include a yard of long French bread, a sausage out of which the garlic sang, some cheese which lay down and cried, and a long-necked straw-covered flask wherein lay bottled sunshine shed and garnered on far Southern slopes. Thus laden, he returned with all speed, and blushed for pleasure at the old seaman's commendations of his taste and judgment, as together they unpacked the basket and laid out the contents on the grass by the roadside.

The Sea Rat, as soon as his hunger was somewhat assuaged, continued the history of his latest voyage, conducting his simple hearer from port to port of Spain, landing him at Lisbon, Oporto, and Bordeaux, introducing him to the pleasant harbours of Cornwall and Devon, and so up the Channel to that final quayside, where, landing after winds long contrary, storm-driven and weather-beaten, he had caught the first magical hints and heraldings of another Spring, and, fired by these, had sped on a long tramp inland, hungry for the experiment of life on some quiet farmstead, very far from the weary beating of any sea.

Spell-bound and quivering with excitement, the Water Rat followed the Adventurer league by league, over stormy bays, through crowded roadsteads, across harbour bars on a racing tide, up winding rivers that hid their busy little towns round a sudden turn; and left him with a regretful sigh planted at his dull inland farm, about which he desired to hear nothing.

By this time their meal was over, and the Seafarer, refreshed and strengthened, his voice more vibrant, his eye lit with a brightness that seemed caught from some far-away sea-beacon, filled his glass with the red and glowing vintage of the South, and, leaning towards the Water Rat, compelled his gaze and held him, body and soul, while he talked. Those eyes were of the changing foam-streaked grey-green of

leaping Northern seas; in the glass shone a hot ruby that seemed the very heart of the South, beating for him who had courage to respond to its pulsation. The twin lights, the shifting grey and the steadfast red, mastered the Water Rat and held him bound, fascinated, powerless. The quiet world outside their rays receded far away and ceased to be. And the talk, the wonderful talk flowed on—or was it speech entirely, or did it pass at times into song—chanty of the sailors weighing the dripping anchor, sonorous hum of the shrouds in a tearing North-Easter, ballad of the fisherman hauling his nets at sundown against an apricot sky, chords of guitar and mandoline from gondola or caique? Did it change into the cry of the wind, plaintive at first, angrily shrill as it freshened, rising to a tearing whistle, sinking to a musical trickle of air from the leech of the bellying sail? All these sounds the spell-bound listener seemed to hear, and with them the hungry complaint of the gulls and the sea-mews, the soft thunder of the breaking wave, the cry of the protesting shingle. Back into speech again it passed, and with beating heart he was following the adventures of a dozen seaports, the fights, the escapes, the rallies, the comradeships, the gallant undertakings; or he searched islands for treasure, fished in still lagoons and dozed day-long on warm white sand. Of deep-sea fishings he heard tell, and mighty silver gatherings of the mile-long net; of sudden perils, noise of breakers on a moonless night, or the tall bows of the great liner taking shape overhead through the fog; of the merry home-coming, the headland rounded, the harbour lights opened out; the groups seen dimly on the quay, the cheery hail, the splash of the hawser; the trudge up the steep little street towards the comforting glow of red-curtained windows.

Lastly, in his waking dream it seemed to him that the Adventurer had risen to his feet, but was still speaking, still holding him fast with his sea-grey eyes.

"And now," he was softly saying, "I take to the road again, holding on southwestwards for many a long and dusty day; till at last I reach the little grey sea town I know so well, that clings along one steep side of the harbour. There through dark doorways you look down flights of stone steps, overhung by great pink tufts of valerian and ending in a patch of sparkling blue water. The little boats that lie tethered to the rings and stanchions of the old sea-wall are gaily painted as those I clambered in and out of in my own childhood; the salmon leap on the flood tide, schools of mackerel flash and play past quay-sides and foreshores, and by the windows the great vessels glide, night and day, up to their moorings or forth to the open sea. There, sooner or later, the ships of all seafaring nations arrive; and there, at its destined hour, the ship of my choice will let go its anchor. I shall take my time, I shall tarry and bide, till at last the right one lies waiting for me, warped out into midstream, loaded low, her bowsprit pointing down harbour. I shall slip on board, by boat or along hawser; and then one morning I shall wake to the song and tramp of the sailors, the clink of the capstan, and the rattle of the anchor-chain coming merrily in. We shall break out the jib and the foresail, the white houses on the harbour side will glide slowly past us as she gathers steering-way, and the voyage will have begun! As she forges towards the headland she will clothe herself with canvas; and then, once outside, the sounding slap of great green seas as she heels to the wind, pointing South!

"And you, you will come too, young brother; for the days pass, and never return, and the South still waits for you. Take the Adventure, heed the call, now ere the irrevocable moment passes! 'Tis but a banging of the door behind you, a blithesome step forward, and you are out of the old life and into the new! Then some day, some day long hence, jog home here if you will, when the cup has been drained and the play has been played, and sit down by your quiet river with a

store of goodly memories for company. You can easily overtake me on the road, for you are young, and I am ageing and go softly. I will linger, and look back; and at last I will surely see you coming, eager and light-hearted, with all the South in your face!"

The voice died away and ceased as an insect's tiny trumpet dwindles swiftly into silence; and the Water Rat, paralysed and staring, saw at last but a distant speck on the white surface of the road.

Mechanically he rose and proceeded to repack the luncheon-basket, carefully and without haste. Mechanically he returned home, gathered together a few small necessaries and special treasures he was fond of, and put them in a satchel; acting with slow deliberation, moving about the room like a sleep-walker; listening ever with parted lips. He swung the satchel over his shoulder, carefully selected a stout stick for his wayfaring, and with no haste, but with no hesitation at all, he stepped across the threshold just as the Mole appeared at the door.

"Why, where are you off to, Ratty?" asked the Mole in great surprise, grasping him by the arm.

"Going South, with the rest of them," murmured the Rat in a dreamy monotone, never looking at him. "Seawards first and then on shipboard, and so to the shores that are calling me!"

He pressed resolutely forward, still without haste, but with dogged fixity of purpose; but the Mole, now thoroughly alarmed, placed himself in front of him, and looking into his eyes saw that they were glazed and set and turned a streaked and shifting grey—not his friend's eyes, but the eyes of some other animal! Grappling with him strongly he dragged him inside, threw him down, and held him.

The Rat struggled desperately for a few moments, and then his strength seemed suddenly to leave him, and he lay still and exhausted, with closed eyes, trembling. Presently the Mole assisted him to rise and placed him in a chair, where he sat collapsed and shrunken into

himself, his body shaken by a violent shivering, passing in time into an hysterical fit of dry sobbing. Mole made the door fast, threw the satchel into a drawer and locked it, and sat down quietly on the table by his friend, waiting for the strange seizure to pass. Gradually the Rat sank into a troubled doze, broken by starts and confused murmurings of things strange and wild and foreign to the unenlightened Mole; and from that he passed into a deep slumber.

Very anxious in mind, the Mole left him for a time and busied himself with household matters; and it was getting dark when he returned to the parlour and found the Rat where he had left him, wide awake indeed, but listless, silent, and dejected. He took one hasty glance at his eyes; found them, to his great gratification, clear and dark and brown again as before; and then sat down and tried to cheer him up and help him to relate what had happened to him.

Poor Ratty did his best, by degrees, to explain things; but how could he put into cold words what had mostly been suggestion? How recall, for another's benefit, the haunting sea voices that had sung to him, how reproduce at second-hand the magic of the Seafarer's hundred reminiscences? Even to himself, now the spell was broken and the glamour gone, he found it difficult to account for what had seemed, some hours ago, the inevitable and only thing. It is not surprising, then, that he failed to convey to the Mole any clear idea of what he had been through that day.

To the Mole this much was plain: the fit, or attack, had passed away, and had left him sane again, though shaken and cast down by the reaction. But he seemed to have lost all interest for the time in the things that went to make up his daily life, as well as in all pleasant forecastings of the altered days and doings that the changing season was surely bringing.

Casually, then, and with seeming indifference, the Mole turned

his talk to the harvest that was being gathered in, the towering wagons and their straining teams, the growing ricks, and the large moon rising over bare acres dotted with sheaves. He talked of the reddening apples around, of the browning nuts, of jams and preserves and the distilling of cordials; till by easy stages such as these he reached midwinter, its hearty joys and its snug home life, and then he became simply lyrical.

By degrees the Rat began to sit up and to join in. His dull eye brightened, and he lost some of his listening air.

Presently the tactful Mole slipped away and returned with a pencil and a few half-sheets of paper, which he placed on the table at his friend's elbow.

"It's quite a long time since you did any poetry," he remarked. "You might have a try at it this evening, instead of—well, brooding over things so much. I've an idea that you'll feel a lot better when you've got something jotted down—if it's only just the rhymes."

The Rat pushed the paper away from him wearily, but the discreet Mole took occasion to leave the room, and when he peeped in again some time later, the Rat was absorbed and deaf to the world; alternately scribbling and sucking the top of his pencil. It is true that he sucked a good deal more than he scribbled; but it was joy to the Mole to know that the cure had at least begun.

X.
THE FURTHER ADVENTURES
OF TOAD

The front door of the hollow tree faced eastwards, so Toad was
called at an early hour; partly by the bright sunlight streaming in on
him, partly by the exceeding coldness of his toes, which made him
dream that he was at home in bed in his own handsome room with
the Tudor window, on a cold winter's night, and his bedclothes had
got up, grumbling and protesting they couldn't stand the cold any
longer, and had run downstairs to the kitchen fire to warm themselves;
and he had followed, on bare feet, along miles and miles of icy stone-
paved passages, arguing and beseeching them to be reasonable. He
would probably have been aroused much earlier, had he not slept for
some weeks on straw over stone flags, and almost forgotten the

friendly feeling of thick blankets pulled well up round the chin.

Sitting up, he rubbed his eyes first and his complaining toes next, wondered for a moment where he was, looking round for familiar stone wall and little barred window; then, with a leap of the heart, remembered everything—his escape, his flight, his pursuit; remembered, first and best thing of all, that he was free!

Free! The word and the thought alone were worth fifty blankets. He was warm from end to end as he thought of the jolly world outside, waiting eagerly for him to make his triumphal entrance, ready to serve him and play up to him, anxious to help him and to keep him company, as it always had been in days of old before misfortune fell upon him. He shook himself and combed the dry leaves out of his hair with his fingers; and, his toilet complete, marched forth into the comfortable morning sun, cold but confident, hungry but hopeful, all nervous terrors of yesterday dispelled by rest and sleep and frank and heartening sunshine.

He had the world all to himself, that early summer morning. The dewy woodland, as he threaded it, was solitary and still: the green fields that succeeded the trees were his own to do as he liked with; the road itself, when he reached it, in that loneliness that was everywhere, seemed, like a stray dog, to be looking anxiously for company. Toad, however, was looking for something that could talk, and tell him clearly which way he ought to go. It is all very well, when you have a light heart, and a clear conscience, and money in your pocket, and nobody scouring the country for you to drag you off to prison again, to follow where the road beckons and points, not caring whither. The practical Toad cared very much indeed, and he could have kicked the road for its helpless silence when every minute was of importance to him.

The reserved rustic road was presently joined by a shy little

brother in the shape of a canal, which took its hand and ambled along by its side in perfect confidence, but with the same tongue-tied, uncommunicative attitude towards strangers. "Bother them!" said Toad to himself. "But, anyhow, one thing's clear. They must both be coming **from** somewhere, and going **to** somewhere. You can't get over that. Toad, my boy!" So he marched on patiently by the water's edge.

Round a bend in the canal came plodding a solitary horse, stooping forward as if in anxious thought. From rope traces attached to his collar stretched a long line, taut, but dipping with his stride, the further part of it dripping pearly drops. Toad let the horse pass, and stood waiting for what the fates were sending him.

With a pleasant swirl of quiet water at its blunt bow the barge slid up alongside of him, its gaily painted gunwale level with the towing-path, its sole occupant a big stout woman wearing a linen sun-bonnet, one brawny arm laid along the tiller.

"A nice morning, ma'am!" she remarked to Toad, as she drew up level with him.

"I dare say it is, ma'am!" responded Toad politely, as he walked along the tow-path abreast of her. "I dare it **is** a nice morning to them that's not in sore trouble, like what I am. Here's my married daughter, she sends off to me post-haste to come to her at once; so off I comes, not knowing what may be happening or going to happen, but fearing the worst, as you will understand, ma'am, if you're a mother, too. And I've left my business to look after itself—I'm in the washing and laundering line, you must know, ma'am—and I've left my young children to look after themselves, and a more mischievous and troublesome set of young imps doesn't exist, ma'am; and I've lost all my money, and lost my way, and as for what may be happening to my married daughter, why, I don't like to think of it, ma'am!"

"Where might your married daughter be living, ma'am?" asked

the barge-woman.

"She lives near to the river, ma'am," replied Toad. "Close to a fine house called Toad Hall, that's somewheres hereabouts in these parts. Perhaps you may have heard of it."

"Toad Hall? Why, I'm going that way myself," replied the barge-woman. "This canal joins the river some miles further on, a little above Toad Hall; and then it's an easy walk. You come along in the barge with me, and I'll give you a lift."

She steered the barge close to the bank, and Toad, with many humble and grateful acknowledgments, stepped lightly on board and sat down with great satisfaction. "Toad's luck again!" thought he. "I always come out on top!"

"So you're in the washing business, ma'am?" said the barge-woman politely, as they glided along. "And a very good business you've got too, I dare say, if I'm not making too free in saying so."

"Finest business in the whole country," said Toad airily. "All the gentry come to me—wouldn't go to any one else if they were paid, they know me so well. You see, I understand my work thoroughly, and attend to it all myself. Washing, ironing, clear-starching, making up gents' fine shirts for evening wear—everything's done under my own eye!"

"But surely you don't **do** all that work yourself, ma'am?" asked the barge-woman respectfully.

"O, I have girls," said Toad lightly: "twenty girls or thereabouts, always at work. But you know what **girls** are, ma'am! Nasty little hussies, that's what **I** call 'em!"

"So do I, too," said the barge-woman with great heartiness. "But I dare say you set yours to rights, the idle trollops! And are you **very** fond of washing?"

"I love it," said Toad. "I simply dote on it. Never so happy as

when I've got both arms in the wash-tub. But, then, it comes so easy
to me! No trouble at all! A real pleasure, I assure you, ma'am!"

"What a bit of luck, meeting you!" observed the barge-woman,
thoughtfully. "A regular piece of good fortune for both of us!"

"Why, what do you mean?" asked Toad, nervously.

"Well, look at me, now," replied the barge-woman. "I like
washing, too, just the same as you do; and for that matter, whether I
like it or not I have got to do all my own, naturally, moving about as I
do. Now my husband, he's such a fellow for shirking his work and
leaving the barge to me, that never a moment do I get for seeing to
my own affairs. By rights he ought to be here now, either steering or
attending to the horse, though luckily the horse has sense enough to
attend to himself. Instead of which, he's gone off with the dog, to see
if they can't pick up a rabbit for dinner somewhere. Says he'll catch
me up at the next lock. Well, that's as may be—I don't trust him, once
he gets off with that dog, who's worse than he is. But meantime, how
am I to get on with my washing?"

"O, never mind about the washing," said Toad, not liking the
subject. "Try and fix your mind on that rabbit. A nice fat young rabbit,
I'll be bound. Got any onions?"

"I can't fix my mind on anything but my washing," said the
barge-woman, "and I wonder you can be talking of rabbits, with such
a joyful prospect before you. There's a heap of things of mine that
you'll find in a corner of the cabin. If you'll just take one or two of
the most necessary sort—I won't venture to describe them to a lady
like you, but you'll recognise them at a glance—and put them through
the wash-tub as we go along, why, it'll be a pleasure to you, as you
rightly say, and a real help to me. You'll find a tub handy, and soap, and
a kettle on the stove, and a bucket to haul up water from the canal
with. Then I shall know you're enjoying yourself, instead of sitting

here idle, looking at the scenery and yawning your head off."

"Here, you let me steer!" said Toad, now thoroughly frightened, "and then you can get on with your washing your own way. I might spoil your things, or not do 'em as you like. I'm more used to gentlemen's things myself. It's my special line."

"Let you steer?" replied the barge-woman, laughing. "It takes some practice to steer a barge properly. Besides, it's dull work, and I want you to be happy. No, you shall do the washing you are so fond of, and I'll stick to the steering that I understand. Don't try and deprive me of the pleasure of giving you a treat!"

Toad was fairly cornered. He looked for escape this way and that, saw that he was too far from the bank for a flying leap, and sullenly resigned himself to his fate. "If it comes to that," he thought in desperation, "I suppose any fool can **wash!**"

He fetched tub, soap, and other necessaries from the cabin, selected a few garments at random, tried to recollect what he had seen in casual glances through laundry windows, and set to.

A long half-hour passed, and every minute of it saw Toad getting crosser and crosser. Nothing that he could do to the things seemed to please them or do them good. He tried coaxing, he tried slapping, he tried punching; they smiled back at him out of the tub unconverted, happy in their original sin. Once or twice he looked nervously over his shoulder at the barge-woman, but she appeared to be gazing out in front of her, absorbed in her steering. His back ached badly, and he noticed with dismay that his paws were beginning to get all crinkly. Now Toad was very proud of his paws. He muttered under his breath words that should never pass the lips of either washerwomen or Toads; and lost the soap, for the fiftieth time.

A burst of laughter made him straighten himself and look round. The barge-woman was leaning back and laughing unrestrainedly, till

the tears ran down her cheeks.

"I've been watching you all the time," she gasped. "I thought you must be a humbug all along, from the conceited way you talked. Pretty washerwoman you are! Never washed so much as a dish-clout in your life, I'll lay!"

Toad's temper which had been simmering viciously for some time, now fairly boiled over, and he lost all control of himself.

"You common, low, **fat** barge-woman!" he shouted; "don't you dare to talk to your betters like that! Washerwoman indeed! I would have you to know that I am a Toad, a very well-known, respected, distinguished Toad! I may be under a bit of a cloud at present, but I will **not** be laughed at by a bargewoman!"

The woman moved nearer to him and peered under his bonnet keenly and closely. "Why, so you are!" she cried. "Well, I never! A horrid, nasty, crawly Toad! And in my nice clean barge, too! Now that is a thing that I will **not** have."

She relinquished the tiller for a moment. One big mottled arm shot out and caught Toad by a fore-leg, while the other-gripped him fast by a hind-leg. Then the world turned suddenly upside down, the barge seemed to flit lightly across the sky, the wind whistled in his ears, and Toad found himself flying through the air, revolving rapidly as he went.

The water, when he eventually reached it with a loud splash, proved quite cold enough for his taste, though its chill was not sufficient to quell his proud spirit, or slake the heat of his furious temper. He rose to the surface spluttering, and when he had wiped the duck-weed out of his eyes the first thing he saw was the fat barge-woman looking back at him over the stern of the retreating barge and laughing; and he vowed, as he coughed and choked, to be even with her.

He struck out for the shore, but the cotton gown greatly impeded his efforts, and when at length he touched land he found it hard to climb up the steep bank unassisted. He had to take a minute or two's rest to recover his breath; then, gathering his wet skirts well over his arms, he started to run after the barge as fast as his legs would carry him, wild with indignation, thirsting for revenge.

The barge-woman was still laughing when he drew up level with her. "Put yourself through your mangle, washerwoman," she called out, "and iron your face and crimp it, and you'll pass for quite a decent-looking Toad!"

Toad never paused to reply. Solid revenge was what he wanted, not cheap, windy, verbal triumphs, though he had a thing or two in his mind that he would have liked to say. He saw what he wanted ahead of him. Running swiftly on he overtook the horse, unfastened the towrope and cast off, jumped lightly on the horse's back, and urged it to a gallop by kicking it vigorously in the sides. He steered for the open country, abandoning the tow-path, and swinging his steed down a rutty lane. Once he looked back, and saw that the barge had run aground on the other side of the canal, and the barge-woman was gesticulating wildly and shouting, "Stop, stop, stop!" "I've heard that song before," said Toad, laughing, as he continued to spur his steed onward in its wild career.

The barge-horse was not capable of any very sustained effort, and its gallop soon subsided into a trot, and its trot into an easy walk; but Toad was quite contented with this, knowing that he, at any rate, was moving, and the barge was not. He had quite recovered his temper, now that he had done something he thought really clever; and he was satisfied to jog along quietly in the sun, steering his horse along by-ways and bridle-paths, and trying to forget how very long it was since he had had a square meal, till the canal had been left very far

behind him.

He had travelled some miles, his horse and he, and he was feeling drowsy in the hot sunshine, when the horse stopped, lowered his head, and began to nibble the grass; and Toad, waking up, just saved himself from falling off by an effort. He looked about him and found he was on a wide common, dotted with patches of gorse and bramble as far as he could see. Near him stood a dingy gipsy caravan, and beside it a man was sitting on a bucket turned upside down, very busy smoking and staring into the wide world. A fire of sticks was burning near by, and over the fire hung an iron pot, and out of that pot came forth bubblings and gurglings, and a vague suggestive steaminess. Also smells—warm, rich, and varied smells—that twined and twisted and wreathed themselves at last into one complete, voluptuous, perfect smell that seemed like the very soul of Nature taking form and appearing to her children, a true Goddess, a mother of solace and comfort. Toad now knew well that he had not been really hungry before. What he had felt earlier in the day had been a mere trifling qualm. This was the real thing at last, and no mistake; and it would have to be dealt with speedily, too, or there would be trouble for somebody or something. He looked the gipsy over carefully, wondering vaguely whether it would be easier to fight him or cajole him. So there he sat, and sniffed and sniffed, and looked at the gipsy; and the gipsy sat and smoked, and looked at him.

Presently the gipsy took his pipe out of his mouth and remarked in a careless way, "Want to sell that there horse of yours?"

Toad was completely taken aback. He did not know that gipsies were very fond of horse-dealing, and never missed an opportunity, and he had not reflected that caravans were always on the move and took a deal of drawing. It had not occurred to him to turn the horse into cash, but the gipsy's suggestion seemed to smooth the way

towards the two things he wanted so badly—ready money, and a solid breakfast.

"What?" he said, "me sell this beautiful young horse of mine? O, no; it's out of the question. Who's going to take the washing home to my customers every week? Besides, I'm too fond of him, and he simply dotes on me."

"Try and love a donkey," suggested the gipsy. "Some people do."

"You don't seem to see," continued Toad, "that this fine horse of mine is a cut above you altogether. He's a blood horse, he is, partly; not the part you see, of course—another part. And he's been a Prize Hackney, too, in his time—that was the time before you knew him, but you can still tell it on him at a glance, if you understand anything about horses. No, it's not to be thought of for a moment. All the same, how much might you be disposed to offer me for this beautiful young horse of mine?"

The gipsy looked the horse over, and then he looked Toad over with equal care, and looked at the horse again. "Shillin' a leg," he said briefly, and turned away, continuing to smoke and try to stare the wide world out of countenance.

"A shilling a leg?" cried Toad. "If you please, I must take a little time to work that out, and see just what it comes to."

He climbed down off his horse, and left it to graze, and sat down by the gipsy, and did sums on his fingers, and at last he said, "A shilling a leg? Why, that comes to exactly four shillings, and no more. O, no; I could not think of accepting four shillings for this beautiful young horse of mine."

"Well," said the gipsy, "I'll tell you what I will do. I'll make it five shillings, and that's three-and-sixpence more than the animal's worth. And that's my last word."

Then Toad sat and pondered long and deeply. For he was hungry

and quite penniless, and still some way—he knew not how far—from home, and enemies might still be looking for him. To one in such a situation, five shillings may very well appear a large sum of money. On the other hand, it did not seem very much to get for a horse. But then, again, the horse hadn't cost him anything; so whatever he got was all clear profit. At last he said firmly, "Look here, gipsy! I tell you what we will do; and this is **my** last word. You shall hand me over six shillings and sixpence, cash down; and further, in addition thereto, you shall give me as much breakfast as I can possibly eat, at one sitting of course, out of that iron pot of yours that keeps sending forth such delicious and exciting smells. In return, I will make over to you my spirited young horse, with all the beautiful harness and trappings that are on him, freely thrown in. If that's not good enough for you, say so, and I'll be getting on. I know a man near here who's wanted this horse of mine for years."

The gipsy grumbled frightfully, and declared if he did a few more deals of that sort he'd be ruined. But in the end he lugged a dirty canvas bag out of the depths of his trouser pocket, and counted out six shillings and sixpence into Toad's paw. Then he disappeared into the caravan for an instant, and returned with a large iron plate and a knife, fork, and spoon. He tilted up the pot, and a glorious stream of hot rich stew gurgled into the plate. It was, indeed, the most beautiful stew in the world, being made of partridges, and pheasants, and chickens, and hares, and rabbits, and pea-hens, and guinea-fowls, and one or two other things. Toad took the plate on his lap, almost crying, and stuffed, and stuffed, and stuffed, and kept asking for more, and the gipsy never grudged it him. He thought that he had never eaten so good a breakfast in all his life.

When Toad had taken as much stew on board as he thought he could possibly hold, he got up and said good-bye to the gipsy, and

took an affectionate farewell of the horse; and the gipsy, who knew the riverside well, gave him directions which way to go, and he set forth on his travels again in the best possible spirits. He was, indeed, a very different Toad from the animal of an hour ago. The sun was shining brightly, his wet clothes were quite dry again, he had money in his pocket once more, he was nearing home and friends and safety, and, most and best of all, he had had a substantial meal, hot and nourishing, and felt big, and strong, and careless, and self-confident.

As he tramped along gaily, he thought of his adventures and escapes, and how when things seemed at their worst he had always managed to find a way out; and his pride and conceit began to swell within him. "Ho, ho!" he said to himself as he marched along with his chin in the air, "what a clever Toad I am! There is surely no animal equal to me for cleverness in the whole world! My enemies shut me up in prison, encircled by sentries, watched night and day by warders; I walk out through them all, by sheer ability coupled with courage. They pursue me with engines, and policemen, and revolvers; I snap my fingers at them, and vanish, laughing, into space. I am, unfortunately, thrown into acanal by a woman fat of body and very evil-minded. What of it? I swim ashore, I seize her horse, I ride off in triumph, and I sell the horse for a whole pocketful of money and an excellent breakfast! Ho, ho! I am The Toad, the handsome, the popular, the successful Toad!" He got so puffed up with conceit that he made up a song as he walked in praise of himself, and sang it at the top of his voice, though there was no one to hear it but him. It was perhaps the most conceited song that any animal ever composed.

> "The world has held great Heroes,
> As history-books have showed;

But never a name to go down to fame
Compared with that of Toad!

"The clever men at Oxford
Know all that there is to be knowed.
But they none of them know one half as much
As intelligent Mr. Toad!

"The animals sat in the Ark and cried,
Their tears in torrents flowed.
Who was it said, 'There's land ahead?'
Encouraging Mr. Toad!

"The army all saluted
As they marched along the road.
Was it the King? Or Kitchener?
No. It was Mr. Toad.

"The Queen and her Ladies-in-waiting
Sat at the window and sewed.
She cried, 'Look! who's that **handsome** man?'
They answered, 'Mr. Toad.'"

There was a great deal more of the same sort, but too dreadfully conceited to be written down. These are some of the milder verses.

He sang as he walked, and he walked as he sang, and got more inflated every minute. But his pride was shortly to have a severe fall.

After some miles of country lanes he reached the high road, and as he turned into it and glanced along its white length, he saw approaching him a speck that turned into a dot and then into a blob, and then into something very familiar; and a double note of warning, only too well known, fell on his delighted ear.

"This is something like!" said the excited Toad. "This is real life again, this is once more the great world from which I have been missed so long! I will hail them, my brothers of the wheel, and pitch them a yarn, of the sort that has been so successful hitherto; and they will give me a lift, of course, and then I will talk to them some more; and, perhaps, with luck, it may even end in my driving up to Toad Hall in a motor-car! That will be one in the eye for Badger!"

He stepped confidently out into the road to hail the motor-car, which came along at an easy pace, slowing down as it neared the lane; when suddenly he became very pale, his heart turned to water, his knees shook and yielded under him, and he doubled up and collapsed with a sickening pain in his interior. And well he might, the unhappy animal; for the approaching car was the very one he had stolen out of the yard of the Red Lion Hotel on that fatal day when all his troubles began! And the people in it were the very same people he had sat and watched at luncheon in the coffee-room!

He sank down in a shabby, miserable heap in the road, murmuring to himself in his despair, "It's all up! It's all over now! Chains and policemen again! Prison again! Dry bread and water again! O, what a fool I have been! What did I want to go strutting about the country for, singing conceited songs, and hailing people in broad day

on the high road, instead of hiding till nightfall and slipping home quietly by back ways! O hapless Toad! O ill-fated animal!"

The terrible motor-car drew slowly nearer and nearer, till at last he heard it stop just short of him. Two gentlemen got out and walked round the trembling heap of crumpled misery lying in the road, and one of them said, "O dear! this is very sad! Here is a poor old thing—a washerwoman apparently—who has fainted in the road! Perhaps she is overcome by the heat, poor creature; or possibly she has not had any food to-day. Let us lift her into the car and take her to the nearest village, where doubtless she has friends."

They tenderly lifted Toad into the motor-car and propped him up with soft cushions, and proceeded on their way.

When Toad heard them talk in so kind and sympathetic a way, and knew that he was not recognised, his courage began to revive, and he cautiously opened first one eye and then the other.

"Look!" said one of the gentlemen, "she is better already. The fresh air is doing her good. How do you feel now, ma'am?"

"Thank you kindly, Sir," said Toad in a feeble voice, "I'm feeling a great deal better!" "That's right," said the gentleman. "Now keep quite still, and, above all, don't try to talk."

"I won't," said Toad. "I was only thinking, if I might sit on the front seat there, beside the driver, where I could get the fresh air full in my face, I should soon be all right again."

"What a very sensible woman!" said the gentleman. "Of course you shall." So they carefully helped Toad into the front seat beside the driver, and on they went again.

Toad was almost himself again by now. He sat up, looked about him, and tried to beat down the tremors, the yearnings, the old cravings that rose up and beset him and took possession of him entirely.

"It is fate!" he said to himself. "Why strive? why struggle?" and he turned to the driver at his side.

"Please, Sir," he said, "I wish you would kindly let me try and drive the car for a little. I've been watching you carefully, and it looks so easy and so interesting, and I should like to be able to tell my friends that once I had driven a motor-car!"

The driver laughed at the proposal, so heartily that the gentleman inquired what the matter was. When he heard, he said, to Toad's delight, "Bravo, ma'am! I like your spirit. Let her have a try, and look after her. She won't do any harm."

Toad eagerly scrambled into the seat vacated by the driver, took the steering-wheel in his hands, listened with affected humility to the instructions given him, and set the car in motion, but very slowly and carefully at first, for he was determined to be prudent.

The gentlemen behind clapped their hands and applauded, and Toad heard them saying, "How well she does it! Fancy a washerwoman driving a car as well as that, the first time!"

Toad went a little faster; then faster still, and faster.

He heard the gentlemen call out warningly, "Be careful, washerwoman!" And this annoyed him, and he began to lose his head.

The driver tried to interfere, but he pinned him down in his seat with one elbow, and put on full speed. The rush of air in his face, the hum of the engines, and the light jump of the car beneath him intoxicated his weak brain. "Washerwoman, indeed!" he shouted recklessly. "Ho! ho! I am the Toad, the motor-car snatcher, the prison-breaker, the Toad who always escapes! Sit still, and you shall know what driving really is, for you are in the hands of the famous, the skilful, the entirely fearless Toad!"

With a cry of horror the whole party rose and flung themselves on him. "Seize him!" they cried, "seize the Toad, the wicked animal

who stole our motor-car! Bind him, chain him, drag him to the nearest police-station! Down with the desperate and dangerous Toad!"

Alas! they should have thought, they ought to have been more prudent, they should have remembered to stop the motor-car somehow before playing any pranks of that sort. With a half-turn of the wheel the Toad sent the car crashing through the low hedge that ran along the roadside. One mighty bound, a violent shock, and the wheels of the car were churning up the thick mud of a horse-pond.

Toad found himself flying through the air with the strong upward rush and delicate curve of a swallow. He liked the motion, and was just beginning to wonder whether it would go on until he developed wings and turned into a Toad-bird, when he landed on his back with a thump, in the soft rich grass of a meadow. Sitting up, he could just see the motor-car in the pond, nearly submerged; the gentlemen and the driver, encumbered by their long coats, were floundering helplessly in the water.

He picked himself up rapidly, and set off running across country as hard as he could, scrambling through hedges, jumping ditches, pounding across fields, till he was breathless and weary, and had to settle down into an easy walk. When he had recovered his breath somewhat, and was able to think calmly, he began to giggle, and from giggling he took to laughing, and he laughed till he had to sit down under a hedge. "Ho, ho!" he cried, in ecstasies of self-admiration, "Toad again! Toad, as usual, comes out on the top! Who was it got them to give him a lift? Who managed to get on the front seat for the sake of fresh air? Who persuaded them into letting him see if he could drive? Who landed them all in a horse-pond? Who escaped, flying gaily and unscathed through the air, leaving the narrow-minded, grudging, timid excursionists in the mud where they should rightly be? Why, Toad, of course; clever Toad, great Toad, **good** Toad!"

Then he burst into song again, and chanted with uplifted voice—

"The motor-car went Poop-poop-poop,
As it raced along the road.
Who was it steered it into a pond?
Ingenious Mr. Toad!

O, how clever I am! How clever, how clever, how very clev——"

A slight noise at a distance behind him made him turn his head and look. O horror! O misery! O despair!

About two fields off, a chauffeur in his leather gaiters and two large rural policemen were visible, running towards him as hard as they could go!

Poor Toad sprang to his feet and pelted away again, his heart in his mouth. O, my!" he gasped, as he panted along, "what an **ass** I am! What a **conceited** and heedless ass! Swaggering again! Shouting and singing songs again! Sitting still and gassing again! O my! O my! O my!"

He glanced back, and saw to his dismay that they were gaining on him. On he ran desperately, but kept looking back, and saw that they still gained steadily. He did his best, but he was a fat animal, and his legs were short, and still they gained. He could hear them close behind him now. Ceasing to heed where he was going, he struggled on blindly and wildly, looking back over his shoulder at the now triumphant enemy, when suddenly the earth failed under his feet, he grasped at the air, and, splash! he found himself head over ears in deep water, rapid water, water that bore him along with a force he could not contend with; and he knew that in his blind panic he had run straight

into the river!

He rose to the surface and tried to grasp the reeds and the rushes that grew along the water's edge close under the bank, but the stream was so strong that it tore them out of his hands. "O my!" gasped poor Toad, "if ever I steal a motor-car again! If ever I sing another conceited song"—then down he went, and came up breathless and spluttering. Presently he saw that he was approaching a big dark hole in the bank, just above his head, and as the stream bore him past he reached up with a paw and caught hold of the edge and held on. Then slowly and with difficulty he drew himself up out of the water, till at last he was able to rest his elbows on the edge of the hole. There he remained for some minutes, puffing and panting, for he was quite exhausted.

As he sighed and blew and stared before him into the dark hole, some bright small thing shone and twinkled in its depths, moving towards him. As it approached, a face grew up gradually around it, and it was a familiar face!

Brown and small, with whiskers.

Grave and round, with neat ears and silky hair.

It was the Water Rat!

XI.
"LIKE SUMMER TEMPESTS
CAME HIS TEARS"

The Rat put out a neat little brown paw, gripped Toad firmly by the scruff of the neck, and gave a great hoist and a pull; and the water-logged Toad came up slowly but surely over the edge of the hole, till at last he stood safe and sound in the hall, streaked with mud and weed to be sure, and with the water streaming off him, but happy and high-spirited as of old, now that he found himself once more in the house of a friend, and dodgings and evasions were over, and he could lay aside a disguise that was unworthy of his position and wanted such a lot of living up to.

"O, Ratty!" he cried. "I've been through such times since I saw you last, you can't think! Such trials, such sufferings, and all so nobly borne! Then such escapes, such disguises such subterfuges, and all so cleverly planned and carried out! Been in prison— got out of it, of course! Been thrown into a canal—swam ashore! Stole a horse— sold him for a large

sum of money! Humbugged everybody—made 'em all do exactly what I wanted! Oh, I **am** a smart Toad, and no mistake! What do you think my last exploit was? Just hold on till I tell you——"

"Toad," said the Water Rat, gravely and firmly, "you go off upstairs at once, and take off that old cotton rag that looks as if it might formerly have belonged to some washerwoman, and clean yourself thoroughly, and put on some of my clothes, and try and come down looking like a gentleman if you **can;** for a more shabby, bedraggled, disreputable-looking object than you are I never set eyes on in my whole life! Now, stop swaggering and arguing, and be off! I'll have something to say to you later!"

Toad was at first inclined to stop and do some talking back at him. He had had enough of being ordered about when he was in prison, and here was the thing being begun all over again, apparently; and by a Rat, too! However, he caught sight of himself in the looking-glass over the hat-stand, with the rusty black bonnet perched rakishly over one eye, and he changed his mind and went very quickly and humbly upstairs to the Rat's dressing-room. There he had a thorough wash and brush-up, changed his clothes, and stood for a long time before the glass, contemplating himself with pride and pleasure, and thinking what utter idiots all the people must have been to have ever mistaken him for one moment for a washerwoman.

By the time he came down again luncheon was on the table, and very glad Toad was to see it, for he had been through some trying experiences and had taken much hard exercise since the excellent breakfast provided for him by the gipsy. While they ate Toad told the Rat all his adventures, dwelling chiefly on his own cleverness, and presence of mind in emergencies, and cunning in tight places; and rather making out that he had been having a gay and highly-coloured experience. But the more he talked and boasted, the more grave and

silent the Rat became.

When at last Toad had talked himself to a standstill, there was silence for a while; and then the Rat said, "Now, Toady, I don't want to give you pain, after all you've been through already; but, seriously, don't you see what an awful ass you've been making of yourself? On your own admission you have been handcuffed, imprisoned, starved, chased, terrified out of your life, insulted, jeered at, and ignominiously flung into the water—by a woman, too! Where's the amusement in that? Where does the fun come in? And all because you must needs go and steal a motor-car. You know that you've never had anything but trouble from motor-cars from the moment you first set eyes on one. But if you **will** be mixed up with them—as you generally are, five minutes after you've started—why **steal** them? Be a cripple, if you think it's exciting; be a bankrupt, for a change, if you've set your mind on it: but why choose to be a convict? When are you going to be sensible, and think of your friends, and try and be a credit to them? Do you suppose it's any pleasure to me, for instance, to hear animals saying, as I go about, that I'm the chap that keeps company with gaol-birds?"

Now, it was a very comforting point in Toad's character that he was a thoroughly good-hearted animal and never minded being jawed by those who were his real friends. And even when most set upon a thing, he was always able to see the other side of the question. So although, while the Rat was talking so seriously, he kept saying to himself mutinously, "But it **was** fun, though! Awful fun!" and making strange suppressed noises inside him, k-i-ck-ck-ck, and poop-p-p, and other sounds resembling stifled snorts, or the opening of soda-water bottles, yet when the Rat had quite finished, he heaved a deep sigh and said, very nicely and humbly, "Quite right, Ratty! How **sound** you always are! Yes, I've been a conceited old ass, I can quite see that; but

now I'm going to be a good Toad, and not do it any more. As for motor-cars, I've not been at all so keen about them since my last ducking in that river of yours. The fact is, while I was hanging on to the edge of your hole and getting my breath, I had a sudden idea—a really brilliant idea—connected with motor-boats—there, there! don't take on so, old chap, and stamp, and upset things; it was only an idea, and we won't talk any more about it now. We'll have our coffee, **and** a smoke, and a quiet chat, and then I'm going to stroll quietly down to Toad Hall, and get into clothes of my own, and set things going again on the old lines. I've had enough of adventures. I shall lead a quiet, steady, respectable life, pottering about my property, and improving it, and doing a little landscape gardening at times. There will always be a bit of dinner for my friends when they come to see me; and I shall keep a pony-chaise to jog about the country in, just as I used to in the good old days, before I got restless, and wanted to **do** things."

"Stroll quietly down to Toad Hall?" cried the Rat, greatly excited. "What are you talking about? Do you mean to say you haven't **heard?**"

"Heard what?" said Toad, turning rather pale. "Go on, Ratty! Quick! Don't spare me! What haven't I heard?"

"Do you mean to tell me," shouted the Rat, thumping with his little fist upon the table, "that you've heard nothing about the Stoats and Weasels?"

What, the Wild Wooders?" cried Toad, trembling in every limb. "No, not a word! What have they been doing?"

"—And how they've been and taken Toad Hall?" continued the Rat.

Toad leaned his elbows on the table, and his chin on his paws; and a large tear welled up in each of his eyes, overflowed and splashed on the table, plop! plop!

"Go on, Ratty," he murmured presently; "tell me all. The worst is

over. I am an animal again. I can bear it."

"When you⁻got⁻into that⁻that⁻trouble of yours," said the Rat, slowly and impressively; "I mean, when you⁻disappeared from society for a time, over that misunderstanding about a⁻a machine, you know⁻"

Toad merely nodded.

"Well, it was a good deal talked about down here, naturally," continued the Rat, "not only along the river-side, but even in the Wild Wood. Animals took sides, as always happens. The River-bankers stuck up for you, and said you had been infamously treated, and there was no justice to be had in the land nowadays. But the Wild Wood animals said hard things, and served you right, and it was time this sort of thing was stopped. And they got very cocky, and went about saying you were done for this time! You would never come back again, never, never!"

Toad nodded once more, keeping silence.

"That's the sort of little beasts they are," the Rat went on. "But Mole and Badger, they stuck out, through thick and thin, that you would come back again soon, somehow. They didn't know exactly how, but somehow!"

Toad began to sit up in his chair again, and to smirk a little.

"They argued from history," continued the Rat. "They said that no criminal laws had ever been known to prevail against cheek and plausibility such as yours, combined with the power of a long purse. So they arranged to move their things in to Toad Hall, and sleep there, and keep it aired, and have it all ready for you when you turned up. They didn't guess what was going to happen, of course; still, they had their suspicions of the Wild Wood animals. Now I come to the most painful and tragic part of my story. One dark night⁻it was a **very** dark night, and blowing hard, too, and raining simply cats and dogs⁻

a band of weasels, armed to the teeth, crept silently up the carriage-drive to the front entrance. Simultaneously, a body of desperate ferrets, advancing through the kitchen-garden, possessed themselves of the backyard and offices; while a company of skirmishing stoats who stuck at nothing occupied the conservatory and the billiard-room, and held the French windows opening on to the lawn.

"The Mole and the Badger were sitting by the fire in the smoking-room, telling stories and suspecting nothing, for it wasn't a night for any animals to be out in, when those bloodthirsty villains broke down the doors and rushed in upon them from every side. They made the best fight they could, but what was the good? They were unarmed, and taken by surprise, and what can two animals do against hundreds? They took and beat them severely with sticks, those two poor faithful creatures, and turned them out into the cold and the wet, with many insulting and uncalled-for remarks!"

Here the unfeeling Toad broke into a snigger, and then pulled himself together and tried to look particularly solemn.

"And the Wild Wooders have been living in Toad Hall ever since," continued the Rat; "and going on simply anyhow! Lying in bed half the day, and breakfast at all hours, and the place in such a mess (I'm told) it's not fit to be seen! Eating your grub, and drinking your drink, and making bad jokes about you, and singing vulgar songs, about—well, about prisons and magistrates, and policemen; horrid personal songs, with no humour in them. And they're telling the tradespeople and everybody that they've come to stay for good."

"O, have they!" said Toad getting up and seizing a stick. "I'll jolly soon see about that!"

"It's no good, Toad!" called the Rat after him. "You'd better come back and sit down; you'll only get into trouble."

But the Toad was off, and there was no holding him. He marched

rapidly down the road, his stick over his shoulder, fuming and muttering to himself in his anger, till he got near his front gate, when suddenly there popped up from behind the palings a long yellow ferret with a gun.

"Who comes there?" said the ferret sharply.

"Stuff and nonsense!" said Toad, very angrily. "What do you mean by talking like that to me? Come out of that at once, or I'll——"

The ferret said never a word, but he brought his gun up to his shoulder. Toad prudently dropped flat in the road, and **Bang!** a bullet whistled over his head.

The startled Toad scrambled to his feet and scampered off down the road as hard as he could; and as he ran he heard the ferret laughing and other horrid thin little laughs taking it up and carrying on the sound.

He went back, very crestfallen, and told the Water Rat.

"What did I tell you?" said the Rat. "It's no good. They've got sentries posted, and they are all armed. You must just wait."

Still, Toad was not inclined to give in all at once. So he got out the boat, and set off rowing up the river to where the garden front of Toad Hall came down to the waterside.

Arriving within sight of his old home, he rested on his oars and surveyed the land cautiously. All seemed very peaceful and deserted and quiet. He could see the whole front of Toad Hall, glowing in the evening sunshine, the pigeons settling by twos and threes along the straight line of the roof; the garden, a blaze of flowers; the creek that led up to the boat-house, the little wooden bridge that crossed it; all tranquil, uninhabited, apparently waiting for his return. He would try the boat-house first, he thought. Very warily he paddled up to the mouth of the creek, and was just passing under the bridge, when ...

Crash!

A great stone, dropped from above, smashed through the bottom of the boat. It filled and sank, and Toad found himself struggling in deep water. Looking up, he saw two stoats leaning over the parapet of the bridge and watching him with great glee. "It will be your head next time, Toady!" they called out to him. The indignant Toad swam to shore, while the stoats laughed and laughed, supporting each other, and laughed again, till they nearly had two fits—that is, one fit each, of course.

The Toad retraced his weary way on foot, and related his disappointing experiences to the Water Rat once more.

"Well, **what** did I tell you?" said the Rat very crossly. "And, now, look here! See what you've been and done! Lost me my boat that I was so fond of, that's what you've done! And simply ruined that nice suit of clothes that I lent you! Really, Toad, of all the trying animals—I wonder you manage to keep any friends at all!"

The Toad saw at once how wrongly and foolishly he had acted. He admitted his errors and wrong-headedness and made a full apology to Rat for losing his boat and spoiling his clothes. And he wound up by saying, with that frank self-surrender which always disarmed his friend's criticism and won them back to his side, "Ratty! I see that I have been a headstrong and a wilful Toad! Henceforth, believe me, I will be humble and submissive, and will take no action without your kind advice and full approval!"

"If that is really so," said the good-natured Rat, already appeased, "then my advice to you is, considering the lateness of the hour, to sit down and have your supper, which will be on the table in a minute, and be very patient. For I am convinced that we can do nothing until we have seen the Mole and the Badger, and heard their latest news, and held conference and taken their advice in this difficult matter."

"Oh, ah, yes, of course, the Mole and the Badger," said Toad, lightly. "What's become of them, the dear fellows? I had forgotten all about them."

"Well may you ask!" said the Rat reproachfully. "While you were riding about the country in expensive motor-cars, and galloping proudly on blood-horses, and breakfasting on the fat of the land, those two poor devoted animals have been camping out in the open, in every sort of weather, living very rough by day and lying very hard by night; watching over your house, patrolling your boundaries, keeping a constant eye on the stoats and the weasels, scheming and planning and contriving how to get your property back for you. You don't deserve to have such true and loyal friends, Toad, you don't, really. Some day, when it's too late, you'll be sorry you didn't value them more while you had them!"

"I'm an ungrateful beast, I know," sobbed Toad, shedding bitter tears. "Let me go out and find them, out into the cold, dark night, and share their hardships, and try and prove by——Hold on a bit! Surely I heard the chink of dishes on a tray! Supper's here at last, hooray! Come on, Ratty!"

The Rat remembered that poor Toad had been on prison fare for a considerable time, and that large allowances had therefore to be made. He followed him to the table accordingly, and hospitably encouraged him in his gallant efforts to make up for past privations.

They had just finished their meal and resumed their arm-chairs, when there came a heavy knock at the door.

Toad was nervous, but the Rat, nodding mysteriously at him, went straight up to the door and opened it, and in walked Mr. Badger.

He had all the appearance of one who for some nights had been kept away from home and all its little comforts and conveniences. His shoes were covered with mud, and he was looking very rough and

touzled; but then he had never been a very smart man, the Badger, at the best of times. He came solemnly up to Toad, shook him by the paw, and said, "Welcome home, Toad! Alas! what am I saying? Home, indeed! This is a poor home-coming. Unhappy Toad!" Then he turned his back on him, sat down to the table, drew his chair up, and helped himself to a large slice of cold pie.

Toad was quite alarmed at this very serious and portentous style of greeting; but the Rat whispered to him, "Never mind; don't take any notice; and don't say anything to him just yet. He's always rather low and despondent when he's wanting his victuals. In half an hour's time he'll be quite a different animal."

So they waited in silence, and presently there came another and a lighter knock. The Rat, with a nod to Toad, went to the door and ushered in the Mole, very shabby and unwashed, with bits of hay and straw sticking in his fur.

"Hooray! Here's old Toad!" cried the Mole, his face beaming. "Fancy having you back again!" And he began to dance round him. "We never dreamt you would turn up so soon! Why, you must have managed to escape, you clever, ingenious, intelligent Toad!"

The Rat, alarmed, pulled him by the elbow; but it was too late. Toad was puffing and swelling already.

"Clever? O, no!" he said. "I'm not really clever, according to my friends. I've only broken out of the strongest prison in England, that's all! And captured a railway train and escaped on it, that's all! And disguised myself and gone about the country humbugging everybody, that's all! O, no! I'm a stupid ass, I am! I'll tell you one or two of my little adventures, Mole, and you shall judge for yourself!"

"Well, well," said the Mole, moving towards the supper-table; "supposing you talk while I eat. Not a bite since breakfast! O my! O my!" And he sat down and helped himself liberally to cold beef and

pickles.

Toad straddled on the hearth-rug, thrust his paw into his trouser-pocket and pulled out a handful of silver. "Look at that!" he cried, displaying it. "That's not so bad, is it, for a few minutes' work? And how do you think I done it, Mole? Horse-dealing! That's how I done it!"

"Go on, Toad," said the Mole, immensely interested.

"Toad, do be quiet, please!" said the Rat. "And don't you egg him on, Mole, when you know what he is; but please tell us as soon as possible what the position is, and what's best to be done, now that Toad is back at last."

"The position's about as bad as it can be," replied the Mole grumpily; "and as for what's to be done, why, blest if I know! The Badger and I have been round and round the place, by night and by day; always the same thing. Sentries posted everywhere, guns poked out at us, stones thrown at us; always an animal on the look-out, and when they see us, my! how they do laugh! That's what annoys me most!"

"It's a very difficult situation," said the Rat, reflecting deeply. "But I think I see now, in the depths of my mind, what Toad really ought to do. I will tell you. He ought to——"

"No, he oughtn't!" shouted the Mole, with his mouth full. "Nothing of the sort! You don't understand. What he ought to do is, he ought to——"

"Well, I shan't do it, anyway!" cried Toad, getting excited. "I'm not going to be ordered about by you fellows! It's my house we're talking about, and I know exactly what to do, and I'll tell you. I'm going to——"

By this time they were all three talking at once, at the top of their voices, and the noise was simply deafening, when a thin, dry voice

made itself heard, saying, "Be quiet at once, all of you!" and instantly every one was silent.

It was the Badger, who, having finished his pie, had turned round in his chair and was looking at them severely. When he saw that he had secured their attention, and that they were evidently waiting for him to address them, he turned back to the table again and reached out for the cheese. And so great was the respect commanded by the solid qualities of that admirable animal, that not another word was uttered until he had quite finished his repast and brushed the crumbs from his knees. The Toad fidgeted a good deal, but the Rat held him firmly down.

When the Badger had quite done, he got up from his seat and stood before the fireplace, reflecting deeply. At last he spoke.

"Toad!" he said severely. "You bad, troublesome little animal! Aren't you ashamed of yourself? What do you think your father, my old friend, would have said if he had been here to-night, and had known of all your goings on?"

Toad, who was on the sofa by this time, with his legs up, rolled over on his face, shaken by sobs of contrition.

"There, there!" went on the Badger, more kindly. "Never mind. Stop crying. We're going to let bygones be bygones, and try and turn over a new leaf. But what the Mole says is quite true. The stoats are on guard, at every point, and they make the best sentinels in the world. It's quite useless to think of attacking the place. They're too strong for us."

"Then it's all over," sobbed the Toad, crying into the sofa cushions. "I shall go and enlist for a soldier, and never see my dear Toad Hall any more!"

"Come, cheer up, Toady!" said the Badger. "There are more ways of getting back a place than taking it by storm. I haven't said my last

word yet. Now I'm going to tell you a great secret."

Toad sat up slowly and dried his eyes. Secrets had an immense attraction for him, because he never could keep one, and he enjoyed the sort of unhallowed thrill he experienced when he went and told another animal, after having faithfully promised not to.

"There—is—an—underground—passage," said the Badger, impressively, "that leads from the river-bank, quite near here, right up into the middle of Toad Hall."

"O, nonsense! Badger," said Toad, rather airily. "You've been listening to some of the yarns they spin in the public-houses about here. I know every inch of Toad Hall, inside and out. Nothing of the sort, I do assure you!"

"My young friend," said the Badger, with great severity, "your father, who was a worthy animal—a lot worthier than some others I know—was a particular friend of mine, and told me a great deal he wouldn't have dreamt of telling you. He discovered that passage—he didn't make it, of course; that was done hundreds of years before he ever came to live there—and he repaired it and cleaned it out, because he thought it might come in useful some day, in case of trouble or danger; and he showed it to me. 'Don't let my son know about it,' he said. 'He's a good boy, but very light and volatile in character, and simply cannot hold his tongue. If he's ever in a real fix, and it would be of use to him, you may tell him about the secret passage; but not before.'"

The other animals looked hard at Toad to see how he would take it. Toad was inclined to be sulky at first; but he brightened up immediately, like the good fellow he was.

"Well, well," he said; "perhaps I am a bit of a talker. A popular fellow such as I am—my friends get round me—we chaff, we sparkle, we tell witty stories—and somehow my tongue gets wagging. I have

the gift of conversation. I've been told I ought to have a **salon**, whatever that may be. Never mind. Go on, Badger. How's this passage of yours going to help us?"

"I've found out a thing or two lately," continued the Badger. "I got Otter to disguise himself as a sweep and call at the back-door with brushes over his shoulder, asking for a job. There's going to be a big banquet to-morrow night. It's somebody's birthday—the Chief Weasel's, I believe—and all the weasels will be gathered together in the dining-hall, eating and drinking and laughing and carrying on, suspecting nothing. No guns, no swords, no sticks, no arms of any sort whatever!"

"But the sentinels will be posted as usual," remarked the Rat.

"Exactly," said the Badger; "that is my point. The weasels will trust entirely to their excellent sentinels. And that is where the passage comes in. That very useful tunnel leads right up under the butler's pantry, next to the dining-hall!"

"Aha! that squeaky board in the butler's pantry!" said Toad. "Now I understand it!"

"We shall creep out quietly into the butler's pantry—" cried the Mole.

"—with our pistols and swords and sticks—" shouted the Rat.

"—and rush in upon them," said the Badger.

"—and whack 'em, and whack 'em, and whack 'em!" cried the Toad in ecstasy, running round and round the room, and jumping over the chairs.

"Very well, then," said the Badger, resuming his usual dry manner, "our plan is settled, and there's nothing more for you to argue and squabble about. So, as it's getting very late, all of you go right off to bed at once. We will make all the necessary arrangements in the course of the morning to-morrow."

Toad, of course, went off to bed dutifully with the rest—he knew better than to refuse—though he was feeling much too excited to sleep. But he had had a long day, with many events crowded into it; and sheets and blankets were very friendly and comforting things, after plain straw, and not too much of it, spread on the stone floor of a draughty cell; and his head had not been many seconds on his pillow before he was snoring happily. Naturally, he dreamt a good deal; about roads that ran away from him just when he wanted them, and canals that chased him and caught him, and a barge that sailed into the banqueting-hall with his week's washing, just as he was giving a dinner-party; and he was alone in the secret passage, pushing onwards, but it twisted and turned round and shook itself, and sat up on its end; yet somehow, at the last, he found himself back in Toad Hall, safe and triumphant, with all his friends gathered round about him, earnestly assuring him that he really was a clever Toad.

He slept till a late hour next morning, and by the time he got down he found that the other animals had finished their breakfast some time before. The Mole had slipped off somewhere by himself, without telling any one where he was going to. The Badger sat in the arm-chair, reading the paper, and not concerning himself in the slightest about what was going to happen that very evening. The Rat, on the other hand, was running round the room busily, with his arms full of weapons of every kind, distributing them in four little heaps on the floor, and saying excitedly under his breath, as he ran, "Here's-a-sword-for-the-Rat, here's-a-sword-for-the Mole, here's-a-sword-for-the-Toad, here's-a-sword-for-the-Badger! Here's-a-pistol-for-the-Rat, here's-a-pistol-for-the-Mole, here's-a-pistol-for-the-Toad, here's-a-pistol-for-the-Badger!" And so on, in a regular, rhythmical way, while the four little heaps gradually grew and grew.

"That's all very well, Rat," said the Badger presently, looking at

the busy little animal over the edge of his newspaper; "I'm not blaming you. But just let us once get past the stoats, with those detestable guns of theirs, and I assure you we shan't want any swords or pistols. We four, with our sticks, once we're inside the dining-hall, why, we shall clear the floor of all the lot of them in five minutes. I'd have done the whole thing by myself, only I didn't want to deprive you fellows of the fun!"

"It's as well to be on the safe side," said the Rat reflectively, polishing a pistol-barrel on his sleeve and looking along it.

The Toad, having finished his breakfast, picked up a stout stick and swung it vigorously, belabouring imaginary animals. "I'll learn 'em to steal my house!" he cried. "I'll learn 'em, I'll learn 'em!"

"Don't say ‘learn 'em,' Toad," said the Rat, greatly shocked. "It's not good English."

"What are you always nagging at Toad for?" inquired the Badger, rather peevishly. "What's the matter with his English? It's the same what I use myself, and if it's good enough for me, it ought to be good enough for you!"

"I'm very sorry," said the Rat humbly. "Only I **think** it ought to be ‘teach 'em,' not ‘learn 'em.'"

"But we don't **want** to teach 'em," replied the Badger. "We want to **learn** 'em—learn 'em, learn 'em! And what's more, we're going to **do** it, too!"

"Oh, very well, have it your own way," said the Rat. He was getting rather muddled about it himself, and presently he retired into a corner, where he could be heard muttering, "Learn 'em, teach 'em, teach 'em, learn 'em!" till the Badger told him rather sharply to leave off.

Presently the Mole came tumbling into the room, evidently very pleased with himself. "I've been having such fun!" he began at once;

"I've been getting a rise out of the stoats!"

"I hope you've been very careful, Mole?" said the Rat anxiously.

"I should hope so, too," said the Mole confidently. "I got the idea when I went into the kitchen, to see about Toad's breakfast being kept hot for him. I found that old washerwoman-dress that he came home in yesterday, hanging on a towel-horse before the fire. So I put it on, and the bonnet as well, and the shawl, and off I went to Toad Hall, as bold as you please. The sentries were on the look-out, of course, with their guns and their ʿWho comes there?' and all the rest of their nonsense. ʿGood morning, gentlemen!' says I, very respectful. ʿWant any washing done to-day?'

"They looked at me very proud and stiff and haughty, and said, ʿGo away, washerwoman! We don't do any washing on duty.' ʿOr any other time?' says I. Ho, ho, ho! Wasn't I **funny**, Toad?"

"Poor, frivolous animal!" said Toad, very loftily. The fact is, he felt exceedingly jealous of Mole for what he had just done. It was exactly what he would have liked to have done himself, if only he had thought of it first, and hadn't gone and overslept himself.

"Some of the stoats turned quite pink," continued the Mole, "and the Sergeant in charge, he said to me, very short, he said, ʿNow run away, my good woman, run away! Don't keep my men idling and talking on their posts.' ʿRun away?' says I; ʿit won't be me that'll be running away, in a very short time from now!'"

"O **Moly**, how could you?" said the Rat, dismayed.

The Badger laid down his paper.

"I could see them pricking up their ears and looking at each other," went on the Mole; "and the Sergeant said to them, ʿNever mind **her**; she doesn't know what she's talking about.'"

" ʿO! don't I?'" said I. " ʿWell, let me tell you this. My daughter, she washes for Mr. Badger, and that'll show you whether I know what

I'm talking about; and **you>'ll** know pretty soon, too! A hundred bloodthirsty badgers, armed with rifles, are going to attack Toad Hall this very night, by way of the paddock. Six boatloads of Rats, with pistols and cutlasses, will come up the river and effect a landing in the garden; while a picked body of Toads, known at the Die-hards, or the Death-or-Glory Toads, will storm the orchard and carry everything before them, yelling for vengeance. There won't be much left of you to wash, by the time they've done with you, unless you clear out while you have the chance!' Then I ran away, and when I was out of sight I hid; and presently I came creeping back along the ditch and took a peep at them through the hedge. They were all as nervous and flustered as could be, running all ways at once, and falling over each other, and every one giving orders to everybody else and not listening; and the Sergeant kept sending off parties of stoats to distant parts of the grounds, and then sending other fellows to fetch 'em back again; and I heard them saying to each other, 'That's just like the weasels; they're to stop comfortably in the banqueting-hall, and have feasting and toasts and songs and all sorts of fun, while we must stay on guard in the cold and the dark, and in the end be cut to pieces by bloodthirsty Badgers!'"

"Oh, you silly ass, Mole!" cried Toad, "You've been and spoilt everything!"

"Mole," said the Badger, in his dry, quiet way, "I perceive you have more sense in your little finger than some other animals have in the whole of their fat bodies. You have managed excellently, and I begin to have great hopes of you. Good Mole! Clever Mole!"

The Toad was simply wild with jealousy, more especially as he couldn't make out for the life of him what the Mole had done that was so particularly clever; but, fortunately for him, before he could show temper or expose himself to the Badger's sarcasm, the bell rang

for luncheon.

It was a simple but sustaining meal—bacon and broad beans, and a macaroni pudding; and when they had quite done, the Badger settled himself into an arm-chair, and said, "Well, we've got our work cut out for us to-night, and it will probably be pretty late before we're quite through with it; so I'm just going to take forty winks, while I can." And he drew a handkerchief over his face and was soon snoring.

The anxious and laborious Rat at once resumed his preparations, and started running between his four little heaps, muttering, "Here's-a-belt-for-the-Rat, here's-a-belt-for-the-Mole, here's-a-belt-for-the-Toad, here's-a-belt-for-the-Badger!" and so on, with every fresh accoutrement he produced, to which there seemed really no end; so the Mole drew his arm through Toad's, led him out into the open air, shoved him into a wicker chair, and made him tell him all his adventures from beginning to end, which Toad was only too willing to do. The Mole was a good listener, and Toad, with no one to check his statements or to criticise in an unfriendly spirit, rather let himself go. Indeed, much that he related belonged more properly to the category of what-might-have-happened-had-I-only-thought-of-it-in-time-instead-of-ten-minutes-afterwards. Those are always the best and the raciest adventures; and why should they not be truly ours, as much as the somewhat inadequate things that really come off?

XII.
THE RETURN OF ULYSSES

When it began to grow dark, the Rat, with an air of excitement and mystery, summoned them back into the parlour, stood each of them up alongside of his little heap, and proceeded to dress them up for the coming expedition. He was very earnest and thoroughgoing about it, and the affair took quite a long time. First, there was a belt to go round each animal, and then a sword to be stuck into each belt, and then a cutlass on the other side to balance it. Then a pair of pistols, a policeman's truncheon, several sets of handcuffs, some bandages and sticking-plaster, and a flask and a sandwich-case. The Badger laughed good-humouredly and said, "All right, Ratty! It amuses you and it doesn't hurt me. I'm going to do all I've got to do with this here stick." But the Rat only said, "**please**, Badger. You know I shouldn't like you to blame me afterwards and say I had forgotten **anything!**"

When all was quite ready, the Badger took a dark lantern in one

paw, grasped his great stick with the other, and said, "Now then, follow me! Mole first, "cos I'm very pleased with him; Rat next; Toad last. And look here, Toady! Don't you chatter so much as usual, or you'll be sent back, as sure as fate!"

The Toad was so anxious not to be left out that he took up the inferior position assigned to him without a murmur, and the animals set off. The Badger led them along by the river for a little way, and then suddenly swung himself over the edge into a hole in the river-bank, a little above the water. The Mole and the Rat followed silently, swinging themselves successfully into the hole as they had seen the Badger do; but when it came to Toad's turn, of course he managed to slip and fall into the water with a loud splash and a squeal of alarm. He was hauled out by his friends, rubbed down and wrung out hastily, comforted, and set on his legs; but the Badger was seriously angry, and told him that the very next time he made a fool of himself he would most certainly be left behind.

So at last they were in the secret passage, and the cutting-out expedition had really begun!

It was cold, and dark, and damp, and low, and narrow, and poor Toad began to shiver, partly from dread of what might be before him, partly because he was wet through. The lantern was far ahead, and he could not help lagging behind a little in the darkness. Then he heard the Rat call out warningly, **"Come** on, Toad!" and a terror seized him of being left behind, alone in the darkness, and he "came on" with such a rush that he upset the Rat into the Mole and the Mole into the Badger, and for a moment all was confusion. The Badger thought they were being attacked from behind, and, as there was no room to use a stick or a cutlass, drew a pistol, and was on the point of putting a bullet into Toad. When he found out what had really happened he was very angry indeed, and said, "Now this time that tiresome Toad **shall**

be left behind!"

But Toad whimpered, and the other two promised that they would be answerable for his good conduct, and at last the Badger was pacified, and the procession moved on; only this time the Rat brought up the rear, with a firm grip on the shoulder of Toad.

So they groped and shuffled along, with their ears pricked up and their paws on their pistols, till at last the Badger said, "We ought by now to be pretty nearly under the Hall."

Then suddenly they heard, far away as it might be, and yet apparently nearly over their heads, a confused murmur of sound, as if people were shouting and cheering and stamping on the floor and hammering on tables. The Toad's nervous terrors all returned, but the Badger only remarked placidly, "They **are** going it, the Weasels!"

The passage now began to slope upwards; they groped onward a little further, and then the noise broke out again, quite distinct this time, and very close above them. "Ooo-ray-ooray-oo-ray-ooray!" they heard, and the stamping of little feet on the floor, and the clinking of glasses as little fists pounded on the table. "**What** a time they're having!" said the Badger. "Come on!" They hurried along the passage till it came to a full stop, and they found themselves standing under the trap-door that led up into the butler's pantry.

Such a tremendous noise was going on in the banqueting-hall that there was little danger of their being overheard. The Badger said, "Now, boys, all together!" and the four of them put their shoulders to the trap-door and heaved it back. Hoisting each other up, they found themselves standing in the pantry, with only a door between them and the banqueting-hall, where their unconscious enemies were carousing. The noise, as they emerged from the passage, was simply deafening. At last, as the cheering and

hammering slowly subsided, a voice could be made out saying, "Well, I do not propose to detain you much longer"—(great applause)—"but before I resume my seat"—(renewed cheering)—"I should like to say one word about our kind host, Mr. Toad. We all know Toad!"—(great laughter)—"**Good** Toad, **modest** Toad, **honest** Toad!" (shrieks of merriment).

"Only just let me get at him!" muttered Toad, grinding his teeth.

"Hold hard a minute!" said the Badger, restraining him with difficulty. "Get ready, all of you!"

"—Let me sing you a little song," went on the voice, "which I have composed on the subject of Toad"—(prolonged applause).

Then the Chief Weasel—for it was he—began in a high, squeaky voice—

> "Toad he went a-pleasuring
> Gaily down the street—"

The Badger drew himself up, took a firm grip of his stick with both paws, glanced round at his comrades, and cried—

"The hour is come! Follow me!"

And flung the door open wide.

My!

What a squealing and a squeaking and a screeching filled the air!

Well might the terrified weasels dive under the tables and spring madly up at the windows! Well might the ferrets rush wildly for the fireplace and get hopelessly jammed in the chimney! Well might tables and chairs be upset, and glass and china be sent crashing on the floor, in the panic of that terrible moment when the four Heroes strode wrathfully into the room! The mighty Badger, his whiskers bristling,

his great cudgel whistling through the air; Mole, black and grim, brandishing his stick and shouting his awful war-cry, "A Mole! A Mole!" Rat; desperate and determined, his belt bulging with weapons of every age and every variety; Toad, frenzied with excitement and injured pride, swollen to twice his ordinary size, leaping into the air and emitting Toad-whoops that chilled them to the marrow! "Toad he went a-pleasuring!" he yelled. "**I'll** pleasure 'em!" and he went straight for the Chief Weasel. They were but four in all, but to the panic-stricken weasels the hall seemed full of monstrous animals, grey, black, brown and yellow, whooping and flourishing enormous cudgels; and they broke and fled with squeals of terror and dismay, this way and that, through the windows, up the chimney, anywhere to get out of reach of those terrible sticks.

The affair was soon over. Up and down, the whole length of the hall, strode the four Friends, whacking with their sticks at every head that showed itself; and in five minutes the room was cleared. Through the broken windows the shrieks of terrified weasels escaping across the lawn were borne faintly to their ears; on the floor lay prostrate some dozen or so of the enemy, on whom the Mole was busily engaged in fitting handcuffs. The Badger, resting from his labours, leant on his stick and wiped his honest brow.

"Mole," he said," "you're the best of fellows! Just cut along outside and look after those stoat-sentries of yours, and see what they're doing. I've an idea that, thanks to you, we shan't have much trouble from **them** to-night!"

The Mole vanished promptly through a window; and the Badger bade the other two set a table on its legs again, pick up knives and forks and plates and glasses from the **débris** on the floor, and see if they could find materials for a supper. "I want some grub, I do," he said, in that rather common way he had of speaking. "Stir your

stumps, Toad, and look lively! We've got your house back for you, and you don't offer us so much as a sandwich." Toad felt rather hurt that the Badger didn't say pleasant things to him, as he had to the Mole, and tell him what a fine fellow he was, and how splendidly he had fought; for he was rather particularly pleased with himself and the way he had gone for the Chief Weasel and sent him flying across the table with one blow of his stick. But he bustled about, and so did the Rat, and soon they found some guava jelly in a glass dish, and a cold chicken, a tongue that had hardly been touched, some trifle, and quite a lot of lobster salad; and in the pantry they came upon a basketful of French rolls and any quantity of cheese, butter, and celery. They were just about to sit down when the Mole clambered in through the window, chuckling, with an armful of rifles.

"It's all over," he reported. "From what I can make out, as soon as the stoats, who were very nervous and jumpy already, heard the shrieks and the yells and the uproar inside the hall, some of them threw down their rifles and fled. The others stood fast for a bit, but when the weasels came rushing out upon them they thought they were betrayed; and the stoats grappled with the weasels, and the weasels fought to get away, and they wrestled and wriggled and punched each other, and rolled over and over, till most of 'em rolled into the river! They've all disappeared by now, one way or another; and I've got their rifles. So **that's** all right!"

"Excellent and deserving animal!" said the Badger, his mouth full of chicken and trifle. "Now, there's just one more thing I want you to do, Mole, before you sit down to your supper along of us; and I wouldn't trouble you only I know I can trust you to see a thing done, and I wish I could say the same of every one I know. I'd send Rat, if he wasn't a poet. I want you to take those fellows on the floor there upstairs with you, and have some bedrooms cleaned out and tidied up

and made really comfortable. See that they sweep **under** the beds, and put clean sheets and pillow-cases on, and turn down one corner of the bed-clothes, just as you know it ought to be done; and have a can of hot water, and clean towels, and fresh cakes of soap, put in each room. And then you can give them a licking a-piece, if it's any satisfaction to you, and put them out by the back-door, and we shan't see any more of **them**, I fancy. And then come along and have some of this cold tongue. It's first rate. I'm very pleased with you, Mole!"

The goodnatured Mole picked up a stick, formed his prisoners up in a line on the floor, gave them the order "Quick march!" and led his squad off to the upper floor. After a time, he appeared again, smiling, and said that every room was ready, and as clean as a new pin. "And I didn't have to lick them, either," he added. "I thought, on the whole, they had had licking enough for one night, and the weasels, when I put the point to them, quite agreed with me, and said they wouldn't think of troubling me. They were very penitent, and said they were extremely sorry for what they had done, but it was all the fault of the Chief Weasel and the stoats, and if ever they could do anything for us at any time to make up, we had only got to mention it. So I gave them a roll a-piece, and let them out at the back, and off they ran, as hard as they could!"

Then the Mole pulled his chair up to the table, and pitched into the cold tongue; and Toad, like the gentleman he was, put all his jealousy from him, and said heartily, "Thank you kindly, dear Mole, for all your pains and trouble tonight, and especially for your cleverness this morning!" The Badger was pleased at that, and said, "There spoke my brave Toad!" So they finished their supper in great joy and contentment, and presently retired to rest between clean sheets, safe in Toad's ancestral home, won back by matchless valour, consummate strategy, and a proper handling of sticks.

The following morning, Toad, who had overslept himself as usual, came down to breakfast disgracefully late, and found on the table a certain quantity of egg-shells, some fragments of cold and leathery toast, a coffee-pot three-fourths empty, and really very little else; which did not tend to improve his temper, considering that, after all, it was his own house. Through the French windows of the breakfast-room he could see the Mole and the Water Rat sitting in wicker-chairs out on the lawn, evidently telling each other stories; roaring with laughter and kicking their short legs up in the air. The Badger, who was in an arm-chair and deep in the morning paper, merely looked up and nodded when Toad entered the room. But Toad knew his man, so he sat down and made the best breakfast he could, merely observing to himself that he would get square with the others sooner or later. When he had nearly finished, the Badger looked up and remarked rather shortly: "I'm sorry, Toad, but I'm afraid there's a heavy morning's work in front of you. You see, we really ought to have a Banquet at once, to celebrate this affair. It's expected of you—in fact, it's the rule."

"O, all right!" said the Toad, readily. "Anything to oblige. Though why on earth you should want to have a Banquet in the morning I cannot understand. But you know I do not live to please myself, but merely to find out what my friends want, and then try and arrange it for 'em, you dear old Badger!"

"Don't pretend to be stupider than you really are," replied the Badger, crossly; "and don't chuckle and splutter in your coffee while you're talking; it's not manners. What I mean is, the Banquet will be at night, of course, but the invitations will have to be written and got off at once, and you've got to write 'em. Now, sit down at that table—there's stacks of letter-paper on it, with 'Toad Hall' at the top in blue and gold—and write invitations to all our friends, and if you stick to it

we shall get them out before luncheon. And **I'll** bear a hand, too; and take my share of the burden. **I'll** order the Banquet."

"What!" cried Toad, dismayed. "Me stop indoors and write a lot of rotten letters on a jolly morning like this, when I want to go around my property, and set everything and everybody to rights, and swagger about and enjoy myself! Certainly not! I'll be—I'll see you——Stop a minute, though! Why, of course, dear Badger! What is my pleasure or convenience compared with that of others! You wish it done, and it shall be done. Go, Badger, order the Banquet, order what you like; then join our young friends outside in their innocent mirth, oblivious of me and my cares and toils. I sacrifice this fair morning on the altar of duty and friendship!"

The Badger looked at him very suspiciously, but Toad's frank, open countenance made it difficult to suggest any unworthy motive in this change of attitude. He quitted the room, accordingly, in the direction of the kitchen, and as soon as the door had closed behind him, Toad hurried to the writing-table. A fine idea had occurred to him while he was talking. He **would** write the invitations; and he would take care to mention the leading part he had taken in the fight, and how he had laid the Chief Weasel flat; and he would hint at his adventures, and what a career of triumph he had to tell about; and on the fly-leaf he would set out a sort of a programme of entertainment for the evening—something like this, as he sketched it out in his head:—

SPEECH. . . . BY TOAD.
(There will be other speeches by TOAD during the evening.)

ADDRESS. . . BY TOAD
SYNOPSIS—Our Prison System—the Waterways of Old England—
Horse-dealing, and how to deal—Property, its rights and its duties—Back
to the Land—A Typical English Squire.

SONG. . . . BY TOAD.
(Composed by himself.)

OTHER COMPOSITIONS. BY TOAD
will be sung in the course of the evening by the. . . COMPOSER.

The idea pleased him mightily, and he worked very hard and got all the letters finished by noon, at which hour it was reported to him that there was a small and rather bedraggled weasel at the door, inquiring timidly whether he could be of any service to the gentlemen. Toad swaggered out and found it was one of the prisoners of the previous evening, very respectful and anxious to please. He patted him on the head, shoved the bundle of invitations into his paw, and told him to cut along quick and deliver them as fast as he could, and if he liked to come back again in the evening, perhaps there might be a shilling for him, or, again, perhaps there mightn't; and the poor weasel seemed really quite grateful, and hurried off eagerly to do his mission.

When the other animals came back to luncheon, very boisterous

and breezy after a morning on the river, the Mole, whose conscience had been pricking him, looked doubtfully at Toad, expecting to find him sulky or depressed. Instead, he was so uppish and inflated that the Mole began to suspect something; while the Rat and the Badger exchanged significant glances.

As soon as the meal was over, Toad thrust his paws deep into his trouser-pockets, remarked casually, "Well, look after yourselves, you fellows! Ask for anything you want!" and was swaggering off in the direction of the garden, where he wanted to think out an idea or two for his coming speeches, when the Rat caught him by the arm.

Toad rather suspected what he was after, and did his best to get away; but when the Badger took him firmly by the other arm he began to see that the game was up. The two animals conducted him between them into the small smoking-room that opened out of the entrance-hall, shut the door, and put him into a chair. Then they both stood in front of him, while Toad sat silent and regarded them with much suspicion and ill-humour.

"Now, look here, Toad," said the Rat. "It's about this Banquet, and very sorry I am to have to speak to you like this. But we want you to understand clearly, once and for all, that there are going to be no speeches and no songs. Try and grasp the fact that on this occasion we're not arguing with you; we're just telling you."

Toad saw that he was trapped. They understood him, they saw through him, they had got ahead of him. His pleasant dream was shattered.

"Mayn't I sing them just one **little** song?" he pleaded piteously.

"No, not **one** little song," replied the Rat firmly, though his heart bled as he noticed the trembling lip of the poor disappointed Toad. "It's no good, Toady; you know well that your songs are all conceit and boasting and vanity; and your speeches are all self-praise and—

and—well, and gross exaggeration and—and——"

"And gas," put in the Badger, in his common way.

"It's for your own good, Toady," went on the Rat. "You know you **must** turn over a new leaf sooner or later, and now seems a splendid time to begin; a sort of turning-point in your career. Please don't think that saying all this doesn't hurt me more than it hurts you."

Toad remained a long while plunged in thought. At last he raised his head, and the traces of strong emotion were visible on his features. "You have conquered, my friends," he said in broken accents. "It was, to be sure, but a small thing that I asked—merely leave to blossom and expand for yet one more evening, to let myself go and hear the tumultuous applause that always seems to me—somehow—to bring out my best qualities. However, you are right, I know, and I am wrong. Hence forth I will be a very different Toad. My friends, you shall never have occasion to blush for me again. But, O dear, O dear, this is a hard world!"

And, pressing his handkerchief to his face, he left the room, with faltering footsteps.

"Badger," said the Rat, "**I** feel like a brute; I wonder what **you** feel like?"

"O, I know, I know," said the Badger gloomily. "But the thing had to be done. This good fellow has got to live here, and hold his own, and be respected. Would you have him a common laughing-stock, mocked and jeered at by stoats and weasels?"

"Of course not," said the Rat. "And, talking of weasels, it's lucky we came upon that little weasel, just as he was setting out with Toad's invitations. I suspected something from what you told me, and had a look at one or two; they were simply disgraceful. I confiscated the lot, and the good Mole is now sitting in the blue boudoir, filling up plain, simple invitation cards."

At last the hour for the banquet began to draw near, and Toad, who on leaving the others had retired to his bedroom, was still sitting there, melancholy and thoughtful. His brow resting on his paw, he pondered long and deeply. Gradually his countenance cleared, and he began to smile long, slow smiles. Then he took to giggling in a shy, self-conscious manner. At last he got up, locked the door, drew the curtains across the windows, collected all the chairs in the room and arranged them in a semicircle, and took up his position in front of them, swelling visibly. Then he bowed, coughed twice, and, letting himself go, with uplifted voice he sang, to the enraptured audience that his imagination so clearly saw.

TOAD'S LAST LITTLE SONG!

The Toad—came—home!
There was panic in the parlours and howling in the halls,
There was crying in the cow-sheds and shrieking in the stalls,
When the Toad—came—home!

When the Toad—came—home!
There was smashing in of window and crashing in of door,
There was chivvying of weasels that fainted on the floor,
When the Toad—came—home!

Bang! go the drums!
The trumpeters are tooting and the soldiers are saluting,
And the cannon they are shooting and the motor-cars are
hooting,
As the—Hero—comes!

Shout—Hoo-ray!
And let each one of the crowd try and shout it very loud,
In honour of an animal of whom you're justly proud,
For it's Toad's—great—day!

He sang this very loud, with great unction and expression; and
when he had done, he sang it all over again.

Then he heaved a deep sigh; a long, long, long sigh.

Then he dipped his hairbrush in the water-jug, parted his hair in
the middle, and plastered it down very straight and sleek on each side
of his face; and, unlocking the door, went quietly down the stairs to
greet his guests, who he knew must be assembling in the drawing-
room.

All the animals cheered when he entered, and crowded round to
congratulate him and say nice things about his courage, and his
cleverness, and his fighting qualities; but Toad only smiled faintly, and
murmured, "Not at all!" Or, sometimes, for a change, "On the
contrary!" Otter, who was standing on the hearthrug, describing to an
admiring circle of friends exactly how he would have managed things
had he been there, came forward with a shout, threw his arm round

Toad's neck, and tried to take him round the room in triumphal progress; but Toad, in a mild way, was rather snubby to him, remarking gently, as he disengaged himself, "Badger's was the mastermind; the Mole and the Water Rat bore the brunt of the fighting; I merely served in the ranks and did little or nothing." The animals were evidently puzzled and taken aback by this unexpected attitude of his; and Toad felt, as he moved from one guest to the other, making his modest responses, that he was an object of absorbing interest to every one.

The Badger had ordered everything of the best, and the banquet was a great success. There was much talking and laughter and chaff among the animals, but through it all Toad, who of course was in the chair, looked down his nose and murmured pleasant nothings to the animals on either side of him. At intervals he stole a glance at the Badger and the Rat, and always when he looked they were staring at each other with their mouths open; and this gave him the greatest satisfaction. Some of the younger and livelier animals, as the evening wore on, got whispering to each other that things were not so amusing as they used to be in the good old days; and there were some knockings on the table and cries of "Toad! Speech! Speech from Toad! Song! Mr. Toad's song!" But Toad only shook his head gently, raised one paw in mild protest, and, by pressing delicacies on his guests, by topical small-talk, and by earnest inquiries after members of their families not yet old enough to appear at social functions, managed to convey to them that this dinner was being run on strictly conventional lines.

He was indeed an altered Toad!

After this climax, the four animals continued to lead their lives, so rudely broken in upon by civil war, in great joy and contentment, undisturbed by further risings or invasions. Toad, after due consultation with his friends, selected a handsome gold chain and locket set with pearls, which he dispatched to the gaoler's daughter with a letter that even the Badger admitted to be modest, grateful, and appreciative; and the engine-driver, in his turn, was properly thanked and compensated for all his pains and trouble. Under severe compulsion from the Badger, even the barge-woman was, with some trouble, sought out and the value of her horse discreetly made good to her; though Toad kicked terribly at this, holding himself to be an instrument of Fate, sent to punish fat women with mottled arms who couldn't tell a real gentleman when they saw one. The amount involved, it was true, was not very burdensome, the gipsy's valuation being admitted by local assessors to be approximately correct.

Sometimes, in the course of long summer evenings, the friends would take a stroll together in the Wild Wood, now successfully tamed so far as they were concerned; and it was pleasing to see how respectfully they were greeted by the inhabitants, and how the mother-weasels would bring their young ones to the mouths of their holes, and say, pointing, "Look, baby! There goes the great Mr. Toad! And that's the gallant Water Rat, a terrible fighter, walking along o' him! And yonder comes the famous Mr. Mole, of whom you so often have heard your father tell!" But when their infants were fractious and quite beyond control, they would quiet them by telling how, if they didn't hush them and not fret them, the terrible grey Badger would up and get them. This was a base libel on Badger, who, though he cared little about Society, was rather fond of children; but it never failed to have its full effect.

國家圖書館出版品預行編目資料

柳林中的風聲（中英雙語典藏版）/ 肯尼斯・格雷厄姆
（Kenneth Grahame）著；亞瑟・拉克姆（Arthur
Rackham）、曾銘祥 繪；謝世堅 譯
臺中市：晨星，2022.11.
　面；　公分. --（愛藏本；115）

譯自：The Wind in the Willows

ISBN 978-626-320-252-8

873.596　　　　　　　　　　　　　111014467

愛藏本：115

柳林中的風聲（中英雙語典藏版）
The Wind in the Willows

作　　者｜肯尼斯・格雷厄姆（Kenneth Grahame）
繪　　者｜亞瑟・拉克姆（Arthur Rackham）、曾銘祥
譯　　者｜謝世堅

責任編輯｜呂曉婕、江品如
封面設計｜鐘文君
美術編輯｜王宜容
文字校潤｜呂昀慶、江品如

創 辦 人｜陳銘民
發 行 所｜晨星出版有限公司
　　　　　台中市 407 工業區 30 路 1 號 1 樓
　　　　　TEL：04-23595820　FAX：04-23550581
　　　　　http://star.morningstar.com.tw
　　　　　行政院新聞局局版台業字第 2500 號
法律顧問｜陳思成律師

服務專線｜TEL：02-23672044 / 04-23595819#212
傳真專線｜FAX：02-23635741 / 04-23595493
讀者信箱｜service@morningstar.com.tw
網路書店｜http://www.morningstar.com.tw
郵政劃撥｜15060393（知己圖書股份有限公司）

初版日期｜2004 年 12 月 01 日
二版日期｜2022 年 11 月 15 日
　　ISBN｜978-626-320-252-8
　　定價｜新台幣 330 元

印　　刷｜上好印刷股份有限公司

填寫線上回函，立刻享有
晨星網路書店50元購書金